MW00861140

LAKE
OF
FLOWERS

A LORD HANI MYSTERY

N.L. HOLMES

WayBack Press
P.O.Box 16066
Tampa, FL
⚑

Lake of Flowers

The Lord Hani Mysteries™ 2020

Quotes from *"The Instructions of Any"*, *"Love Poems"*, and *"The Instructions of Amenemope"* from *Ancient Egyptian Literature* by Miriam Lichtheim, University of California Press (1976).

Cover art and map© by Streetlight Graphics.
Author photo© by Kipp Baker.

Dedicated to the excavation team at Kommos,
who introduced me to orpiment.

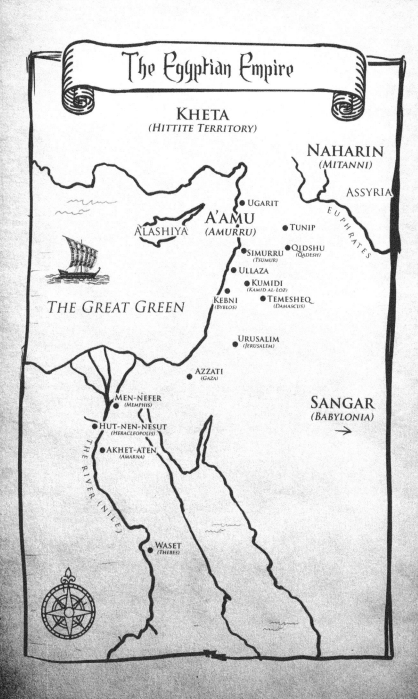

HISTORICAL NOTES

Our story takes place in the seventeenth and final year of Akh-en-aten's reign (by the reckoning of this account, his twelfth alone on the throne) and immediately thereafter, so about 1338 BCE. Those who deny him a coregency with his father would put the date five years later. We are entering one of the murkiest moments in Egyptian history, where the very identities of the monarchs are held in question. This is because the later successors of the "Heretic King" completely obliterated from the record him and his immediate successors. Scholars debate whether Ankh-khepru-ra Smenkh-ka-ra held a coregency with Akhenaten or ruled alone. Indeed, we don't even know who he was—Akh-en-aten's brother? His son? His wife, under a masculine name? A Hittite prince? Was Ankhet-nefru-ra the same person or a female ruler sharing essentially the same name? The novelist has to make some choices, and they're not always the most likely in the historical sense.

Similar problems arise with the parentage of Prince Tut-ankh-aten. He may have been Akh-en-aten's son or

Smenkh-ka-ra's… or someone else's. DNA suggests that he was the son of two unidentified mummies that have been tested, and that those parents were brother and sister (or double cousins). I have tried to respect the genetic evidence, but the reader should bear in mind that this story is fiction.

We know from Hittite documents about the journey to obtain a husband for a certain widowed queen of Egypt, as yet unidentified. Some scholars believe she was the widow of Tut-ankh-amen, others that she was one of the queens who preceded him, that is, Nefert-iti or Meryet-aten. I have adopted the latter scenario and tried to construct a plausible motivation. Hani was historically the emissary sent to carry this mission out.

Because this period has been blanked out of Egyptian records, we don't know what happened after the death of Akh-en-aten, but one may imagine that, given the dissatisfaction of a large number of important people, there would have been civil unrest of some kind.

As for Maya, the treasurer of Tut-ankh-aten, he is certainly not our Ptah-mes/Maya, but I have taken the liberty of conflating them.

The Egyptians had a sense of the circulatory system, the meaning of a pulse, and so forth, but they thought that air as well as blood was pumped throughout the body through the same vessels (which is more or less true on the cellular level). Turnips are attested in Egypt at a later period, but there's no reason to think they didn't enter the country earlier. And finally, a real wooden prosthetic toe was found in an ancient Egyptian burial.

CHARACTERS

(Persons marked with an * are purely fictitious)

HANI'S FAMILY

A'a*: gatekeeper of Hani's family.

Amen-em-hut: Nub-nefer's brother, Third Prophet of Amen.

Amen-em-ope known as **Pa-kiki*** (The Monkey): Hani and Nub-nefer's younger son.

Amen-hotep known as **Hani:** a diplomat.

Amen-hotep known as **Aha*:** Hani and Nub-nefer's elder son. Later takes the name **Hesy-en-aten**.

Amen-hotep known as **Anuia:** Amen-em-hut's wife, a chantress of Amen.

Amen-hotep called **Tepy*:** Maya and Sat-hut-haru's eldest son.

Amen-mes known as **Maya***: Hani's dwarf secretary and son-in-law, married to Sat-hut-haru.

Baket-iset*: Hani's eldest daughter.

Bener-ib*: Neferet's partner and fellow *sunet*.

Bin-addi*: a servant from Kharu, working for Hani.

In-hapy*: Maya's mother, a royal goldsmith.

Khawy*: an orphaned student taken in by the household.

Khentet-ka*: Aha's wife.

Mai-her-pri*: Maya's third child and second son.

Meryet-amen*: Mery-ra's widowed lady friend.

Mery-ra: Hani's father.

Mut-nodjmet*: Pipi's daughter, the wife of Pa-kiki.

Pa-ra-em-heb known as Pipi*: Hani's brother.

Neferet*: Hani and Nub-nefer's youngest daughter, a physician to the royal women.

Nub-nefer*: Hani's wife, a chantress of Amen.

Sat-hut-haru*: Hani and Nub-nefer's second daughter, married to Maya.

OTHER CHARACTERS

Ankh-kepru-ra Smenkh-ka-ra: Akh-en-aten's coregent and brother.

Ankhet-khepru-ra Nefer-nefru-aten: former queen Nefert-iti, ruling briefly as king after her husband's death.

Ay: father of Nefert-iti, a cavalry officer and uncle of Akh-en-aten, who bore the title God's Father.

Ba-ba-ef*: servant of Pentju and Djefat-nebty.

Djefat-nebty*: a female doctor treating the royal women. The teacher of Neferet and Bener-ib.

Har-em-heb: a general of the infantry and son-in-law of Ay.

Ipuki*: a laundryman, widower of Tuy.

Khuit*: an old neighborhood healer and midwife.

Mahu: chief of Akh-en-aten's police at Akhet-aten.

Mai: First Prophet of Amen-Ra until deposed by Akh-en-aten.

Mane son of Pa-iry: former ambassador to Naharin and Hani's friend.

Menna*: a young infantry officer, whose life Hani had once saved.

Meryet-aten*: Akh-en-aten and Nefert-iti's eldest daughter, who served as nominal Great Royal Wife to her father, to Smenkh-ka-ra, and even to her mother.

Nakht-ef-mut*: Bener-ib's father. A *wab*-priest and teacher of medicine at Sau who had just been appointed physician to the crown prince.

Nakht-pa-aten: vizier of the Upper Kingdom under Akh-en-aten.

Nefer-khepru-ra Wa-en-ra Akh-en-aten: the "heretic king" under whom the Egyptian pantheon was replaced by a sole god, the Aten.

Pa-ra-mes-su: adjutant of Har-em-heb.

Pentju: royal physician, priest of the Aten, and chamberlain under Akh-en-aten.

Ptah-mes son of Bak-en-ren-ef: Hani's friend and former superior, who had been stripped of office for countering the king.

Ra-nefer*: vizier of the Lower Kingdom. His real name is unknown.

Sen-nedjem: nephew of Ay and tutor to Prince Tut-ankh-aten.

Si-mut: Second Prophet of Amen-Ra, deposed by Akh-en-aten.

Tut-ankh-aten: crown prince under Akh-en-aten.

Tuy*: a midwife, late wife of Ipuki.

User-hat*: a laundryman, son of Ipuki and Tuy.

GLOSSARY OF PLACES, TERMS, AND GODS

akh: the combined souls of a person in their blessed state after death.

Akhet-aten: "Horizon of the Aten", capital of Akh-en-aten.

Amen-Ra: chief god of New Kingdom Egypt, supplanted briefly by Akh-en-aten's "reform."

the **Aten:** the visible sun disk, probably identified with Akh-en-aten's father, Amen-hotep III, who became the chief then only god under Akh-en-aten.

Azzati: center of Egypt's rule among the northern vassals. Today's Gaza.

bennu **bird:** symbol of the reborn soul; it was thought to look like a heron. Later identified with the phoenix.

birthing bricks: the blocks on which a woman squatted during childbirth, to raise her so the baby could be lowered to the ground between her feet.

Crocodiles: Hani's term for the rebellious priests of Amen-Ra and their sympathizers who plotted a return to the old ways.

Djahy: the lower half of the Levant, corresponding more or less to Roman Palestina. It had been held by Egypt since the beginning of the eighteenth dynasty.

Djehuty: (Thoth) judge of the soul after death and patron of scribes.

Double House of Silver and Gold: the treasury, although technically much of Egypt's wealth was held in commodities.

Feast of Drunkenness: a festival in honor of Hut-haru (Hathor), goddess of joy, sex, beauty, music, and abandon. According to myth, she had once been so angered at the human race that she went on a destructive rampage, ready to drink its blood. But humans outsmarted her by dyeing beer red like blood and letting her drink her fill until she was drunk and forgot about her anger.

Field of Reeds: the Egyptian paradise where blessed souls lived in an environment like earth, only perfected.

Gem-pa-aten: a temple of the Aten in Thebes in which Akh-en-aten tried out his shocking new artistic style for the first time.

Great House: "Per-a'o," meaning the palace. It came to refer to the king himself. Our word *pharaoh* derives from this.

hapiru: a loose, nomadic group of bandits and social outcasts that terrorized the eastern borders of Egypt's Syrian vassals.

Haru (Horus) in the nest: the title of the crown prince.

House of Rejoicing: Amen-hotep III's jubilee palace in Waset, from which he ruled for the remainder of his reign.

House of Royal Ornaments: the name of the king's harem.

Hut-nen-nesut: also known as Hnes, a city near the Fayyum Oasis. Later called Heracleopolis.

Inpu (Anubis): jackal-headed god of embalming.

Ipet-isut: Greatest of Shrines, the temple of Amen-Ra at Thebes.

iteru: a unit of distance, approximately a mile.

Kap: the royal nursery where the king's sons were brought up with the sons of high aristocrats and vassal princes.

Kheta Land: the Hittite empire, in modern Turkey.

Lake of Flowers: the lake which the soul, once judged worthy, had to pass over before reaching the Field of Reeds.

Men-nefer: Memphis, capital of the Lower Kingdom.

menut: a mourning dove.

orpiment: a yellow pigment made from a crystalline form of arsenic. Repeated contact, even without ingestion, can slowly poison a person.

Osir: Osiris, king of the underworld. A deceased person was often referred to as "an Osiris."

Pa-maru-en-pa-aten: Sunshade of the Aten, one of several pleasure parks in Akhet-aten designed for members of the royal family as a place where the beauties of the Aten were visible.

Per-nefer: a port at the mouth of the Nile through which ships sailed for the Mediterranean.

Red Land: the desert, as opposed to the Nile valley, the Black Land.

Sangar: Babylonia.

Sau (Saïs): city in the delta, home to the cult of Sekhmet and a seat of medical training.

Sekhmet: lion-headed goddess of plague and of healing.

senet: a board game similar to checkers, played by two people.

Serqet: scorpion-tailed goddess who protected from stings and other harm.

Seyawt: modern Asyut, in Middle Egypt.

shebyu: a heavy gold collar with lens-shaped beads, awarded by the king to those he wished to honor.

Shu and **Tefnut:** Air and Moisture, the first generation of gods—siblings and spouses—after the primal All divided.

Sutesh: (Seth) god of chaos and the desert.

sunet (f., m. *sunu*): a physician of the more scientific sort, as opposed to priestly or magician healers.

Ta-nehesy: Kush or Nubia, the land to the south of Egypt (today's Sudan), held by Egypt as a viceroyalty in the New Kingdom.

Teni-menu: the palace built by Akh-en-aten at Thebes, when he was still coregent with his father.

Waset: Thebes, the capital of the Upper Kingdom, ancestral home of the Eighteenth Dynasty, and center of the worship of Amen-Ra.

Way of Haru: one of several roads up the coast of Djahy and Amurru, maintained for the rapid movement of Egypt's armies.

CHAPTER 1

HANI WOULD FOREVER REMEMBER WHAT he was doing the day he learned of the coregent's death. He and his father, Mery-ra, were strolling in the garden before dinner, on their leisurely way to the garden pavilion where they would eat on warm summer evenings. As if they were synchronized everywhere on earth, the cicadas roared in rhythmic waves, and the late-afternoon sun was a golden liquid dripping through the leaves of the big sycomore fig and spattering the gravel of the path. Hani breathed deeply of the shady air. Despite all the troubles in the world around him, he couldn't help but believe that life was good. Jasmine and lilies were in bloom, as well as earthy aromatics and white daisies—the air was syrupy with their perfume as if scent had mass. *Could a man ask for more?*

"Look, Father," Hani said with a smile.

He pointed to where Qenyt, his pet heron, stood on one leg in the shallows of the pool, as still as a statue, her gray color making her almost invisible among the reeds that swayed there—a whisper of feathers, a deadly shadow of bird. All at once, her long neck unfurled, and her dagger-sharp beak plunged into the water. A moment later, she stood with a twisting silver fish in her bill, which almost immediately disappeared down her throat.

"She's ruthless."

Mery-ra chuckled, his belly bouncing. "I've found that to be true of females generally, son. Haven't you ever noticed that with all the devious ladies you've had to serve over the years?"

Hani joined him in his laughter. "You have a point. Certainly, the royal women are a cutthroat bunch." But he added with a twinkle in his eye, "Of course, *our* women are very different."

"I should think," said Nub-nefer from behind him. She emerged from among the bushes, a tray in her hands, upon which were arranged a variety of cheeses and pickled vegetables and bread cut into chunks. "However, our *men* tend to get hungry before a meal." Hani's wife set the tray down on a little folding table in the pavilion. "I'll bring you some beer. The kitchen girls have had it cooling in the well. Dinner will be a while yet."

"Thank you, my dove," Hani stroked her coppery arm. As Nub-nefer's name proclaimed, she was pure gold—his golden treasure. Even after thirty-six years of marriage, he felt she had perfections he had yet to plumb.

The two men settled into their chairs on the porch of the pavilion and stretched out their legs. Mery-ra expelled a big breath with a whoosh. "Hot." He folded his arms over his head to cool his armpits.

"That shouldn't surprise you, Father. It's almost time for the Inundation."

Without lowering his arms, Mery-ra scrubbed his close-cropped gray hair. "I'm not surprised, but it's hot nonetheless. These are the *heriu-renpet*, the intercalary days. The old year is fast coming to an end. What will the new one bring, do you suppose?"

Nub-nefer and one of the serving girls approached with the beer pot and its stand. "Here you are, my hungry men," she called from the porch of the pavilion, her voice rich with affection.

Suddenly, Hani heard wild footsteps hammering down the gravel path from the gate, and his youngest daughter, Neferet, burst into the open, red-faced and panting. "Mama! Papa! Grandfather! Ankh-khepru-ra Smenkh-ka-ra is dead!"

Hani and Nub-nefer exchanged a stunned look. Hani struggled to swallow, wondering if he'd heard his daughter correctly. *The coregent, only in his twenties, has died?*

Mery-ra was the first to regroup. "When, my girl? How?"

"The plague, Grandfather. It just took him off like that." She snapped her fingers. "It hasn't even been made public yet." Neferet, a physician of the ladies attached to Ankh-kheperu's court in Waset, would have been one of the first to know about this turn of events.

"That's what happens when the king doesn't perform the Appeasement of Sekhmet ritual," Mery-ra said in a dire tone. "She gets mad."

"Today's the birthday of Sutesh," Hani murmured. "A day of ill omen."

They all got to their knees and scraped up dust to strew on their heads in a gesture of mourning. Hani climbed heavily to his feet, sweat beginning to spring out on his forehead. *This is the first brick falling out of the edifice King Nefer-khepru-ra has built. Now what will happen? The building is starting to crumble.*

Nub-nefer's face lit up with hope. She fastened huge glowing eyes on her husband, and Hani knew she was thinking the same thing but with a more unambiguous joy. Hani stared around him, the tableau of his family fixing itself in his memory. This wasn't just an occasion to tie on the white headband of mourning and participate in the lavish funeral rites of a king. Something significant had shifted— far more significant than the young deceased himself, who had been none too bright and was undoubtedly under the sway of others, probably his brother—or his wife. The likelihood of civil war breaking out when the present king died had just grown immeasurably greater.

Everyone stood there without moving until Neferet, unable to remain silent any longer, said, "Can I stay for dinner?"

Hani finally returned to the world around him. He laid a paternal hand on the girl's shoulder. "Of course, my duckling. Where's Bener-ib?" Neferet's fellow *sunet* and friend was always to be found trailing after her.

"She's staying late tonight. One of the queen's handmaids is sick." No doubt seeing her family's horrified expressions, she hastened to add, "But it's not plague. The poor handmaid just had a stillborn baby, and things aren't looking too good."

"Come, my love." Nub-nefer took her daughter by the elbow. "Help me bring out the food." She caught Hani's eye, and he could see her ill-dissembled joy, the ember beneath the ash that threatened to leap into flame.

Hani watched his wife and daughter as they set off through the garden for the house, Nub-nefer almost as trim and lovely as she'd ever been at an age when many women would have sunk into the evening of their beauty. Behind her, Neferet nearly skipped. She was grown but so full of energy that she was unable to walk sedately. Hani's heart warmed with love, as always, when he thought of his little duckling. In appearance, Neferet was a female version of her father, square jawed and stocky, with small brown eyes and the same winsome gap between her front teeth. But whatever she lacked in beauty, she more than made up in personality, the irrepressible girl. Hani saw less of his daughter than he might wish, even though she lived in Waset, assigned to the coregent's court. She'd married Hani's friend and superior Lord Ptah-mes and resided, with Bener-ib, in her husband's magnificent villa while Ptah-mes himself was all but banished to far-off Azzati, a victim of the king's antipathy. Hani declined to think about the strange arrangement of convenience that defined that marriage.

He turned to his father. "What will happen now, I wonder?"

Mery-ra said, with a twinkle of false innocence in his eye, "I suspect we'll eat dinner."

"I meant with the kingdom, revered Father." Hani pretended to punch Mery-ra in the arm. "Ankh-khepru-ra was supposed to outlive the king and provide a transition to the reign of the little prince, maybe make him coregent with himself for a while when the boy was older. Who's left except the great queen now? And that seemed to be something the king was trying to avoid."

Two servants arrived, bearing between them the couch of Hani's eldest daughter, Baket-iset. Paralyzed after a terrible fall from a boat when she was only fifteen, she'd remained strong souled and cheerful. Hani's nose twinged every time he thought about her, his swan, who was all the more precious after her brush with death the previous year. "Papa, Grandfather, wait till you see what Mama had the cook make." Baket-iset turned her sunshine smile upon the two men as the servants set her down.

Hani drew down the reed mat that shaded one end of the pavilion from the long rays of afternoon and resumed his seat. "I can't wait." He cleared his throat and asked in a lower voice, leaning toward his daughter, "Did Neferet tell you what has happened?"

"About the coregent? Yes. I'm very sorry for him. He was so young."

"I guess we'll have to trot out the white scarves again," Mery-ra said without much sorrow. He popped a slice of pickled turnip into his mouth and leaned toward his beer straw.

Nub-nefer and Neferet soon emerged from the house, leading a procession of servants, who arranged the dishes on small tables in front of the assembled family's seats. All talk ceased as they tucked into the delicious fish baked on fennel leaves.

"Lady Meryet-aten told me to tell you she wants to see you after the funeral, Papa." Neferet said into the silence, her mouth half-full.

Mery-ra shot his son an uneasy glance. Hani stopped

chewing, frozen in his tracks. He hoped this was nothing serious. The last time the younger Great Royal Wife had called him in was to find out the real mother of the Haru in the nest. He was aware that the younger queen harbored designs on the throne after her father's death.

"Do you know why, little duckling?" Hani finally asked.

"I have no idea, Papa." Her eyes shifted guiltily, and Hani suspected she did indeed know.

The family settled back to their meal, Hani careful not to let his uneasiness show. They had made their way through the quails and grilled endive and were starting in on figs when there was a loud, breathless exchange of voices coming from the gate. A moment later, Hani's son-in-law and secretary, Maya, came pounding down the path on his short legs, crying, "My lord! My lord! The coregent has died!" He mounted the porch, his face flushed with excitement.

"I know, son." Hani motioned to a stool, and Maya hoicked himself up onto it.

"I already told them," Neferet informed him, smug.

A flash of annoyance flittered across Maya's face, but he said handsomely, "Of course you would have, my girl. You work in the palace, don't you? I just found out at the barracks."

"What else were they saying, my boy?" Hani said, trying to soften the blow—Maya liked to be indispensable.

"They're saying that the king isn't long for this world either—"

"I told them that a long time ago," said Neferet, not easily put into the shade.

"And that there will be a civil war between Lord Ay's

party—that is, Lady Nefert-iti and the crown prince—and her daughter's party, which wants to return the country to the old ways."

Hani and his wife locked eyes. A smile of carnivorous delight spread across Nub-nefer's face. "May the Hidden One bless the girl. She's stood firm through all the indoctrination of her childhood."

The end of this awful nightmare may be in sight, Hani told himself, hardly daring to hope. *But I fear it won't come bloodlessly. Today is a day of bad omen indeed.*

⊠

Seventy days later, the Osir Ankh-khepru-ra was inducted into the afterlife in a splendid ceremony at the capital, in which Hani, an increasingly upper-level functionary, found himself involved at rather close rank. All the diplomats abroad had been called home. To Hani's amazement, Lord Ptah-mes was actually among the grandees chosen to help sledge the late coregent's coffin to its burial place in the valley in the mountains east of Akhet-aten. As Hani stood in the sun, sweltering in his neck full of gold *shebyu* collars while he waited until he and his peers were to join the procession, he wondered who had made that decision. Certainly not the king, who was no friend of Ptah-mes. Perhaps the Osir's young widow. Hani asked himself whether things might soon be going Ptah-mes's way for a change. Nefer-khepru-ra had made a point of bypassing Ptah-mes for promotion and, indeed, degrading him in rank over and over, driving the commissioner deeper and deeper into rebellion. *And now this honor…*

The royal family, including the eighteen-year-old

widow, attended the ceremonies under a flower-decked marquee, cooled by servants with ostrich-plume fans, while everyone else tried not to pass out in the glaring sun of early Inundation season. Ironically, the burial took place on what had once been the collective festival of the Gods of the Two Lands. *Are they planning their return?*

Hani shaded his slitted eyes with a hand and stared around. The bleak Great Place, where kings had been buried on the west bank of Waset from time out of mind, was a verdant garden in comparison to this fissure in the cliffs of the eastern desert. Here were no royal mortuary temples, with their carefully tended trees and shrubs, to soften the harsh reddish stone. Indeed, Hani wasn't even sure where the mortuary chapel of the deceased coregent was. Perhaps it had yet to be constructed—no one had expected him to die.

Hani's mind was full of turmoil. *No question but that the death of Ankh-khepru-ra is the end of something, and the gorgeous facade that remains standing is hollow and doomed.*

Nefer-khepru-ra opened the mouth of the coregent's coffin so the dead man might enjoy the food and perfumes of the Field of Reeds—even though, Hani was sure, the Atenist creed made no provision for a Field of Reeds. This was a role usually played by the deceased's son. At royal burials, the ritual signaled that he had been designated as his father's successor. But of course, Ankh-khepru-ra had had no children.

What does it mean that his older brother, not the little nephew who is the Haru in the nest, took this role today? The king looked drained by the weight of his duties. He could have let his energetic nine-year-old take over the burden, but somehow, the symbolism had been important enough to for him to undertake it himself.

At last, the ceremony was over. The royal family made their way, in their carrying chairs, back to the palace, and little by little, the lesser participants untied their scarves. The image of the black-clad, bare-breasted mourning women, wailing and strewing their hair with dust and tearing their clothes, lingered in Hani's mind like a bitter aftertaste.

In a reflective mood, Hani spotted his old friend Mane. His heart brightened. They waved at one another, and Mane scurried against the current to walk beside his friend.

"I haven't seen you for over a year," Hani said, slapping Mane delightedly on the back. "How are you managing at Artatama's court?"

Mane rolled his eyes. "I'm retired, my friend. There's not enough of Naharin left to justify an ambassador, and our government isn't interested in talking to the Hittite viceroy at Karkemisa. It seemed like a good time to say my goodbyes to the foreign service."

"We're the poorer for that, but I'm happy for you. I wish I could do the same." Hani thought queasily of the threat of promotion that hung over him in spite of his resistance to the king's policies. He'd almost quit once. But he'd known that those who chafed against the king's reforms wanted loyal men to pack the bureaucracy so that when their day came, the transition would be smoother. Having seen the pale ghost of Nefer-khepru-ra, Hani wondered if that time were upon them.

"Your family's not here?" Mane asked in his booming voice as they walked.

"My father, sons, and son-in-law are. Nub-nefer refused to come, and the girls stayed with her, except for Neferet."

"My wife's not here either. She had no desire to stand out in the sun for hours."

The two of them trudged in silence over the stony ground toward the city.

"What does it mean that our kings are now to be buried in the east?" Hani mused. "What does that say about the afterlife?"

Mane shot him a wry look. "We'll all get to flutter around Nefer-khepru-ra's altar, remember? He'll shine like the sun upon us." He wiggled his fingers to indicate the joyous throng of fluttering souls.

Hani snorted. It occurred to him that he'd heard more and more of this sort of open scorn, even among the diplomatic corps.

"Do you want to join me on my boat?" Mane asked. "I'm leaving this evening for Waset, even though I won't get far before nightfall."

"Thanks, my friend, but my family and I are to meet at my firstborn's house, where we'll spend the night. I'm hoping to see Lord Ptah-mes before I get away."

Mane nodded. "Where is he these days? He used to be my superior, but then he disappeared."

Hani heaved out a breath of disgust, dangerously close to saying something he would regret. "He was demoted and sent to Azzati. I saw him last year when I was up there."

"Demoted, eh?" Mane's cheerful face twisted in a momentary sneer. "His honesty was too much of a thorn between someone's toes, I suppose."

"Undoubtedly."

"My lord! My lord!" called a voice from behind Hani, making him turn. Maya was trotting up from out of the press. With his short stride, he fell into step alongside the two diplomats. "I can hardly believe I found you in this crowd. Lord Mane." He nodded respectfully to Hani's friend.

Hani smiled down at his son-in-law with affection. Maya was still wearing his pen case over his shoulder, reluctant to abandon the symbol of his literacy even in a crowd composed mostly of literate bureaucrats.

"Here's where I split off. I'm docked downriver," Mane said. He and Hani clasped forearms. "Come see me. I'm always home now."

"With pleasure, my friend."

As they entered Akhet-aten proper, Mane disappeared into the crowd while Hani and his secretary turned south on the main processional street. He observed, as they passed the central palace, that the red banners signaling the king's presence stirred lazily in the sluggish air. Hani's thoughts were confused, a mixture of dread and hope.

As if he'd read Hani's mind, Maya asked in a quiet voice, "What will happen next, my lord?"

"I don't know. There'll almost certainly be an uprising as soon as the king dies. That may be the moment this whole bizarre experiment falls apart. I can't imagine there are many real believers. Most people, like our Aha, are committed only to please the king and advance their careers."

Maya made a ruminative humming noise.

"Whether that's a good or a bad thing, I'm not sure. The restoration of the Hidden One may come at a bloody cost." The thought sat like a weight on Hani's chest, making it impossible to rejoice as he wanted to.

"It depends on whom the army supports, doesn't it?"

"I suspect it does." Hani thought about the young officers he knew—the noncommittal Menna and the fervently anti-Atenist Pa-aten-em-heb, who'd wasted no time returning to his own name of Har-em-heb as soon as he was posted outside the Two Lands. "I guess our friend the new commissioner of Kumidi is back for the funeral. Is that why you were at the barracks?"

"No, Lord Hani. I was visiting a comrade, a young standard bearer. His wife is Sat-hut-haru's friend, and I thought it might be useful to cultivate another contact in the infantry. Maybe we'll see Har-em-heb somewhere here today."

Hani looked about him at the throng. Many people had peeled off to their separate destinations, but it was still quite a crowd that streamed toward the River or up or down the processional street. It would be miraculous to encounter the commissioner among all these people—this flock of noisy lapwings.

"You know what I want?" Hani asked.

"For there not to be a war? For the Hidden One to be reinstated?"

Hani turned a humorous eye to his secretary. "I want lunch."

⊠

At Aha's house that evening, the male members of the family gathered in the garden after dinner to enjoy a pot of beer or some honeyed tamarind drink. A sweet pearly twilight had descended. The cicadas were hushed, the crickets had taken up their watch, and a musky perfume of aromatics wafted from the well-tended flowerbeds edged with white stones that glowed in the fading day. The men settled themselves in comfortable silence, and the liquid notes of a nightingale rose over the quiet evening. It was hard to imagine civil war disturbing this pleasant tranquility.

Hani, sitting on the step of the garden pavilion alongside his second son, Pa-kiki, put an arm around the boy's shoulder. "We don't see much of you these days, now that you're stationed in Kumidi."

Pa-kiki said enthusiastically, "That may end soon, Father. Lord Har-em-heb has been promoted to general. He's being withdrawn from the commissioner's post."

Hani and Maya, seated on the other side of Pa-kiki, exchanged a look. "His wife will be happy," Hani said neutrally, mindful of Aha's presence, but in fact, he could barely contain his delight. Their fervent friend was making his way rapidly into a position of influence.

"And so will I. It's pretty boring up there. But now that Lord Har-em-heb is a general, we can return to put those rebel vassals in their place with as many troops as we need."

Hani pondered this development. It seemed the cause of the Hidden One was advancing nicely.

Seated in his chair above Hani, Aha was pontificating. Mery-ra pretended interest, but his jaw trembled with a suppressed yawn. He finally interrupted Aha. "What will become of your job if the old gods make a comeback, my son?"

Aha bridled. "The Aten isn't going anywhere,

Grandfather. Maybe they'll open the temples back up, but the Dazzling One will always rule over our kingdom."

"And when he dies?" Hani asked.

"The Aten die? What do you mean?"

"You know who the Aten is, don't you?"

But Aha seemed confused. "He's the sun…"

"He's the king."

Aha's bushy eyebrows drew down. He appeared to have stopped in his tracks.

You'd better give some thought to that, son. You're employed by the temple of the Sun Disk, and you may soon be forced to try to look faithful to Amen-Ra, just as you've tried to look zealous for the Aten. Saying nothing, Hani bent to take a pull on his straw.

⊠

The next morning, as soon as the sun had risen, Hani, Neferet, and Maya made their way to Ptah-mes's splendid villa in the capital. Hani was eager to speak to his superior, whom he had not seen for the better part of a year. Their last meeting had been after their illegal arrest of Amen-nefer, the former commissioner at Kumidi, the two of them having taken it upon themselves to punish a corrupt and demonic man. At the very recollection, Hani's lip curled up in a sneer. He was far from feeling guilt about the matter. Amen-nefer had been the cause of Baket-iset's terrible fall. It was only by the grace of the Weigher of Souls that he and Ptah-mes didn't have the commissioner's blood on their hands. They'd certainly intended to execute the man, guilty of murder or not, but his nefarious allies, the *hapiru* brigands, had taken care of that instead.

"*Djehuty sits by the balance,*" Hani told himself in the words of one of his aphorisms. *Justice is more important than the law, my boy. Ma'at was well served.*

They approached the lofty gate of Ptah-mes's "modest place," where the commissioner stayed when he was unavoidably required in the new capital. Hani was interested to see that Neferet wanted to greet her husband. She seemed eager, striding along beside her father with a spring in her step, chattering away about potions and puppies. Bener-ib trailed quietly in her steps.

"Papa, did you know that henbane is used in medicine?"

"What's that?" Hani asked uneasily.

"It's a plant with pretty flowers," said Bener-ib in her timid little-girl voice.

Neferet continued her friend's explanation. "It stinks, though. It's poison if you eat enough of it, but a little is all right. Mostly, it's used in salves for various things. Like impotence."

Hani stared at her, round-eyed. "What do you know about that, duckling? I thought you only treated the young queen and her ladies."

Neferet shrugged, her eyes twinkling with the pleasure of shocking her father. "But that involves the queen, doesn't it? I mean, after all, who's on the receiving end of—"

"Stop right there, my girl," Maya cut in. "Say you're not applying salve to men's parts."

She snickered but left the question unanswered.

They marched along in silence for a few paces more, a clamminess moistening Hani's forehead that had nothing to do with the heat, before he was able to say what was going through his mind. "Do you mean to tell us that the Osir

Ankh-khepru-ra wasn't able to…?" He coughed, distinctly uneasy discussing such a thing with his twenty-one-year-old daughter and her friend.

"I can't tell the coregent's secrets, Papa," Neferet said with a virtuous lift of her chin. "But if someone twisted my arm, I'd have to say yes."

Hani and Maya exchanged a look of discomfort. "Please keep that to yourself, my duckling," Hani warned her. But he remembered his first meeting with Queen Meryet-aten more than a year before, when a comment about not bearing any heirs had slipped from her lips. Suddenly, it made sense. No doubt about it—Ankh-khepru-ra's foreseeable lack of children made his choice as coregent clearer, despite his modest intelligence. It had been intended to make Prince Tut-ankh-aten's claim to the throne more secure. Too many regents had taken the power from their wards and passed it along to their own offspring.

They passed through the beautifully painted gate of Lord Ptah-mes's villa. He hadn't inscribed the usual catalog of his offices on the lintel. Instead, it simply read, *Ptah-mes son of Bak-en-ren-ef.* No doubt, "First Prophet of Amen-Ra" wouldn't have sat well in Akhet-aten, where the Hidden One was never to be mentioned.

Under his breath, Hani asked Neferet, "When was the last time you saw your husband?"

"Just once, right after we were married—you were there," she said matter-of-factly. "But I've written to him."

"Yes, he told me. Good for you, little duckling."

The gatekeeper immediately welcomed his new mistress and her companion with a deep bow. Then he saw Hani and Maya, and a smile lit his formal face. "My ladies. My lords. What can I do for you?"

"Is Lord Ptah-mes in?"

"He is, my lord, and I'm sure he would be happy to see you and the mistress of the house."

"Thank you. Please announce us."

"He's in the garden, eating breakfast, Lord Hani. Feel free to join him there."

Hani had virtually lived in this house for years, staying in it whenever he made a visit to the capital. He knew the way to the garden pavilion and made his way past the long pool, the orchard, and the beautifully manicured flowers. A pair of finches was fussing and screeching, invisible in the bushes, and they filled him with the desire to laugh. Nature could not be completely tamed.

Ahead, he saw the flash of white garments and called out, "Lord Ptah-mes? It's Hani."

Ptah-mes rose from his chair under the shady grapevine rich with hanging clusters. His austere face lit up with pleasure. "Hani, my friend. I'm so glad we crossed paths. Maya." He nodded courteously, then he turned to Neferet, who was bouncing on her toes at her father's side with Bener-ib standing shyly behind her. "Lady Neferet. Lady Bener-ib." The high commissioner's face never changed its pleasant expression, but his eyes flickered sideways.

He's ill at ease, Hani thought. And well he might be. His marriage with Neferet was undoubtedly the most unconventional in the Two Lands, each serving as cover for the other's unwillingness to engage in the normal rules of matrimony. Ptah-mes had lost his beloved wife only three years before and was still in mourning—perhaps would always be—while Neferet had no interest in men and lived under Ptah-mes's roof with her lady friend.

"Lord Ptah-mes," Neferet said, bobbing in a bow. But that was the extent of her formality— Neferet was spontaneous and not too concerned with etiquette. She beamed at her husband with her broad gap-toothed smile and waggled her fingers in a wave.

Hani saw, with a thrill of unease, that Ptah-mes's expression softened into something resembling fatherly affection. *She's made him start to care for her—just through her letters, I suppose.* The gods knew his own children were no comfort to him.

"I had hoped to catch you before you went back to Azzati, my lord," Hani said.

Ptah-mes gestured for them to be seated. "Please forgive me my lack of courtesy, my friends." They settled themselves on his beautifully carved stools, and Ptah-mes crossed his legs, linking his fingers around his knee. "Any news, Hani?"

"Nothing since we last met, my lord. I wonder what's going to happen now?"

"Me too." The high commissioner's lips spread in a sly smile.

"Queen Meryet-aten is going to rebel against her mother and brother, that's what." Neferet burst out. "And since the king is sick, it shouldn't be long." She stared at Ptah-mes with sparkling eyes, no doubt delighted to take him off guard.

Ptah-mes sat up. He caught Hani's glance and lifted an eyebrow in surprise. Maya groaned and hung his head. Hani could have spanked his daughter, who was ever ready to spill any secret to draw attention to herself. Along with that impulse came a twinge of guilt that he had not informed his superior of this earlier. It hadn't seemed to be his news to share.

"How do you know this, my dear?" Ptah-mes asked smoothly.

Smug, Neferet smiled. "I work at the Teni-menu, of course. I'm the young queen's physician."

Ptah-mes nodded slowly. "I've heard that Lady Nefert-iti is to be raised to full coregency and that Lady Meryet-aten is to become Great Royal Wife in her place."

Maya gasped, and Hani widened his eyes in stunned silence. Neferet said, in the flat voice of disappointment, "*Iyi!* I didn't know about that!"

"It sounds like the whole royal family is a set of *senet* pieces to be moved around the game board at the king's will," Hani said, poorly disguising his disgust. "All this shuffling of roles smacks of desperation to me."

"Doesn't it?" Ptah-mes smiled. The idea seemed to please him. He looked more genuinely cheerful than Hani had seen him in a long time—certainly since Nefer-khepru-ra had come to the throne. "Perhaps the end is upon us, Hani."

"That's what I feel, too, my lord." Hani turned to Neferet and said urgently, "But no one must express that in public, my duckling. Not a word of it. Dying animals often bite."

She smirked. "Good thing I'm a doctor, isn't it?"

Hani had to laugh in spite of his anxiety. *The clever little demon.* He saw Ptah-mes smile indulgently and thought once more, *Oh dear. He's under her spell.* "I suppose we're still in our old assignments. The coregent wasn't in charge of foreign service appointments."

"No. It's still Ra-nefer." Ptah-mes's lips grew thin. Hani knew how he held the vizier of the Lower Kingdom in contempt. "But I suspect he'll be distracted with all the coronations coming up. You might as well enjoy some time with your family until someone remembers we have a foreign policy."

Maya suppressed a snort, and Neferet giggled outright.

"I was pleasantly surprised to see you as one of the late coregent's pallbearers, my lord," Hani said. "Does this mean things are... looking up for you?"

"As you have probably guessed, that honor was at the request of Lady Meryet-aten. Perhaps the king didn't even know until he saw me there. I understand he's delegating a lot more decisions than he used to."

Hani nodded. "It was a little risky for both you and her. She's declared her independence of her father in full public view."

Ptah-mes smiled caustically. "All the colleagues who abandoned me in disgrace have started creeping back to remind me how they've always admired me."

"I wonder what's made her change her mind. Does she know you well?"

"In a word—Mai." Ptah-mes exchanged a significant look with Hani. "She's been listening to him."

Mai, the First Prophet of Amen-Ra, had watched his god dishonored, his temples shuttered, and his priests and personnel dismissed, with no apparent resistance. The Hidden One's estates had been confiscated and his treasuries stripped. But Mai and his fellows had not given up, Hani knew. Quiet on the surface, they were seething below, fomenting rebellion among the bureaucrats and the army, enlisting the support of allies... and even enemies.

Hani goggled at Ptah-mes, dumbfounded. "The Crocodiles? She's in with them?"

"Who's Mai? Who are the Crocodiles?" Neferet asked, gaping from face to face.

"Perhaps it's safer for you not to know, my dear," said her husband with that same softened expression as before. "Since you work at the palace."

Hani saw the beginning of a stubborn lip outthrust, but then his daughter's eyes grew round as she cried, "Oh, wait. Will anybody be living in Waset now that Ankh-khepru-ra is dead?"

Ptah-mes shrugged. "A good question. I doubt it. It was never clear to me what the king hoped to accomplish by that anyway. Perhaps just to keep an eye on our fair city, full of sedition as it is."

Neferet turned to her father, her little brown eyes squinting with anxiety. "Do you think Lady Djefat-nebty will send us permanently up to Hut-nen-nesut to tend the king's harem, now that nobody will be at the Teni-menu? It's so-o-o far away..."

"How can we know, my girl?" Maya answered irascibly.

Hani chuckled inside. He could imagine how irritated Maya was at Neferet for monopolizing everyone's attention for so long.

At last, Ptah-mes rose with a brush of his skirts, and the others followed suit. "I know you need to get away to Waset, Hani. And for that matter, so do I. There's nothing holding me here at the moment. Can I prevail upon you to join me on my boat?"

"I thank you, my lord, but my father and brother are with me."

Ptah-mes tipped his head in a gracious gesture of welcome. "I would be delighted for them to join us. Shall I meet you at the embarcadero after lunch?"

"With pleasure, Lord Ptah-mes. That's very kind of you."

"But anyway, it's my boat, too, Papa," said Neferet with a grin as if she'd just realized this delightful fact. She caught Ptah-mes's eye with merry complicity.

This is still a game for her, Hani thought uneasily. *I just hope Ptah-mes doesn't really fall in love with her only to have her repulse him. It would be too cruel.* "Then we take our leave, my lord. We'll see you at the boat."

Ptah-mes saw them off with perfect grace, and Neferet decided to go back to Aha's with them for lunch rather than remain at her husband's villa. Through the garden shaded with sycomore fig and plane trees, the four of them set off. A pair of ducks floated serenely on the water of the long pool, and Hani eyed them with affection. *They have no idea what's about to break over the Black Land. But then, no one really does.*

With a nod to the gatekeeper, who threw back the heavy doors for them, Hani and his secretary and his daughter passed out into the street. The heat and glare hit them on the dusty road like a slap across the face.

"What do you think about what Lord Ptah-mes told us, Lord Hani? That's what you tried to get for the queen years ago," Maya said.

"But *iy*, to marry your own daughter?" Neferet's nose wrinkled.

"I suspect it's just a pro forma marriage, my duckling." *And you should know about that.* "The Great Royal Wife has many ceremonial duties, and if Lady Nefert-iti is really a full-fledged king, she can't perform them. Perhaps that's why Nefer-khepru-ra didn't formally make her king back then, even though she had all the powers of one."

Maya nodded. "That's probably true."

They strode on in the silence of the noon hour, while the sun beat down upon them mercilessly. There were scarcely any shadows at that time of day. Fortunately, Aha's place was also in the southern suburb of the city, so their way was not long.

"Well, here you all are at last," cried Mery-ra as soon as the little party had entered the gate. "We'd begun to think that slavers had kidnapped you and dragged you off to Sangar." He heaved himself up from where he was sitting on the steps of the garden shrine. Pipi, hunkered beside him on the gravel path, managed to rise gracelessly, bottom first, nearly losing his wig.

"You'll both be overjoyed to know that Lord Ptah-mes has invited us to join him on his yacht for the trip home."

"*Yahya*! Oh, Hani, you know how I love that boat!" Pipi cried, a grin lighting up his square-jowled face until he nearly quivered with excitement.

Hani laughed. "Why are you coming down to Waset, anyway, little brother? Don't you have duties at the Hall of Royal Correspondence here?"

"It's the Feast of the Purification of the Hearts of the Gods. I'm off work."

Mery-ra snorted. "Don't tell me they gave you *that* day off in Akhet-aten."

"And a lot of other festivals are coming, Father."

"There's something nearly every day of the year. But they're not all holidays, you know, son."

Pipi's smile faded, and he hung his head and looked up guiltily from under his eyebrows. "I told them I was sick. But I want to see Mut-benret and the grandchildren."

Forcing the rebuke out of his voice, Hani said in a neutral tone, "Not even Pa-kiki is coming down, and they're his wife and children. He has duties, and his superior is stationed in Akhet-aten at the moment, so there he stays." *Like a grown-up.* Pipi was nearly fifty, but he was still just a big ten-year-old at heart, with no sense of responsibility.

Pipi was quiet during lunch, undoubtedly suspecting he'd disgraced himself in his father's and brother's eyes yet again. But Aha, Mery-ra, and Neferet kept the conversation lively. As for Hani, he was sunk in troubled thought. *How do I figure into the queen's plans?* Despite the possibility of a much-desired outcome in the short term, this summons foreboded nothing good.

CHAPTER 2

AFTER THREE DAYS, THE TRAVELERS had reached Waset, and Hani was happy enough to enjoy an afternoon in his family's company. They settled all together in the pavilion for dinner, the twilight starting to twinkle with oil lamps hanging over the tables.

"We have snails, Hani. I know how you love them." Nub-nefer kissed the top of Hani's wigless head then probed his close-cut curls with a finger. "It's getting pretty gray up here, my love."

"Nothing a big dish of snails in garlic sauce can't cure." He winked at her.

They fell to their dinner, and silence descended while everyone savored the snails. *There's fennel in there*, thought Hani with pleasure. At a moment like this, every little thing about his life made him happy. He could give himself up to the company of those he loved best and pretend he wasn't about to get sucked into some dangerous political assignment.

"You know, I think I'd like to have a yacht like that.

Look how it shortens our travel time," said Pipi wistfully. Clearly, he was still reliving the trip on Ptah-mes's boat.

Hani hoped another of his brother's ruinously expensive passions wasn't about to take root. He and his father exchanged an uneasy glance behind Pipi's back.

Mery-ra said neutrally, "I think that's outside the range of most scribes, son. Even Hani doesn't have one, and he's Master of the King's Stable."

"It wouldn't have to be that big…" Pipi's eyes had taken on a dreamy look.

The worst of it is that Nedjem-ib would probably go right along with him, Hani thought in exasperated amusement. *Their children won't have any inheritance at all.*

Nub-nefer said dryly, "Perhaps you can find something stolen that's on sale cheap to a gullible buyer."

The others laughed, including Pipi, who grew red in the face. Everyone remembered his disastrous attempt at horse trading. Laughter defused the tension, and they finished their meal in a genial mood.

Hani and Nub-nefer went to bed early. *Perhaps Meryet-aten will forget all about me tonight*, Hani thought before he fell asleep.

⊠

But the next morning, Hani sat up in bed and told himself, *I can't avoid it any longer, or the young queen'll get suspicious. I have to go see her and learn what she wants to talk to me about.* He got reluctantly to his feet, rubbing the sleep from his eyes, then knotted a kilt around his hips and lurched downstairs and into the kitchen in search of something to eat. To his surprise, he found his father standing at the outside door, surreptitiously eating the last of the snails from the night before.

"Ah, Hani, my boy." Mery-ra licked his fingers, looking guilty. "I had hoped to finish these off before you showed up."

Hani, overcome with affection, wrapped an arm around his father's shoulders and grinned. "As if nobody would be able to tell who had eaten the garlic snails, you old rogue."

"It was mostly Pipi I was hoping to beat to them." Mery-ra dug the last of the tasty mollusks from its shell and swallowed it. "There's bread and some figs left."

"I'm not too proud to eat your sweepings." Hani found milk in the big jug and poured himself a cup then broke off half a flatbread. "Let's go out into the garden. I don't want to wake everyone up."

They made their way barefoot out to the pavilion through the peaceful twilight of an early morning still not light enough to cast shadows. Ta-miu, Baket-iset's cat, appeared on the path with some small victim in her mouth, froze, then slid away into the bushes.

"That had better not be a bird." Hani pushed the good low-backed chair over to his father and seated himself on a stool. "I need to go see the young queen," he said, breaking off a chunk of bread.

Mery-ra looked suspicious. "What's Neferet dragged you into now, son?"

"I don't know yet. Did I ever tell you about the last time Meryet-aten called me in?"

"Oh, my boy, stay away from those royal women. They mean trouble." Mery-ra's face grew suddenly serious.

"For sure. But when a man is commanded, he has to obey his queen."

Hani's father sat forward as curiosity overcame anxiety. His voice dropped. "Tell, tell. Why did she call you before?"

"She wanted me to find out who Prince Tut-ankh-aten's real mother was."

Mery-ra drew back, surprised. "Was there any doubt?"

Hani told him what Neferet had revealed to him some years before—how Queen Nefert-iti's stillborn baby had been switched with that of a servant from the Hall of Royal Ornaments. "Needless to say, no one must ever know this, or Neferet would be in terrible trouble."

Mery-ra widened his little brown eyes and blew out an exaggerated breath as if to say that was an understatement. "How do my family members get into these things? My life at your age begins to look quite bland."

Hani laughed in fond accusation. "I understand you were a spy of some sort and not just an ordinary military scribe. How bland could that have been?"

"Bland, son. Bland. There were no royal women involved."

"Speaking of which…" Hani rose and stretched. "I've procrastinated as long as I can. Say a prayer, Father."

"May the Hidden One watch over you, my boy."

Hani made his way into the house, where he encountered a groggy Pipi shambling toward the kitchen. They exchanged an affectionate mock punch, and Hani headed up the stairs to where Nub-nefer was sitting at her cosmetic table, grinding kohl for her eye paint on a stone palette.

"Good morning, my love," she said with a smile, tilting

her face up to him for a kiss. "Where are you off to so early?"

He winked at her. "I'm going to see another woman."

☒

Maya at his side, Hani made his way to the Theban palace of the young dowager queen, his stomach aflutter with trepidation. He found he had little to say as the two men trudged along.

"What do you suppose this is about, my lord?" asked Maya after a while.

Hani shook his head and let out an uneasy puff of air through his nose. "I don't know, but I can't imagine it's anything safe to be seen doing."

They passed the massive walls of the Ipet-isut, the temple of Amen-Ra, now deserted and locked, its flagpoles bare and its massive gilded doors barred. A hand visoring his eyes, Hani squinted at the undulating silhouette of the wall against the morning sun. *Is a new day dawning for the Hidden One, in fact?*

At the pylon of the Teni-menu palace, Maya took a seat outside the walls, where the morning shade still made it endurable, while Hani proceeded alone across the deep court planted with rows of young shade trees like the living hypostyle hall of some temple. He experienced the unease he might have felt upon entering a temple—the same sense of getting into something that dwarfed and crushed him. *Please say there's no conspiracy afoot here against the Great House that will suck me into it.* He mounted the wide steps of a porch with a pair of elaborately costumed Nubian soldiers in leopard skin and ostrich plumes guarding them at either end. There a doorman bade him wait.

A short while later, the majordomo, with his long bronze-shod staff, appeared. "Follow me if you will, my lord." The servant turned and, barefoot and soundless except for the clicking of his staff, made his way through the reception hall and back into the more private areas of the palace, Hani clopping after him.

Hani had entered palaces before, and in fact, the Teni-menu was considerably smaller than most. It was a residence the king had built when he was still coregent and Waset was the capital of the Two Lands. Like everything Nefer-khepru-ra set his hand to, the place was exquisite, the walls painted in rich colors with scenes of marsh life and animals frolicking—praising the Aten who sustained them. Mercifully, there were none of the shocking distorted images that the coregent had set up in the Teni-menu's sister buildings, like the Gem-pa-aten.

The cool, dark hall was gradually lit as they approached a portico that opened into a court. Between the painted water-lily columns, gauzy curtains of fine linen billowed inward with the slightest breeze, filtering the sunlight of morning into a dreamlike pearly glow, blurring the silhouettes of what had to be solid stone into a substance more ethereal. Outside, the low, sweet voice of a *menut* dove called. Hani fully expected that the curtains might open at any moment to reveal some goddess. Instead, a stoutish middle-aged woman in court dress came forward up the steps out of the garden, parting the gauze with her hands.

"Lord Hani?" she said.

Not sure of the woman's rank, Hani bowed deeply. She led him back through the curtains into the lush greenery of a garden centered with a long T-shaped pool and shaded by persea trees, their bright-green fruit hanging like gems among the richer green of their leaves. Hani gasped. Nothing moved him as much as a beautiful garden... except a beautiful bird. As if the vision were tailored to his own idea of perfection, an extremely large heron the color of twilight stood like a statue in a corner of the pool. *It's the* bennu *bird, the symbol of the reborn soul!* Surely some important rebirth was promised. Hani felt his anxiety slipping away, leaving eagerness in its wake.

His guide left him and disappeared among the trees. A moment later, a slim girl in a short wig with an elaborate jeweled sidelock appeared. Hani recognized the coregent's queen from their meeting a year before. She was a strikingly beautiful young woman, with her mother's juicy cheekbones and her father's pointed chin and full, curved lips.

Her green-painted eyes lit up. "You came!"

"If my lady the queen commands, I must obey," Hani said gallantly with another bow that aimed his nose to the ground.

Meryet-aten's eyes glittered. "Remember those words, Hani." She turned to the lady at her side. "Bring your husband, Sit-djehuty."

The older woman melted away through the trees while Hani and the young queen stood face-to-face in silence. Finally, a heavy tread on the gravel signaled the approach of someone large. Hani looked up at the blur of white clothing materializing through the curtains as the man emerged, and his jaw dropped in shock.

"Lord Mai!" he cried.

"Hani, my friend," said Mai in his deep, fruity voice. He smiled and extended his hands. Hani clasped them, still not quite able to absorb it. "Our time has finally come."

Hani nodded stupidly. *Ptah-mes was right. Lady Meryet-aten is one of Mai's revolutionaries.* These were the men and women Hani thought of as the Crocodiles, and they had come out of the water at last. "May it be so, my lord," he managed to say.

"Now is the time you can be of service to us, Hani," Meryet-aten said fervently, her cheeks flushed. She was no longer just a girl but a true queen marshaling her troops for the dangerous battle to come. "Neferet said you would help us, as you promised Lord Mai before."

Oh, merciful gods—Neferet is involved in this? "What would you have me do, my lady?"

"Tell him our plans, Lord Mai." She turned to the priest, but her burning eyes were still fixed on Hani.

Mai lowered his voice. "The king is ill, Hani. It wouldn't take much to push him into the arms of Osir."

Hani swallowed and nodded. *Are they planning an assassination, then?* This sounded more like the wild-eyed fervor of Hani's brother-in-law than the tempered resistance Hani expected from Mai and the other priests. He stared at Meryet-aten. "You're prepared to assassinate your own father?" *Am I even prepared to go so far?*

The queen dropped her eyes and looked uncomfortable. "He's dying anyway. It's a mercy, really."

"And then what? Your mother becomes king? Regent?"

"Father is already about to make her his coregent—a

full-blown king. I'm to become his Great Royal Wife, a ceremonial position."

"What about the Haru in the nest?"

Meryet-aten's face hardened, and her voice grew harsh with resolve. "Hani, that child must not come to the throne of my ancestors, do you hear? Our divine blood must be preserved at all costs."

And yet you'd murder your father? Not for the first time, Hani saw that fanaticism wasn't always consistent. He wondered if Meryet-aten's aim were not so much the restoration of Amen-Ra as her own ascent to power. "Then you foresee taking the throne after your mother dies? Won't you need a consort to perpetuate your line?"

Mai smiled gravely. "She will seek one who will bring us a peace treaty and trade monopolies."

A Hittite. Mai had hinted at this in their first meeting years before. It had seemed like a remote and far-fetched possibility, but now only the failing lives of Meryet-aten's parents stood between the idea and its fulfillment.

"I refuse to marry one of my own subjects," the queen said, lifting her chin.

"How do you see my role in this, my lady?" he asked uneasily.

Mai was the one who answered. "Just do your job, Hani." He was tall and robust with a wise, shrewd, heavy-jowled face and a majesty about his movements that no doubt came from years of liturgical pomp.

Hani remembered that Mai had replaced Lord Ptah-mes as high priest when the latter had been jerked from office by Neb-ma'at-ra. The two men seemed to have overcome their differences. Hani wondered what Ptah-mes would make of Hani's present circumstance.

"And your job will be to investigate a possible Hittite rapprochement," Mai continued.

Hani said skeptically, "I reported to the vizier a willingness on their part last year, my lord, my lady. I don't know if it was ever acted upon."

"It was not," said Meryet-aten. "My father has been too busy with his religion. And with his succession." There was something frightening about the coldness of her voice. The sweet-faced girl was a relentless predator.

"What can I do, then? I can hardly dodge my official duties to make a two-month journey to a semihostile country."

"You can if your queen commands you." Meryet-aten fixed Hani with her big dark painted eyes. "And as soon as my mother is king, I *will* command you. Then it will become your official duty."

Hani felt trapped. He could feel a trickle of perspiration under his wig. "Forgive me. You know I'm sympathetic to your cause. But are you so sure that Lady Nefert-iti herself won't abandon the religion of the Aten? Perhaps she has only been under the influence of her royal husband..."

"She has been under the influence of Lord Ay," Mai said. "And she will continue to be until his death."

"Is he really such a convinced ideologue, then?" Hani thought of something Har-em-heb had said years before—that Ay would change allegiance if he saw that the party of Amen-Ra was winning.

"My mother will be faithful. She won't persecute

anyone, but neither will she yield her status as the one priest of her god."

Hani heaved a dubious sigh. "Then for the moment, I simply wait?"

Mai smiled. "We've all become experts at that, have we not, my friend?" He clapped Hani on the back. "Stand ready to respond as soon as the time is ripe. And it's coming."

Hani's face seemed to be on fire. "Who else is with us, my lord? If we act before we have sufficient support, it could be fatal."

"We have all the priests and former employees of the temples of the entire kingdom. That's tens of thousands—hundreds of thousands—in itself. We have men in the Double House, in the Hall of Royal Correspondence, and—what is more important—in the army. And many who seem to be worshipers of the Aten now will change over as soon as they see the ruler is no longer persecuting us."

"We are everywhere, Hani," said Meryet-aten, her eyes like coals.

Hani shifted uncomfortably. "My lord and my lady must know that even among those who await the return of the Hidden One, there will be many who can't stomach the idea of putting a man of Kheta on the throne."

With a dismissive flick of his hand, Mai said, "What the people at large think isn't an issue. They'll respect the decisions their betters make for them. And we have the infantry. That's where the ultimate question will be debated. Our men in other key places will come with us. Nakht-pa-aten will turn."

The vizier of the Upper Kingdom. He controls half of the

Two Lands. Something leaden sat in Hani's middle. If he let himself be drawn into this, he would turn out to be as much a radical as his brother-in-law, the fiery Amen-em-hut. Mai and Meryet-aten were discussing regicide and a political alliance that might well be seen as treasonable. Mai and the coregent's widow didn't seem to understand the depth of the opposition they were going to encounter. And the cavalry, as might be expected, was still on Ay's side.

"So stand ready, Hani," said Meryet-aten, an exalted light inflaming her sweet girlish face.

She's certainly not what she seems, Hani thought, his flesh creeping. *She's younger than Neferet and already utterly implacable.*

Hani made a deep bow and backed from her presence. When he next raised his eyes, she and Mai had gone. The curtains blew softly along the edge of the empty porch, and Hani heard the clack of the majordomo's bronze-shod staff as he came to escort him away.

⊠

The coronation of the Great Queen Nefert-iti Nefer-nefru-aten as King Ankhet-khepru-ra Nefer-nefru-aten was to take place a few weeks later. In preparation for that glorious spectacle and the raising to queenship of Lady Meryet-aten, the capital was in perpetual festival, with beer and bread and even meat handed out to all, assuring—*if not buying*, Hani thought cynically—the satisfaction of the people. Hani couldn't help remembering the first time Nefert-iti had been crowned, elevated to a rank he'd understood as kingship but which had turned out to be something different. In his innocence, he had thought his work successfully accomplished on that day because Nefert-iti no longer considered herself in rivalry with the Beloved Royal Wife, Kiya. Yet eventually, she'd managed to have Kiya expelled from the kingdom. Hani wondered if this event, too, was going to prove to be less of a blessing than it appeared.

He'd decided not to tell his family anything about what he'd heard from Meryet-aten. Ignorance seemed like the only hope for remaining safe. Indeed, Hani wished he could un-know what he'd heard at the Teni-menu. He hoped above all that Neferet was not involved in any way with the girl who was now her royal father's wife.

But Hani wondered what Nub-nefer already knew. She'd started singing for longer periods of time lately, with a rapt expression on her face, as if practicing to resume her duties as a chantress of Amen-Ra—as if, in her heart, the liturgy of the Hidden One had already picked up where it had left off twelve years before. Hani wondered if her brother had told her something about what was afoot.

⊠

Maya had shaved freshly and put on his nicest wig and was readying himself to head to Lord Hani's for a morning of dictation when he was stopped halfway out the door by the sound of knocking at the outer gate. The heavy portal was amply strapped with bronze—because their house had formerly been a goldsmith shop—and the knock was faint. Sat-hut-haru was still in bed, having spent much of the night tending to their youngest, Mai-her-pri, who had a fever, and the servant girl had yet to arrive, so Maya slipped into his sandals and crunched across the modest garden.

Every time he saw his garden, it tucked a blanket of peace and contentment around his soul—the square pool in the middle with its waterlilies and the four flower beds edged with stones, a small tree at the center of each, separated by clean gravel paths. It wouldn't be long until the rich shade of persea and doum palms cooled the walled garden and fed the family. In the back court, he'd planted dates, pomegranates, and jujube trees, which he tended carefully himself. He had redesigned the property completely, changing it from the barren work yard of his childhood to his little piece of the blessed Field of Reeds, and Maya was inordinately proud of it. How often had he repeated to himself the beautiful words of Lord Hani's aphorisms: "Make a garden, enclose a patch. Set out trees within it as a shelter about your house. Fill your hand with all the flowers your eye can see. One has need of all of them." Every day, he called down blessings on his mother for giving the property to him and Sati.

"I'm coming," he called peevishly as the feeble knock sounded again. He slid back the bolt and heaved open a leaf of the gate. To his surprise, Khuit, the neighborhood healer, stood in the doorway.

"If it isn't my little dear," she cried happily, raising her hands.

She was no more surprised than Maya. "Come in, come in, mistress," he stammered.

Khuit, unchanged in the eight or nine years since he'd last seen her, was a tiny spindle-shanked husk of a woman, her skin as leathery and darkened by sun as if she had lain in the embalming salts. Her wrinkled old face was wreathed in smiles. "Where's In-hapy, love? I just thought I'd drop in on her for a bit of dirty gossip." She cackled with crafty good humor.

Maya was hard put to imagine his busy mother taking time for any gossip, let alone the salacious sort. He suspected some other motive. "She doesn't live here anymore, mistress. The shop has moved to Akhet-aten. It's me and my family here now. I was actually on my way out…"

She craned her neck to see the garden behind him. "Well, haven't you done a nice job, dearie. I'd love to see how you've fixed the homestead up."

Maya contained his impatience and said through gritted teeth, "Of course, Khuit. Everything's newly planted right now. We've only been here a few years." He led her to the pool, where she turned around, admiring.

"The neighbors said you were doing real nice things with the place. I'll bet you have more fruit than you can eat, heh heh." She poked him in the chest with a gnarled finger. "You wouldn't miss a few pieces for an old lady, would you?"

He blew a frustrated breath through his nose. "I'll be sure to send you some dates when they're ripe."

"May the Hidden One and the Aten and everybody else bless you, sonny! And how's our little Neferet these days? Did she stick with her studies? She got so upset sometimes over worms and things I wasn't sure she'd ever be a *sunet*."

"Yes, she did. She's one of the physicians for the royal women."

"Well, now, isn't that lovely! The king's women." She nodded several times as if to make this astonishing truth slide down her throat better. Then she looked at Maya with a sly twinkle in her eye. "D'you know what, little friend? I used to take care of the king's women too."

Oh, I'm sure, thought Maya cynically. Aloud, he said in a polite tone, "Oh?"

"Not his wives, I have to admit. But their servants. I've midwifed ever so many of them little ladies. Of course," she added modestly, "it's been a long while. From the time the Osir Neb-ma'at-ra moved the only capital up here until about—oh, I don't know—fourteen, fifteen years ago." Khuit cackled. "Not one of them was anything but a beauty. The old king, he had an eye for the pretty ones. Wanted nothing but beauty around him. Heh heh. Quite a man was our king."

I'm surprised he let you *through the door.* "Uh, mistress, forgive me, but I'm late for work." Maya edged suggestively toward the gate, but Khuit didn't seem inclined to take his hint.

"I'm fond of your little wife, Maya. If she ever needs a healer or a midwife, think of me, eh. I'm just around the corner. Was my forecast about the first boy right, or wasn't it?"

"It was, it was," he assured her, trying to conceal his impatience. "The next time Sati is expecting, we'll let you know." He herded her discreetly in the direction of the gate.

Finally, she patted him on the shoulder and gave it an affectionate shake. "A fine young man like you—it shouldn't be long before there's another one, eh?" She turned and tottered out into the street. "Remember me to your mother, little friend."

"I most certainly will, mistress. Goodbye." Maya slipped out the gate in her wake and drew it shut behind him. She'd already turned and was hobbling down the lane toward her street on her skinny little legs, the ends of her knotted scarf hanging like rabbit ears down her back.

He heaved a sigh of relief. Lord Hani would wonder what had happened to him—Maya always tried to be irreproachably punctual. He set off at a good clip, as fast as he could go without jogging and looking ridiculous. *Khuit took care of the royal servant girls, did she? That's likely.* He gave a derisive snort. *As if a working-class village healer would have been entrusted with palace personnel.*

He arrived at Lord Hani's house just as Lady Nub-nefer was leaving. She brightened at the sight of him and stroked his cheek with an affectionate hand. "Maya, dear! How is Sati? How are the children?"

"Well, my lady. Mai-her-pri is doing fine. Sati was going to come over this morning when she woke up, but if you're going off…"

"I'll be back shortly." Nub-nefer's lips curled up in a secretive smile, and her voice dropped. "I'm going to visit my brother. It won't be long before he can come out of hiding, Maya. Anuia will be so happy!"

"May it be so." Maya wondered if it was going to be so easy as that. It all seemed to hinge on who made it to the throne after Nefer-khepru-ra.

Nub-nefer passed, wreathed in smiles, and disappeared down the lane, a basket on her arm. Maya fervently hoped she didn't get Sat-hut-haru into trouble somehow. Maya had the utmost respect and affection for Lady Nub-nefer, but she was a fiery sort, like that hothead brother of hers. After five years in hiding, separated from his family, Amen-em-hut still hadn't stopped calling for the assassination of the king—unlike Lord Hani, who managed to stay friends with both sides even as he quietly pursued the path of his conscience. *There's nobody like my father-in-law,* he told himself, love and gratitude warming him, as it always did, at the thought of Hani. The man was as solid as he looked, a rampart of strength against every danger. Humorous, kindhearted, principled—he was admirable in every way. *I'm so blessed.*

⊠

"Forgive me, my lord, for being late." Maya entered, puffing with exertion, all apologies. "Just as I was leaving, Khuit appeared at the gate, looking for Mother, and I ended up having to spend time showing her around."

"That's all right, son. I'm not sure you actually are late." Hani smiled.

"Guess what Khuit told me? She said she used to work at the House of Royal Ornaments here back in the days of Neb-ma'at-ra. Can you imagine? She said she took care of the serving girls." Maya gave a skeptical bark of laughter.

Hani grinned. "Maybe she's misremembering. Maybe it was really a weaver's shop."

Maya hooted with laughter.

"I have some correspondences to translate and pass back to the vizier. Why don't you have a seat, and we'll get started." Hani folded his legs and sank to the floor amid a scatter of clay tablets. He'd begun to read the first of them haltingly, translating them into Egyptian in his mind—they could always make it more elegant later—when he heard voices at the outer gate.

A moment later, A'a appeared in the doorway. "Lord

Hani, there's a messenger here from Lord Ra-nefer. He says it's urgent."

"Send him in, my friend." Hani scrambled to his feet.

The pursy little secretary who had once served Ptah-mes pushed aside the doormat and entered with a strut. He said officiously, "Lord Ra-nefer, vizier of the Lower Kingdom, commands your presence at the earliest possible moment."

"Very well," said Hani, shooting Maya a look. "Tell him we'll set out this afternoon."

Having delivered his message, the secretary bowed and strutted out.

"I don't suppose our venerable superior could have sent a written message so I'd actually know why he wanted to see me." Hani gave an amused sniff. "Well, my friend, let's get some lunch and pack up."

"I'll need to run by the house, then, my lord, and grab some clean linen."

Hani nodded, already preoccupied with what might be coming. *Why would the vizier want to see me?* With all the turmoil of the multiple coronations, it seemed unlikely that much foreign policy was being implemented. It occurred to Hani that it wouldn't be a bad idea to see Lord Ptah-mes before he left. The high commissioner always seemed to know what was happening at court, even though he was now domiciled far away.

Hani packed quickly and called for his litter. It turned out that Mery-ra had it at his lady friend's, so Hani told A'a where he was going, in case Nub-nefer should return before him, and set out on foot. It was well into the fourth month of Inundation, and the weather was pleasantly mild. Hani breathed deeply of the sun-kissed air. The trash-strewn lanes and beggars huddled against the walls of empty villas could be ignored if one concentrated on the flock of ibises beating their way toward the River against a sky like blue frit.

He reached the sparser suburbs where the old wealth of Waset had homes along the water, and behind Ptah-mes's high-walled property, Hani saw his friend's yacht tied up at the private jetty. *Good. He hasn't left for Djahy yet.*

Hani presented himself at the gate and was ushered in by a beaming porter. He'd no sooner headed up the path to the house when a speeding whirl of white linen, accompanied by a pounding of bare feet on the path, struck him, nearly knocking him off balance. Neferet threw her arms exuberantly around her father. "Papa! What are you doing here?" She stretched up to kiss him. Some cubits farther along, Bener-ib stood, blank faced, eyes averted.

What's wrong with that girl? Hani asked himself, his heart pained. *Something terrible must have happened to her.* "I'm here to speak to Lord Ptah-mes, my duckling. He's home?"

"I'm not sure, Papa, but we can ask." She took her father by the hand, and the three of them made their way up the porch and into Ptah-mes's elegant salon. Neferet was bubbling over with energy and cheer, as usual. "I'm glad you came. You can see something new Bener-ib and I are working on." Then, unable to keep her own secret even for the purposes of a surprise reveal, she added proudly, "It's a toe."

Hani was caught off guard. Recovering, he said with a jiggle of amusement, "I think those have already been around for a very long time, my girl."

"Oh, not a real toe, silly, but a fake toe so people who've lost one can still walk."

"Is that a common problem?" he asked dubiously, thinking he'd never, in fifty-three years of life, met anyone who had no toe.

"I don't know, but we have a patient who lost one. It was hurt so badly Lady Djefat-nebty had to cut it off. And now the poor woman is terribly unsteady on her feet. You'd be surprised how important toes are."

At that moment, the steward entered, bowed, and inquired, "May I be of service to my lord?"

"Is your master home?"

"He is, Lord Hani. I'll tell him you're here."

A short while later, Ptah-mes himself came down the staircase, dressed in the latest fashion and wigged to perfection. "Hani," he called, his lean, handsome face lighting up. "You just caught me before I left this afternoon." He nodded graciously to the two women. "My dear. Lady Bener-ib."

Hani laid a hand on Neferet's shoulder. "Duckling, I need to talk to Lord Ptah-mes in confidence. Can I see your toe later?"

"Of course, Papa. Come on, Ibet." The two young *sunet*s went flouncing off up the stairs.

"See her toe?" Ptah-mes asked with a curl of amusement at the corners of his mouth. "Is something the matter with it?"

Hani laughed. "No, no. She and her friend have invented an artificial toe for people who have lost theirs."

"You should be proud of your daughter, Hani. She seems to be a very devoted doctor." That gauzy look Hani had noticed was back, softening the high commissioner's severe features.

"We're very proud of her." Hani smiled. "I wanted to see you before either of us left, my lord, because the vizier has sent for me. Do you have any knowledge of what it might be about?"

"Perhaps the king is determined to promote you?" Ptah-mes suggested dryly. Once before, Hani had come dangerously close to being named high commissioner of foreign affairs in the north, supplanting Ptah-mes, who'd been demoted from that post.

"May the Hidden One protect me! I hope not. I thought perhaps you'd heard…"

"In fact, there are whispers that the queen is interested in you. But I can't verify that."

Hani could feel the blood draining from his face. *The queen? Has she already found out that I've spoken to her daughter?* He said in a low voice, "I must tell you what has happened, my lord. No one must hear this."

Ptah-mes drew him out into the garden, where the men made their way to the dining pavilion. There they were alone with the ducks. Barely whispering, Hani told Ptah-mes about his interview with Lady Meryet-aten and Lord Mai.

Ptah-mes listened intently, eyes in his lap, his face growing drawn. "I can only hope they're as prepared as they think they are. Ay won't stand by idly if he sees his granddaughter make a move for the throne."

"They seem to think they have the support of the vizier of the Upper Kingdom and of the army."

"I think this effort to put a Hittite on the throne is

a very desperate move. It may alienate some people who might have been our supporters."

"So it seems to me," Hani said. "Although Lord Mai explained it fairly convincingly."

"Of course, *he* intends to be the real power behind the throne, I suppose."

Hani thought that was cynical but not necessarily wrong. The stranger, who probably wouldn't even speak Egyptian, would need guidance, and that guidance should be pointed toward the restoration of the Hidden One. "In all honesty, my lord, Lady Meryet-aten may have a certain legitimate claim to the throne." And Hani revealed to his superior a story he'd never told him before about the switching of babies at birth and the discovery that the little crown prince's mother was no better than a servant at the House of Royal Ornaments.

Ptah-mes lifted his eyebrows in surprise. "Meryet-aten will use that, of course. Who is the father?"

"I have no idea, my lord. It was only pure chance that led me to the mother's identity. I just hope my name never comes up in association with this. Or Neferet's."

"She's in a very dangerous position, Hani," the commissioner said. "The queen and her father would do anything to ensure this never comes out, I'm convinced."

"I'm not sure Nefert-iti knows. Neferet said the dead baby was never shown to the coregent. She may honestly believe she's the mother of the prince." Hani fervently hoped this to be true—although Ay alone was dangerous enough. "Well, I feel better now that someone else bears the weight of the secret with me," he said with a rueful grin. "Thank you for hearing me out."

"When are you planning to go back to Akhet-aten?"

"This afternoon, my lord."

"Then perhaps you'd like to accompany me on my boat as far as the capital. I'm going on to Per-nefer, of course, to catch a ship back to Azzati. Or if the sailing is already too bad at this time of year, I may take the Way of Haru overland." Ptah-mes's mouth twitched in his almost-shy smile, as if simply being a friend was a faculty so rarely exercised that he'd almost forgotten how it was done.

"I'd be delighted, Lord Ptah-mes. Thank you once again for your generosity."

The commissioner turned and headed back into the rear of the house, his elegant turned-up sandals clopping in the silence.

Neferet caught Hani before he'd reached the vestibule door and called, "Papa, can you see our toe now?"

"Briefly, my duckling. I have to leave right away for the capital."

She bounced up to her father and unveiled something wrapped in a linen napkin. Hani almost laughed. It was indeed a big toe carved from wood—very well carved, with a nail and everything—and stained the reddish color of a person's skin. Attached to it was a harness of leather straps.

"Why, this is amazing, my girl. Did you carve this?"

"Bener-ib did. She's very good with a knife," Neferet said, as proud as if she herself had been singled out for praise. "But I made the halter. Look how this piece fits around the wide part of the foot and ties so it will stay on."

"You girls will be famous for this. Who knows what body part you'll be called upon to make next! You might even carve phallus clappers for the Feast of Drunkenness!"

Neferet laughed uproariously and gave Hani a bone-cracking hug of delight. "How long will you be gone, Papa?"

"I'm not sure, my dear."

"We may be sent back to Akhet-aten too. Maybe I'll see you there."

"That would be wonderful." Hani embraced his daughter once more, and then he set off for home, where Maya should be waiting.

⊠

As always, the trip to the capital was substantially faster on Ptah-mes's sleek yacht than on a public ferry.

"You should get one of these," Maya said after they'd bidden Ptah-mes a grateful goodbye and marched down the gangplank onto the gravelly dry slope of the embarcadero.

Hani sighed as if exhilarated by the swift journey. "I'll just use Pipi's." He shot Maya a wry grin. "And I'm hoping that the capital will soon be back in Waset."

"May it be so, my lord." Maya trudged along beside his father-in-law, his writing case bobbing on his shoulder. After a moment, during which their steps crunching on the hard-packed earth of the road was the only sound, he asked, "Do you know what this audience is about?"

"I do not. Lord Ptah-mes said he'd heard whispers that it might be the qu—the soon-to-be coregent who wants to see me." Hani rolled his eyes. "The person I least want to see upon the earth, except for her husband."

Maya made a hum of assent and sank into thoughtful silence. After a minute, he noticed that they were heading to the center of town and not to the southern suburbs, where Ptah-mes's place was located.

Hani seemed to read his mind. "I want to check in with the vizier right away. If it's a royal audience he's going to announce, it won't happen immediately, and we can go leave our baggage at Ptah-mes's first."

With their traveling baskets under their arms, Maya and Hani made their way, as they so often had over the last twelve years, up the broad ceremonial road with its necklace of king-headed lions. They passed through the parklike forecourt of the smaller of the two Aten temples, which had once extended to the very water's edge. A mammoth addition to the palace, constructed by Ankh-khepru-ra during his brief reign, had taken much of the temple's place. But along the road, the park flourished, its plane saplings growing nicely, and Maya had to admit it was a pleasant place to walk, a bit of welcome shade in a sunbaked desert city. And then they passed through the gate of the bridge over the road and found themselves once more in the royal precinct. Rather than following the high white wall of the center-city palace north, they turned right into the humbler cluster of buildings of the Hall of Royal Correspondence. Hani strode briskly toward the office of Lord Ra-nefer, vizier of the Lower Kingdom, as if he feared nothing. But Maya knew his father-in-law was uneasy about what the vizier would tell him.

"Wait here, Maya," Hani said when they had entered the still, shadowed reception room and the vizier's secretary had ushered Hani toward Ra-nefer's office door. Maya sat down on the floor in a corner and pulled out a scrap of papyrus. He thought he might jot down a few scenes for the Tales he was writing about his and Lord Hani's adventures. The children would love to hear about the palace.

CHAPTER 3

HANI ENTERED THE OFFICE AND pulled the door shut behind him. He was conscious, as he bowed low, of the rotund little figure of the vizier seated on his chair, looking petulant.

"Here you are, Hani," said Ra-nefer in his high-pitched, weary voice.

Hani felt he was expected to respond, so he said with a straight face, "Here I am, my lord."

Ra-nefer suppressed a belch and clasped his pudgy ringed hands across his belly as if it might slip off otherwise. "The queen Nefert-iti Nefer-nefru-aten wants to see you. I can't tell you what about, but she seemed in a hurry. I suggest you announce your presence right away."

"I'm honored, my lord," Hani said, bowing low, hands on knees. "Was there anything else?"

"Not yet. Things are going to be reorganized soon, of course, since the entire government has returned to Akhet-aten."

Hani, who had no reason to think any part of the

government had actually accompanied the Osir Ankh-khepru-ra Smenkh-ka-ra to Waset in the first place, murmured, "Understood, my lord."

Ra-nefer dismissed him, and Hani backed his way out, bowing. Once he'd shut the door behind him, he straightened up and made his way to Maya's corner, where the young man was writing with such concentration that he didn't even see Hani until the latter cleared his throat.

With a mortified expression on his face, Maya scrambled to his feet. "Oh, forgive me, my lord."

"Nothing serious, son," Hani said with more good cheer than he felt. "Pack up your writing tools. We're off to one or another of the palaces to visit the elder queen."

"The queen, eh." Maya nodded knowingly. "She wants to see you after all?"

"So it seems." Hani's smile faded. "And I can't think of any possible reason that won't mean trouble."

"Is she at the palace here or at the north residential one?"

"No idea. Although I don't see the flags flying, so let's assume she's at the residential palace."

They emerged back onto the processional way, and this time, they headed north toward where the larger palace lay. It was some distance, a long walk. But to his satisfaction, Hani noticed that the red banners that indicated the royal presence were fluttering to either side of the gate. Apprehension was beginning to gain on him, leaving the hair on his arms standing up like the hackles of an uneasy animal.

Hani and Maya were stopped at the pylon to the outer court of the palace by a quartet of soldiers in lavish garb, one from each quadrant of the empire. Hani gave his name and said he was responding to a summons from the Great Royal Wife, and an officer made them open their traveling baskets and rifled through the smallclothes and shaving kits. At last, the soldiers lowered their spears, and the two scribes passed through the lofty gates into the outer court.

Maya let out a whistle under his breath. "I've never seen anything so enormous!"

The vast paved area, surrounded by colossal seated figures of Nefer-khepru-ra, swallowed up favor seekers, turning them into ants. Ahead, a second pylon with closed gates was designed to accommodate chariot processions, but to either side, a smaller pedestrian door stood open. Hani and Maya made their way toward one of them—this, too, guarded by soldiers with crossed spears.

"I don't remember quite this many troops before," Hani murmured. "It seems the king is feeling insecure."

Maya smirked. "I wonder why." But his saucer eyes, as he stared around, were anything but cynical. This palace, only one of four in the city, was awe-inspiring by any standards.

They breached the second pylon and strode endlessly across the smoothly paved expanse of the inner court. A few tiny figures came and went in the distance, and Hani could see the glint of armor every few cubits on the steps at the far end. To either side, two obelisks pierced the sky, their golden caps blinking in the strong sunlight like malevolent eyes. Hani's knees grew wobbly as he thought about the coming interview and pictured all the terrible possible outcomes. Could he deny any knowledge of the young queen and her plot?

Eventually, the guards on the steps grew larger until they were the size of men. "Why don't you wait here, my friend, and look out for our baggage?" Hani whispered to his secretary. "I don't know when the coregent may deign to call me into her presence. You can go back to Lord Ptah-mes's to wait if you prefer."

But Maya said loyally, "I'll wait here for you, my lord."

Hani left him and trudged up the steps past the soldiers and across the richly painted porch, with its papyrus columns and murals of marshes and birds and predatory animals praising the Aten. The majordomo met him at the door as before and padded silently into the interior of the palace to find out Nefert-iti's will, while Hani stared at the unimaginable splendor and luxury that surrounded him in this public passage. Even the lily-like column capitals were touched with gold.

How can anyone ever overthrow such power? he asked himself hopelessly. *We're going to have a civil war for nothing.*

A moment later, the servant returned and bade Hani wait until he was called. Hani, who hadn't expected to be admitted that day, took a seat on the cool gypsum floor and entertained himself by trying to identify the shore birds depicted in the marsh scenes on the wall. Some time passed—he could watch the transit of the hours from the changing angle of the sun through the clerestories. Servants came and went, more elegantly dressed than the average grandee. A group of musicians headed down the hall, instruments in hand.

Eventually, Hani's stomach growled, and he realized it was the lunch hour. *I hope Maya has gone back to Ptah-mes's house and gotten something to eat.* He'd just drifted off into a half-waking dream of fresh bread and stewed onions when the majordomo's staff came clicking through the corridor. Hani sprang to his feet.

"The Lady of the Two Lands will receive you. Follow me, my lord." The majordomo walked off, and Hani followed, anxiety mounting in him once more. He found it uncommonly hard to draw a satisfying breath all of a sudden.

The servant led Hani through a maze of the most lavishly decorated corridors, painted with delicate scenes of nature, as if one shouldn't have to abandon the gorgeous dream even to pass from room to room. At last, they saw light ahead, and soon the corridor became a colonnade around a garden. Small rooms, encircling, beckoned, their walls brilliant with color, the atmosphere heady with perfume, but it was the garden that drew Hani's eye. The rectangle within the walkway was steeply sunken, with a long pool in the center and flowers planted in narrow terraces up the sides—chamomile, poppies, yellow daisies, and little white chrysanthemums with their pungent fragrance, colonized by a fluttering population of butterflies. Four short flights of granite steps descended to the water's edge, where a serving girl crouched, filling a large jar. Hani gasped in spite of himself. He did love a beautiful garden, and this one was magnificent. In each of its four corners stood an olive tree. They were the first he'd ever seen growing in the Two Lands. Olives in the market were something new—costly and imported from Djahy—but the Great Royal Wife had four whole trees. In the shady cloister, Hani saw naked handmaids and magnificently dressed ladies-in-waiting, in fashionably sheer caftans, walking and chatting, with only an occasional glance at the male visitor. Soldiers stationed every few cubits kept watch.

"Wait here," the majordomo said to Hani with a twinkle of haughty amusement in his eye. Hani couldn't hide his awestruck reaction. This was a palace he'd never visited before.

The official strode away, leaving Hani to draw deep breaths of perfumed air into his lungs and feast his eyes. He noticed how the red poppies reiterated the red bindings of the water-lily columns. The girl with the water jug, now mounting the steps, even had a red ribbon tied around her head. *I've got to hand it to Nefer-khepru-ra*, Hani admitted grudgingly. *He has extraordinarily good taste.*

At last, the servant returned and drew a reluctant Hani away from the view. He knocked at the gilded door of one of the rooms on the periphery of the cloister, opened it, and gestured Hani within. There Nefert-iti sat on a low chair, with her father at her side.

Strangely informal. Hani dropped into a court bow, hand to mouth.

As he rose, he could see that the eight or nine years since he had last spoken with the Beautiful One had not been kind to her. The chiseled face with its firm square jaw was puffy and softened. She had, as Hani's father had observed some time ago, put on weight, and the seductive curves of old were starting to look dowdy. She didn't seem altogether well. But there was something riveting about her nonetheless, with her full lips and long, elegant neck. At her side, Ay was the same lean, bright-eyed fox as ever. *He must be nearing sixty.*

"Hani, ever our faithful servant, is it not so?" the coregent said in her smoky, breathless voice.

Hani dipped another little bow. Such a question made his stomach tighten with unease. The gods knew what sort of spying she had in mind for him. "I am yours to command, Great Lady."

"We knew you'd say that," Ay said cheerfully. "You're a principled man, and you would show yourself grateful for all the favors the king has lavished on you."

So, they were trying to buy me with all those suspicious honors of the last few years.

"I want you to investigate something for me," said the queen, "and it must be carried out with the greatest discretion."

Ay added with a chuckle, "Not the sort of thing you'd set our friend Mahu on." Mahu, the chief of the royal police, had missed no chance to wreak his animosity on Hani in the past.

Curiosity was rising in Hani's middle like a tide of warm effervescent liquid. "I'm at my lady's service."

"There have been thefts from the royal household. This has been going on for nearly a year in a minor way. But lately, things are disappearing at a faster rate."

"We could just torture all the servants," said the queen's father, "but it isn't so simple. More than once, we've changed out part of the staff until there was almost completely new personnel, but the thefts have continued."

"Is this your royal husband's household or yours, my lady?"

"Mine. The objects that have disappeared include jewelry but also baskets, small chests, cosmetic spoons—

things like that. Beautiful objects but of no great value, really."

"The disappearances aren't constant. There'll be a flurry of them, then they'll stop for a while," said Ay. "And the strangest thing is, eventually, the things come back."

Hani stroked his chin thoughtfully. "That's strange indeed—the thief isn't trying to sell them or melt them down. How long are the objects gone?"

"It's hard to say. I don't call for the same piece of jewelry every day. It might be months before we'd even notice. The other things—they seem to return in a short while."

"And you're sure these items are actually missing? They're not mislaid in some way?" Hani pressed, intrigued in spite of himself.

Ay said, "Oh, we've looked for them quite zealously since we noticed what was going on."

Hani nodded slowly. "The king is aware of this, I suppose."

But Lady Nefert-iti said dryly, "The Lord of the Two Lands is too busy to worry about missing baskets, Hani."

"So, can you help us?" Ay rose to his feet and clapped Hani on the shoulder as if there weren't years of undeclared enmity between the two men.

With a bow, Hani said, "I'll do my best, my lord. My lady."

"There's another thing." The queen looked him up and down with her languid kohl-rimmed eyes. "We want you to tutor the Haru in the nest in foreign languages."

Hani gaped. "Surely I'm of more use to my Sun God in the foreign service. I fear I have little experience as a teacher."

Ay's long mouth stretched in his friendly, foxy smile. "But you're a father, Hani. You understand boys. We need someone to teach him the arts of war as well, but don't worry." His amber eyes twinkled. "We don't expect you to do that too. You can come once a week—that should be sufficient. We know you have other duties."

"My lady's commands are the breath of life to me." Hani murmured the formulaic words with confusion in his heart. He'd be under the eye of the queen's father constantly.

"We'll notify you when to start. At some point, you'll need to meet the prince, but not now." Nefert-iti dismissed him, and Hani was backing from her presence in a deep bow when Lord Ay called out, "By the way, Hani, you'd do well not to listen too hard to my granddaughter. I'm not sure her activities are in the best interest of the kingdom. It would befit a Master of the Royal Stable to keep an eye out for her trouble-making friends, maybe let us know what they're up to, eh? Your own father had similar duties back in his day."

A pall of dread descended over Hani, chilling the puzzlement of a moment before. *This is what this interview was really about*, he thought somberly. He regained the corridor, and the majordomo led him through the magnificent halls to the golden doors. Hani drew in a deep draft of air as if he'd scarcely breathed for some time.

He saw Maya sitting on the porch steps in the one corner that was shady at that hour, almost at the feet of one of the guards. The secretary sprang up to meet him, wide-eyed with curiosity. "Has there been a murder?" he asked in a stage whisper.

Hani shook his head and laughed wryly. "No. Someone has stolen the queen's basket."

Incredulity and then disgust galloped across Maya's features. "And so she's calling in an investigator?"

"There must be more to it than that. They must suspect something."

"By 'they' you mean she and the he-king?"

"No. She and her father, Lord Ay. I got the impression that Our Sun God—life, prosperity, and health to him, of course—is too busy to be informed of such trivial matters."

Maya snorted. "I'm glad they realize it's trivial. This is almost an insult to you. Maybe they just want to keep you busy so you won't look into more important things."

"They also want me to teach Prince Tut-ankh-aten languages."

The little secretary goggled. "Is that good or bad, my lord?"

Hani shrugged and raised his eyebrows. He wondered how much it was safe for Maya to know. After the two men had walked on in silence for a ways, he said in a low tone, "There was something else. They know what Meryet-aten is up to, and they know I'm involved." He curled his lip. "All my honors of recent years have clearly been with the idea of buying my loyalty. I'm expected to report on her to Lord Ay."

Maya clenched his fists in outrage. "They want you to spy? How base. Of course, you won't do it, will you, my lord?"

Hani heaved a sigh and shot Maya a distressed look from the corner of his eye. "They've studied up on Father. They're watching my family, Maya." Hani thought uneasily of Nub-nefer's unsuspecting visits to her proscribed brother in hiding.

Maya paled, and his eyes grew round as doum fruit. His wife was Hani's daughter, after all. In silence once again, they strode along through the city until Ptah-mes's gate came into sight. The more Hani thought about Ay's parting words, the more his throat grew tight with fear. *They must know Neferet is involved with the younger queen too. Mut, mother of us all, protect her.*

He said at last, "We have to find Neferet and warn her. She's got to stay out of this business. I wonder where she is right now."

"Would the steward here know? She would surely be staying here if she's come back."

Hani, with Maya in his wake, entered the house through the porch and called out for the steward, who appeared instantly, bowing and smiling. "My lord requires something?"

"Would you happen to know where the mistress of the house is at the moment? Has she come back to the capital, do you know?"

"It's unlikely she could have gotten here so fast, though, my lord," Maya said. "She was in Waset when we left five days ago, and we just arrived today."

But the steward said, "She's here, my lord. She arrived two days ago in Lord Maya's yacht. Shall I call her?"

"Please." The servant started off, and Hani, remembering that Ptah-mes went by "Maya" now, turned to the other Maya, his heart brightening with relief. "She must have left right after we did."

A moment later, a thunder of bare footsteps sounded

on the staircase, and Neferet flew toward them across the painted gypsum floor. "Papa! I beat you here!" She threw her arms around him so hard she practically jumped on him.

Hani embraced her with a desperate intensity, as if he could protect her with his arms. "My duckling, I need to tell you something very important. I beg you to take it seriously."

She drew back, seeming surprised at his gravity, and said earnestly, "I swear I will, Papa. May the seven-headed demons pull out my tongue and the *ba*s of our ancestors tie it in a knot if I don't. May my toenails turn blue and—"

Without waiting for her to finish, Hani drew her back outside to the pavilion, where no one could hear, and the three of them seated themselves once more. He spoke quietly. "I had an interview with the Great Royal Wife and her father today, my little duck." She started to say something, but Hani hushed her with a hand. "They know about Lady Meryet-aten and her plans. They even know about my involvement. *They've watched the family*, Neferet. Whether they know specifically that you're part of it, I couldn't say, but you must be exceptionally careful. Try to stay away from the young dowager queen. It's worth as much as your life."

Never one to yield without an argument, she said, "But she's under my care, Papa."

"Do your job as a *sunet*, but don't discuss anything else, do you hear? 'Stay away from hostile people—keep your heart quiet among fighters. One who knows nothing is not bound in fetters.'"

Neferet stared at her father for a few heartbeats as if absorbing his words.

"The elder queen has commanded me to spy on you all, my love. I'm supposed to report to her anything I find out about her daughter's plot. You see what a terrible position this puts me in."

She nodded, wide-eyed with horror.

"You must keep me out of things. Tell Meryet-aten not to contact me. I'm sure her mother has other sources who will tell whether I've visited or not. So I must not. Is that clear?"

"Yes, Papa."

"And you, little duckling—do nothing that would bring down danger on your head. Be suspicious of everyone. Trust nobody."

Neferet nodded but said, "Papa, don't you want to see the Hidden One returned to his rightful place?"

"Of course, Neferet." Hani's soul writhed with anguish. "But they threatened the family. I had no choice but to obey their command. So you must give me nothing to report, any of you. Be sure Mai understands." He pulled the girl against his chest and laid his cheek on her shaven head. "Don't do anything that would draw attention to you, duckling. The safety of our dear ones may be in your hands."

⬛

The next morning, Hani and Maya found a ferry and set off for Waset, Hani's heart like lead. Five days later, as soon as he'd set down his baggage and kissed his wife, he told Nub-nefer about the upshot of his interview with the queen. Her face grew dark as she listened.

"Lord Ay is determined not to lose control of the throne, even if it means putting that little commoner on it," she steamed. "Hani, you mustn't help him. The Hidden One will never be able to come into the light if Ay and the queen win."

She was more beautiful than ever with her great dark eyes aflame and the flush of anger on her cheeks, but that didn't lift Hani's mood. "What could I do, my dove? I couldn't refuse a direct command. And they hinted at something befalling my family if I didn't help them. I couldn't bear to lose you—any of you." He kissed her forehead and drew her closer to him. "I wouldn't even have told you, but you need to be watchful. There's danger now. I keep thinking of how vulnerable Baket-iset is."

"You did right, Hani. What happens after the king's death concerns us all. It will make the difference in whether Amen-em-hut can emerge from hiding." She looked up at him, her black kohl-rimmed lashes starting to grow starry with tears. "Five years, he's been hiding—five years without his family. And for doing what? Remaining faithful to the god he has served all his life."

Hani might have said, "Your brother has been spreading sedition and calls for an assassination—that's what they're mad at him for." But he didn't. He admired Amen-em-hut's singleness of purpose. Instead, he said, "It concerns me that Neferet is so involved. Can she hold her tongue?"

"I'm proud of her, Hani. She's faithful to the Hidden One."

Hani had to agree. No one could say his youngest

daughter lacked courage. *But prudence...?* He sighed, anxiety a murmuring background noise in his mind.

"Sat-hut-haru was here this morning. She brought the children over. Mai-her-pri is all recovered. And that Tepy— he seems so much older than his nine years sometimes. He takes charge of the others like a real little man. It's adorable!" Nub-nefer smiled fondly.

Pain clutched at Hani's heart. All of these beloved ones were at risk because of him. "I'm going to have to spend more time in Akhet-aten for a while, my dove. They want me to tutor the crown prince in foreign languages."

"Use your influence on him. If he loves the King of the Gods himself, then eventually, Ay's impact will be undone. Maybe that's why the gods have permitted this." Her gaze was luminous with hope.

"May it be so. Let me go say hello to Baket before I clean up." Hani gave his wife's arm a light squeeze—she was ever his pillar of strength—and went out through the porch, into the garden, and around the side of the house where the pavilion sat. Baket-iset's couch had been set up there in the shade to take advantage of the pleasant winter weather.

She cast her eyes upward as Hani approached from behind her. "Papa! I heard your voice inside. Welcome home." She smiled, her whole face alight with love and happiness.

Hani's heart was choked with painful tenderness for this brave and beautiful daughter of his, who had never once complained or cried injustice in the twenty-one years of suffering since her accident. *Although it was no accident*, he thought, gritting his teeth. He was bitter enough for the two of them. Hani still felt bilked that her assailant had managed to find death without Hani's hand on the knife. But at least he could picture the monster in perpetual torment in the Lake of Fire.

"My swan. I wanted to see you all and spend some time with you, but it looks as if I'll have to go back to the capital more frequently." He stooped to kiss his eldest daughter and patted her affectionately on the arm. "They want me to teach the little Haru in the nest foreign languages."

"But you'll be gone for years, Papa!" Baket's disappointment was written all over her face. Then she conquered herself and added more cheerfully, "That's a great honor. I'm sure you'll win him over... to our cause."

"That's what your mother hopes too."

"And her mother says dinner is ready," said Nub-nefer, smiling, from the path.

The two servants following her picked up Baket-iset's couch, and Hani and Nub-nefer led the way, arm in arm, back into the salon. They sat down at their small tables, and Hani's mouth watered at the savory aroma of the roast duck. He experienced a twinge of conscience, since he knew and loved those ducks, but that was nature's way—the big ones ate the little ones.

And you, my boy—are the big ones going to eat you too? To Nub-nefer, who was feeding Baket her mouthfuls, he said, "The cook has outdone herself, my dove. You certainly know how to coax the best out of her."

She beamed, her happiness at his presence undisguised.

"Where is Father?" Hani asked.

"At Meryet-amen's house. She apparently has an even

85

better cook." Nub-nefer's eyes twinkled. The whole family was onto Mery-ra's motives and teased him mercilessly.

Hani laughed. Then he thought of the orphaned boy of an artisan family whom Mery-ra had taken as a pupil when his uncle, a witness in one of Hani's cases, had been killed. "And young Khawy? Is married life agreeing with him?"

"I think it is. He's working in the Place of Truth now, so we don't see so much of him. He's apprenticed to the new chief draftsman."

"Then he's fulfilled his dream," Hani said. "It's nice to have some good news for a change. He can't have learned enough in four years to serve as a scribe in the Hall of Royal Correspondence, but I'm sure he's capable of copying on the wall what someone hands him on a piece of papyrus. And he's very artistic—his whole family was."

Nub-nefer's smile tarnished a bit. She said in a hushed voice, as if she'd been holding the words back from the moment Hani arrived, "Amen-em-hut has changed his hiding place. He's back home with Anuia."

Hani's first reaction was delight, but it was quickly tempered by uncertainty. "Is that safe? The king is still alive. I can't see that anything has changed."

He could see that Nub-nefer was equally uneasy. "That's what I thought. But I'm so glad to see him openly again that I've put that in the back of my mind." She gave Hani a pleading look. "I don't want anything to happen to him, Hani."

Hani stared at his dish full of duck bones, making the effort to summon up some optimism. Finally, he raised his eyes and tried to sound reassuring. "It's quite possible that the king has forgotten all about him, my dove. It's been years since he disappeared, after all. And Nefer-khepru-ra has had a lot to think about lately, what with all the funerals and coronations."

Baket-iset, whose eyes had switched from one parent's face to the other as they talked, said, "Perhaps they wouldn't think to look for him in such an obvious place as his own home."

"May your words come true, my little swan." In his heart, Hani sighed. *The last thing we need is for Mahu and the police to start harassing the family again.* Like Neferet, his brother-in-law wasn't lacking in courage, but he sometimes showed remarkably little good sense.

Having fed her daughter, Nub-nefer took her seat at Hani's side and nudged his empty dish away to make room for her own. "Did you know that Pa-kiki's officer has been made a general?"

"Why, yes. Pa-kiki told me the last time I saw him. Are they stationed here or in the capital?"

"Akhet-aten, I believe—more's the pity. Mut-benret and the children are going to move up there eventually, but I'm sure Pa-kiki will travel anyway. You always traveled as a military scribe." She lifted a duck wing between delicate fingers and began to nibble.

Suddenly, an idea signaled its presence in Hani's mind like the metallic ring of a sistrum. *Har-em-heb is the perfect man to teach the young prince the arts of war. I need to talk to him.*

They finished dinner and sauntered out into the garden together. Twilight had descended, a cricket-rhythmed late-winter evening with air like warm milk. The day birds gave their last twitters, and from not too far away came the liquid notes of a nightingale on its spring migration. The frogs had begun their courtship bellows in the pool. After a moment, Qenyt appeared from the bushes and directed her angular footsteps toward the pavilion where the two humans sat.

"Come here, my girl." Hani held out a hand to the heron. He was feeling more at ease after a good dinner. The frightening possibilities around them seemed further away. She approached him, head tilted to see better, but apparently found nothing of interest and drifted off. Hani heaved a sigh of satisfaction.

"How long are you going to stay there, my love?" Nub-nefer asked, snuggling against his arm.

"I can't say. As briefly as I can manage."

She was silent for a while—in contentment, Hani would have said, but then she turned her face to his, and he saw that it was twisted with apprehension. "Be careful. What would happen to us all if something befell you? Oh, be careful."

Hani's mellow mood chilled. *Be careful indeed. The stakes couldn't be higher.* Trying to sound more relaxed than he felt, he said, "I thought I'd stay here until they summon me. I need to think about how to go about this instruction—what languages are most important for the prince to learn. If the vizier needs me, he'll let me know."

A commotion from the gate made Hani look up. He heard A'a laugh and then Mery-ra's jolly voice reply. A crunch of multiple footsteps marked the passage of the litter bearers toward the stable in back.

"Father?" Hani called. "Is that you?"

"In the flesh, my son—and plenty of it. You're back.

For how long?" Mery-ra toddled up the porch steps and pulled up a stool beside Hani and Nub-nefer.

Hani gazed at him affectionately. The old man was past seventy but still hale and sharp. He was broad and solid to the point of squatness, remarkably like Hani—all the men of his family resembled one another to a conspicuous degree. Mery-ra's face was red from the heat of his journey in a closed litter, his little brown eyes twinkling, his tufty eyebrows just as black as ever.

"Why, Father, do you realize you're twice as old as most people ever live to be? And look at you, the picture of health. That's remarkable!"

Mery-ra lifted an authoritative finger. "I owe it all to having my teeth. Whatever you youngsters do, don't lose your teeth."

Hani and Nub-nefer laughed.

"I try never to lend them to anyone," Hani said with a broad grin. "People always forget to give back things they borrow."

His father looked smug. "You laugh, but I'm right. Once you lose your teeth, you can't eat anything but porridge. Once you eat nothing but porridge, you lose your will to live. And then—poof!" He smacked a fist into the other palm. "Into the West with you."

"I take it that means no more porridge in the family diet, Father," Nub-nefer said, smiling. "Then I'd better go in and have the kitchen girls change the menu for tomorrow's lunch." She rose, kissed Hani, and gracefully made her way into the house.

Hani watched her go, his heart warm with love, then he grew more serious and turned again to his father. "I may have dragged the whole family into danger. You need to be very careful about what you say and where you go." He proceeded to explain the terrible commission the elder queen had laid upon him in addition to finding the basket thief and to teaching Prince Tut-ankh-aten. And he described how Lord Ay seemed to know too much about Mery-ra's career.

Mery-ra's eyes grew wide with misgiving. "*You* be careful, my boy. These are dangerous waters in which you find yourself. You're caught among three generations of a ruthless family."

Hani scrubbed his face with his hands. "I had no choice. And now I have to go back to Akhet-aten every week. I'll spend all my time traveling."

"Well, at least you'll see plenty of Aha and Pa-kiki. Neferet too. I suppose you'll be living under her roof, in fact."

It seemed to Hani that was more of an uncomfortable reality than otherwise, considering that he would be the guest of his daughter's absent husband. After a while spent in companionable—if somewhat anxious—silence, Hani stood up and clapped his father on the shoulder. "I think I'm going on to bed, Father."

Mery-ra caught his hand and squeezed it fervently. "Don't take too many chances, eh, son?"

⊠

The coronation of King Ankhet-khepru-ra Nefer-nefru-aten was as splendid as all of Nefer-khepru-ra's spectacles. But royal pageantry had become so common in the last few years that Hani found himself a bit jaded. To be sure, it was rather novel to see the former queen in the red and white crowns of the Two Lands, the crook and flail crossed over her breast as she was lifted high above the heads of the crowds in her carrying chair. No woman had sat upon the throne for generations. But Hani couldn't help but notice how small a role the male king played in the ceremonies. It had been so long since Nefer-khepru-ra had been crowned alongside his father that Hani was no longer able to remember whether that absence was normal. The words of Mai kept resonating in his ears: "The king is ill. It wouldn't take much…"

After the ceremonies had concluded, the streets began to empty of celebratory crowds laughing and talking and carrying their bread and cuts of meat that had been offered in sacrifice and then dispensed to the onlookers to take home. Hani, fearing events were rushing toward something ominous, was far from festive. He waited pensively beneath the Window of Appearances, where they had agreed to meet, until his father, brother, sons, and Maya joined him from their respective ranks.

"Let's gather at my house for a little party," Aha suggested jovially. He was all red-faced and exalted, as he always was by royal pomp. Khentet-ka, on his arm, gazed around brightly. "The offices will be closed."

But Pa-kiki had to get back to his barracks. Sati and Maya pleaded that they needed to take the children home to their grandmother before the little ones grew cranky. Hani and Mery-ra cited weariness and too much sun. Only Pipi and his wife, despite their overstimulated twins, seemed up for a celebration—everyone else dispersed, leaving Aha looking confused.

By the time Hani reached Lord Ptah-mes's house in the company of his father, the afternoon shadows were long. Neither of them had brought any of the food on offer, since they were only guests in someone else's house. They'd just settled under the pavilion, its bare tendrils veiled in palest green, when they heard Neferet's voice calling wildly from the salon, "Papa? Grandfather? Where are you?" A moment later, she emerged through the delicate greenery of late winter, her eyes wide open as if she had seen the *ba* of an ancestor. "Papa—she's dead!"

CHAPTER 4

NEFERET, PANTING, RAN UP THE steps of the pavilion, Bener-ib in her wake. Hani jumped up in alarm. He'd just seen his daughter earlier in the morning, and then they'd all separated for the coronation because Hani and his sons had official parts to play in the procession.

"What is it, my duckling?" he cried, his stomach leaping into his throat. "Who's dead? The coregent?"

"No, Papa. The old midwife who delivered the prince. I'm just sure the new king had her put to death so she couldn't tell what she knew!" She plopped with a grunt to a seat on the floor at her father's feet.

Hani and Mery-ra exchanged an apprehensive glance. They both knew what this might mean for Neferet, another witness. Hani said, "How did she die? When was she found?"

"I don't know. Ibet just heard some servants talking when we got back to the palace after the ceremony. They sounded scared. They said, 'On a propitious day like this?'"

Hani turned to Bener-ib, his voice grave. "Tell me

everything they said, my girl. Lives may depend on this—yours and Neferet's among them."

The girl stepped forward, clearly uncomfortable in the center of everyone's attention. In her little-girl voice, she began expressionlessly, "One of them said, 'Have you heard about Tuy? She was just found dead.' And the other one said, 'On a propitious day like this? Sutesh is afoot, my dear. Don't think he isn't. Strange things have happened in this palace for the last few years. Didn't you think it odd that a lady-in-waiting just dropped dead a few weeks ago?' And then the first one said, 'Keep your thoughts to yourself, my girl, if you know what's good for you.'"

It was all Hani could do not to urge her impatiently on. But Bener-ib had been told to reveal everything the women had said, and she was going to do it, so he nodded and gave her an encouraging look. "Anything more?"

Bener-ib went on, her eyes aimed at the grapevine overhead as if she were reciting something from memory. "The second one said, 'We ought to go pay our condolences to her husband. Maybe he knows more.' And the other one said, 'Where did she live?' And the second one said, 'Somewhere near that jeweler's workshop, near the River. Her husband is a laundryman.'"

"Which jeweler's workshop—did they say?" Hani interrupted, an idea forming in his mind.

"I don't know, Lord Hani. One near the River. And then the second girl asked, 'How did she die?' And the first one said, 'They found her in the water, half eaten by crocodiles.'"

Mery-ra made a noise of revulsion. "How do they know she didn't die of natural causes? Being eaten is usually fatal."

"That's what the second maidservant asked. And the first one said, 'I don't think a crocodile slit her throat. Now, don't tell anybody I told you this, or else we're both going to die young.'" Bener-ib looked from Mery-ra to Hani, gnawing her lip, like a little girl who wasn't sure she'd given the right answer to a grown-up's question. Neferet beamed and squeezed her friend's hand triumphantly.

Hani turned to his father, fixing him with a meaningful stare. "I think we need to pay a visit to In-hapy." In-hapy was Maya's mother.

"You think she might know something?"

"It's a start. She's the only goldsmith with a workshop by the River—that I'm aware of, at any rate. She might at least know where the woman lived if they're neighbors." Hani rose. "Thank you, ladies. And please, please be careful. Whoever killed her must know that you two are witnesses as well."

"But it has to be the coregent and her father, doesn't it?" Neferet cried. "Who else would be hunting the people who saw the switch?"

"We can't say that without proof. And we can't bring them to justice in any case. But they may have a spy in the queen's household. I want to know so we can try to protect you two." He gave his daughter a quick hug and said to Mery-ra, "I'm off, Father."

"Wait, I'm coming too," the old man said, hauling himself to his feet. "You know how good I am at pulling things out of people."

Despite his anxiety, Hani had to laugh. "I certainly do. Pipi and I couldn't hide anything."

"I want to come too, Papa." Of course Neferet wasn't about to be left out.

Hani could see her stubborn lip creeping forward. He said sternly, "No, my duckling. This is extremely dangerous. I don't think you quite realize that."

"Why is it dangerous to visit In-hapy? She's my sister's mother-in-law."

Hani exchanged a look with his father, who gave a shrug. "All right. But nothing else. You're recognizable as the royal *sunet*. It would be too easy for someone to wonder why you're traipsing all over the city, asking questions."

Neferet broke out into a victorious grin that bared the roguish gap between her front teeth. "You'll be glad you let me come."

◻

Early the next morning, they set off toward the center of the city, an even more motley gang than usual. Hani's daughter strode along with an excited air. Her friend had begged off, saying she had a patient who needed her attention. Nothing had changed overnight to lessen Hani's misgivings about letting Neferet involve herself further in this perilous affair, but at least it wasn't an official investigation. With the foreign office in a state of hibernation after the elevation of the coregent, Hani had the leisure to find out what was going on with the little crown prince.

"I'm almost sure Lord Ay is behind the murder of this woman," he said under his breath to his father as they walked.

"Then do you have to investigate it further, son? Nothing good can come of crossing that old fox."

"At first, I was afraid that he might try to silence Neferet too. But she's already told the story to Lady Meryet-aten, which Ay must be aware of if he has a spy in his granddaughter's household. All this makes me more determined than ever that Ay's party not win. He knows the Haru in the nest isn't really his grandson, but he doesn't care as long as the boy's accession keeps Ay in power."

Mery-ra said nothing. Only his puffing breath and the tread of six feet disturbed the stillness of the early hour. There weren't many birds in the desert city, but Hani observed a flock of ibises taking off from the River not far away, their black-barred white wings flashing as they ascended in the rosy light of the rising sun. *The servants of Djehuty, the Weigher of Hearts. Let* ma'at *be done, my lord*, Hani prayed with a discouraged sigh.

As they approached the palace zone, warehouses and long, vaulted magazines stretched before them nearly to the water's edge. The narrow streets were utterly bleak and none too clean where the north wind had blown trash into piles at every corner—torn hempen sacks, fruit peels, and loose grains of wheat that attracted rats. The houses were small. Palace artisans tended to set up their workshops here, in proximity to their clientele.

At last, Neferet pointed and said, "That's it."

The last time Hani had seen In-hapy's residence was before the building was even completed, and the encircling mudbrick wall had been only a few cubits high, still under scaffolding. It certainly looked secure now. They approached the heavy gate and knocked. Things seemed very quiet. Clearly, the day's work had yet to begin.

The old Nubian gatekeeper pulled back the panels and

peered out. "Who's there at this hour—" Then he recognized Hani. "My lord! Come in. The mistress of the house is just setting things up for the day's work." He turned to Neferet. "Welcome back, young mistress."

Hani looked at his daughter in surprise. "He recognizes you?"

Neferet looked smug. "Oh, I've been in and out, Papa." The gods knew, the girl was memorable enough in appearance, with her shaven head and determinedly working-class shift.

The porter ushered them in and barred the gate. Even before he could announce their presence, In-hapy appeared in the doorway of the workshop, pushing under the loosely woven straw mat that protected the interior from flies. Her face lit up in delight, and she came waddling out to meet them on her bowed little legs. "Lord Hani! Lord Mery-ra! Neferet, did you bring your father to see it?"

Neferet made frantic shushing motions and cast an uneasy glance toward Hani. She said with forced innocence, "No, In-hapy. Why? Is Lady Bener-ib's bracelet finished?"

"Not yet, mistress. I'll be sure to tell you when it is."

Hani saw with amusement how quickly the diminutive goldsmith had caught on and regrouped. *They're up to something.*

"If you've come to see Maya, he's in the back court, eating breakfast. Sat-hut-haru is still sleeping, and so are the children."

She led the way through the silent workshop into the rear court. There Maya sat on a log near the woodpile that fed the forge, a bunch of dried dates in his hand. At the emergence of his father-in-law and other relatives by marriage, the secretary leaped to his feet and cried in delight, "My lords! Neferet! You're still here?"

"Don't stop eating, son. We've actually come to talk to your mother." Hani added in a low voice, "The midwife who witnessed—*ahem*—the birth of the crown prince has just been found murdered."

Maya's jaw dropped.

"How can I be of service, Lord Hani?" In-hapy inquired politely.

"My dear, do you know of a midwife in your neighborhood?"

In-hapy's lips spread in her half-toothed smile. "Nobody knows their neighbors here too well—we're all new. But I do know her by hearsay. Apparently, a very good midwife who was even hired by the palace on occasion. I understand she's died."

Hani nodded gravely.

"I need to offer my respects to her family. I think her husband is a laundryman for the king. It's him I see around occasionally."

"If you go, would you mind if we joined you?"

"Not at all, my lord." She looked at Hani then at her son. "Should I get cleaned up?"

"You look fine, Mother," Maya assured her. "You'll be back before it's time to open the shop."

She straightened her scarf and brushed down her shift, and the five of them set out. The midwife's house was just around the corner and rather more nicely kept than one would expect of a place belonging to a laundryman. When they knocked on the modest gate, a servant girl appeared in the opening. She looked at them inquiringly but said nothing.

"Hello, my good woman. We're here to pay our condolences to the Osir's family. Are they home?"

"I'm a colleague of Tuy from the palace," Neferet added.

The girl tipped her head in polite acquiescence but said nothing.

Is she mute? She was certainly a beautiful thing with a sweet, rounded face, full lips, and large doe eyes. Only a strawberry mark on one jaw marred her perfection, but even that was mostly hidden by her natural hair, which was dust-strewn and disheveled with mourning. Her dress hung down to the waist. Hani forced himself to keep his eyes off her breasts, which were as attractive as the rest of her. He saw with amusement that Maya and Mery-ra were making the same transparent effort and perhaps Neferet too.

The girl led them into the salon, where ten or twelve other people had gathered, filling the single-columned room with the smell of sweat and funeral banquet meats. *The five of us are going to make things rather congested*, he thought ruefully. The servant forged a path through the crowd toward a man a little older than Hani, shaven headed and lean, his beard beginning to show. He had on no shirt, and his face was disfigured with dust. He was talking animatedly to several younger adults with mourning scarves.

The servant laid a respectful hand on his elbow, and the man looked around, his eyes widening at this party of strangers in his small salon. "Welcome, my friends," he said in a voice hoarse from weeping. "How can I help you?" Then he seemed to see In-hapy among the taller people. "Mistress In-hapy. How good of you to come."

In-hapy laid a consoling hand on his forearm. "I heard the terrible news and had to pay my respects, Ipuki."

"I'm a *sunet* from the palace, and we worked together," Neferet added. "I could hardly believe it when someone said she was murdered."

"Is that what they said?" Ipuki looked around uneasily.

One of the young men to whom Ipuki had just been talking had moved up behind him. "I'm Tuy's firstborn. My family and I thank you for coming to see us in our grief. Please help yourself to the food." Both he and his father, despite their humble status of washermen, were well-spoken.

"My own father and I and young Maya here are investigators in the king's service," Hani said in a low voice. "We want to understand better the circumstances of your mother's death in order to appease her *ba* and make sure *ma'at* is restored. Might we talk to one or the other of you privately?"

The two men exchanged a look, and Ipuki said, "User-hat, here, will talk to you. About time somebody from the palace showed any interest." He turned back to his conversation.

The son led Hani, Neferet, Maya, and Mery-ra through the kitchen and into a tiny courtyard partly covered over with reeds to mitigate the sun's heat. In-hapy remained behind to mingle with the other mourners.

"Tell us what you know about your mother's death, User-hat. It's our understanding that she was probably dead when... everything else happened."

The youth nodded, his face congested with grief.

"Her throat was slit, my lord. Who would kill a midwife, someone who did nothing but good?"

Hani laid a compassionate hand on the man's shoulder. "That's what we need to find out, son." *Although we have some pretty strong suspicions.*

"I worked with Tuy at the palace," Neferet said earnestly. "As far as I could see, everybody loved her whenever she came."

User-hat nodded, struggling to control his mouth. "Please tell your masters that this woman was consecrated. She was... she was eaten by crocodiles, chosen by the Lord of the Waters. She should have a special high-status burial, which we certainly can't afford." He dashed at the trickle running from his nose.

"I'll do that. I'm sure the young queen will be amenable to honoring her, as is only right."

"I don't know what these Aten people believe and don't believe," the youth said bitterly. He glared at the king's investigators, defying them to object to this heresy.

"We understand, son," Mery-ra said in his most soothing tone. "We don't either."

"That's all we know, my lords. Her body was found in the reeds just upriver from here, not so far as Waset. Half her body. How she got up there, nobody knows."

"Might she have been visiting a patient?" Neferet asked. Hani wished she would keep a lower profile, but these people didn't seem likely to turn her in.

"Maybe," said the youth, his chin trembling. "We used to live in Seyawt, about a day's sail upstream. She had left for a few days and told us to take care of each other until she got back. Maybe that's where she was."

"Thank you, User-hat," Hani said. "We won't trouble you anymore. You have our deepest sympathy."

User-hat hung his head and nodded, his mouth a thin downturned line.

"Is that girl who answered the gate part of the family?" Maya asked as they were turning to leave.

"Her? No. She's one of Mother's charity cases. Some servant who had her tongue cut off and was thrown out on the street." Hani and his companions flinched in unison. "Mother brought her home to nurse her, and she's stayed to work for us—out of gratitude, perhaps. We don't even pay her."

"When did she come to you, do you remember?" Hani asked blandly.

User-hat pushed back his wig and scratched his scalp. "I don't know exactly. Nine or ten years ago. Maybe eight."

They departed, leaving In-hapy to socialize with her neighbors, and made their way back to her workshop, where Maya peeled off to see if Sat-hut-haru was awake. "Take some time to be with your family, son," Hani called after him. "Now, while things are quiet."

Hani and his father and daughter pursued their way southward toward Lord Ptah-mes's villa. "You know what, Papa? I feel like I've seen that servant before," Neferet said as they walked along.

"She's certainly memorable," Mery-ra agreed with a waggle of his eyebrows.

"Who would have cut out a girl's tongue, though? She's not much older than me."

Hani gave a dark snort. "Somebody who wanted to shut her up." The idea came to him suddenly that the servant might have been a witness to the exchange of babies, like the lady-in-waiting and the midwife, who had just been silenced in the most radical way. The hair rose on his neck. "Neferet, we need to get you and Bener-ib away from the palace. It's no longer safe for you."

"But, Papa," she objected, "the ladies need us. The coregent needs us. Ibet's little patient needs us."

"Let Lady Djefat-nebty deal with them, as she did before. Oh, wait—she witnessed this too. Either she's in line to die, or she's complicit."

"I thought our girl said Djefat-nebty gave the order to go get the other child." Mery-ra laid a hand on his granddaughter's shoulder.

"That's right, Grandfather."

"True. I was thinking of warning her, but maybe she's the one to flee from." Troubled, Hani blew out a great breath.

They strode along in silence, Mery-ra as brisk as the others in his rocking gait. It was midmorning by that time, and the streets had begun to fill. The sky had hazed over with a strange colorless veil that did nothing to temper the heat.

Mery-ra eyed the air. "Sandstorm's coming."

"Stay here till morning, Father. There's no point in catching a ferry tonight. You'd just have to hole up until the storm blew over."

"Very well, son."

By the time they entered Lord Ptah-mes's gate, the air had grown thick and red and hot as a blast from the oven. Hani felt a cough working its way up his throat. "Let's go into my bedroom, where we won't get as much sand."

He found the servants closing all the doors and putting wet rags across the cracks. A boy on a ladder was even blocking the ceiling ventilator and high windows in the salon with soaked linen.

The steward greeted them. "I thank the gods you're home, my lords, my lady. Anybody outside will be sliced up by this sand."

Bener-ib came running out from the stairwell with relief all over her pointed little face.

"I hope Aha and his family are safely in shelter," said Mery-ra.

"And Sati and Maya," Neferet added. She turned to Hani, beaming, her hands on her hips. "I was helpful, wasn't I, Papa?" She shot her friend a crafty glance. "He can't deny it, Ibet. I made the man feel more at ease by saying everybody loved his mother."

Hani threw an arm around her shoulders and gave her an affectionate squeeze. "You did, my duckling. You clearly take after your grandfather." Then he turned serious and said to the two girls, "I think we need to get you two out of Akhet-aten."

Before Neferet could object, Mery-ra said, "I'll bet Ptah-mes has plenty of agricultural properties around Waset. You could hide up there someplace."

"But I don't want to hide out," Neferet cried. "I'm not afraid. We face the plague every day."

"No, my love. But the plague is blind. It isn't stalking you personally."

"We need to go," Bener-ib said in a small, frightened voice. "They'll kill us both. We could take Weneb with us."

"A flower? Why would you take that with you, my duckling?"

"That's the name of Ibet's patient, Papa. We're afraid to leave her alone. She's losing blood, even though she's up and working."

"Listen to your friend, my girl." Mery-ra faced her, arms akimbo. "Somebody in this household needs to show some sense."

Neferet's face grew thunderous. Hani watched her fighting against her stubborn streak. She didn't like to be told no.

"But I'll have to tell Lady Djefat-nebty that we won't be back for a while. She counts on us."

"I think the less you tell her, the better."

"But we'll never see anybody."

"That's the purpose of hiding out, my duckling." Hani managed a stern face. In truth, he was genuinely fearful for his daughter. Anybody who knew her could predict that whatever she had seen would eventually become public.

After lunch, the girls withdrew to their room, and Hani and his father were left in the salon. The air was so heavy it could hardly be breathed. Outside, Hani heard the groan and whistle of the rising wind. *Sutesh is prowling. The Lord of the Red Lands has attacked. This can't be an omen of anything good.*

The two men sat in uneasy silence, both listening to the wind. Eventually, Mery-ra said, as if to confirm Hani's thoughts, "This can't mean anything good."

⊠

The next morning, the heat had shot upward, and sand lay

all over everything. In the garden, it had drifted over the paths and the pavilion floor and turned the tattered leaves red and festered looking. Even inside, it had breached the wet cloths and powdered the gypsum floors. Striking a cushion raised a cloud of dust. The servants were already at work sweeping it up when Hani came down the stairs. He heard Mery-ra hawking and spitting even before he saw him at the door of the porch.

"Let's see what the Lord Sutesh has left in the wake of his passage," Hani said loudly.

Mery-ra turned. "Ah! Good morning, son. Hopefully, I can sail home today, eh?" He nearly blew backward with the force of an enormous sneeze.

Hani gave a laugh, which ended in a cough. "Is Neferet still asleep?"

"Apparently. I asked the steward about some of Lord Ptah-mes's estates that might be a good place to hide. Most of them are around Waset, but he has a few places near Men-nefer as well—emoluments from his days as vizier, no doubt. He suggested one in particular which is essentially a date grove. The residence is small and the staff minimal. They've never even seen the new mistress of the house."

"Sounds good. Thank you for being so prompt on this, Father. I feel like something could happen to her from one day to the next." Hani clapped Mery-ra affectionately on the shoulder.

His father gave a wag of the eyebrows. "Wouldn't you think Bener-ib's parents would want to know what's happening? They might prefer to shelter her at home."

"I can't figure those people out," Hani admitted. "They've never made the least overture to see her since

107

we've known her, and that must be four or five years now. What gives me pause is that we don't know where they stand regarding the political situation."

"Didn't Neferet say the girl's father was a priest of Sekhmet?"

"Yes, but also a friend of Lord Pentju." Hani heaved a sigh. "Let's leave them in the dark for now."

The two men got some breakfast—rather more elegant than their usual day-old bread and milk, which they would eat while leaning on the kitchen door frame—and had risen from their stools when Neferet and her friend came sleepily down the stairs. Neferet approached her father and gave him a groggy kiss then stretched luxuriously and kissed Mery-ra as well. "Are you going back today, Grandfather?"

"Yes, my girl." He gave her a squeeze. "Maya will take my place at your papa's side while I renew my acquaintance with Meryet-amen's cook."

The girl snickered. "I'm going to tell Mama!"

⊠

By midmorning, Hani had accompanied his father to the embarcadero and seen him off. He'd returned to Ptah-mes's villa and was standing at the gate, preparing to knock, when the sound of running footsteps behind him made him turn. It was the vizier's plump little secretary. Far from his usual smug self, he was panting and red-faced, his expression wild.

"Lord Hani! Lord Hani!" he cried. "Lord Ra-nefer wanted you to know—the king has died!"

For all that he'd been predicting this for months, Hani was shocked. "You mean Nefer-khepru-ra?"

"Yes, my lord. They found him dead in bed a few hours ago. We haven't even gotten scarves yet."

Hani gasped for breath as if someone had punched him in the stomach. Part of him wanted to rejoice that the long nightmare was nearing its end. But part of him—the part that knew civil war was getting closer—was deathly afraid. "It… it was natural, wasn't it?"

"As far as I know. The vizier wants you to come to his office. All the diplomats will be recalled, of course. All missions are suspended."

Hani thanked the man, who turned and left at a more sedate pace than that at which he'd arrived. There was a tense fluttering in Hani's stomach as he reached up and knocked on the gate. *Now it begins.*

"Papa!" Neferet came hurrying down the path toward him with her usual exuberance, a folded piece of papyrus in her hand. "I just got a letter from Lord Ptah-mes. He said to greet you." But she must have seen her father's grim face because she murmured in alarm, "What is it, Papa? Is Grandfather…?"

"He's fine, my duckling. Someone from the Hall of Royal Correspondence just told me that Nefer-khepru-ra has died." Hani felt as if he were caught in some strange dream. *Dead less than a year after his coregent. Things are rushing to a climax.* "You… you didn't have anything to do with this, did you?" he whispered.

"No, Papa. I don't treat the king." She looked more disappointed than shocked—no doubt she would have liked to be the one to bear this extraordinary news to her father and not the other way around.

His heart pounding, Hani got heavily to his knees and

strewed his head with a handful of gravel from the path, and Neferet, still looking unsure of what to think, did the same. Kneeling there, they stared one another in the eye, and Hani grabbed his daughter's arm. "You have to get away to safety immediately, Neferet. This very minute." He hauled himself to his feet. "Pack your things and Bener-ib's, too, if she wants to come. There will be no one to stop Ankhet-khepru-ra now."

But Neferet stood and said stubbornly, "I don't want to hide, Papa. They need me at the palace."

"No!" he said forcefully, angry with fear for his youngest child. *Has the mule-headed girl no common sense?* "For once, you need to obey me without arguing about every word."

Her voice rising, she shot back, "I'm a married woman. I don't have to obey you at all."

"Then consider me as transmitting a message from your husband."

"He told me he was ver-r-ry proud of my courage. He said now was the time for us to push back." She brandished the letter in her fist, her lips compressed in defiance.

Hani's heart fell to the bottom like lead. How could he argue against her husband's words? Ptah-mes, once the most prudent of men, had grown quite reckless since the death of his first wife. He had nothing left to lose. But Neferet... Hani let out a furious breath through his nose. He wished he had Nub-nefer's bronze will, but he wanted the children to make good choices on their own, uncoerced by their parents.

"So be it," he said, abruptly releasing his clenched hands. "Let the responsibility fall on him."

But Neferet was still having none of it. "Let the

responsibility fall on *me*, Papa. I am a grown-up, after all."
She stood there, planted as firm as a rock, fists on her hips.

In spite of himself, he was proud of her. So many
people wanted to take responsibility for nothing. His heart
aching with tenderness, he smiled ruefully. "Yes, you are,
my duckling." He drew her to him and murmured into her
stubbled scalp, "Just don't take chances, all right?" He held
her to him for the space of a slow heartbeat then stepped
back, his eyes blurred. "We couldn't bear it if..."

"I'll be careful, Papa. May Sekhmet toast my ears and
make my elbows turn green if I'm not."

Hani didn't think he could face sitting down at
lunch with Neferet, knowing this conversation still hung
between them, so he decided to return to the Hall of Royal
Correspondence immediately. He was almost certain he
knew what the vizier would tell him—the government was
in an interregnal stasis. As he was already aware, all missions
were canceled. All correspondence suspended. Preparations
for the royal funeral would consume every working hour
and every flake of gold over the next seventy days. Ankh-
khepru-ra, the late coregent, had been a minor king by any
definition, but his brother had ruled for seventeen years,
from the moment he'd assumed the throne beside his father.
Hani could see it now in hindsight—Nefer-khepru-ra had
exercised a determining influence over his father even
while the old king lived, and little by little, the son's whole
campaign to humiliate the Hidden One and exalt the Aten
in his place had begun to take shape, unnoticed.

They found scarves to don—the house had known too
much of death, alas. As he strode back toward the center of
the city, Hani was ruminating darkly on the upheavals of

the Osir's reign—*Is the late king an Osir if he didn't believe in Osir?*—when he heard a familiar voice behind him.

"Lord Hani! Wait!"

He turned to see Maya running toward him on his stubby legs. Hani's throat clenched. *Is there trouble at home?* He managed a calm smile. "I thought you'd gone back to Waset with the family, son."

"No, my lord." Maya was panting as he caught up. "I sent them on, and I decided to stay one more night with Mother." He caught Hani's eye and added sardonically, "We heard about the king. I guess he ran out of life, prosperity, and health, eh?"

Hani cringed. The habit of reverence was hard to break. "I guess so. Were you on your way to the chancery?"

"Yes. I figured I'd catch you here."

They turned in to the maze of low buildings and dusty courtyards that housed the Hall of Royal Correspondence. As they walked, Hani told Maya about the how the midwife's throat had been slit. He described the visit to her grieving household and the servant whose tongue had been cut out.

The young secretary's eyes bugged. "Lord Ay's trap is closing. Soon, no one alive will be able to testify that the Haru in the nest isn't really a royal child at all." After a moment, as if it had finally sunk in, he cried, "Neferet! She witnessed the exchange!"

His frustration and anxiety welling up afresh, Hani heaved a sigh. "Yes, and she refuses to hide anywhere. She insists on continuing to serve at the palace. I don't know whether to admire her courage or carry her away by force."

Maya whistled under his breath. "The queen—I mean the king—must know about the exchange, then, eh, my lord? Otherwise, how would Lord Ay know? He surely wasn't present at his daughter's lying-in."

"He undoubtedly set it in motion, in any event. He must have found a servant who was due on the same day as the Great Royal Wife, just in case she bore another girl. He couldn't afford to let his daughter lose her husband's favor."

"But how could they be sure this servant was going to have a boy?"

"Remember how our friend Khuit forecast that little Tepy would be a son? There are ways. I think they make the woman pee on barley."

Maya brightened. "That reminds me. I wonder if Khuit would know anything about all this. She said she took care of the royal servants from time to time."

"Perhaps, although Neferet didn't say anything about her being present at the birth." Hani smiled, trying to push back his fears. "We might talk to her when we get back to Waset."

They'd entered the court of the vizier's office. Only a few scribes were about, scurrying back and forth, their wigs bound by white scarves. Hani left Maya to sit in the shade of the building while he entered the dark, lofty reception room and presented himself to the secretary on duty.

The man disappeared into Ra-nefer's office then reappeared a moment later. "Lord Ra-nefer, vizier of the Lower Kingdom, will see you, my lord."

Hani remembered how he used to enter the presence of his vizier and superior and find Lord Ptah-mes there, with his incisive intelligence and endless knowledge of court politics. Even Ptah-mes's successor, Aper-el, had been a capable administrator despite his rather blind military obedience. Of Ra-nefer, Hani couldn't say much good. He had the feeling that the stout little man was someone's brother-in-law who'd been given a sinecure but found himself in over his head in real demands. Half the kingdom and its foreign policy were relying on the vizier's decisions. Hani folded in a formal bow, hands on knees.

"Ah, Hani," said Ra-nefer in his vague, displeased way. He had, if anything, grown stouter since their last visit, his chins straining to stay afloat above the heavy gold *shebyu* collars that hung, too numerous, around his short neck. "Here we are, bereft again, our missions all suspended. We await the official installation of the new king in seventy days to see who remains in office and who doesn't."

Hani imagined that he heard a note of wistfulness in his superior's voice. Perhaps Ra-nefer hoped he would *not* remain in office.

"Until then, you and the other diplomats are free of official duties. But the Great Royal Wife wants to see you."

A shiver of alarm ran up Hani's back. His first thought was that Nefert-iti sought him, but she was now the king, and her daughter Meryet-aten was queen—the new Great Royal Wife. Perhaps that was even more frightening. Ay would certainly be watching him.

"She's at Pa-maru-en-pa-aten." The vizier stifled a belch.

Hani bowed again, and Ra-nefer rose. Clearly, the audience was ended. At the look of anxious confusion on Ra-nefer's round red face, Hani almost felt sorry for him.

"This is getting to be a tradition," Hani said wryly as he emerged from the vizier's office. "Meryet-aten wants to see me again. No wonder Ay knew I was visiting her, if she goes through Ra-nefer to contact me. I hope Neferet warned her I'm being used as a spy."

Maya made a hum of uneasiness. "You're the frog contended over by two herons again, Lord Hani. Someone will end up eating you alive, I fear."

〼

By the time Hani and Maya had trudged to the far southern edge of town, where Pa-maru-en-pa-aten, the Sunshade of the Aten, stood, Maya had begun to understand why the grandees drove their chariots to the Hall of Royal Correspondence every day. It was deep into harvest season, and after the sand-laden winds, the heat beat down on the two men with murderous intensity.

Maya took off his wig and fanned his face with it. "I wouldn't mind having a sunshade myself."

Lord Hani was distracted, almost grim—not his usual cheerful self at all. Although the perspiration rolled down his face and his shirt stuck to his thick body with sweat, he hardly seemed to notice, he was so lost in his own thoughts. After a moment, Hani appeared to come to himself and realize Maya had addressed him. A wide grin split his face, and he said with a semblance of cheer, "You've never been here, have you, son? Wait till you see this place! I'll ask if they'll let you accompany me to the audience."

A warm wave of pleasure rose to Maya's cheeks. *I'm going to meet the Great Royal Wife! Be a coconspirator with men of highest birth like Lord Mai! Not bad for a working-class boy.* What a story this would make for his Tales. If he survived…

The *maru* was a tall, featureless enclosure that stood

by itself, well into the desert that flanked the arid City of the Horizon. Its whitewashed walls, fringed with palm fronds, shimmered in the heat of the sand, looking as if they floated on the surface of a silvery lake.

Hani must have read Maya's thoughts because he said, "Do you suppose that's what the Lake of Flowers looks like?"

"What's that, my lord?"

"The beautiful lake that the blessed souls will cross to enter the Field of Reeds. Is it glimmering and evanescent like that?"

Maya didn't want to ask what *evanescent* meant lest he look low-class, so he just nodded knowingly and said, "Probably."

As they drew closer, Maya saw that the single pylon gate was heavily guarded by soldiers in the costumes of every part of the empire. Hani identified himself to the porter. "It's important that my secretary accompany me. I foresee the need to take notes."

The gatekeeper bowed, and Hani slipped Maya a sly wink. They were bidden to enter the cool, dark hall, which was really a deep, columned portico that edged the inner space. More soldiers stood sentinel between columns. Beyond, blinding in its sun-drenched brightness, a garden stretched—a fabulous paradise of greenery and flowers, of pools and pavilions, shimmering in the sun of a late-summer morning.

Maya gasped. "This? Out in the desert?"

He'd never seen such a place. No house was visible, just porticoes, pavilions, and ponds with the most luscious vegetation waving gently in a dry wind. The large rectangular pool that centered it all had a kind of stone jetty extending out into the middle of the waters, and on it stood an airy curtained pavilion with a tented roof, rising and falling with the breeze like the breathing of some magical beast. The air was richly perfumed by early summer's flowers, and a waving line of palms against the wall blended reality seamlessly into the garden painted upon it. Maya let out a whistle of amazement.

"This used to belong to Lady Kiya," Hani said under his breath.

Maya thought cynically, *How fickle is the royal pleasure. But also, how opulent.*

A servant in fashionable court clothes and a long wig approached the two men and, with a bow, ordered them to follow. The three of them trooped through the immaculate beds of chrysanthemums and chamomile, alive with butterflies, and set out along the jetty across the pool. Under the summer sun, the sparkle of the water was almost blinding. Maya shaded his eyes with a hand and saw Hani doing the same. Maya felt conspicuous, being so visible—and, he feared, risible—trailing at Hani's back, his short legs making a dignified passage impossible. At last, they reached the kiosk at the end. The sheer linen curtains billowed under a ceiling of richly woven tapestry from some foreign land.

Within, a slender and extremely attractive girl stood, with a jeweled sidelock over her wig and the crimped red sash of queenship around her waist. The three men folded in a full court bow. *So, this is the young queen up close. Surely her mother's daughter.*

Her face lit up at the sight of Lord Hani. "Hani! You're

here at last." But then, the queen's eyes flickered to Maya, and her smile cooled. "Who is this?"

Maya bowed again deeply to cover his confusion. He knew his face must be turning scarlet with embarrassment.

"My secretary, my lady. He is utterly trustworthy, and I suspected his services might be required."

Maya rose and puffed out his chest proudly. He lived for these moments of Lord Hani's approbation.

The queen nodded. "Very well. We'll need a secretary."

She drew her skirts about her and sank into the embroidered cushion of a throne-like chair then gestured to the two men to be seated. Maya took his seat on the floor and prepared his ink, ready to write. Meryet-aten dismissed the servant, who bowed out of the pavilion and disappeared down the causeway.

Then her voice dropped. "The time has come to make a little trip to Kheta Land." Her dark kohl-edged eyes pierced Hani's, full of meaning.

Hani paled, despite the amiable smile with which he nodded his understanding. "So soon, my queen? Your mother—life, prosperity, and health to her—is still on the throne. Is it legal for you to be conducting foreign policy?"

Meryet-aten lifted her chin. "Foreign rulers approach me all the time, Hani. I'm already conducting foreign policy. And besides, nobody is going to miss you right now. The whole Hall of Royal Correspondence is in suspension—you're not likely to receive any conflicting orders. My mother isn't officially the sole king until she opens the mouth of Father's coffin, anyway. So we have seventy days."

Hani drew in a deep breath through his nose. "On the

contrary, my lady. Your mother has already given me three assignments, among them to tutor your... er, brother in languages."

"You must go to Kheta, Hani." Her soft, lovely face grew hard with intensity. "If anything should happen to Mother, *that boy* will be on the throne. We must stop him."

"What about my duties to tutor him? No one has told me when that will begin—I'm just to await word."

"I'll take care of that—don't worry." She smiled a fierce, wolfish smile. "I can stand up to my grandfather."

Poor Lord Hani. For once, he doesn't know what to say.

A flicker of reluctance and even fear crossed Hani's face, but he only dipped his head in a little bow. "Tell me what you want me to say, my queen."

"Secretary, take this down. You can put it into proper diplomatic language, Akkadian or whatever, but here's the gist of the message. Take the Great King of Kheta gifts—I'll provide those—and take some to his wife, too, and to his vizier. And tell him"—for the first time her mask of self-confidence wobbled—"that I have no son and I need one of his sons to be my consort. He'll be more than a consort. He'll be my coregent, and his sons will rule over the Two Lands, and our great kingdoms will be as one."

Hani seemed to absorb these shocking words silently, then he said in a low voice, "My lady must be aware of the kind of resistance a proposal like this is going to arouse here. It will look to some like traducing the kingdom to an enemy."

"But it won't be, will it? Because the real enemy is right here in Kemet. The real enemy is my grandfather, who

119

would do anything—lie, cheat, kill—to preserve his own power."

A wave of heat flushed Maya's face, and his hand was none too steady as he took down the queen's words. This was a coup d'état, and he was in the middle of it. He thought of Sat-hut-haru and the children. *What will happen to them if I'm burned alive for treason?*

"Do you know what to say now, Hani? Make them understand that I'm serious—and that there must be absolutely no delay. We only have seventy days. And this must all be carried out in the uttermost secrecy. If anyone found out…" She swallowed, letting the two men imagine the worst.

"That's what worries me, my queen. Ay is already clearly aware of your plotting and of my participation. He charged me to report to him on your actions. I'm sure someone in your household is watching us both. They'll know the moment I set out—and I probably won't get far."

Meryet-aten's face darkened, and she stared at the floor for a long time. At last, she looked up at Hani, her shapely eyebrows knotted. "Thank you for telling me this, Hani. Let's just stand by, then, until Grandfather's suspicions die down. But while my mother is yet living, we must open negotiations. Otherwise, the deadline will be too close to come and go in time."

Hani bowed and murmured an appropriate protestation of obedience, and the two men backed from the kiosk. Once out of the queen's presence, they turned and walked quickly back down the causeway. Maya's emotions were sparking like freshly lit tinder and threatened to engulf him in a conflagration of horror.

Hani walked faster and faster, as if he couldn't wait to get away, and Maya pattered after him without dignity, only wanting to be gone. The beautiful artificial paradise around them seemed less benign, more sinister than before. At the shore of the pool, the servant who had conducted them into the *maru* led them out past the flowers, cicadas, and butterflies... past the shadowy colonnade and its watchful soldiers. At last, they were through the pylon's majestic doors and into the road. Around them, the desert stretched, rocky, silent, and barren. The whole thing was suddenly like a dream.

CHAPTER 5

Hani strode along toward Lord Ptah-mes's residence, his pace urged on by nerves, until Maya cried out, "Slow down, please, my lord."

The secretary jogged up to join him, and Hani said, "Sorry, my friend. I just want to run away and hide where no one can find me. Maybe one of Lord Ptah-mes's country properties." He forced a smile.

"This is the most ridiculous scheme I've ever heard of! Is the queen serious?"

"I'm afraid she is, and so are a lot of admirable people. She'd just better be sure she has the support of the army." They strode on for a bit. Hani said, "I wish Ptah-mes were here. I'm sure he's on his way back for the funeral."

Maya sneered. "I'll bet he won't be a pallbearer at *this* funeral."

"No. But he might be a good ally in the wild-eyed business we're caught up in. I know he's lost a lot of his former inhibitions"—*and prudence*—"but he knows what's going on everywhere." Hani sighed. It would be days, if not weeks, before his superior returned from Azzati, and by that time, Hani would be committed to teaching the crown prince Akkadian. He smiled a bit more anxiously than he would have liked. "Listen, son, whenever this... diplomatic mission comes about, you don't have to come with me. This could put us both in danger. Ay will almost certainly be trying to stop it. Perhaps it would be better if you stayed with Sat-hut-haru and the little ones. I don't want my grandchildren to grow up fatherless."

That thought seemed to sober Maya. His eyes became round, and he considered Hani's words in silence. Then he said with feeling, "I want to go with you, my lord. You'll need a secretary, and it wouldn't be wise to let anyone else in on our secret."

Hani smiled at him, touched and deeply grateful. Maya didn't lack for courage. He clapped the little man on the shoulder and gave him a squeeze of affection.

They walked on with a purposeful stride toward Lord Ptah-mes's villa. Finally, Maya said, "What about the jewel thefts and the death of the midwife, my lord? Have you learned anything helpful?"

"I haven't had a minute to investigate. And that's something we can start to do right now before we head back to Waset."

"Who do you have in mind to talk to?" Maya asked, eyes wide with eagerness.

Hani chuckled. "I was hoping you could tell me! It's possible that Neferet or even Lady Djefat-nebty might have noticed something. Anyway, I've been thinking how bad I'd feel if Djefat-nebty were innocent of collusion in the matter of the false prince and I let her continue in danger without warning her."

"How could she be innocent if she gave Neferet the order to change the babies?"

Hani pursed his lips in thought. "I can see why she might have approved it for other reasons than political ones. Maybe she was afraid it would affect the queen's health to find that, yet again, she'd failed to produce an heir."

Maya snorted skeptically. "And if her reasons *were* political? If she's in the pay of Ay? She might be dangerous if she thought you knew about it."

"We don't have to tell her we know. We'll simply notify her that the midwife was killed. Actually"— Hani brightened—"we can just interrogate her about Tuy. She must know her if the woman worked at the palace from time to time."

Instead of heading directly to Ptah-mes's villa, the two men turned aside in the same neighborhood and set off inland to the house of Pentju and his wife.

"I hope this is a good idea," Hani murmured as they stood at the gate. He idly read Lord Pentju's titles on the lintel. *He seems to have been indispensable to the late king. I wonder what his status is now.*

The gatekeeper admitted them, and a few moments later, Hani was waiting in the shadowy vestibule while Maya sat on the step of the porch. Despite the mounting warmth, it was almost nippy out of the sun, but that was normal for the time of year. The chill that fluttered up Hani's back might have nothing to do with the temperature.

As he entered, he noted through the inner door that the elegant salon was being repainted—scaffolding was up along one wall, and the two columns had been whitewashed over their previous decorations. Eventually, he heard footsteps approaching. From the interior door appeared the tall, mannish figure of Neferet's much-admired superior, Lady Djefat-nebty, the *sunet* in charge of the health of the royal ladies.

"Lord Hani," she greeted him in her dry, cold voice, which, he knew, concealed a considerably warmer heart. "Are you looking for your daughter?"

"No, my lady," Hani replied with a bow. "I am here in my formal capacity as a royal investigator. As you may or may not be aware, the midwife Tuy, who sometimes worked at the palace, was found dead. Murdered, it would seem."

Djefat-nebty's eyebrows rose in surprise. "How unfortunate. A very capable person."

Hani cleared his throat, uncomfortable. "Do you have any idea why someone might want to murder a midwife?"

The *sunet* stared out into the empty room as if her eyes were focused on something behind Hani. At last, they returned to Hani's face, and she said flatly, "No. Perhaps the angry husband of someone she wasn't able to save? Midwives, even the best, are not gods."

"Have you ever known that to happen?"

"No, actually."

"It's my understanding that one of the coregent's former ladies-in-waiting has died violently as well. Are you aware of anything that might tie the two murders together? Anything the women had in common? Any secret they might have shared?" Hani hoped to guide her memory into a significant path without making it too obvious that he knew about the exchange of babies.

Djefat-nebty looked pensive, her mouth pursed. "Maybe..." She shot a penetrating glance at him. "What I'm about to tell you must never be revealed to anyone, Hani. Understood?"

"I swear upon my mother's *ka* never to reveal it to a living soul—who doesn't already know."

Her gaze sharpened into flint, but her mouth quirked with amusement. "I perceive that you may already be aware of what I'm about to reveal to you. And for her sake, I hope it wasn't Neferet who told you."

She turned back into the interior and beckoned Hani to follow. They entered the splendid room in which he'd first met her and her husband, with its shining gypsum floors and the dais where two throne-like chairs sat between the pair of fine columns. But she pointed to stools, and as Hani seated himself, so she did, too, drawing hers forward until their knees were almost touching.

"Nine years ago," she began in a low voice, "our king, who was then queen, gave birth to a seventh daughter. I'd been instructed that should that happen, we were to exchange the baby with a male child. You can imagine why. Not only for the queen's own peace of mind, but because the king was desperate for an heir."

Hani nodded. "How could you just go out and find a male baby in the moment like that?"

"The... the person who was orchestrating this exchange had provided another young mother about to give birth. We had reason to believe her child would be a boy, but failing that, there would be another attempt with the queen's next pregnancy."

Hani was more than a little surprised at her frankness. "And who was behind this, if I may ask?"

Djefat-nebty straightened up and said tartly, "You may ask. But I won't tell you. The reasons offered me seemed compelling at the time, and if I have grown less convinced over the years, that's between me and my conscience." She stared at Hani as if defying him to accuse her of anything untoward.

"I believe you were laying this background to explain the death of the midwife?" he urged.

"Tuy was present at this event. And perhaps the lady-in-waiting you mentioned was also. There was some such person around, but I don't know her name."

"Then the other witnesses may be in danger as well. You and Neferet. The princess Meryet-aten. Don't you think?"

"Up until this moment, Hani, I knew nothing of these deaths. If we had all survived for nine years, I had no reason to think we were in danger. I don't know what has changed, but now it seems there is peril. Please look out for your daughter." The *sunet* looked quite serious, her severe face set. "The princess—the Great Royal Wife now—is on her guard and well protected. I'll be leaving the capital."

"Whose child was substituted for the girl baby, my lady?"

"I was told she was the king's sister, Lady Sit-pa-aten." She avoided Hani's eye.

She's aware it isn't true. She must have known Sit-pa-aten and recognized that the other mother wasn't she. But at least, Hani felt satisfied that Djefat-nebty had nothing to do with the two deaths. She was not a person who would lie if asked point-blank for an answer. He sat for a moment, pensive.

"Do you think the person who orchestrated this exchange is now eliminating the witnesses?" he finally asked.

Djefat-nebty's thin mouth turned down in the effort to control a wry smile. "I doubt it. He's dead."

She can only mean the late Nefer-khepru-ra, Hani thought in surprise. A royal command would have made it impossible for the *sunet* to refuse, no matter how dishonorable she found the deceit. And perhaps it had been justified. Anything that might have obviated a civil war would have had merit. Only it hadn't worked.

Hani rose, and his hostess followed suit. "I'm trying to convince Neferet to lie low for a while, but she insists she's needed here."

"And she's very right. My husband is thinking of returning to Sau, and that would mean that Neferet and Bener-ib would be solely responsible for the court ladies— who now include the king."

Hani felt a twinge of pride in spite of himself. "We're honored by your trust, my lady."

"They've deserved it, both of them. Bener-ib has trained longer, but Neferet has an exceptional eye for symptoms and a deep compassion for her patients. Sometimes that's all a doctor can offer." A crooked smile broke out upon her face at last, and her dark eyes twinkled. "Has she shown you her toe?"

Hani laughed. "She has. It's astonishing."

"It was her idea. She's a remarkable young woman. You should be proud."

Hani made a little nod of a bow, and Lady Djefat-nebty turned to go. But before she'd breached the door into the interior of the house, Hani called out, "Do you know anything about a series of petty thefts in the former queen's household, my lady?"

She turned a severe face to him, one eyebrow lifted. "What have I to do with the queen's domestic goods, Hani? I'm a doctor." Then she exited.

⊠

When Lord Hani finally emerged from the palatial house, evening was falling. Maya had stood up to avoid the encroaching long rays of the sun and was walking back and forth, sounding out in his mind some especially felicitous phrasing for his Tales. "How did it go, my lord?" he asked eagerly.

"It was interesting. I'll tell you when we get out into the street."

They set off down the long path through Pentju's elaborate garden, where the plane trees were still not fully in leaf, exposing more of the plantings than usual. As they drew nearer to the gate, two male voices could be heard approaching from that direction. A moment later, Lord Pentju and a smaller man came into view. Pentju was a tall, fleshy fellow, and his mass made the other person look even more diminutive and desiccated.

"Ah—Hani, is it not?" Pentju said in his deep rumble as the men encountered one another. "I present to you my friend Nakht-ef-mut. We were students together." He was more cordial than Maya expected, considering the skimpy acquaintance he and Hani enjoyed.

"Honored, my lord," Hani said with a bow and his warmest, most genial smile.

It was met by a tense and haughty expression on Nakht-ef-mut's part. He was a slim, stooped man about Hani's age with an angular, pointed face, long sharp nose, and uneasy mouth. His head was smoothly shaven, marking him as a *wab* priest, and although he wasn't on priestly duty, he wore no wig. He acknowledged the introduction with a brusque nod.

"Hani, you may have met his daughter. She's one of my wife's apprentices."

"Ah," Hani said. Maya could see surprise in his little brown eyes, although Hani managed to keep his bland composure.

Pentju must have exhausted his courtesies, because without so much as a nod, he and his guest continued toward the house, leaving Maya and Hani staring after them.

"Is that Bener-ib's father, then?" Maya whispered incredulously. "He really exists?"

"So it seems," Hani said with a lift of his eyebrows. "I can see a resemblance now that I think about it. I wonder if he's finally come to visit her."

The pair made their way out the gate and turned toward their lodging at Lord Ptah-mes's villa. Hani strode along in preoccupied silence while Maya eagerly awaited his report on the meeting with Djefat-nebty. At last, he said, "How was your interview, my lord?"

"Oh." Hani seemed to snap out of his reverie. "She told me about the exchange of babies."

Maya's jaw dropped. "Really? She actually admitted it?"

"It was engineered by the late king. She had to do what she was ordered."

"Not Lord Ay, then. I'm amazed."

"Although he certainly has an interest in perpetuating the deceit. Djefat-nebty seemed unaware of the death of the midwife, so my warning may have saved her life." Hani fell silent, concern deepening the lines between his straight, bushy eyebrows. "There's not much chance of Neferet getting away to safety now. Djefat-nebty is returning to Sau, and she's leaving the entire care of the court ladies to our girls."

Maya let out a whistle. "I'm impressed. But won't that make them vulnerable to... to elimination?"

Hani looked at his secretary, his eyes bright with fear. He said nothing, but Maya knew the answer was yes.

It was deep into twilight when they knocked on Ptah-mes's imposing gate. The porter admitted them with a smile. "The master of the house is here, my lord."

Hani and Maya exchanged a look of surprise and delight. "When did he arrive?"

"Just an hour or so ago. He may be in the garden. I can announce you, if you like."

"Don't bother. We'll go into the house that way, and if we see him, we see him." They headed around through the side garden, Hani with a fresh bounce in his step. Maya realized how much his father-in-law must have missed Ptah-mes's sardonic humor and intelligent advice.

A flash of white clothing in the gloaming announced that someone was under the arbor.

"Lord Ptah-mes?" Lord Hani called. "Welcome back."

Ptah-mes, a cup of wine at his elbow, rose and broke

into a smile. He looked tired after his long journey but in good spirits. "Hani, my friend! What a pleasure. Neferet told me you were my guests." His black eyes sparkled in amusement.

"I'm sorry if our presence inconveniences you, my lord—you would probably prefer some time alone to relax." Hani clasped forearms with Ptah-mes. "You made unbelievably good time."

"I happened to be on my way when the message came. What brings you to our fair capital?"

"We're just here for some brief investigation."

"Ah." Ptah-mes indicated stools then reseated himself and called to the servants inside, "Bring two more cups out here, and light some lamps!" By the flickering light of the oil lamps, Maya noticed that the high commissioner was wearing a beautiful shirt with a thin border of embroidery around the neck and down the placket below the ties.

"Let me commend you on that handsome shirt, my lord," Hani said. "I've never seen one like it."

"Why, thank you. It was a gift from your daughter." Ptah-mes smiled dryly. Maya wasn't sure how to interpret either the gift or the smile. When the serving girl had set the cups on the table and discreetly disappeared, Ptah-mes said in an undertone, "What case are you working on, Hani?"

Lord Hani filled him in on all that had happened in his absence—the conflicting commissions from Ankhet-khepru-ra and her daughter. The matter of the thefts from the former queen's establishment. The order to undertake the crown prince's linguistic education.

"No doubt to keep you under their eyes and out of

trouble," Ptah-mes said. "There won't be any journeys to Kheta while you're in the classroom."

And finally, Hani revealed the murder of two who had witnessed the switching of babies nine years before. "Lady Djefat-nebty admitted to the switch, and she said it was the king who'd planned the whole scheme. I guess he can present whomever he wants as his heir."

"Case closed, I suppose," Ptah-mes agreed reluctantly.

"Djefat-nebty said she and her husband are returning soon to Sau and that Neferet and Bener-ib would be the official doctors of the royal women."

Ptah-mes raised an eyebrow. "That's a mark of great confidence, my friend. There must be many older, more experienced women—and men too—competing for this honor."

"That's no doubt true, my lord. The only thing that concerns me is that Neferet will be exposed to the killer of the other witnesses."

Ptah-mes nodded somberly. "It's up to us to protect her, Hani."

Maya didn't see how they could do that if Neferet insisted on going to court every day. They could hardly trail her into the palace and stand watch. The stubborn girl would be the last to put up with such a thing.

"Oh, it seems Bener-ib's father is in town," Hani added. "Perhaps he's come to protect *her*."

Maya gave a dubious snort. He wondered how much Lord Ptah-mes even knew about the girl's past. Ptah-mes's eyes cut between Hani and Maya, but he said nothing, the corner of his mouth twitching.

"Lord Ptah-mes!" Neferet's voice rang through the

half-bare garden, and she burst into view and stopped at the sight of her father. "Papa!" she cried, running to him and throwing her arms around him. "You're here. I was beginning to think you and Maya had gone back to Waset."

"That's a beautiful shirt you bought your husband." Hani smiled at her, but she evaded his gaze.

"Isn't it? It was embroidered by people from Djahy. I thought that would be appropriate," she said, drawing back to admire the shirt.

Ptah-mes accepted her scrutiny without self-consciousness. He'd taken on that soft smile again. "Your father tells me you're in danger, my dear. Please be careful."

"I know, I know," she said with a world-weary sigh. "But what can I do? Life is full of dangers."

Hani's tight grin said he was suppressing a laugh. He squeezed his daughter tenderly around the shoulders. "Never change, little duckling."

⊠

At dinner that evening, the three men and Neferet shared a superb meal—without Bener-ib, who'd remained late at the palace, tending her patient. They feasted on dishes from both Kemet and Djahy, prepared with the finest ingredients from Ptah-mes's own farms. *How can he eat like this and stay so slim?* Maya wondered enviously.

Hani remarked again about how fast Lord Ptah-mes had gotten back from Azzati. "But you said you'd already left before the message came announcing the king's death?"

"That's right," Ptah-mes said with a bitter smile as he wiped his plate of the rich pomegranate sauce with a rolled-up piece of flatbread. "I was coming back to tender my resignation."

A stunned silence fell upon the diners. Neferet, looking confused, stared from her husband to her father and back again, her eyes wide. Maya felt he couldn't close his jaw, which had dropped like a stone.

At last, Hani managed to say, "Was there a particular reason, my lord?"

"An endless stream of vassals left unprotected, cronies getting out of their punishment, officials bought off—especially after Har-em-heb left Kumidi. You know the symptoms, Hani. I had been so fatuous as to think I might be able to make a difference, but my hands were tied at every moment. I was seen as more of an enemy of the crown than the malefactors were."

Hani let out a breath and said between gritted teeth, "Surely, the corruptions of the former regime have hit new lows."

"Wasn't there supposed to be an invasion or razzia or something to show the *hapiru* we meant business?" Maya said.

"There was, yes. But I never saw any signs that it was actually going to take place. Now, of course…"

"What will they do to you?" Neferet asked in a hushed voice.

Ptah-mes gave a bark of laughter. "Why, it's absolutely moot at this point. With a new king, our posts are all up in the air anyway."

"I wish I had your courage, my lord," Hani said.

"So, you're here until the funeral?" Maya asked.

"Perhaps forever, my friend."

Maya wondered what that was going to mean for Neferet and Bener-ib, who had counted on a house empty of its master. Perhaps Ptah-mes would reside in Waset. The girls would certainly need to remain in Akhet-aten.

Finally, Hani rose. "With your permission, my lord, Maya and I are hoping to catch an early ferry tomorrow morning. I think it might be a good idea to go to bed before it gets much later."

Ptah-mes nodded graciously. "As you like, Hani. Don't feel constrained by my hours."

As Hani and Maya made their way to their rooms, Maya said in a low voice, "You didn't mention to Neferet that Bener-ib's father is in town?"

Hani raised his eyebrows. "I don't want to cause any tensions, and anything I told Neferet would reach Bener-ib as soon as she got home. Either Nakht-ef-mut's coming to visit his daughter, and she knows he's here, or he came for some other reason, and she doesn't want to see him. They seem to have a strange relationship."

"I'll say." Maya thought of how close Lord Hani was to his daughters—and he himself to his little Henut-sen—and had to shake his head in disgust.

⊠

Despite his intention to get an early start, Hani awoke rather late the next morning. The two young doctors were at a small folding table in the salon, sharing a loaf of bread and discussing in quiet tones the latest case they'd encountered at the palace. As Hani passed through the room, they rose and headed up the stairs.

Ptah-mes stood in the garden, his arms crossed,

gazing idly out over the newly burgeoning flowerbeds, his expression pensive but more relaxed than usual. He looked up as Hani approached, shirtless and holding a cup of milk.

"Did you sleep well, my friend?" Ptah-mes asked.

Hani laughed. "Well and long. I dreamed about the Lake of Flowers. Maybe that means we're coming to the end of our tribulations and a happier world is approaching."

"May it be so." Ptah-mes had opened his mouth to say something else when voices from the gate drifted toward them.

A moment later, the porter came crunching up the path. "My lord, there is a gentleman here to see Lady Bener-ib. Should I get her, or would you like to talk to him first?"

Ptah-mes exchanged a glance with Hani. "Send him to me."

The two men stood in silence while the servant fetched Ptah-mes's visitor. Hani suspected who it was, and he was uneasy about the reason for the visit. He wondered how Nakht-ef-mut knew where his daughter lived. *Has he come to take her home? That would break Neferet's heart.*

The *sunu* appeared shortly and made a deep bow. His eyes flickered over to Hani's—he might or might not have remembered they'd been introduced—but it was to the much-better-dressed Ptah-mes that he spoke. "My lord, my name is Nakht-ef-mut. I am a *wab* priest of Sekhmet from her temple in Sau. I've been told that my daughter resides here, and I would like to see her, if I may."

Hani could well imagine that he was asking himself why Bener-ib lived in the mansion of a grandee and what her status might be. *Does he think she's his mistress, I wonder? Or does he know about the girl's proclivities?*

Ptah-mes, gracious but cool, indicated a chair, and the three of them seated themselves, the priest perching nervously on the edge of his seat, his hands clenched together in his lap. His lofty expression was clearly a mask. Ptah-mes nodded. "Of course. Her condition is wholly honorable, I can assure you. She is a colleague of my wife, and it is convenient for them to live here, near the palace, while I'm away in Djahy."

Nakht-ef-mut's sharp face stiffened, but he tipped his head politely. "I've been assigned to the palace myself, to replace Lord Pentju. I thank you for your hospitality, my lord, but it would probably be more appropriate if she lived with me from now on. Her stepmother will be moving up shortly."

Oh dear. This won't make the girls happy. Where have you been for the last five years of your daughter's life, my man? Never an attempt to contact her. Never a feast-day gift...

"As you will," Ptah-mes said smoothly. He rose. "Let's get her. Come, Hani."

Nakht-ef-mut shot an anxious glance at Hani and hesitated.

"Don't worry. He's my father-in-law." Ptah-mes caught Hani's eye, and a wry smile twitched at his mouth.

The three men made their way into the salon, which was cooler than outside. Hani, following the priest, saw that his neat back was tense, his steps self-consciously precise. Hani didn't altogether like the man, but he couldn't say why, other than that he had a ratlike look about him. Nakht-ef-mut's manner was a mixture of hauteur and nervousness. Perhaps he dreaded this encounter and was fortifying his self-confidence behind a supercilious facade.

Ptah-mes instructed his steward to bring Lady Bener-ib, and he and the guests seated themselves.

"You're a *sunu*, then?" asked Ptah-mes in a conversational tone.

Nakht-ef-mut tipped his head. "I am. I served at court briefly in my youth, but more recently, I've been teaching at the school in Sau." He volunteered no more.

At last, Hani heard the thunder of bare feet on the stairs—mostly Neferet's, he suspected. Whispered voices emerged from the corridor—Bener-ib's high-pitched "Come with me" and something reassuring from Neferet. A moment later, Bener-ib appeared in the doorway. She looked pitifully childlike and unsure of herself. Neferet stood behind her protectively. As soon as her eyes landed on her father, Bener-ib stiffened and made as if to run away. Neferet pushed her gently forward. The girl from Sau was trembling.

Nakht-ef-mut rose and took a tentative step toward his daughter. He cleared his throat. "Bener-ib, my dear, I'd like to put the past behind us. We're going to be living in Akhet-aten now. I want you to come home with me."

"Father," she said in a small voice, her eyes avoiding his. She made no move to come toward him.

Nakht-ef-mut looked embarrassed at this public lack of warmth. He said rather too sharply, "It's more appropriate for you to be with your family until you're married. I've been putting him off for years by saying you were studying, but your betrothed is getting impatient."

With a cry, Bener-ib turned and tried to break out the doorway, but Neferet blocked her. Neferet put her arms around her friend and said in her most defiant voice, "She's a grown woman, my lord. Maybe she doesn't want to marry that man, and you can't make her."

"Who is this person?" the priest cried, his face flushing.

"My wife," Ptah-mes said in a voice both casual and laden with warning. "She's right, of course."

Hani, saying nothing, watched the strange confrontation play out. His face warmed with pride at his lioness of a daughter, although he could well imagine Nakht-ef-mut's frustration at finding these strangers interfering with his parental rights.

As if he'd heard Hani's thoughts, Nakht-ef-mut said tensely, "With all due respect, my lord, this is a matter between myself and my daughter." His face flaming, he cut uneasy eyes toward Hani, perhaps seeking an ally. But Hani said nothing, just looked on with a bland expression.

Nakht-ef-mut moved slowly toward his daughter, saying in the reasonable voice one might use to lull a frightened animal, "Bener-ib, dear, don't make a scene. I'm your father, after all. You're making the whole family look foolish."

Bener-ib, who was caught in a corner of the room, gave a whimper. Her expression was so distressed and conflicted and her face so beaded with sweat that Hani was tempted to say, "Enough. You should leave the poor girl alone, father or not." But he appreciated that it was really none of his business, and he felt sorry for the embarrassment the priest was going through. Some of his own confrontations with Neferet hadn't gone well in the past either. Still, at least, he'd known when to give up. Nakht-ef-mut kept drawing closer and implacably closer to his daughter, who, eyes bugging from her head, was sucking up great desperate drafts of air as if preparing to dive into the water and swim away.

Nakht-ef-mut was near enough to reach her and was stretching out a hand, more beseeching than peremptory, when Bener-ib began to scream. It was a wild, high-pitched, scarcely human scream of terror. She tunneled past Neferet and balled herself up in the corner, shrieking something that might have been "No! No!"

As one, Hani and Ptah-mes rushed forward and held Nakht-ef-mut back. He didn't seem angry or determined to get at his daughter. In fact, he looked frightened and shamed. His hands were shaking. Neferet huddled over Bener-ib, trying to calm her friend, who was almost having a seizure, her eyes rolling up, clawing at the wall as if to escape. And that awful panting, hysterical scream trailed off into wails.

"What is the meaning of this?" Ptah-mes asked neutrally, but there was a hard edge to his voice. "The girl is obviously terrified of you."

Hani's hair was standing on end. *What's going on?* Nakht-ef-mut turned a miserable scarlet face to the two men and cried in an unsteady voice, staring at them in turn as if to convince them, "I swear to you, I've never laid a hand on her. She's been this way for years. I... I was sure she would have calmed down by now. My wife thought that if we left her alone for a while, she would work her way through this stubbornness..."

"Take her away, my duckling," Hani called to his daughter. Neferet lifted up her writhing friend, who fortunately wasn't very big, and bundled her off up the stairs. The girl was still weeping incoherently.

The three men were left staring at one another, breathing hard.

"I'd like an explanation for this, my lord. This is, after all, my house, and your daughter is my guest." There was frosty menace in Ptah-mes's voice.

Nakht-ef-mut covered his face with his hands, his narrow shoulders jerking. "It was wrong, wrong," he moaned. "We should never have done it."

"Let's all sit down, and you'll explain what's going on." Ptah-mes was wholly the magistrate now, calm but implacable.

Hani helped Nakht-ef-mut to a stool. The man seemed to be in shock, his haughty manner completely crumbled and shaken to the ground. "*What* was wrong?" Hani urged, dreading lest the *sunu* should admit to abusing his daughter.

Nakht-ef-mut took a big shaky gulp of air. "I must first tell you the shame the girl has brought upon our family, my lords. She... she refused to marry. She showed no interest in the nice young men of our acquaintance—quite the contrary. We set her up with some very eligible and fine students of mine, but she was adamant. And worse, she threatened to harm herself if we forced her. Then I found out that... that she liked females." He dropped his face into his hands once more as if the humiliation were more than he could bear.

Hani knew the shock of that discovery only too well. But they'd never pushed Neferet to be who she was not.

"We locked her up. We kept her away from other girls, never knowing if they were just friends or something worse. She's shy—it's not as if she had many friends. Finally, my wife suggested that we encourage her fiancé to... to have her before they were married. We thought she'd find out what a pleasure it was, and that would cure her, you know?

I wanted it to be something gentle and... well, pleasant. But she became hysterical, fighting and screaming and going half-mad. The poor young man was frightened to death by her reaction, but he dutifully carried out his job. She hasn't been normal since. She's afraid of her shadow—won't even look you in the eye. We thought it would be best to send her away to study with Pentju's wife." His face twisted with grief.

Hani was torn between rage and pity for the man's stupidity. He said in a low voice, "You had your own daughter raped?"

Nakht-ef-mut's voice rose wildly. "That wasn't my intention. I wanted her to enjoy the experience, to be cured. But I was wrong, so wrong. May the gods forgive me. My only daughter. What have I done to her?" He covered his face yet again. "She was such a good, meek little girl. This all started when she had her sidelock cut off."

Well, of course, Hani thought, exasperated. *You, a doctor, should know how things change when a child enters adolescence.* But his heart was heavy for both of them—for the traumatized girl and for her father, who, in apparent good faith, had made a cruel and terrible mistake. He found that he couldn't be judgmental. *We might have done that, too, and it would have been Neferet screaming in the corner.*

Ptah-mes, who'd stood in frozen silence during this recital, let out a heavy breath. "I think you should go, my lord. To insist would be good for no one. We appreciate your honesty."

Mopping his face, Nakht-ef-mut nodded and staggered to the door, looking broken, and Hani heard his ragged footsteps making their way out the vestibule. Lord Ptah-mes stared at Hani, a sheen of sweat on his face. Ptah-mes, too, was the father of daughters.

Suddenly, Maya came running into the room, eyes wild. "I heard screaming! Is everything all right?"

Hani forced himself to smile, despite his heavy heart. "No one has been murdered. Bener-ib's father just showed up." He described for his son-in-law the harrowing meeting and its cause.

Maya gaped. "Who would do such a horrible thing?"

Hani said cynically, "Remember what Neferet told us about the girl's hostile stepmother? Her motives might not have been so benign as her husband's. Nakht-ef-mut must be under her influence. Let's leave Bener-ib to the care of Neferet. You and I will head back to Waset." Hani exchanged a look of sorrow with Ptah-mes. "I'm grieved this has been inflicted upon you, my lord. After all your generosity."

Ptah-mes said nothing for a moment then asked, "Did I understand that her father is the new royal physician? He and his daughter will almost inevitably run into one another at the palace, won't they?"

Hani's heart chilled. *How awful that would be.* "What can we do about it? Perhaps they can time their coming and going so as not to meet."

Ptah-mes raised a skeptical eyebrow.

"Well, I guess we're ready to go home, eh, Lord Hani?" said Maya, looking as drained as Hani felt.

But Hani said, to his own surprise, "No. I think we'll hold off a day after all. I want to ask around about those disappearing baskets."

CHAPTER 6

To no one's surprise, the young doctors didn't show up for lunch. Hani, Maya, and Ptah-mes ate without much talk. Afterward, as they were sitting back, enjoying some herb-flavored beer, Hani said, "It's just occurred to me that Neferet may know something about the thefts from the king's household. Once things have calmed down, I'd like to talk to her."

Ptah-mes nodded somberly. He'd been pale and pensive since the scene of the morning. "Should we have some food sent up to them, do you think?"

"I'm sure that would be appreciated."

Ptah-mes had no sooner called out to the steward than the sound of thudding bare footsteps down the stairs announced that Neferet was approaching. She headed for the three men, put her arm around her father's shoulders, and kissed his wigless head. Her usually cheerful face was sad and her little brown eyes red lidded.

"How are you two holding up, my duckling?"

She shrugged then said with feeling, "Her father is a

ba-a-ad man, Papa. How could anybody do that to their own child?"

Hani said with a sigh, "I think Nakht-ef-mut meant well, my love. I wonder if it wasn't the stepmother who pushed him to this. He was overcome with remorse."

"Well, he should be. How would he like it if somebody *he* loved turned him over to be raped? And Ibet was only fifteen. And her mother had died only three years before."

Ptah-mes lowered his eyes, and Maya bent to take his straw in his mouth.

"It was a terrible thing." Hani patted the empty stool at his side, and Neferet plopped down, probing her father's plate for uneaten bits of cucumber. Hani watched, his heart swelling with tenderness, thinking how they might have lost her. At last, he said, "Neferet, my little duck, are you in a condition to answer a few questions for me? I'm not sure where else to start."

"About what, Papa?" she said as a servant set her own dish before her.

"There's been a series of petty thefts from the king's household over the last few months or maybe a year. Jewelry, little coffers, baskets—things like that. But they were always returned eventually. Nobody seemed to see anyone doing it, so it must have been someone whose presence was taken for granted."

"I've heard that, actually." She stopped to chew a bit of fried fish and swallowed it, tiny bones and all. "It wasn't me, if that's what you're thinking."

"That reassures me," Hani said with a mischievous smile. "Do you have any idea of who it might have been? Maybe you've overheard people talking…"

She knit her brows and appeared to be thinking hard. "Nothing, Papa."

"Why do you think someone might have taken those things, some of which aren't worth much in the first place, and then brought them back? Could they have been using them for something? To cast a spell, maybe?"

"Perhaps you should ask Khuit about that," Maya said wryly.

Neferet looked thoughtful, then she squinted in a suppressed snicker. "Maybe they spat on them or something."

"I can't imagine why the person had to take the objects away to do that."

Neferet shrugged. "You asked me if I had any ideas." Having finished her lunch, she pushed her stool back and rose. "Forgive me, everybody, but I need to take Ibet some food... if she wants to eat."

"The cook is preparing something, and one of the servants will take it up. I suspect Bener-ib needs you," said Ptah-mes kindly.

He's not the piece of flint a lot of people think he is, Hani told himself, his heart warming with friendship for this man who had suffered so much and conducted himself with dignity through it all.

"Do we have any more investigations to do here, my lord?" Maya asked.

"I would like to find out more about that lady-in-waiting who died. We've been assuming she was murdered—Bener-ib said the maidservants used the words *dropped dead*—but maybe her death was just a coincidence."

147

"Take my litter, Hani," Ptah-mes offered. "Whom do you plan to interrogate?"

"Perhaps one of the palace servants. For once, we don't have to go skulking around without the king's knowledge."

"That's right." Ptah-mes smiled thinly. "This is an official investigation."

⌧

Maya followed Lord Hani to the king's quarters—the she-king, as he and Hani had once distinguished her. Only now she was the sole king. Her apartments were as fabulous as imagination had painted them. Maya's heart was beating so hard he could hardly swallow—overwhelmed that a boy from the working class might actually present himself in this place of gold and gems, of color and gardens. Of silent servants better dressed than he. Surely the status of scribe had opened to him exalted worlds. As the wise man had once said, "Be a scribe—he makes friends with those greater than he."

The two men waited in the vestibule while the king's subchamberlain sought the permission they needed to interview several of the king's handmaidens. To Maya's amazement, that worthy official was none other than Sheshi, the tall, thin, dark-skinned brother of one of Lord Hani's lower secretaries. Maya had interrogated him, but he couldn't be sure the man recognized him. He decided not to recall the event to the official, who had reported Maya, with nearly fatal consequences.

Some time passed. Maya gaped about him in a state of euphoria, drinking in the priceless objects and rich colors, daring to inhale the musky floral scent of incense and the honeyed sweetness of bouquets of water lilies. Eventually, the subchamberlain returned, as haughty as a grandee. His fuzzy hair was concealed under a long court wig, except for a rim over the brow. "Our Sun God—life, prosperity, and health be to her—says you may question whomever you like, my lord. I am to round up the maidservants who are on this shift and present them to you."

"Thank our ruler for her most gracious generosity. Her favor is the breath of life in my nostrils." Hani bowed humbly, and it was all Maya could do not to roll his eyes. Hani was far from being a toady of the king—he'd cast his lot with the party of rebels who hoped to return the land of Kemet to the old gods. But his courtesy was always perfect.

Sheshi spun on his heel and a moment later returned with a dozen or so beautiful young women—most clad in diaphanous gowns, others naked except for girdles of beads around their hips. They looked anxious, clustering together as if their very nearness could give them strength to endure what was coming. They were like the mythical Lovelies of Hut-haru, handmaids to the goddess of beauty. It was all Maya could do not to goggle at them.

Lord Hani beamed. "My ladies, I have a few questions for you. Anyone may answer at any time. My secretary here will take notes. You're all aware of the petty thefts that have been taking place in our Sun God's household, I'm sure."

There was a murmur of assent and a nodding of pretty heads. The girls' eyes were universally round under the elegant makeup, their nervousness palpable.

"Since before she became sole king," one offered hesitantly.

"Have any of you seen anything on anyone's part that

might seem suspicious? Any of your number or other servants or visitors who might have looked furtive, for example? Anyone whose visits coincide with the disappearance of objects?"

Another flurry of head-shaking and terrified glances. They were too frightened to be helpful.

Hani smiled with his broadest paternal smile and said in a teasing voice, "I won't bite, you know. I'm here to help your mistress. She's afraid these disappearances and returns have some sinister meaning. Anything you can tell might help us. Keep in mind, you may all be in danger."

Nice one. Nothing like self-interest to loosen up the tightest tongue. But nothing was forthcoming, just a shaking of heads and a murmured "No" or two.

Hani gnawed his lip then tried another tack. "Who all has visited the king's court? This could go back a few years, but I want people who show up repeatedly. Who visits her in her apartments?"

"The wigmaker," said one girl timidly. "Merchants of jewels and fabrics."

Another offered, "The captain of her guard. The God's Father, Lord Ay."

"The princesses. The chamberlains. Pages. Messengers."

"Now we're getting somewhere!" Hani said genially. "Who else?"

"The doctors and magicians. Her chamberlain. Litter bearers."

"But they don't actually come in," someone objected. "They just let our lady out in the vestibule."

"All the girls who work at night," said the first handmaid to speak up. "Ladies-in-waiting."

"What about laundrymen or people from the kitchen?" Hani prompted.

"They just leave things at the door, and we take them in."

"She talks to the viziers and diplomats in one of the throne rooms."

The suggestions trickled off into silence as the maids' ideas were exhausted. Lord Hani started again. "Who was the woman who died recently—not the midwife but the lady-in-waiting? How did she die, do you know?"

"That was Lady Henut-tawy, the king's dresser," said one of the girls. "I think she just died of disease. She'd been getting sicker for a long time. In fact..." She cast an anxious glance at her neighbors as if afraid she was violating some secret. "In fact, a lot of us haven't felt well. It's unusual, you know? Many of us, including the king."

Another one held out her arm. "Look at these pale spots. We're almost all starting to get them."

Lord Hani bent to get a better view—there were clearly lighter patches on the inside of the girl's tawny arm. And on the outside was a dense dark spatter of freckles. He reached out to touch it but pulled his hand back.

Strange. Maya's heart started hammering. Here was a line of questioning that seemed significant.

Hani appeared to be interested too. "Do you think someone could have poisoned you?"

"No, because the tasters have never gotten sick," someone else said.

"Has Lady Djefat-nebty seen this?"

"Yes, my lord," one of the other girls said. "She thought it didn't look like anything."

"Well, then, I guess she should know. But I thank you, ladies. You've given me much to think about." Hani tipped his head to the handmaids. "I may come back later to talk to your colleagues who stay the night."

Hani shot Maya a knowing glance. They were on the trail of something—but what? It was true that if the tasters were healthy, poison was unlikely. But Maya remembered one of their investigations when people had been deliberately infected with the plague. Things weren't always what they seemed.

⊠

They retraced their steps, Sheshi in the lead, through the magical beauty of the palace and into the drabber real world outside the gates, where they stood while their eyes adjusted to the glare of the street.

Hani blew a deep breath out his nose. He was baffled. *How is the king's whole household feeling sick if the tasters have had no ill effects from any of the food? Perhaps the well is bad. At any rate, it seems that the lady-in-waiting died of natural causes.* "Sounds like there's more than one mystery going on at the palace, eh, my friend? But I'm not sure this has anything to do with our investigation. We just need to find out who has been borrowing personal items from the king and why."

They mounted Ptah-mes's litter again and took off for the southern part of the city. Hani was quiet, sunk in thought. After a while, he said, "I completely forgot that I promised the dead midwife's family to see to a special burial for her. She was eaten by crocodiles, after all."

Maya pushed back his wig and scratched his head. "I'm

confused now that there's no reason to think that Lady Henut-tawy was murdered. Maybe the midwife's death had nothing to do with the exchange of babies after all."

"I don't know, but let me gather a couple of silver *deben*s, and we'll pay the family a visit. She deserves that respect."

They made the long journey back through the city to Lord Ptah-mes's villa, only to find he'd set out for Waset. From his room, Hani gathered a handful of the silver scraps he always took along on foreign missions in case he needed to bribe someone. He said with a grim smile as he hefted his small bag, "Let's go appease the Lord of the Waters."

They were clopping their way through the cool, quiet salon with its polished gypsum floors when Neferet came down the stairs and called, "Papa!"

He turned and opened his arms to his daughter. She was more precious than ever to him. "How is Bener-ib, my duckling?"

"Better. When I told her that her father had left, she calmed down. But you know, if he's going to be the new royal *sunu* like you said, she's going to see him again. I didn't dare tell her."

Hani shook his head and grunted sadly, then he brightened. "My duckling, could you do me a favor? I didn't think to ask when I was at the king's apartment just now. Could you bring me one of the items that was stolen and returned? Get permission from the king, though—we don't want anyone to think you were the thief."

"Of course," she said cheerfully. "I'm on my way there now."

Neferet, toting her big, lidded wicker basket, set off

with her father and brother-in-law, but the two men veered off toward the poorer neighborhood near the River while she continued up the processional street northward.

After a moment, Maya cried in surprise, "There's Mother!"

Sure enough, his unmistakable little mother, in her habitual scarf, was waddling down the narrow alley that ran alongside the edge of her workshop.

"Mother!" Maya hailed her.

Lord Hani waved a genial hand. "Where are you off to in the middle of the day, In-hapy? It's almost lunchtime."

"Lord Hani! My son! Were you coming to see me? I was just going to take some food to Tuy's family. They're all men now. I don't know if anybody knows how to cook."

She held out a big clay pot wrapped in towels. A fragrance of onions and garlic and herbs wafted up, and Hani realized how hungry he was. "What about the mute girl?"

"Well, there's her. But I don't know what her skills are. I rather wish she could get away, to be honest. Alone with all those grown sons... I don't think any of them are married, and they're getting a little long in the tooth."

Hani nodded in understanding. "We'll go with you, if you don't mind." The three of them continued down the block together and turned on the next street. The neighborhood wasn't well cared for, despite the fact that many royal artisans had to live there in the vicinity of the midtown palace. People didn't seem to have rooted themselves in the City of the Horizon or to take pride in their surroundings. It was as if they wanted to camp lightly and leave as little investment of their hearts as possible.

Hani, Maya, and his mother drew near to the house, a modest cube of whitewashed mudbrick already peeling and streaking. An adolescent boy stood in the doorway, chewing on something.

"Good morning, my boy," In-hapy called.

The lad looked around, unsmiling.

"Is your father home?"

"No." The youth was closer to an adult than a child, though he still had his sidelock—a tall, lean boy like his father and brother. "He's at the riverside. I'm going back as soon as I finish."

"Are you the only one home, then?" Hani asked in a friendly voice.

"No. My older brother is here."

"Then give him this stew, my dear. I thought it might be nice for you not to have to cook for once." In-hapy extended the pot.

The boy's sullenness evaporated. She'd touched him in the adolescent's weak spot—his stomach. He took the vessel gratefully. "Thank you, mistress."

Hani asked, "Could I speak to your brother, please? That's User-hat?"

"Yes, my lord." Then, as if he had just remembered his manners, the youth added, "Come in."

The three of them trooped after the lad into the diminutive salon with its low masonry benches and single crudely painted column. With the sun directly overhead, the small, high windows left the room very dark. User-hat was just emerging from the back of the house, picking his teeth with a fingernail. He stopped short as he saw them.

Hani could see him struggling to place these strange men who'd invaded his house.

In-hapy, he recognized. "Mistress. My father is at work."

"He was the one I wanted to talk to, but I'm sure you'll do nicely." Hani's voice dropped. "I've brought silver from the king—life, prosperity, and health be to her—to pay for your mother's funeral as one consecrated to the Lord of the Waters."

He handed the young man the clinking bag he'd brought. As he slid open the drawstring and peered in, User-hat's eyes widened in astonishment. At first, he seemed unable to speak, then he fell to his knees and tried to kiss Hani's foot.

"Easy," Hani said with a smile, drawing him to his feet. "I'm just the messenger."

Behind User-hat, Maya shot Hani a knowing look.

"We're eternally indebted to you, my lord. If there's ever anything my family can do... wash your clothes for free?"

Hani laughed. "You're very kind, but I live in Waset, my boy. There is one thing, though. That servant girl—the mute one. Could I by any chance engage her services?"

"She's yours, my lord. I know my father would say the same." User-hat let out a piercing whistle, and the servant appeared in the inner doorway. "You're to go with this gentleman, girl. If you have any things, gather them up."

It took her only a moment to wrap her few poor belongings in a cloth and follow Hani and his party to the door. She was completely dressed, and her once-disheveled hair was neatly covered with a workaday scarf—the period of mourning was long past—but even in nondescript garb, she was a lovely young woman. *She rather resembles Lady*

Meryet-aten, Hani thought with amusement. *The gods bestow their gifts without distinction of class and wealth.*

After an exchange of thanks that threatened to become endless, Hani and Maya took their leave, the servant in their wake. As they walked, Hani dropped back to exchange a few words with the young woman. She was respectful but not abject. She'd been, perhaps, a servant in a wealthy household, who was accustomed to having some dignity.

"My dear, who did this to you?" Hani asked in compassion, not expecting an answer. But the servant made a bulbous gesture over her head, her face drawing up with tears that were somehow harder than mere sorrow.

"What's that?" Maya looked puzzled.

An idea had come to life in Hani's head. He stopped walking. "Is that a crown you're making?" The idea awoke a thrill of something between delight and fear within him. This was extremely useful information for their investigation—but it also made their every move more dangerous.

She nodded, her mouth pulled down, and tears beginning to trickle from her eyes.

Hani glanced around him uneasily and nearly whispered, "The he-king or the she-king?"

The girl looked desperate, then she pointed to herself and shook her head—*Not like me*. She pointed at Hani and Maya and nodded—*Like you*.

"Oh no!" cried Maya, horror-struck. "Now we're in trouble."

"At least he's dead," Hani observed wryly. "The she-king is the bigger danger." He drew the girl against a wall and blocked her with his mass from prying eyes. "Did you

157

witness an exchange of babies at the time the Haru in the nest was born?"

The servant nodded fiercely, her face suddenly bitter. She sketched another bulbous shape out in front of her, mimed rocking a baby in her arms, and threw them wide, as if relinquishing their contents.

The hair stood up on Hani's neck. *Dear gods! Can she be the mother?* Almost afraid to ask, he said, "Were you brought up here from Hut-nen-nesut?"

She nodded, her face twisted and tear streaked.

"Bes have mercy!" Maya murmured, his eyes round with horror. "No wonder they cut out her tongue."

"I'm surprised they didn't kill you," Hani told the girl earnestly. "They seriously underestimated your eloquence, even without words." He laid a proud hand on her shoulder, and still tearful but defiant, she nodded.

It was past lunchtime, and Hani's stomach told him in no uncertain terms that they needed to get back to Ptah-mes's house. With a significant glance at Maya, he led the way down the sun-scorched back streets toward the southern suburbs. As they strode along, he asked the girl the question he wanted more than anything to know the answer to. "Who is the father, my dear?"

She grew rigid and stopped walking. Then she made once more the bulbous shape overhead. Her eyes caught Hani's, burning with rancor. Hani couldn't suppress the cry of astonishment that escaped his lips. "Sweet gods! King Nefer-khepru-ra?"

She nodded, the wings of her nostrils tense and pale.

Hani's heart froze within him. Some discarded lower-class mistress of the king—perhaps Nefer-khepru-ra had impregnated her expressly to provide a backup in case his wife bore another girl. Hani thought this might be news Lady Meryet-aten wouldn't like to have known—that the little prince was indeed her brother. Her claim to the throne had just evaporated.

The threesome entered Ptah-mes's impressive gate and crossed the long garden, the servant girl trailing behind the two men. When they had entered the house, Hani said to the steward, "Please find lodging for this young woman. She'll be going back to Waset with us."

Hani and Maya found themselves alone in the garden, waiting under the arbor for their late lunch. They exchanged an anxious stare.

"I never saw this coming, my lord," said Maya. "Do you suppose the present king and her father know her identity? If so, the girl's life isn't worth much."

"It's been nine years, and no one has attempted anything against her. No doubt they lost sight of where she'd gone. They might well have thought she'd die without medical care." Although it wasn't especially hot, Hani pushed back his wig and mopped his forehead. "Do we tell anyone? Both sides have reason to want her dead."

Conversation ceased as two servants brought out the food, setting it on their little tables, and Hani fell to with pleasure. The dish was one of his favorites: meat-stuffed pastries with cumin and tamarind. Maya was attacking the meal with gusto. For their respective sizes, the two men were hearty eaters.

They'd just finished off the meal with some dried figs when Hani heard Neferet calling out in the house, "Has my father come back yet?"

The porter murmured something in response, and a moment later, Neferet burst into the garden. Her footsteps came pounding down the path, and then she bounded up the step of the pavilion. "Today was an exciting day, Papa. One of the girls found a dead cat in the well. It must have fallen in and drowned a good long time ago, poor thing. And everybody's been drinking the water. *Iyi!*"

So, Hani thought, grateful. *That explains why people have been getting sick.* He recalled a horrible episode from his childhood, when the well of one of his friends had been polluted and several of the lad's family had died. It had made Hani highly ticklish about well water.

Neferet held out her basket. "I brought you some of the stolen objects, Papa."

"Well, my duckling, you certainly didn't waste any time. Let's see what you have."

Neferet cleared away the empty dishes from Hani's little table and set her wicker pannier upon it. From within, she produced several items—a small inlaid box, such as might hold a lady's jewels, a diminutive basket, a tube of kohl, a mirror. Hani stared at them, looking for some connection. They were exquisite pieces but not priceless compared to the other objects that must decorate the king's apartments. He picked up the kohl tube, with its slender applicator stick. It was made of turquoise faience with the king's names inlaid upon it in white. Hani pulled out the stick and peered inside. Except for a few grains of something yellowish near the rim, the inside was all black like the eye paint it contained. He sniffed and caught the earthy smell of antimony and fat.

"Why would anybody take the king's kohl?" Maya said in disgust.

"And then bring it back? That's what we're trying to figure out."

Hani opened the intarsia jewel box with its shrine-like tilted lid. Nothing was inside. He stared at it, willing it to disclose its secrets. Then he noticed faint traces of yellow in the fine cracks between the inlaid stone pieces around the knob. *Odd...*

The gilded bronze handle of the mirror, cast in the likeness of a papyrus stalk, seemed to be clean. Hani took up the basket. It wasn't much larger than his two fists, woven of delicate reeds of several different colors to form a pattern.

"What's that little thing used for?" Maya asked, eyeing it.

"It must be one of those mysterious weapons the ladies keep in their armory of beauty." Hani smiled. He picked up the lid and examined the interior. And there he saw it clearly—in the interstices between the woven reeds, the bright-yellow residue had piled up, although the outer surface of the reeds was clean. He sat staring at the objects for a while, trying to make sense of it. "It looks like someone actually carried some yellow pigment in this basket—or something with pigment on it. And I've noticed traces elsewhere on these other things. The mirror is too smooth to have retained any of it."

"Could it be left from that sandstorm we had a while back?" Neferet asked.

Hani furrowed his brow skeptically. "I don't remember

it being this bright color. It's as if someone rubbed paint onto these surfaces."

"Is that significant, my lord?" Maya said, running his finger over the reeds and bringing the residue forth to stare at it. "Do you think all the stolen objects were defaced like this?"

"The curious thing is they haven't really been defaced. Unless you were looking for it, you wouldn't even have seen it."

"If it's paint, maybe Khawy would know something about it." Neferet looked up eagerly at her father.

"You think Khawy stole the items, duckling?" Her father smiled. "He lives in the Place of Truth, way up in Waset."

"No, of course not, but… well, I don't know. He might know of someone who had stolen some paint or something."

Eyeing Neferet, Maya said sharply, "But why would anyone put paint on the king's things and then send them back to her, my girl?"

Hani heaved a great sigh. "You're sure you haven't seen her painting her eyelids yellow?"

With a roll of her own eyes, Neferet scoffed, "Nobody paints their lids yellow, Papa."

Hani would have wondered if the yellow substance were somehow responsible for poisoning the queen's household, but the polluted well was so much more likely. That relieved him. This was only a case of theft—or appropriation.

"Well, Maya," he said, rising, "it looks like it's time for us to head home. I think we have some questions to ask in Waset."

"But what about your lessons for the crown prince, my lord?"

Hani shrugged. "No one has contacted me yet. Maybe Lord Ay thinks my investigations of the theft will keep me busy enough not to go on any missions for the Great Royal Wife."

He'd just turned to make his way into Ptah-mes's house when the steward came bursting out, his face grave. "Lord Hani, may I speak to you, please?"

His flesh creeping with dread, Hani shot Maya a look. *Please say no one in the family is in trouble.* "Speak, man. It's not a secret from these people."

"My lord, a messenger just came from Lord Pentju, the royal physician. He said he thought Lady Bener-ib lived here, and I told him she does." He swallowed, out of breath. "He said her father has been killed."

"Oh no!" cried Neferet, clapping her hands to her mouth in horror. "Oh, poor Ibet!"

But Hani wondered whether Bener-ib might not be so sorrowful after what her father had done to her. He thanked the servant then turned to Neferet. "Where is she now, little duck? We need to tell her."

Neferet's face puckered in distress. "I thought she'd be here by now. She was coming as soon as she looked in on her patient, that girl I told you about who had the stillborn baby. I ran ahead to show you the king's things."

"Well, let's go look for her. We may find her en route."

The three of them thundered to the gate, almost stumbling over one another. *Dear gods, what will the poor girl suffer next?*

In a ragged block, they pounded down the street.

Neferet steered them away from the main road and into the byways. "This is the way we always come," she panted.

It was the end of the afternoon, the hottest part of the day, and although it was not oppressively warm at this late spring season, Hani felt as if he were being roasted. The white walls radiated heat, his face was on fire, and the sweat threatened to blind him with its burning trickles. After they'd pelted along at top speed for several blocks, he had to stop and breathe or he would explode. Maya was trailing already. Hani wondered what they must look like to the few passers-by who jumped aside and stared at them.

"Hold up," he called, his chest heaving. "I can't do this anymore. Neferet, dear, if you want to run ahead, feel free."

Hitching up her skirts, Neferet shot off, leaving Maya and Hani bent over, trying to recover their breath.

"We look like we're making a court obeisance." Maya tried to laugh, but he was panting too hard.

After a few moments, his pulse no longer pounding in his neck, Hani felt restored enough to continue at a more sedate pace, but it wasn't long before the two doctors appeared around a corner, Neferet with her friend's basket in one hand and the other arm around the girl's shoulders. Neferet appeared to be holding her upright. Bener-ib's pointed little face was red and tear streaked. She had a stunned, expressionless look, as if she couldn't grasp what had happened.

Mindful of her fear, Hani approached gently as he might have done with an injured bird. "Bener-ib, my dear. I guess Neferet has told you the sad news."

She nodded stiffly, her face a frozen mask. Then, to

Hani's surprise, she said, "Yes, Lord Hani." Biting her lip, the girl dropped her face.

That's almost the first time she's ever voluntarily addressed a word to me, Hani thought in pity. "Do you two want me to walk you back?"

But Neferet said, "I can do it, Papa."

Helping her friend, who staggered like an unseeing ghost, she headed back south.

Maya and Hani continued until Hani said aloud to himself, "Where are we going? I thought we were just looking for Bener-ib."

Maya gave a bark of humorless laughter. "Looks like trouble found her first, my lord. A star-crossed girl."

Hani shaded his eyes and looked around absentmindedly, his attention ensnared in his thoughts. "I wonder why the man was killed—and how. Right after he was appointed royal physician." He turned to Maya. "Seems strange, doesn't it, along with all the other things happening at the palace?"

"But what connection could he have had with all that? He'd been in Sau until just a few days ago."

"I wish I knew..." Hani took an uncertain step forward, not sure what he should be doing. Then he said with determination, "Let's go to Pentju's house and see what he knows. We can make it look like a call of condolence. And it is, I suppose. I didn't know Nakht-ef-mut at all well, but Pentju did introduce him to me as his friend."

They veered off back in a southerly direction, through increasingly affluent villas, until they arrived at the *sunu's* gate. Hani knocked, and the porter, who knew him well, opened. The servant had on a mourning scarf.

"We've come to pay our respects to Lord Pentju and his wife on the death of their friend."

The servant ushered them inside, and they followed him through the garden to the door of the house, where they waited in silence until his return.

"The master and mistress of the house will receive you, my lords. Please enter."

In the salon, Hani encountered the two physicians seated in splendor upon their beautifully carved chairs, just as they'd been when he first met them years before. Pentju, a massive figure, towered above his tall, bony wife. They both looked somber, with mourning scarves about their heads.

"My heartfelt condolences to you both, my lord, my lady. Nakht-ef-mut had just been at Lord Ptah-mes's villa yesterday—this came as a terrible shock," Hani said soberly.

"That's what he said," rumbled Pentju. "It seems the meeting with his daughter didn't go well. He was quite distraught when he arrived at the house yesterday."

"Your messenger said your friend was killed. Did he have an accident?"

Lady Djefat-nebty gave a bark of disgust. "I rather doubt it was an accident. Someone hit him in the head with a rock and, while he was down, stabbed him repeatedly."

Hani and Maya exchanged a look full of unease. This was indeed a murder. *What motive could anyone in the capital have to slay a visitor? Unless...* "Was he robbed, do you think?"

Pentju shrugged. "Probably. He had a fair bit of silver on him, since he was prepared to buy a house."

Is it possible this had anything to do with all the

mysterious events at the palace? But Hani couldn't see what the connection might be. Nakht-ef-mut seemed like a complete outsider. "This saddens me to hear it. And after the sorrow of his meeting with his daughter."

"What was that all about?" Djefat-nebty asked in her brusque way. "He didn't say much, although we knew he wanted her to come live with the family again."

Hani took a deep breath. "Apparently, at some time in the past, Lord Nakht-ef-mut had tried to cajole or force his daughter into being more receptive to marriage by having her fiancé take her by force. It seems to have left her traumatized."

The lady of the house shook her head and forced a long, angry breath out between her teeth. "It's that wife of his. Nakht-ef-mut could never stand up to her. Or to anyone else, I'm afraid."

Her husband's eyebrows drew down into a grim frown. "I wish we could find out what happened and bring the killer to justice. I'm afraid our friend's unhappy *ba* may haunt us otherwise."

Hani hesitated. He had so many diverse commissions already that he didn't see how he was going to juggle everything. But poor Bener-ib was almost a part of his family. She deserved to know how her father had died. "My lord, my lady, I've carried out an occasional investigation for the king—life, prosperity, and health to her—and for her predecessors. Perhaps I could look unofficially into this sad case, if you like."

Lady Djefat-nebty's long mouth twitched in knowing humor.

Her husband said, "Very well. I'm aware his only child

lives with your daughter and Ptah-mes—what's he calling himself now, Maya? Investigate away."

"Were there any witnesses to the murder?"

"No. Just the fellow who found the body on the street. He went to the police with it, and they told us Nakht-ef-mut had a note from me in his purse."

"Do you know this man?"

"Not at all. Apparently, just a passer-by." But Hani thought, *The one who finds the corpse is often the one who produced the corpse.* "Where was your friend found, do you know, my lord?"

"Somewhere down near the River, where a lot of the artisans live, south of the magazines. Don't ask me why."

Hani pondered this. "That may give us a hint where to start interviewing. With your permission, we'll retire. We have work to do."

"I hope Neferet and Bener-ib will be able to work in the morning, but if not, have them let me know." Djefat-nebty's face was severe and her voice chilly, but compassion leaked out around the edges.

Once he and Maya were out in the street, Hani let out a huge breath. "What have we gotten ourselves into?" His heart was heavy for Bener-ib, who was such a timid, fragile creature. But he wasn't keen on going to the police barracks.

Maya was apparently thinking the same thing. "Do we have to ask Mahu for the man's name, my lord? He won't be happy to think you're investigating his case."

In fact, Hani and Mahu had a long and painful history between them, much of it due to Mahu's jealousy over their respective jurisdictions.

"I'm afraid I can't honestly say this is an official matter

for the foreign service," Hani said with a dry smile. "We're going to have to be subtle. How can we find out who the man was without openly asking the police?"

"If it happened down near the warehouses and the River, perhaps my mother would have heard something. You know how gossip travels down there."

Hani turned to his secretary, beaming. "Brilliant, my friend! Let's go right now, before it gets any later."

They set off briskly toward the center of the city. Just before the palace and the temple of the Aten, they veered left and followed the narrow alleys down toward the river. *Seems like I've been here a lot lately*, Hani thought in grim appreciation.

In-hapy took off her apron and came to greet them as soon as she saw them in the courtyard. "What can I do for you, my lord?"

Hani turned to Maya and gestured to him to explain.

"Have you heard anything about a dead man being found around here, Mother?"

Her weathered old face puckered with distress. "Alas, yes, my lord. Only yesterday, a man was beaten and stabbed just around the corner. Imagine—this close to the palace. What's the world coming to, I ask you?"

"Do you know who found him, mistress?"

"No. Just somebody passing by, I think. He may have been a neighbor, but I haven't heard. We're busy all day, and I don't get much of the gossip." As Hani lifted the rolled-up mat that hung at the door, In-hapy called after him, "Please tell Lady Neferet that her order is ready, my lord."

"I will, In-hapy. Thanks again."

They made their way down the narrow street and

around the corner, Hani asking himself what Neferet had ordered at the goldsmith's. *She's settled comfortably into the role of very rich wife*, he thought with amusement. Ptah-mes seemed happy to indulge her, so it wasn't up to Hani to advise her to frugality.

Looking around him at the dusty, unkempt little alley with its blind houses, Hani wondered whether anyone could have witnessed the crime. He murmured, "I guess we just start randomly knocking on doors."

"There's a woman up on that terrace. Do you suppose she saw anything?" Maya pointed. The woman stood up, folding a length of fabric over her arm, perhaps just cut off the loom. She gazed idly down at the men.

Hani brightened. If the woman worked or slept on her roof terrace, as many people did, she might well have heard or witnessed the attack. "*Yahya*, my good woman," he called, waving an arm. "Could we talk to you?"

She came closer and leaned over the parapet of the terrace. Hani would have put her in her thirties, but there was a worn, leathery quality about her that made her seem much older. She stared at him for a moment then said in a gritty, world-weary voice, "Who are you?"

"I'm investigating the death of the royal *sunu* for the palace." Hani massaged the truth a bit, but the woman wouldn't care that Nakht-ef-mut had been the *sunu* designate and that *the palace* meant Lord Pentju, who was, after all, the king's chamberlain. "Did you see or hear anything out of the ordinary last night? Perhaps a scuffle? Cries?"

The woman gave a snort. "Ain't nobody on our street who didn't see'r hear somethin'. It was still daylight—not even dinnertime."

"Can we talk in a more private place?" Hani called up with his most disarming grin.

After a hesitation, she nodded, and a brief while later, the gate of the courtyard was thrown back. The woman stood there, looking not so much hostile as wary, her eyes cutting back and forth from Hani to Maya. "Look, I have a weavin' quota to meet. I've got to put food in my children's mouths."

"I'd only like a few moments of your time, mistress." Hani pulled the faience ring from his finger and slipped it to her.

She seized the ring, her eyes widening in disbelief. No doubt it was worth more than several days of her piecework as a weaver.

"There was a murder committed in this neighborhood last night. Did you happen to see or hear anything?"

Suddenly, she was eager to talk. "Come to think of it, I did. I was foldin' up my loom on the terrace, same as I was just now. The children were up there with me, but my husband was still at work. He's a quarryman. I heard footsteps—somebody walkin' past in a bit of a hurry. Nothin' strange about that. But then there was a big thump and a scuffle and somebody crying out and then footsteps runnin' away."

"Did you go look? Did you see anything?" Hani prodded.

"You bet I did. I saw a man lyin' in the street, arms and legs every which way. A *wab* priest, I figured—shaven headed. Blood on his head and on his back. Looked dead to me. I run right down and out the gate, and there he was, not one house down from us. Right about there." She pointed. "Then one of the other neighbors come out to see. He yelled for the watchman. Before long, there was a whole crowd of us."

"Anything else unusual?" Hani asked, his heart leaden. What a terrible way for a man to die—violently in a strange city, having been rejected by his own child. "Was the knife still in his back?"

"I sure didn't see it, but I wasn't none too keen on gettin' any closer. Oh, and there was a big bloody rock nearby, the size of my two fists. They must've knocked him on the head and then jumped him while he was stunned."

Hani thanked the woman, and he and Maya headed off toward the processional street in a pensive mood.

"Sounds like a professional assassin, doesn't it, my lord? Pulling out the knife behind him so no one could track it down?" Maya nodded knowingly.

"That's probably true. We just need to find out who paid him and why."

CHAPTER 7

T HEY WALKED IN SILENCE BACK to Ptah-mes's villa.
The shadows were already long. Over the tree-shaded
garden, twilight and a drowsy hush had fallen. Only a
nightingale somewhere nearby proclaimed that there was
any life in the neighborhood.

Within the house, Ptah-mes's steward informed the two
men that his master had left for Waset. Hani heaved a sigh.
"That's where I want to be. I haven't written Nub-nefer
because I kept thinking every day we'd be coming home."

"And here we still are." Maya blew a loud breath through
his nose. "Strange and violent things keep piling up, but we
don't have any clues at all."

"If only that woman had caught a glimpse of the
murderer before he ran away."

Hani and his secretary pulled out stools and sank down,
while servants brought them dinner. Silently, Hani began
to eat the tempting skewers of pork and bits of fruit basted
with pomegranate syrup. He was quickly distracted from
his discouragement. Any life that could provide delicacies

like this wasn't so bad. But still, there was a leaden lump in his stomach. *How could Nakht-ef-mut have attracted a mortal enemy in the capital in a matter of days? Did someone follow him down from Sau? And if so, why?*

"I guess someone will have to tell his wife," Maya said.

"I'm assuming Lord Pentju will do that. They were friends, after all." Hani stretched and pushed back from the table then leaned over to sip his beer. "What time is it? I'm surprised the girls aren't here by now."

The garden around them was dark, beginning to yield up the perfumes it had absorbed all day from the sun. No moon showed its face. The crickets had launched into their song, and there was a soft rustle of breeze in the bushes as if some small animal were slinking through the vegetation. Hani realized, now that his mind had seized upon it, that he was uneasy about the young women's absence, so everything sounded a bit sinister. He couldn't forget that they were both witnesses to the exchange of babies.

"So, will we be going home tomorrow or investigating Nakht-ef-mut's murder?" Maya finally asked.

Hani said with an understanding smile, "Listen, son, you don't have to stay. I know it's been a long time since you saw your family. But I feel I owe it to Bener-ib to resolve this for her."

He could see Maya struggling, his eyebrows arcing up at the pleasant prospect of going home then down in resolution. "I should stay with you, my lord. I'll write to Sati. She'll understand."

Hani smiled affectionately at his son-in-law, who was always full of courage—and more than a little eager to please Hani.

They finished their meal. The servants took away the dishes and folding table and left the two men sitting comfortably in their expensive low-backed chairs. Hani wished Ptah-mes were there to talk to. He always offered excellent advice. The evening deepened into night, and the night stretched on, the pair speaking little. Hani could feel his eyelids sag. The time for bed had clearly come… and gone. It was fully dark, yet the girls had not arrived home.

Anxiety began to gnaw at Hani's gut. "There's something wrong," he finally said. "Neferet would have sent a message if they were detained at the palace."

"Should we look for them, Lord Hani?" Maya offered, jumping up from his seat.

"We should. Let's retrace that route they always use between here and the royal residence. After Nakht-ef-mut…" Hani dared not finish. His throat was far too tight.

They got torches from the servants and set out through the dark streets. It was like a city of the dead—not a soul around, the quiet broken only by the crickets. Their torches flickered with a nervous orange light against the expressionless walls to either side of them. Here and there, Hani saw illumination from the high windows of a household still awake, dim and distant. Within, families were talking and enjoying one another until they all drifted off to a late bed.

Hani's eyes burned. *Let her be all right…*

He and Maya strode relentlessly on, peeking up alleys, calling from time to time. Once, a head peered over the parapet of its terrace, no doubt awakened by the voices. "Have you seen two young women?" Hani asked in a desperate stage whisper.

"At this hour? Not likely, unless they were prostitutes."

At Hani's side, Maya's face was troubled. "Where could they be, my lord?"

Let's just hope it's not the Mountains of the West, Hani told himself in misery. His duckling, his favorite daughter—he could admit it now—was too full of life to be lying somewhere in the silence of death. He wondered if he should send a letter to Nub-nefer and have her come up to be with him. If something had happened, he wasn't sure he could bear it alone.

They walked all the way to the northern palace, its whitewashed wall phosphorescing in the mute, moonless darkness. *It must be the middle of the night.* Hani wiped his forehead and found that his hand was none too steady. He felt chilled, even in the milky warmth of a spring night.

"Where can they be?" Maya put Hani's fears into words. "Wouldn't we see bloodstains if... if something had befallen them?"

That depends on what *befell them*, Hani thought grimly. "You're probably right. Perhaps we should look down by the River."

"I can't imagine that would do any good in the dark, my lord. Maybe we should head back. Perhaps they've showed up in our absence and will laugh like anything when they see us."

Hani, unable to trust himself to speak, nodded. Fear beat in his veins like the wings of a bird that had found itself caught in a fishnet hung to dry. There was no way out. He would have to accept whatever the gods permitted. But how could he face Nub-nefer?

They trudged back upriver. At some point, Maya broke

the silence. "Why would anybody waylay them? They never carried any silver."

"Because they're two young women without protection, that's why." Hani's imagination refused to go there.

"*Yahya!*" a voice cried from the darkness. Both men whirled toward it.

We're unprotected too, flashed through Hani's thoughts. But he would sell his life dearly if it came to a fight.

No brigand emerged into the ruddy light of their torches but rather a dried-up beggar, toothless and stooped. He didn't seem like much of a threat, unless he was the decoy for others.

"What is it?" Hani asked brusquely, too distraught for his usual courtesy.

"I heared you talkin'. You lookin' for them two girls?" The beggar drew nearer. "I might know sumpin' about 'em." He looked up hopefully and extended a gnarled hand.

He might or he might not know sumpin'. Hani had nothing but a thinly gilded bangle to offer, but the beggar snatched it with a sunken grin and slipped it on his skinny wrist. The effect was bizarre, since he had nothing else on but a loincloth.

"I seen 'em a while back, afore it was dark, walkin' down the street an' talkin' to each other. Then a troop of *medjay* policemen come along, with a baboon and all. They said, 'Which of you's the daughter of—somebody? I don't remember the name. The little bit of a girl said she was, an' then they said, 'You're under arrest for the murder of... that fellow. Nakht-sumpin'."

"Dear gods!" Maya cried in a screechy voice, staring wild-eyed at Hani.

At first, Hani was too dumbfounded to speak. He reached out and clutched the beggar by the arm until the old fellow winced. "What else happened, man?"

"Why, they started to tie up her hands—she was, like, stunned, if you know what I mean. But the other girl—she was a sturdy-lookin' one—flew at 'em, cursin' and hittin' at 'em." The beggar chuckled in spite of himself. "It were quite a show. Took three men to get her down. She was bitin' and kickin' at they's legs and buckin' so's they couldn't hardly get her tied up. They had to carry her over one of they's shoulders. But they got 'em both."

Hani exchanged a look of horror with Maya, and then—more horrible still—he remembered who "the police" undoubtedly meant. Mahu. Hani's hair stood up on the back of his neck. *Mahu has Neferet...*

"Thank you," he remembered to say over his shoulder, already loping off toward the inland complex of government buildings. He was half-winded by the time he saw dimly ahead the three-story tower of the police barracks, profoundly black against the black sky. Maya was almost running at his side, panting loudly, but the little secretary never suggested slowing down. Torch upheld, Hani pounded on the door of the dark building. After a heartbeat or two, he pounded again and then kept it up in a furious hailstorm of blows. Eventually, he could hear the unbarring of the door from within.

A surly head appeared in the opening, and a shirtless policeman, his hair rumpled with sleep, growled, "What do you want at this hour? Come back in the morning after daybreak."

But Hani snarled, "My daughter is in there. I demand to see her."

The officer's mouth curled up skeptically. "No daughters here. Just a couple of she-cats accused of murder."

He made as if to slam the door, but Hani had already inserted his foot. "Those women are the king's physicians, and my daughter is the wife of Ptah-mes—er, Maya—son of Bak-en-ren-ef. You'll regret it if you don't let them go immediately."

The *medjay* looked suddenly uncertain. "You'll have to take that up with Lord Mahu."

"Believe me, I will." The man started to close the door again, but Hani forced his way inside. "I want to see them now. If they've been harmed, you'll answer to the king."

The policeman reluctantly lifted his oil lamp and turned toward the bowels of the police tower. Everyone else seemed to be asleep at that hour. Holding his torch high, Hani crowded the man's steps with Maya on his heels, looking truculent. Their flickering orange flames cast monstrous shadows on the walls as they passed down a dark corridor that Hani had traversed before and came to the door of one of several cells. The *medjay* didn't use imprisonment as a punishment—criminals would be bastinadoed or have their nose or ears cut off—but until a judge assigned their sentence, they might be held there. Hani's heart was hammering. The Hidden One alone knew what indignities Mahu had subjected the young women to. The heavy bolt slid back, and the policeman pushed open the panel. Hani could see the *sunet*s curled up on the floor. As the brightness assaulted them, they awoke and struggled to their feet.

"Stay away from her," Neferet warned in a dangerous voice, planting herself between her friend and the door. Then, in the flickering orange light, her face lit up. "Papa! I knew you'd find us!" She rushed toward him and threw herself into his arms. "Oh, Papa, they're trying to say Bener-ib killed her father, but she didn't. Get us out of here."

Hani saw with pain that his daughter's eye was swollen black and dried blood draped her upper lip. Her shift was dirty and torn from where she'd been thrown to the ground, and blue-black finger marks on her arms revealed that she'd been grabbed and manhandled. Fury grew within him like a sandstorm gathering in the desert. *Mahu will pay for this, the son of a jackal.*

"My duckling, what have they done to you? *You're* not accused of anything, surely." He pressed her to him, his nose burning. Over her shoulder, he called, "Bener-ib, come, my girl. We'll get you out of this."

She crept shyly forward and embraced Neferet on the other side.

"They sprang at us on the street and said Ibet was accused of murder, and they tied her hands. I fought them like anything, but there were four of them and a baboon. They knocked me to the ground and got my feet shackled, although I kicked at them for all I was worth. It was awful, Papa. We were so scared. That Mahu is a ba-a-ad man."

Hani asked as gently as he could manage, although hatred was stoking its fire within him, "It was Mahu in person, then?"

She nodded, and he swore silently that he would see the man fall. Hani turned to the policeman and said loftily, "I'm taking these women under my own recognizance.

They must be returned to Our Sun God immediately—life, prosperity, and health be to her—or you'll all be sorry."

"I don't know, my lord. I need to talk to my superior," the officer said, still bleary-eyed and looking distinctly confused.

But Hani said with an air of menace, "You need to obey your king, whose representative I am."

The man hesitantly stepped back for the foursome to leave, but Hani was certain he would notify Mahu as soon as they'd gone. Whatever Hani did would have to be done quickly. Managing an aspect of outraged rank, Hani hustled the others before him into the street, where he whispered to Maya, "Where's the closest place we can hide them before Mahu sends out a search party? They'll head for Lord Ptahmes's immediately."

"My mother's workshop, my lord?"

Desperate to be out of sight before an angry Mahu emerged, they turned their hasty steps toward the royal warehouses. It was a ragtag group, fleeing with no pretense at dignity—a broad man, a dwarf, and two young women rather the worse for wear. The pallor of dawn had begun to suffuse the eastern sky, and Hani extinguished his torch. It was better that they remain invisible for the brief night that remained to them.

At In-hapy's house, all was in darkness. Except for frogs roaring and popping somewhere from someone's well, it was as quiet as the land of the dead. Hani's stomach was knotted. He could imagine only too clearly what would happen if the police caught them.

Maya hammered on the gate. A long while passed, punctuated only by the pounding of Hani's heart. Then the old Nubian slid open the window in the gate. "Who's there at such an hour?"

"It's me, Maya," the little secretary hissed. "Let us in."

The bar slid back with a clatter, the gate swung open, and Hani and his companions fell inside on a wave of desperate gratitude. Behind the astonished gatekeeper, In-hapy emerged, blinking, from her door, her graying hair all over her shoulders.

"Mother," Maya said in a hushed voice, "we need to hide Neferet and Bener-ib. The police are after them. I don't think Mahu knows you have any connection with Lord Hani."

"But of course, my lord," the little goldsmith said without hesitation. "Come inside, all of you." They followed her into the modest salon, where In-hapy lit a lamp from the dying coals in her brazier. "I have an extra room for when the children stay overnight," she said, leading the way up the narrow staircase.

At the landing, she gestured to a small room to the left, furnished with one bed and a stool. The straw mattress was high and freshly filled, the linen immaculate, and a gauzy mosquito net hung open over it. "Will this do, Lord Hani?" Her lined old face was earnest. "I'll bring them another headrest."

"It will more than do, mistress," Hani assured her. "This is only temporary anyway. I want to see the king immediately and then take the girls to Waset, maybe to the country."

Neferet objected, "But, Papa, I don't want—"

"Enough, Neferet. Bener-ib's life is danger," Hani said roughly.

The girl fell silent, gnawing her lip.

Hani turned to his secretary. "Come on, Maya. Let's get out of here before someone sees us." To the young doctors—but especially to his daughter—he said, "Stay out of sight, whatever you do. You're safe for the moment, but I'm sure Mahu has spies. Don't so much as stick your nose outside the courtyard."

After a quick kiss to Neferet, Hani dodged out the gate with Maya. Day was rising—that pearly hour before shadows could be seen. They strode hurriedly down the narrow lanes, keeping to back streets, Hani praying no *medjay* search party would spot them in the twilight. With immense relief, they regained the safety of Lord Ptah-mes's villa just as the sun sent its rays streaming across the walls and trees, and Hani finally dared to breathe again, though he still felt anxious and harried. The steward appeared in the door to greet them, his eyes growing wide as he looked at the two men.

"Too bad Ptah-mes has taken his boat to Waset already," Hani said, "I hate to risk a ferry. Mahu may be watching the embarcadero."

The steward stood, alert, his hands clasped, no doubt perceiving Hani's tension. "He has another one, my lord. A smaller one—it's not so fast, but it can be boarded from his lordship's private stretch of riverbank."

Thank you, great Hidden One! "This evening, then, my friend. Can you have it ready? We'll send it back from Waset."

The servant bowed and took a few steps toward the door.

"We still have to get the girls here," Hani mused. "The police will be dragging the city."

"Can we disguise them somehow, my lord?" Maya asked.

"Or put them in the litter and close the curtains. But no. It would be like Mahu to search every litter that passed. He's not altogether stupid." *Although close enough.*

Still, he wasn't sure disguises would work. The people of the Two Lands weren't heavily dressed—it wouldn't be easy to make two young women pass for anything else. Hani tried in vain to think of a better alternative, something less perilous, but his thoughts were too agitated. He wiped at his face with a none-too-steady hand.

The steward cleared his throat from behind Hani. "Perhaps my lord could load them in baskets or roll them in carpets and put them on donkey backs, like some merchant's wares..."

Hani looked up, hope's faint embers flickering to life in his heart. "Could some of the servants lead them? I'm afraid Mahu would recognize Maya or me."

With a reassuring nod, the servant faded into the other room and left Hani and Maya staring at one another.

"I can't believe this is happening," Maya said at last with a shake of the head. "There's no way that tiny woman could heave a big rock at someone's head and then have the strength to stab a grown man, even if he was stunned."

"Unless she was angry enough..." Hani had seen some remarkable acts of violence seemingly beyond the strength of the perpetrator.

Maya looked incredulous. "You don't think she did it, do you?"

"We don't know yet," said Hani, letting out a dispirited sigh. "Although one would think she'd have been blood spattered afterward."

"But when? She was with us."

"Ah, but remember—that was one of the evenings she was late. Neferet had been home a long time before she showed up. Maybe she even had time to clean herself off."

Maya fell silent, his eyebrows troubled.

The gods know I don't want her to have done it, but I could only too easily understand if she had. Hani said pensively, "Let's get everyone's things packed and ready to board as soon as the girls are back. We need to get out of here as fast as possible. Maya, take dictation. I want to tell the king what's happened to her doctors. We'll have a servant run it to the palace."

But all at once, he wondered why Mahu had come after the girl at all. Who had suggested Bener-ib as the murderer?

🔲

They arrived in Waset five days later, mentally and physically exhausted. Bener-ib looked like a walking ghost—colorless, dead-eyed. Neferet appeared to have regained some of her perky good cheer, but her father could see that it was a facade she displayed so as not to drag the others down. When she thought no one was looking, her mouth fell, and her little brown eyes stared mournfully off into space. Hani's heart was wrung with pity for the two of them.

Nub-nefer came flying to the door when she heard Hani's voice. "Oh, Hani! You were gone so long, and we never heard a word from you. I was starting to get worried."

She flung herself into his arms, and Hani clung to her,

inhaling her warmth, her fragrance of sweet flowers... her strength. "Neferet and Bener-ib are here too. We've had some bad luck, my dove. We need to find the girls a safe hiding place."

Her eyes widened in horror. "What's happened? They're all right, aren't they?"

As if to reassure her, the two young women entered, lugging their baskets.

"Mama!" Neferet cried and, dropping her baggage, ran to her mother and locked her in a wholehearted squeeze. "You won't believe all the awful things that have happened!"

"Tell me, my dear." Nub-nefer reached out touch her daughter's swollen purple eye then shot Hani an anxious look. "Come into the salon. Are you hungry? Do you want to rest first?"

Maya dragged himself in with a huff of weariness. "Greetings, Lady Nub-nefer. I don't suppose Sat-hut-haru is here?"

His mother-in-law embraced him. "She just left, Maya. She was here with the children all day."

"Then I think I'll go on home, my lord, my lady."

"Come by tomorrow morning," Hani called as his son-in-law left. "We have plans to lay."

Nub-nefer went off to tell the servants to bring beer, and when she returned, Mery-ra came toddling in with her. "Son! Girls! What's this Nub-nefer tells me—you have to hide?"

They all withdrew to the garden pavilion, and Hani sank wearily onto the stool. "Neferet, do you want to tell your grandfather what has happened?" he said, thinking he couldn't face all the disturbing facts again until he'd had some beer.

Neferet, who needed no urging to tell a story, launched into an exuberant explanation complete with gestures and different voices. She told them about how Bener-ib's father had showed up and tried to take her back then how he'd sent the poor girl into hysterics and the sad reason behind it. Then the shocking news of Nakht-ef-mut's murder and how the police had accused Bener-ib.

Mery-ra made a noise of objection. "That girl's no stabber. If you took a notion to kill someone, you'd poison them, wouldn't you, my dear?"

Nub-nefer wrapped a motherly arm around the young doctor's shoulders while Bener-ib sat huddled and whey-faced, as if in shock still. "You poor child. What a traumatic few days."

"That awful Mahu took us to the police barracks, but Papa found us and got us out—"

"Somebody's going to be after Hani's hide," Mery-ra said direly. He shot Hani a knowing look.

"And we hid with In-hapy, then they brought us back to Lord Ptah-mes's house rolled up in carpets on the backs of two donkeys. It was unbeli-i-e-evably exciting."

The servants had set up the beer stands and placed the jars around. Hani sucked up a deep draft. He didn't find the situation exciting—he understood the stakes and was tingling with fear for his daughter and her companion. "We have to keep the girls out of sight until I hear from the king. They're her *sunet*s, after all. I don't think she'll let Mahu get away with this."

Hani's father said, "How is it he's still in office, anyway? His deeply lamented protector, Nefer-khepru-ra, is dead."

Hani smiled dryly. "Easy on the sarcasm, Father. Mahu seems not to have lost a tittle of his power. And you know how he loves our family. I fully expect him to show up here any day. He may be more interested in punishing Neferet, who defied him, than Bener-ib."

"We have to find them a hiding place he would never think of. Not anywhere on our property or Ptah-mes's," Nub-nefer said firmly.

"Any ideas? Your family members are the experts on hiding, my daughter." Mery-ra chuckled, his belly bouncing. Everyone knew about Amen-em-hut.

Neferet, who had been chewing her lip in cogitation, finally said, "What about Khuit? I'll bet she could use some help."

Yahya! Hani thought, hope winking on like the first star of evening. "That's a marvelous plan, my duckling. As soon as it's dark, we'll take you down there. And I have a new serving girl for her too."

⊠

They ate an early dinner, and as the twilight began to swallow the garden into its shadows, Hani and his father and the two young women tiptoed to the gate, where the litter awaited them. The mute serving maid was there as well. The girls climbed in and pulled the curtains, and with Hani leading a donkey loaded with their baggage, they set out to the clopping of hooves through the silent evening.

"We're not exactly furtive," murmured Mery-ra. "We're like a small invading army."

"But no one's likely to be looking for us in Waset yet. Mahu is still probably combing Akhet-aten."

"You managed to get Tuy's servant away from her family?" Mery-ra rolled his eyes toward the unspeaking young woman who followed.

"I found out some things about her, Father. She needs to be hidden too. I'll tell you later." Hani heard a giggle from within the litter and realized Neferet was trying to cheer up Bener-ib.

Over the crunch of their footsteps and the slow, rhythmic thud of the donkey's hooves, the old man said quietly, "I'm not sure Khuit's is the best place to hide anything, son. She seems only too willing to tell the latest gossip. It may be more than she can resist, having three fugitives at her house."

Hani shrugged, but not because he didn't care—the whole affair had him tied in knots of anxiety. Still, he didn't know what better he could do. The neighborhood healer's little abode would be the last place anyone would expect to find two wellborn young women.

They passed Maya's house, and Hani remembered that his secretary was supposed to meet him the next morning. *I'll have a lot to tell him.* The darkness was growing profound around them, and only the lingering phosphorescence of the white walls closing in on either side of the lane made it possible to find their way. They reached Khuit's tumbledown house, and Hani knocked on the door, hoping she hadn't already gone to bed. But a faint orange light through the high windows told him someone was still up.

After a moment, the door bolt slid back, and a small moringa oil lamp flickered into view, illuminating the shrunken face behind it into a suspicious mask. "Who's that?" She peered at them, and a toothless smile lit her countenance. "Why, Lord Hani! What an honor. Come in, come in. You can leave the donkey right there in the courtyard." She stepped back and let the men and the litter bearers pass inside, the servant girl at the rear, while from under a table, a cat with knowing golden eyes observed them. The tiny room, cluttered with dried herbs, mortars, and baskets of bark and berries from floor to ceiling, barely accommodated them all. Then Khuit carefully eased the door closed once more. Surprise was clear on her face, her toothless jaw hanging.

Out of the litter climbed Neferet and Bener-ib, and the bearers retreated. Neferet threw her arms around her former teacher. "Khuit! It's me! This is my friend, Bener-ib. We're going to stay with you for a while."

"Well, now, dearie. Isn't that nice?" The old woman didn't seem to know how to react.

"But no one must suspect we're here."

"I'm aware this is an inconvenience, mistress, and I'll certainly recompense you." Hani extended a pouch that clinked appetizingly. "This young woman will be your servant to keep as well. Let's just say, the girls must be hidden from the danger that hangs over them, and knowing how Neferet loves and respects you, you were the first person to come to mind." Hani smiled his most winsome smile as he sank into professional flattery.

Khuit beamed at Neferet. "You remembered your old Khuit, eh? Now that you're the king's physician, you aren't too good to come back, eh, my love?" She turned to Hani and Mery-ra. "What's the danger?"

Mery-ra shot an uneasy look at his son, but Hani said blandly, "It won't be forever—just a while."

The healer stared at Hani with her sharp black eyes, undeceived. "And this little lady is a *sunet*, too, is she?"

Neferet was quick to answer. "Yes. She studied in Sau and has been here with Lady Djefat-nebty for eight years, like me. She's very advanced and is so-o-o good at diagnosis."

"And this girl is...?"

"That's your new servant," Hani said, drawing the girl forward kindly. "She's mute, but she can hear, and she's uncommonly good at making herself understood." He shot the servant a conspiratorial glance.

Khuit eyed her up and down appraisingly. "You're strong, are you?" The old woman walked around her as one might inspect a horse. Suddenly, she stopped. "Why, I know this child. I midwifed her twenty-four, twenty-five years ago. She's turned out right pretty, which is no surprise."

The servant's eyes widened as Hani tried to steer Khuit back to the topic of protecting the two young doctors' whereabouts. But Khuit wasn't to be deflected. "She was born at the House of Rejoicing, weren't you, dearie? I was the midwife to the king's household when the court was in Waset, you know." She cackled, pleased to have surprised them. "See, I recognize that strawberry mark, Lord Hani. Do you know who this girl is?"

Hani exchanged a look of confusion with his father. "No," he admitted.

"Her mother was a handmaid of Lady Tiyi, wasn't she? And do you know who the father was?" She obviously enjoyed holding them all in suspense.

"No," Hani said dutifully, wishing he could get her back to the matter of Neferet's jeopardy.

"Why, King Neb-ma'at-ra."

A stunned silence fell over the group. Hani could feel the hair on his arms rising. He and Mery-ra locked gazes, confounded to the core. *But that means she was Nefer-khepru-ra's sister after all. The Haru in the nest isn't just half-royal.* "How do you know that, mistress?"

"Oh, Lord Hani. You think there's no gossip in the palace? Everybody knows everything. And it's really no surprise. Her mother was a beauty—like one of Hut-haru's Lovelies—and our old king had an eye for beauty, didn't he?"

The servant looked stupefied. Little by little, tears began to overflow her big eyes, and she buried her face in her hands. A broken noise escaped her. *What a shock this must be for the poor girl.* And it was another source of bitterness. The late king's father had begotten her but hadn't even taken the care to recognize her. She might have grown up as a princess rather than a maidservant.

"Khuit, you must keep this girl hidden too. Any number of people would want her dead if they knew what you've just said." *And you can't be the only person who knows.*

"You can trust me, my lord. Some people thinks I tell everything I know, but that's only because they don't know all the things I *don't* tell." A smile, both proud and sly, split Khuit's wrinkled old face.

"*Iy*," murmured Neferet, as stunned as the rest of them. "Lady Meryet-aten isn't going to be happy about this. Even Khuit will be in danger."

Hani said firmly, turning first to Neferet then to Khuit,

"That's why no one must ever tell anyone, do you all understand? No one. 'Broadcast not your words to others.' People's lives are at stake."

Khuit assured him that their secret was safe with her and that she would put the two *sunet*s to useful work making potions and poultices.

When the men emerged, Mery-ra refused to take the litter, so Hani sent the litter bearers ahead, and he and his father walked elbow to elbow through the darkness of the narrow streets. Beneath a star-sequined sky, crickets were chirping, and now and then, a voice was raised in laughter from inside one of the blind houses that closed in on them. The donkey clopped patiently behind the pair.

Finally, Mery-ra said, "Well, I never expected that. I guess you won't be sharing this tidbit with Lady Meryet-aten."

Hani blew out a deep, agitated breath. "I most assuredly will not. I'm conflicted about my service to her anyway, Father, I have to admit. She says she wants to restore the Hidden One to his rightful place, but I can't help suspecting that what she really wants is to be in a position of power. I'm not sure it would make the slightest difference to her to know that her brother really is her brother and that he's fully royal—more royal than she. She still won't recognize him."

"She has nothing on you, Hani, my boy. Your brother really is your brother too."

Hani laughed, relieved to be out from under his grim burden, if only for an instant. Then he sobered. "Should I spy for Ay in fact? He's likely to put her and Lord Mai to death if he has proof of their sedition, and I don't want that either."

"Do we know that Ay and his daughter genuinely plan to keep the Aten on his heavenly throne?"

Hani had to admit that they did not. "But nothing has changed so far."

"Still, Ankhet-khepru-ra has only just come to the throne." Mery-ra scratched his head. "Why did she take the same name as her predecessor, anyway?"

Although he knew it was invisible in the darkness, Hani shrugged. "Perhaps she thought people might not even notice the change of regime. Nobody but bureaucrats here in the capital ever see the king anyway. No more public festivals up and down the River."

His father gave a grunt of skepticism, and they walked on.

Once A'a had admitted them to the garden, Hani said, "I wonder what time it is. I'd like to tell Ptah-mes what's happened as soon as possible, but I don't want to wake him up."

"It looked like most people were still awake back in the town. And he certainly doesn't strike me as a man who spends a lot of time sleeping."

"All right. Tell Nub-nefer where I've gone. This is urgent." Hani took A'a's torch and headed back out into the street and upriver toward the expensive suburbs where Ptah-mes lived. Alone, the hush of night was even more profound. He heard the wild yelp of a jackal from off in the desert and the quiet lapping of the River while pale shadows flashed overhead on silent wings—a pair of barn owls was hunting. Hani wished he felt more optimistic about Bener-ib's case. *Could she have killed her father after all? She had a motive. She had the opportunity to do it. And I'm not sure she's as weak as she looks—she seemed to hoick that big basket of hers around pretty handily.*

By the time Hani reached Lord Ptah-mes's splendid gate, he was in a somber mood. To the porter, he said, "Is your master awake?"

"Yes, my lord. Shall I announce you?"

"Please."

A moment later, Ptah-mes appeared in the doorway to the salon, as impeccably dressed as if he were sitting in his magistrate's chair in the Hall of Royal Correspondence, despite the hour. All he lacked was the gold of honor around his neck. "Hani. You're back. Are Neferet and her friend still in the capital?"

"No, they're here, my lord—in hiding. Something very bad has happened."

Ptah-mes's eyes widened uneasily. "Come in, Hani. Tell me what's going on."

They seated themselves, and Hani began his recital. He told of how Nakht-ef-mut had been killed in the street. How Mahu had arrested Bener-ib for murder. How Neferet had been incarcerated for putting up a resistance. How Hani had managed to get the pair out of prison. Ptah-mes listened, his face grave, his eyes downcast.

"We just now hid the girls at the house of an old neighborhood healer here in Waset. Neferet had studied with her before."

"You did well, Hani." Ptah-mes's mouth was hard, a muscle ticking in his jaw. "That reprobate Mahu must be brought down."

"There's something else, my lord. You recall that I had discovered that the servant girl who lost her tongue was the mother of the crown prince? I found out that Nefer-khepru-ra was the father."

Ptah-mes looked up sharply.

"And the girl herself is a bastard of Neb-ma'at-ra. The late king's sister."

To Hani's surprise, his friend let out a bark of laughter. "Could it be any more complicated? I wonder if Nefer-khepru-ra knew who his chosen broodmare was."

Hani indulged in a strained smile. "My father always says men pick women who look like them for their attentions."

Ptah-mes gave a snort. Then his manner sobered. "We must protect Neferet and her friend. Now they're targeted by the killer of the witnesses to the crown prince's birth *and* by Mahu."

"I wrote to King Ankhet-khepru-ra to let her know her physicians had been arrested. I can't imagine she'd let that stand. Is Mahu even working for her?"

"Who knows?" Ptah-mes expelled a breath through his nose and fell silent.

Hani bade his friend good evening and hastened home, where Nub-nefer was still waiting up for him.

⊠

The next morning, Maya showed up at Lord Hani's comfortable villa, bright-eyed and ready to work.

"Ah, my friend," Hani greeted him. "Father and I were just talking about our cases. We need to plan our next moves."

Maya followed his father-in-law into the salon, where Lord Mery-ra already sat. He was a big, broad man with formidable shoulders, but at his age, his silhouette was loosening into fat, and his arms were not as thickly muscular as they'd once been. "Maya, my boy. Come join the war council," Mery-ra said genially.

Hani and Maya seated themselves on stools, but Hani said, "Perhaps you'd like to take notes for us, my friend. I find it's getting hard to keep the facts straight. Regarding Lord Nakht-ef-mut, we need to find his killer so we can exonerate Bener-ib."

"*If* we can exonerate her," Mery-ra said with a significant lift of the eyebrows.

Maya's jaw dropped in surprise. "You think she's guilty, my lord?"

"I'd have killed him if he'd treated me that way."

Maya had to think about this—he wasn't convinced. He looked up from his page. "Anything else about the murder?"

"Not yet. We need to do some investigation. See what our victim was doing down in the warehouse district. Try to find out who he might have seen besides Pentju. Regarding the mysterious yellow paint on the king's toilet articles, somebody has to tell us what that stuff is and why it might be there. Then maybe we'll get a sense of who might have put it there. I have a funny feeling it's some kind of poison."

"Our young friend Khawy is a former paint boy. He should recognize it, whatever it is." Mery-ra leaned forward, forearms on his thighs.

"Right—Neferet said the same thing. Father, why don't

you and Maya look into that while I do a little sniffing around Nakht-ef-mut?"

"Are you going back to Akhet-aten, Lord Hani?" asked Maya in surprise. "Won't Mahu be looking for you?"

"I'll wait until I hear from the king. If she's willing to protect the girls, then let Mahu try to do his worst to me. His hands will be tied."

Maya gazed up at his father-in-law in worshipful admiration. *What a man! Nothing fazes him!*

Mery-ra got to his feet and rubbed his big hands together. "Well, let's get going before it's too hot. Off to the Place of Truth, Maya, my friend."

"Take the litter," Hani said, suspecting his father would protest. "I expect a reply from Ankhet-khepru-ra from day to day. Maya, whenever you find I've gone, feel free to join me in the capital."

"Right, Lord Hani," Maya said with something nearing a salute. *Another adventure!* His heart swelled with pride when Hani set him independently on an investigation like this.

Mery-ra called up the litter, and he and Maya climbed in. The Place of Truth—the workmen's village attached to the royal tombs on the west bank—was both distant and a difficult trip, and Maya was relieved that they were making it by litter. If Lord Mery-ra were to fall on the loose rocks and steep paths, Maya certainly couldn't pick him up.

At the quay, they hailed a ferry and headed to the opposite bank of the River, litter and bearers and all. Despite the sun, it was cooler on the water, but once they stepped onto the land, the heat hit them like a merciless load of bricks. Up the steep scree, they jounced and bounced, the only sound in this land of the silent dead the grunts and scuffling of their litter bearers. A few times, Maya's stomach lunged for his mouth as one of the lads seemed, for a moment, to go down on a knee. He watched the great red cliffs, the Mountains of the West, that rose to his right, fissured and inhospitable. Out there somewhere was the ravine where kings were buried—until Nefer-khepru-ra.

Eventually, the secretary perceived a leveling off of their path, and ahead of them, in a kind of cup in the plateau, lay the blinding whitewashed wall of the Place of Truth. "Do you know where Khawy lives, my lord?"

"I do. He has a nice place, as befits the chief draftsman's assistant." Mery-ra smiled smugly—through his instruction, the boy had learned to read and write and so opened to himself this choice position. "It's the end-of-week holiday, so he's likely to be home."

They left the litter bearers to wait inside the village gate, where a beer house beckoned. Maya and Lord Mery-ra made their way on foot down the lane of finer houses in which the upper echelon of workmen lived: overseers, foremen, and the literate—scribes and draftsmen. They stopped before a freshly painted gate in a wall crested with palms.

Nice. A garden. Our boy's doing all right for himself.

At their knock, a thin, pretty young woman with a baby in a sling on her back and a scarf on her head opened the gate. She brightened. "Lord Mery-ra! Please come in."

The two men entered, leaving their litter bearers in the street. The garden was small but well tended and attractive. Despite being government issued, the limewashed house set in the midst looked prosperous.

"I guess you want to talk to Khawy, my lord. He's in the salon." The woman, smiling, led them through the front door, which was open except for the rolled-up reed mat.

It was dim inside, the morning sun hitting the high windows only obliquely, and the young draftsman was sitting cross-legged on the floor in the single beam of light. He had a colorful scroll across his knees and, from the array of pots and brushes laid around him, appeared to be engaged in painting something. He looked up, and delight bloomed across his face.

Khawy sprang to his feet and came forward, arms outstretched. "Lord Mery-ra! What a wonderful surprise! I was just working on your *Book of Going Forth by Day*." The two men embraced, then Khawy clapped Maya fraternally on the shoulder. "Lord Maya, my friend."

Lord Maya. Maya liked the sound of that.

"My boy, Hani and Maya and I are investigating a crime. We thought you might be able to help us." Mery-ra held out the diminutive basket that had been taken from the king's household. "There are traces of something yellow between the reeds. It looked like paint to us. Can you figure out what it is?"

Khawy took the container to the light and stared at it, turning it this way and that. Finally, he reached inside, scratched with a nail, and brought forth a few grains of the residue. "It looks like orpiment to me, my lord. See?" He stooped and picked up one of his little pots of paint. "It's the only thing with that beautiful yellow color. Yellow ocher can't touch it for clarity and brilliance."

Maya peeked at the contents of the pot. It was indeed

a sunny shade of yellow, just like the residue in the basket. "Orpiment, you say? Is it from some flower?"

"No. It's a yellow crystal found in the rocks sometimes. You grind it up, and it looks like this. It can be a little orangey, but this is the best color. Then you add gum or rabbit-skin glue and water, and you have a paint. It's much better than vegetal pigments, which are best used on papyrus. Sometimes they don't last well on a wall, but this does."

"Interesting," murmured Maya, although in fact, Khawy's explanation only raised more questions.

"We thank you, son." Mery-ra beamed at Khawy, catching Maya's eye. "Don't let me keep you away from my *Book*."

Khawy assured him that the book was almost finished, and the two men withdrew. They mounted the litter in silence, and neither was quick to speak as they set off across the rough path back to the River.

Finally, Maya said, perplexed, "Why would anybody put paint on the king's things? And not even enough to beautify them. In fact, you'd never see it unless you examined them as carefully as we did."

"I'm sure I don't know, my boy. Let's hope Hani will have some insights."

He will, thought Maya confidently. *He'll know what this is about.*

CHAPTER 8

B UT HANI DIDN'T HAVE ANY more ideas than Mery-ra or Maya had. "Something will come along that will illuminate this, I'm sure," he said, forcing himself to be optimistic.

The whole affair was so irregular in every detail that it left him confused. He was chafing to get back to Akhet-aten and sniff around Nakht-ef-mut's last activities. After seven days, he finally received a reply from the king, delivered by the hand of a royal messenger. Ankhet-khepru-ra was outraged by the arrest of her two physicians and demanded they be brought back.

"I hope she tells Mahu the same thing. Did you explain to her why they were in hiding, my lord?" Maya said after Hani had read the contents of the letter aloud.

"Yes. It sounds like she discounts the accusation of murder, but I can't be sure. Which makes me a little leery about turning the girls over to the palace again. If Mahu convinces her that Bener-ib really is guilty, she may yet throw them overboard."

Maya said, with a brow wrinkled in concern, "Do you have any choice? If the king wants them back…"

Hani gave a bark of laughter, but his thoughts were heavy. "No, I have no choice. I guess we'll have to take them from their refuge."

Nub-nefer bit her lip. "Oh, Hani, do you think it's safe? Once they're out in the open, Mahu can do anything."

As if the mention of the chief of police had conjured up his henchmen, A'a appeared in the outer doorway with a worried and apologetic look on his face. "My lord, there are some *medjay* here to speak to you."

A pang of fear shivered along Hani's neck. Nub-nefer clutched at him and cried, "Oh no! Don't let that terrible man get the girls, my love."

Hani laid a calming hand on her arm and said in what he hoped was a serene voice, "Show them in, A'a."

A clatter of heavy footsteps in the vestibule proclaimed the entry of the policemen, Mahu at the head of his troop. He was a heavyset, hard-faced man, violence always simmering just below his well-dressed surface. Under their mantle of flesh, his black eyes were as mean as hornets.

"Well, Hani," he said with a smirk. "We meet again. You just can't stay out of trouble, can you?"

"I don't have Amen-em-hut," Hani said coldly.

"Oh, it's not him I'm looking for this time. I'm looking for the little murderer you're harboring and her attack bitch, your daughter."

"They live in Akhet-aten now, Mahu." Hani refused to dignify this man with his honorific title. "They're the king's trusted physicians. You'll have to ask her about their whereabouts."

"Oh, I'm sure." Mahu curled his lip in a skeptical sneer.

"If you doubt me, here is a message from Our Sun God Ankhet-khepru-ra—life, prosperity, and health to her." Hani pulled the letter from his waistband and flashed it at Mahu, then he read, "We desire that our physicians be present to us. See to it that they arrive as soon as possible." He dared Mahu to object.

The policeman looked uncertain for a moment then snorted with a fresh flush of bravado. "So, you *are* hiding them."

"From those who would hinder their prompt return to their sovereign."

"Maybe we should search for them, eh." Mahu's malevolent eyes narrowed.

Hani remembered with horror the search Mahu had made of Lord Ptah-mes's house, killing his cattle and draining his granaries, ravaging even his smallest possessions out of sheer spite. Ptah-mes was rich enough to absorb the loss, but it would ruin Hani. *And then there's Baket-iset.*

He let anger neutralize his fear and said coolly, "I'm answerable to the king. How about you?"

Mahu's face grew apoplectically crimson. He cast a hate-filled glance at Nub-nefer, who stood arm in arm with her husband as if to make a living barrier against the *medjays'* intrusion. Hani could almost see the fury rising from his wife like heat from the desert sand. She wasn't meek, but if either of them gave way to the desire to yell at their tormentor, his men would be on them in a minute. Hani and Mahu stood almost nose to nose, quivering.

Hani added disdainfully, "If you think I would be so stupid as to hide anyone in my house, you're judging me by your own standards, Mahu. Who is your protector these days, anyway, since we know the will of the king?"

Mahu seemed to swell with impotent rage. No doubt he realized Hani had the upper hand. Even the chief of the royal police wouldn't dare to go against a written order from the Lady of the Two Lands.

He spun on his heel and marched heavily to the door, his men behind him in a block. In the vestibule, he turned and snarled, "I don't let murderers get away unpunished, Hani. We'll find them." He slammed the door behind him, and the forces of order stumped audibly down the gravel path and away.

Hani dared to breathe for the first time in a long while. He turned to Nub-nefer, whose golden face was fierce with contempt.

"That man is an abomination. I'll kill him before I let him touch the girls again," she growled between her teeth.

"I'm just wondering how to get them back to the capital safely. Mahu may have men waiting at the embarcadero. I'm not so sure he'll be restrained, even by a royal order. This is his chance to pay us back for all the humiliations he thinks he's suffered at my hands." Little by little, Hani's hackles were subsiding, but he was stiff with anxiety still.

"Lord Ptah-mes's yacht? It can outrun any police boat."

Hani stroked his chin. "That's not a bad idea. Although Ptah-mes's is probably the next place Mahu'll go look." He pinched the bridge of his nose between his thumb and forefinger. *Blessed Hidden One, guide me here.* "I feel I need to go get them ready now, but I'm afraid the police will be watching the house and follow me."

"Who could we send? Maybe Bin-addi?" Nub-nefer

suggested. Hani had freed the young slave from Djahy and now employed him to take care of the animals.

"Maybe. The rug trick worked pretty well to transport the girls. But I'll have to alert Lord Ptah-mes first so the boat can be at the ready. Don't visit your brother until this dies down."

After night had fallen, Hani wrapped himself in a dark woolen cloak from Kharu and set out by back streets for Ptah-mes's villa. He was suffocatingly hot in the heavy garment, but it would make him less visible than his white linen. He took no torch, navigating by the pale light of the young moon, which peeped over the roofs of the houses that closed in around him. He feared to trip over some sleeping beggar or steaming pile of donkey droppings. Still, he arrived at Ptah-mes's gate without incident and knocked furtively.

Hearing the approach of steps on the inside, Hani hissed, "Open, my man. It's Hani."

The little window in the door cracked a bit then shut. To his amazement, Lord Ptah-mes himself pushed back the panels. "Come in, my friend," he urged in an equally quiet voice then bolted the gate behind his visitor. "I was walking in the garden when I heard your knock. The gatekeeper is off duty. What brings you here so late?"

"Something urgent, my lord. Mahu came to my house this afternoon, looking for Neferet and Bener-ib. We have to get the girls back to the palace immediately and in secret. The king seems willing to protect them, but I'm afraid that if Mahu finds them first, before they're under Ankhet-khepru-ra's mantle, he'll arrest them and maybe even put Bener-ib to death."

A frown pleated Ptah-mes's brow, and his mouth grew hard. "He came by here too—as you may imagine."

"I thought that perhaps if we smuggled them onto your yacht, we could get them back to the capital and to the king before Mahu could do anything. I had a royal summons, and that seemed to stop him for the moment."

"I wonder how official he is these days. Did the new king even renew his mandate?"

Hani shrugged. *I would give a lot to know the answer to that.*

Ptah-mes seemed lost in thought, then he said, "By all means, put them on the boat. I'll deliver them myself. Even if Mahu leaves today, he won't catch up with us."

"May I accompany you, my lord? I urgently need to talk to the king about this. And then there's my investigation into the real murderer. That's the only thing that will clear Bener-ib for good."

"But of course, Hani. We share responsibility for your daughter, after all," Ptah-mes said with a wry smile.

⊠

Hani took a long, circuitous route to Khuit's house, stopping at Maya's on the way to tell him what was afoot. The old healer met him at the gate. To her surprised face, he whispered, "We have to move the girls out immediately, Khuit."

She hobbled ahead of him into the house.

Neferet appeared in the doorway to the kitchen, rubbing her eyes. "Papa?"

"The two of you, get ready. We're going to get you on

Ptah-mes's boat and back to the capital and into the king's protection immediately."

A moment later, Neferet and Bener-ib appeared, each carrying a large chest-like basket full of their medical supplies. Donkeys were so slow that Hani had decided to rush the girls back to the grandee's villa on their own feet, swaddled, like him, in dark cloaks of Djahy. They would stick to the bitumen-black back lanes and carry no torches. At the first sound of approaching footsteps, they were to separate and crouch down against the wall or in a doorway, making themselves invisible. Maya had already left on his own.

His heart pounding, Hani led the young women out into the street and turned south. "Hold hands," he whispered, "so we can stay together." He had faced danger many times, but at this moment, it was his daughter, his little duckling, in peril, and his every sense was sharpened by fear. Silently, they crept upriver in their bare feet, the handles of their baskets over their shoulders. The moon had barely risen, and they were oriented only by the faint starshine between the upper floors of houses close around them. The road unrolled endlessly as if it were *iteru*s long.

They'd been en route for what seemed like days, the houses around them growing less packed as they made their way into a more affluent area, when a tramp of footsteps made Hani freeze in his tracks. He held out a hand to stop the girls. *Yes, someone's approaching.*

"Go!" he hissed, and the two young women dodged into a doorway like beggars, their faces obscured in the somber wool of their cloaks.

Hani stretched out on his stomach and hoped he

would look like a drunk should he be discovered. His heart was hammering. He could all but feel the ghost of cold bronze skewering him from behind. Fortunately, the person proceeding up the lane didn't seem to be interested in them but kept the beam of his clay lantern straight before him. Peeking out from under his arm, Hani caught sight of the little man ambling down the road. He had to be the neighborhood watchman. He passed right by them with a yawn, never seeing the blacker patches in the darkness outside the range of his light.

As soon as the man's steps had disappeared, echoing, into the silence, Hani called the girls quietly, and once they'd scrambled to their feet, they all took hold of one another's hands again. They had entered the broader streets nearing the River, where widely spaced villas stood, and the fugitives' shadows danced before them by the light of the newly risen crescent moon. Tiptoeing silently across the open area toward Ptah-mes's gate, Hani experienced a sudden chill of fear. *What if Mahu is watching the house?* But no one stopped them.

At the gate, Hani knocked in the prearranged code, and the porter swung one panel open and shut it carefully after the three of them had entered. "Lord Ptah-mes is on board, my lord. Down at his private quay," he whispered. The porter lent Hani his torch, since no one would see them within Ptah-mes's walled property, and the fugitives scurried across the garden and through the orchard and barnyard to the small gate leading to the River.

The beautiful black-and-green yacht lay rocking at the water's edge, its gangplank extended, its torches lit. How sleek and dangerous its silhouette looked by moonlight, with the water sparkling beneath it in a landscape otherwise like kohl. Across the River lay the City of the Dead; no lights broke the darkness of the west bank. A hunting nightjar gave its buzzing cry, and the clapping of the water against the boat's hull was the only other sound. As they neared safety, Hani grew tenser and tenser, his heart in his mouth. He shepherded the girls up the plank and followed, once again imagining an arrow between his shoulder blades. But they boarded with no incident. Ptah-mes was waiting for them and helped each of them step down to the deck without a word.

"Into the cabin, ladies," Hani hissed, and the two *sunet*s obediently made their way out of sight. Hani and Ptah-mes stood looking at each other grimly, the grandee's eyes glittering in the torchlight like the inlaid eyes of a statue. Then he came to life and gestured to the waiting captain to set sail.

Once the sailors had cast off the painter, the boat edged diagonally into the stream, its low-set torches reflected in the water like shooting stars. Hani felt the stream catch the hull, and he heard the hushed splash and drip of paddles in rhythm as the crew began to row ahead of the current. A great weight lifted from his chest, and he drew a deep breath of relief. There weren't any other boats on the River after dark, and even if some *medjay* should see and recognize them, there was no way they'd dare to come after them by night.

"So far, so good," said Ptah-mes quietly. "The hard part is going to be getting them from the boat to the palace."

"Doesn't the king have a private quay?"

"Yes, but I don't know if we can get clearance to dock

there. You may have to flash your royal command at someone."

Hani nodded somberly. "I probably shouldn't be seen with the girls. Mahu knows I'm protecting them. He'll be looking for a party of three."

"If we can disembark at the king's landing, they'll be able to run inside without fear. You and I can go ashore later."

Since the young women occupied one of the rooms in the cabin and Ptah-mes the other, the servants prepared for Hani a comfortable pallet in the shelter of the curtained kiosk at the stern. Hani wanted to sleep—he knew he'd need all his wits about him once they reached the capital—but slumber eluded him. He lay awake, staring at the tented ceiling of the kiosk and listening to the quiet splash of paddles and the creaking of the boat as it shot downstream. Off along the bank, a hippopotamus roared. Little by little, his anxieties grew blurry and faded, and sometime in the early morning, he fell asleep.

⊠

Maya inquired at Hani's house the next morning, only to find that his father-in-law had departed secretly the previous night to deliver the girls to the king's custody. Having asked Lady Nub-nefer to transmit word of his departure to Sat-hut-haru, Maya took off for the quay, and five days later, he set foot in Akhet-aten as well.

Twelve years had mellowed the starkness of Nefer-khepru-ra's capital a bit but not enough for Maya's taste, formed as it was by the millennial city of Waset. Akhet-aten, an outpost perched in the barren desert with a backdrop of hostile ocher cliffs, still had a raw, unfinished air about it. The trees had grown up over the course of time, but they had the exhausted look of something that had to try too hard to prosper under the worst conditions.

Not knowing where he should seek Lord Hani, Maya headed for Ptah-mes's house. There he found both Ptah-mes and Hani. In the elegant salon, Maya greeted them eagerly. "How did it go, my lords? Did the girls make it to the palace? Is the king willing to protect them?"

Hani looked tired, but he grinned. "They did indeed, Maya. She was miffed that her son's new physician had been killed, but she doesn't think Bener-ib did it. So, for the time being, I suspect Neferet and her friend are safe." He caught Ptah-mes's eye. "I guess the next task is to investigate the last days of Nakht-ef-mut. Whoever he saw shortly before he died may be able to shed some light."

"And maybe they would know why he was wandering around in the warehouse district when he was killed."

"Be careful prowling around town, asking questions, my friend. Mahu may still be looking for you here." Ptah-mes shot Hani a pointed look.

"We will, my lord."

After reassuring his host, Hani took his leave, and Maya followed him out into the street. "Where do we start?" Maya shaded his eyes with a hand and stared around.

"I suppose Lord Pentju may have some insights into our victim's destination if anyone does. Let's pay him a little visit."

At the impressive entrance to the royal physician's villa, they knocked and were greeted by the gatekeeper. He set off to notify his master of their arrival, and a moment later, Lady Djefat-nebty appeared on the garden path, her steps crunching brusquely in the gravel. "Lord Hani. My husband is not here. Can I assist you in some way?" Her long face was as severe as always between the lappets of a heavy wig, but the corner of her mouth twitched in wry humor.

"I hope so, my lady," said Hani with a polite bow. "I don't know if you've heard, but the police have accused Nakht-ef-mut's daughter of murdering him."

The physician's eyes widened, and her expression hardened. "Let's go inside, where it's more private."

She led the two men into her elegant salon. A palette for grinding was propped against the foot of the dais, and several pots of color stood around. Maya would have thought the former decorations had been more than splendid enough, especially since the couple seemed on the verge of leaving the city. Perhaps they had been damaged.

After they'd all been seated, Djefat-nebty said with heat, "Bener-ib, did you say? That's ridiculous. She can hardly kill a mosquito."

"I've had to hide the girls for several days from the chief of police, who had them in jail. Now Neferet and Bener-ib are under the protection of the king."

"She appreciates them both. No one will try anything against them there."

"Thanks be to all the gods. But the surest way to keep Bener-ib safe is to find the real killer."

"No doubt," said Djefta-nebty, crossing her arms. She looked thoughtful.

Hani said, watching the *sunet* closely, "One thing I want to check out is why Nakht-ef-mut might have been in the working-class area south of the palace that night. Whom he might have seen."

"Perhaps I can answer the first part of that question. My husband and he had a long talk the day after his interview with his daughter. It seemed, I may say, serious if not agitated—but the two of them were friends, so I let them argue each other out. Eventually, as evening fell, Nakht-ef-mut set out for the palace. He was a stranger here. Perhaps he got lost looking for the entrance."

Hani nodded, his forehead wrinkled in thought.

He certainly took an odd route to the palace, Maya thought.

"Was there no one he might have been going to see on his way?"

Djefat-nebty lifted an eyebrow. "The only person we know in that neighborhood is a paint merchant." She gestured at the salon in chaos behind her, her mouth twitching in a dry smile. "Suddenly, we know all about paint."

Hani stared into space, his brow furrowed. "Thank you, my lady. At least this gives us something to think about."

He bowed and turned to go, but the *sunet* called after him, "I'll go see the girls next time I'm at the palace. We all wondered where they were."

The two men departed and stood outside the gate in thoughtful silence. At last, Maya said, "Paint again. Do you think he was after some of that orpiment substance?"

"But why?" said Hani. "He wasn't involved with the king's household. He just arrived from Sau. The one I wonder about is Djefat-nebty."

They walked wordlessly in the direction of Lord Ptah-mes's house, then Hani stopped in his tracks. "While we're here, let's look around in the warehouse district. Maybe In-hapy would know about a paint grinder's shop in her neighborhood."

Maya shrugged. "I can't imagine she's using paint for anything, but it's worth a try."

They set off with quick footsteps downriver until they were surrounded by the long, vaulted magazines and storehouses where the palace's supplies were stocked. Just before entering the first row of magazines, they turned left toward the River, and ere long, they were at In-hapy's goldsmith workshop.

Maya's mother slipped off her stool and came to them as soon as the old Nubian gatekeeper admitted them. "Lord Hani! Maya, my son! Can I help you?"

"I hope so, mistress," said Hani in a bland, pleasant voice. "Do you happen to know of any paint merchants around here?"

She fingered her chin thoughtfully. "To be honest, my lord, I've never even heard of a paint merchant. I thought artists ground and mixed their own."

"But they must have to buy the pigments somewhere," Maya insisted. "Where do you get things like bitumen or glue?"

"Well, you're certainly right, son—we buy them from a supplier. But paint pigment? I haven't heard of any such thing around here. Maybe some of the neighbors would know."

"Where did you get paint when you had this workshop and house built, Mother?" Maya was beginning to grow frustrated. *Are we on a meaningful trail or not?*

"The artists got the dry pigments and mixed their own. I'm sorry, Lord Hani. I don't think I can help you."

They took their leave, Hani pensive, Maya steaming. *Has there ever been a case with so few clues?* "We should have asked Khawy where he bought his pigments."

"They wouldn't be from the same supplier, surely. The Place of Truth is several hundred *iteru*s from here."

Maya snorted in disgust. "So, what do we do now?"

"Well, we don't even know that Nakht-ef-mut was coming to see the paint merchant. Djefat-nebty just said she didn't know any other businesses here—assuming she was telling the truth. What if, as she speculated, Nakht-ef-mut got lost on his way to introducing himself to the king? He didn't know the city." Hani gnawed his lip.

"At that hour?" Maya asked incredulously. "None of this makes any sense anyway. He was a physician, not a painter."

They stared at one another in discouragement. "Let's pay a visit to the palace. Maybe your friend Sheshi would tell us something." A sly smile curled the ends of Lord Hani's wide mouth.

Maya gave a *hmph*. "He's no friend of mine."

⊠

They strode on to the processional way that cleft the city north to south. A few scattered pedestrians speckled the broad, dusty road, and at one point, a chariot thundered past, the horses slinging foam at the two men.

"There's someone late for work," said Hani with a grin. But he wasn't all that cheerful, really. This was the most sterile investigation he could remember—and the stakes were higher. *I don't even know what to look for.* "Maya, do we know whether Nakht-ef-mut was coming from or going to the palace?"

Maya said, exasperated, "How was Lady Djefat-nebty so sure he was even heading for the palace?"

True. Hani heaved a sigh. "I think we need to figure out both of those things. Let's pay a visit to the Great House and see if we can get an audience with the king or someone close to her."

Morning was getting along, a golden day with a sky nearly white overhead. It would be hot later. The two men strode along to the center-city royal residence. After the endless crossing of courts and corridors, Hani was told to wait while the majordomo who had accompanied them went to notify the king. As he sat on the polished gypsum floor, observing the shadow of his outstretched hand on the wall—fingers shaped into a goose's head—he saw a small party of young women floating down the hall toward him. In the lead was Lady Meryet-aten, the Great Royal Wife, in a sheer, voluminous caftan and the red sash of queenship. Her ladies-in-waiting and handmaids followed her like a trail of goslings, armed with tall ostrich-plume flabella and pipes of steaming incense. One led a slim hound on a leash, as elegant as its mistress.

Hani scrambled to his feet and folded in a court bow, hand to his lips.

"Is that you, Hani?" The queen approached him in her golden sandals and said under her breath, "Are you here to see me?"

"No, my lady. I need to speak to the Lady of the Two Lands about Neferet and Bener-ib."

"I've heard they're in trouble. My mother is sheltering them for the moment."

"Lady Bener-ib is accused of murdering her father."

The queen's lovely face grew suddenly pale. "Oh?" she said in a pinched voice. She made a brief gesture as if she intended to say more but stopped herself. "Be ready, Hani." She continued her perfumed progress down the corridor.

Almost before the queen and her ladies had passed from sight, the majordomo returned. "The God's Father Lord Ay will see you, my lord."

The back of Hani's neck crawled. This was not who he wanted to see—ever. But if Ay could help him convince the king of Neferet and Bener-ib's innocence, then Hani wouldn't scorn his help.

He trailed the servant to a pair of more modest doors than the tall gilded ones to which Hani had become accustomed and was admitted to a chamber that appeared part of a residential suite. High windows with ornamental stone grilles let in a soft, vaporous sunlight. Lord Ay, the king's father, was waiting, seated in a throne-like chair, his legs crossed, his air informal. *He must be at least sixty,* Hani thought, but the old cavalryman was still lean and good-looking, with his square jaw and wide, mobile mouth.

He lifted a hand in friendly greeting. "Hani. It's been a while. Have you learned anything about my granddaughter's plan?"

"No, my lord," Hani said with a bow. "I haven't encountered the queen since our last meeting, except for passing her in the hall just now."

Ay nodded pleasantly. "So, what is it that brings you to see my daughter the king?"

"I'm here about her two young physicians. Perhaps you know what's happened in their regard…"

Ay nodded.

"We deeply appreciate the king's protection, but Mahu, the chief of police, may well try to convince her of Bener-ib's guilt. I believe the only way to assure the girl's safety is to find the real murderer of her father."

"And of course, you're concerned for your own daughter. I would be too."

Remembering what Har-em-heb had said about the old fox's treatment of his youngest child, Har-em-heb's wife, Hani wondered about the sincerity of Ay's words.

"Our Sun God is indisposed, but she told me to speak to you. What can I do for you, my friend?"

"Do you know if Nakht-ef-mut, Bener-ib's father, was at the palace the night of his murder?"

"Not in person, but he sent a message. I daresay he was on his way to follow up on that when he was cut down." Ay tilted his head and considered Hani shrewdly with his reddish-brown eyes.

Dear gods, I can't just ask the man what was in that message, Hani thought. He had a hunch that it was something related to the priest's murder. It might, in fact, be his best clue.

As if he'd read Hani's mind, Ay said smoothly, "But you're an investigator. Perhaps you're the very one I should tell." He flashed Hani his charming smile. From the breast of his caftan, he drew a folded sheet of papyrus and handed it over.

Hani read silently, *I speak as the crown prince's new physician. Someone is poisoning the king and her ladies. Be wary. One who appears to be is not her friend.* He stared up at Lord Ay, his mouth agape.

Ay said in a hard voice, "Find him."

⊠

Hani came out of his audience, shaken. *So, my hunch after interviewing the handmaids was correct. Did someone deliberately throw the cat into the well in an effort to sicken the king's household?*

He rejoined Maya in the courtyard and set off without a word, his secretary pattering alongside, his face all curiosity. They'd passed outside into the street when Hani turned to Maya and said under his breath, "Nakht-ef-mut had just warned the king that someone was poisoning her and her ladies. And then he himself was killed."

Maya sucked in a gasp of shock. "But how did he know? He had barely arrived from Sau."

"That's for us to find out. But it certainly explains his own murder—the poisoner was trying to shut him up. Perhaps whoever that was didn't know that our *sunu* had sent a message ahead of him, telling the king at least the bare outline of the plot. I wonder what he would have said had he been able to reach her in person. Did he know who the culprit was?"

Maya gave a whistle. "'Was poisoning' sounds like something that happened over a long period. How long was that cat in the well and nobody noticed?"

"From Neferet's description, it sounds as if it had been in there a while."

Hani knew little more about the mechanisms of that crime than he had before he visited Ay. What he *had* learned was that Bener-ib wasn't the only person with a motive for killing her father. He heaved a sigh. "We also need to find out something about the mysterious thefts." The two men continued southward down the processional street until Hani stopped suddenly in his tracks. "Can you even do that?"

"What's that, my lord? Investigate the thefts?"

"No. Poison someone a little at a time with polluted water. Wouldn't they get sick and die with the first swallow?" Hani's thoughts were floundering. Nothing made any sense.

"We could ask Djefat-nebty."

"I've bothered her a lot lately. Maybe Neferet would know. She was telling me all about henbane—the girls must have gotten solid training in poisons." The thought struck him with a sickening thud: *What if Bener-ib was the one who'd contaminated the well? But why would that cross your mind, my boy? Is it because Father said something about her being a poisoner rather than a stabber? Yet what could her reason possibly be?* "We're heading back to the Great House. I want to talk to Neferet."

The men made an about-face and set off at a good clip back toward the palace. Hani wished he could rinse that unwelcome suspicion from his mind. It would break Neferet's heart if her friend really was a murderer after all. And if Nakht-ef-mut had discovered her attempt on the king, his daughter might well have wanted to stop him at any cost. Another motive.

This time, Hani could honestly state to the majordomo of the royal residence that he'd come as the king's investigator. He requested to see Neferet, and before too long had passed, the servant returned with the young *sunet* in tow.

"Papa! You're back so soon? Is something wrong?" Her brown eyes were anxious.

"No, my duckling, I don't think so. But I need to ask your professional opinion about something. Would it be possible to poison someone a little at a time?"

"Oh, good!" she cried, a mischievous smile baring the gap between her teeth. "If you're going to poison that Mahu, I'll help you!"

Hani had to laugh. "No, my dear. Much as I'd like to." His voice dropped. "We just learned that someone has been poisoning the king and her ladies for a while."

"Bener-ib would probably know more about that than I would. Let me call her—"

But Hani held her back. "I'd, uh, rather she didn't know we're investigating this. Do you think the dead cat in the well could have sickened people over a period of time?"

Neferet looked at him quizzically but only said, "I think it could do that. But somebody would surely notice before long, and they'd take the carcass out. You'd have to keep replacing it."

Hani pondered this. It didn't help him much. "Thank you, little duck. You'll keep this to yourself, I hope."

"May Sekhmet shrivel my toes and make my teeth fall out if I breathe a word, Papa. May—"

"And not to Bener-ib either."

Neferet's lip crept out stubbornly, but then she said with reluctance, "All right. But I don't see why."

Hani enfolded her in his arms and kissed the top of her shaven head. "Be careful, little girl. Don't drink anything in the king's apartments, eh. You're in danger from two directions."

"Don't worry, Papa." She returned the hug with a squeeze and bounced back off into the interior of the palace.

"I hope she'll keep her mouth shut," muttered Maya.

Mut, the mother of us all, watch over us—so do I.

CHAPTER 9

"Well," Maya said with a huff. "What do we do now?"

Lord Hani smiled. "We stop and think. I believe lunch at the nearest beer house would help that endeavor."

They made their way to the neighborhood beer house, which Hani had last visited when interviewing a witness in one of his other cases. At the noon hour, it was packed with people, mostly workmen taking advantage of their lunchtime to socialize and rest their weary bones. The atmosphere was heavy with sweat and smoke and fried onions and the yeasty smell of beer. They found a low table with a couple of free stools and settled themselves comfortably. Before long, the potbellied servant had brought them a jar of herbed beer and a plate of toasted melon seeds. With a big fresh loaf of bread, it was a feast to match any that Lord Ptah-mes's cook could confect. Hani's mouth was watering by the time the plates were set in front of them.

They ate in hungry silence. Then, once they had pushed

back their stools, Maya said in an undertone, "Who do you reckon is trying to poison you-know-who, my lord?"

The talk and laughter in the big room, echoing against its low ceiling and smoky rafters, made it difficult to hear— but that was good, Hani decided. "Someone Nakht-ef-mut knew about."

"So, we're back to trying to figure out who he saw the night he died. Apparently, he never got to the palace." Maya stuck out his lip pensively. "Do we try to find that elusive paint merchant?"

He'd said it only half seriously, but Hani sighed and shrugged. "That's all we can do. Maybe he at least saw our man pass by."

"Would he have been in his shop so late, though?" Maya frowned and stared at the table in thought.

"Only one way to find out." Hani threw a few copper bangles on the table and stood up with a satisfying stretch of the arms. He saw their server making his way eagerly among the tables in their direction and called out, "I have a question, my man. How well do you know this neighborhood?"

"Well, my lord. I live around here." The man's eyes kept dropping to the jewelry on the table.

"Another bracelet is yours if you can tell me if there's a paint merchant around here," Hani said with a friendly smile.

The servant, whose bare hair was thin and graying, was no doubt asking himself how many extra tips he could tuck away for his old age. After a moment of anxious quiet, his face lit up. "I do know, my lord. The next street toward the

River, up near the warehouses. There's an awful lot of royal artists around here, as you can imagine."

With a wink, Hani dropped another of his bangles on the table. "Thank you. Treat your friends to a round on me."

They made their way out the door, pushing aside the rolled-up fly mat, while the servant bobbed up and down in gratitude.

"Well, let's find the place. It sounds like it's near your mother's workshop after all."

"I guess she can't be expected to know all her neighbors," Maya said in an offhand way that sounded suspiciously defensive.

Hani chuckled silently. His son-in-law was still touchy about his working-class origins.

They passed through streets teeming once more after the siesta hour, jostled by artisans with their tools, donkeys loaded with all kinds of cargo, and a few brusque, well-dressed bureaucratic types in carrying chairs or chariots, who seemed insulted by the presence of other people in their path. Hani drank it in with a smile. For all the late king's attempt to make of his capital a neat, sterile environment, it had become the messy, colorful, noisy hive that was any city of Kemet.

"We're almost to the end of the street. Keep your eye out for something that looks like a paint merchant," Hani said. Shading his eyes with a hand, he combed the stalls set out before houses with his gaze. "I wonder if there's a market someplace."

"Is that it, Lord Hani?" cried Maya excitedly.

Hani followed his pointing finger and saw a few trestles

against the wall to their right. Upon them were displayed rows of clay pots filled to the top with a rainbow of colors, from red and yellow ochers to the pure, rich cerulean ground from blue frit. A wiry older man with a gray tuft of beard on his chin squatted in the narrow shade beside them, swatting at flies with a trimmed palmetto frond.

He hauled himself up as the two scribes forged their way through the crowd toward him. "Can I show you gentlemen some of my beautiful pigments? Look at these blues. Look at that red—and it won't change color even on the plaster."

Hani flashed him his warmest smile. "Actually, we're interested in yellow. Maybe orpiment."

The old man, who was taller than he'd first appeared, shot Hani a conspiratorial look. "My lord is a man of taste. A lot of wellborn people have been asking for it." He gestured toward a pot of powdered pigment like a bowl full of sunlight. "Not a bit orangey, see? The best there is."

Hani feigned interest in the orpiment then asked casually, "You say a lot of people have been seeking it?"

"Well, several, and they weren't artists neither. I'd say rich folks planning to change the decorations in their house. Maybe that's what my lord wants to do?"

"I'm thinking about it," said Hani blandly. He considered the pot of yellow. "How much does this run?"

The merchant looked evasive. "It's one of the more expensive pigments, my lord. It's ground from crystals, and they don't occur just everywhere. But I'm sure my lord is equal to the price." A snaggle-toothed, ingratiating smile split his old brown face.

Why would anybody put this expensive stuff on the king's

stolen toilet articles? Or were their hands covered in it, and they just happened to get some on the objects? Could it have been a painter? "Who all has been buying it of late?"

But the man shook his head virtuously. "I can't tell you about my customers, my lord. I hope you understand."

Hani quietly slipped off a faience ring and pressed it in the merchant's hand. "Are you sure, my friend?"

The old man's eyes grew round, and he closed his fist over the ring avidly. "There was the old witch woman down the street. Well, she calls herself a healer. She said she wanted to use it in a salve that takes off the hair. Like for ladies who don't want a mustache." He snickered. "There was a fellow who's an artist foreman working on the tombs to the east. He comes in now and again. He got other colors too."

The merchant rolled up his eyes and twisted his little tuft of beard as if thinking hard. "A young woman buying it for her mistress. Some servant of a rich man—don't know who. He said his masters were redecorating. That was the only color they got. He'd gotten some before."

One of these people had to be the thief. "What did he look like?" Hani asked.

"Solid. Youngish. Not well shaved. He had a drooping eyelid and a scar down the side of his face. A kind of rough-looking fellow for part of a rich household."

"Did a *wab* priest by any chance come in? A small, spare man with a shaven head and a northern accent?" Hani fixed the old man in the eye.

"In a way, my lord. But he didn't buy anything."

"Did he seem especially interested in orpiment?"

"Not enough to buy any."

But he did stop by, Hani thought with a sense of elation. They were getting somewhere at last. "Did the priest say anything?"

"No, my lord. He just kind of slowed down and looked things over, then he moved on. It was pretty late in the evening. I had already started to put my wares away, so I put them all back out when he came over. But no sale." The merchant looked disgruntled. "That's why I remember him."

Maya reached out to touch the golden powder with a finger, but the old man made a quick move to prevent him. "Be careful with that, little man."

The secretary swelled with injured dignity. "I assure you, I'd pay for any I spilled."

"It's not that. This pretty stuff is poison. You don't want to get it on your hands then touch your mouth. A lot of pigments is poison. I've seen many an artist die young from shaping their brush on their tongue."

Maya jerked back, his eyes wide. Hani was tingling with a sudden intuition that he'd stumbled upon something important. Perhaps it was not the contaminated well that was making people sick after all. Had an enemy deliberately painted the king's toilet articles with poison, hoping she would touch it then ingest it? That would explain why the other women of her household had felt poorly—they must all have handled the royal mirror or jewel casket from time to time.

He shot Maya a brief look then turned to the merchant. "Thank you, my man. You've been very helpful."

The old man bobbed a complaisant bow, and Hani and Maya took their leave.

As soon as they were out in the street, Hani turned to Maya with a triumphant grin. "That, I think, was important information, my friend. The disappearance and reappearance of the king's toilet articles finally makes sense. That's how they were trying to poison her."

Maya nodded, but he looked more reflective than excited. "How do you suppose a person managed to sneak those things out? They're not huge, but you certainly couldn't stick a jewel casket under your shirt."

"That's what we need to find out." *But how?* "I guess it depends on who the person doing the sneaking is. Maybe a merchant could slip them in with his wares."

"But don't they check those things at the gate? Remember when we had our traveling baggage with us? They looked all through it."

"Presumably, the culprit is someone trusted. Someone who comes regularly. The guards may not have bothered."

"So, do we find out the name of everyone who makes a regular appearance at the palace?" Maya asked. "You said the handmaids listed scores of people."

Hani heaved a deep breath. He didn't know what their next move should be. Until he reported to Lord Ay or his daughter, the mysterious slow poisoning might continue to happen. Hani had to ponder how upset that made him. The life of the king was all that stood in the way of a restoration of the old ways. But the God's Father would still be there to guide the young prince in the Atenist paths... unless Lady Meryet-aten could successfully gain the throne in the interim. That idea disquieted Hani—he found the Great Royal Wife frighteningly ruthless. Yet men like Lord Mai supported her, counting on their own influence to moderate her fanaticism, perhaps. Certainly, Ay was no less ambitious than his granddaughter.

Hani shook his head. *There's no good choice.* "I wonder if Mai is still here in the capital."

Maya shrugged. "I can't imagine he'd be very welcome here for long periods of time—the First Prophet of Amen-Ra."

"True. Well, let's go back to Lord Ptah-mes's and plot our next steps."

⊠

Almost the minute they returned to Ptah-mes's luxurious place by the River, Lord Mery-ra popped up in front of them.

"Father," cried Lord Hani in surprise and trepidation. "Nothing's wrong at home, is it?"

The old man's cheerful, conspiratorial grin gave the lie to that idea even before he spoke. "No, no, son. I've come to help you investigate."

Hani threw back his head in a laugh. "Have things gotten that boring in Waset?"

Mery-ra lowered his eyes evasively. "Meryet-amen is at her country place..."

"And her cook went with her, eh? I don't know what to assign you to do, Father. We've run into a wall. But let me fill you in on what we've found out recently."

They all seated themselves in the salon, and Hani brought his father up to date.

Lord Mery-ra pursed his lips in a whistle. "You're closing in on something now, son. But it seems to me that bright-yellow orpiment is one of the more conspicuous forms of poison. So many other things are invisible."

Lord Hani said, "It wasn't really as visible as all that. We were peering at the objects as closely as we could and barely saw it. Maybe they'd mixed it into a solution and that was just the dried residue. I can't imagine the king or her ladies paid that much attention."

Before anyone could respond, the steward appeared in the doorway. "My lord, a courier from the palace just delivered a message before you arrived." He held a folded packet of papyrus out to Hani with a bow.

Hani took the letter with an uneasy flutter in his throat. *Has something happened to Neferet?* He tore the sealing string away and unfolded the papyrus.

Maya and Mery-ra crowded around without shame. "What is it?" Hani's father asked eagerly.

Hani read for a moment and then looked up, his heart sinking. "The king is ready for me to begin tutoring her son."

"Right in the middle of this case, my lord?" Maya cried in disappointment.

"Maybe somebody doesn't want you to solve it," said Mery-ra darkly.

Suppressing a curse, Hani refolded the missive. How many times had this happened—that he'd been taken off one investigation in midstream and switched over to another one? In this case, the new task was far from his actual qualifications. But at least it was only one day a week.

"Is your master home?" he asked the steward.

"No, my lord. But he should be back soon."

Hani turned to his father. "Tell him where I am when you see him, all right? I'm off to the palace."

"Steer clear of Ay, if you know what's good for you, son," Mery-ra called after him.

Hani trudged back up through the city, only to find that the crown prince was not at the central palace at all but rather at the one in the northern edge of the settlement—beyond it only more of the prosperous suburbs. Blowing a disgusted breath through his teeth, he stumped onward. It was a good *iteru* and a half away—half an hour's additional walk.

Hani tried to put aside his annoyance and concentrate on the pleasure of walking. Before long, despite the heat and glare, he found his stride becoming rhythmic and his thoughts more organized. *What we need to do is find who had an opportunity to steal numerous items over a period of months—maybe years—and then replace them.* As for motives, too many people might be interested in ending the king's life, not least among them her own daughter. *Dear gods, say it's not Lady Meryet-aten. Who would she have used as her thief? Neferet?* The hair rose on Hani's arms at the thought. Would his duckling have done something like that? She seemed almost as eager as her mother to see the Hidden One back on his throne.

But once he'd started to picture one of the girls nipping items from the king's bedroom, the thought of Bener-ib came to mind. All those mysterious evenings when she came home late, she could have been up to anything. Hani shook his head, wanting to clear it of such suspicions. All the same, it might not be a bad idea to see if there were any pots of yellow pigments at Lord Ptah-mes's house, where the girl would surely have prepared her poison if she was guilty.

He was stopped at the pylon of the palace by the exotically uniformed guards. Overhead flapped the red banners that marked the presence of the Lady of the Two Lands. Hani took a deep breath and hitched up his kilt— he'd be seeing more of this place. He strode in.

Through endless gorgeously decorated corridors perfumed with incense, past gardens and cloistered walks, the majordomo led him until they emerged into a broad courtyard planted with date trees in rows like an orchard. In the shade of the trees played a dozen or so boys of various ages, running and screaming after one another, hacking away with wooden swords, or squatting in groups of four over a handful of knucklebones. Laughter and raucous little-boy chatter bounced off the walls of the court. This, it seemed, was the famous Kap, the royal nursery, where the king's male children grew up with the sons of vassals and of the high Egyptian nobility. Across the court, Hani could see in the shadow of the colonnade a cluster of women—the king and her maids. One fanned her with an ostrich-plume fan while another painted her fingernails with henna then offered her a cooling beverage from a golden ewer. Hani followed the majordomo into the royal presence, where he prostrated himself.

"Rise, Hani," said Ankhet-khepru-ra in her smoky voice. Hani hauled himself to his feet, conscious of how heavy and ungainly he was in the midst of these lithe, beautiful women. "You are here to meet the Haru in the nest, are you not?"

"I have that honor, my Sun God."

Over her shoulder, the queen instructed one of her handmaids to call the prince and his tutor. In a moment, a well-built, serious-looking man in his late thirties approached, holding by the hand a boy of about nine, who was dancing around, tugging impatiently at his tutor's firm grip. Hani noticed with surprise that the prince limped badly—one of his feet was twisted so that he couldn't walk on the flat of it. He nonetheless had plenty of energy. A warm fatherly affection stole over Hani—how often had he seen the same irrepressible frenzy of motion in his own children.

The king smiled and opened her arms to the boy, and he leaned up to kiss her. *How could we never have noticed how much he looks like the rest of the royal family?* Hani asked himself. The coincidence would have been too much had his parents been some anonymous servants.

"This is my son, the Haru in the nest," the king said, her face softening with motherly pride. She drew the boy against her knees. "Tut-ankh-aten, my little lion, this is Hani. He's going to teach you foreign languages."

The child's eyebrows cocked skeptically. "Don't I have to learn enough things already, Mother?"

Hani almost snorted with laughter. With a respectful little bow, he assured the boy, "This will give you a secret language to talk about private matters, my prince. Only very few people will understand you."

The boy looked up at his tutor with cheerful malice. "You mean Sen-nedjem won't know what I'm saying?"

"Only if he speaks Akkadian, my lord."

"I want you to discuss a schedule with Sen-nedjem, see what days best accommodate his other studies, Hani," said the king. "You can let the prince play with his fellows while you talk."

The two men made a deep court obeisance and backed away until they stood in the tree-shaded court, with the children of the Kap running all around them. The king turned her attention back to her ladies-in-waiting, and Hani and Sen-nedjem drifted off toward the edge of the playground, where they confronted one another in appraisal. Tut-ankh-aten skipped lopsidedly off to play, his jeweled sidelock bouncing.

Sen-nedjem eyed Hani up and down. "Good luck getting him to concentrate on anything," he said dryly.

Hani laughed. "I have two sons, my lord. I doubt that anything he can do will surprise me."

"Of course, you can't spank the Haru in the nest when he's naughty. Don't think he won't take advantage of that. He can be very manipulative."

"Do you like him?" Hani asked in genuine curiosity, because all he had heard so far from the lad's tutor was negative. To Hani, the boy seemed attractive—not only his fine-featured, full-lipped face but also the mischievous twinkle with which he confronted grown-ups. He was devoid of the pomposity one might have expected in the heir to the double throne.

"He's quick," Sen-nedjem said. "But it's hard to keep his mind on anything. I'm afraid he's going to turn out to be half-lettered. I wish you luck with Akkadian."

"Perhaps he'll be one of those people who is drawn naturally to languages," Hani said amiably. While Sen-nedjem didn't act hostile, Hani wondered if there weren't some jealousy at the thought of sharing his pupil with another tutor. "What are you teaching him already?"

Sen-nedjem's eyes were on the group of children playing knucklebones, among whom the young prince had inserted himself. Without looking at Hani, he said, "Basic reading and writing. Court behavior. Piety. How to be a gracious gentleman. I know Our Sun God wants him trained in horsemanship and the military arts as well, but he seems a little young to me. His health isn't too strong."

"Perhaps the exercise will be good for him. It will certainly make him less restless in the classroom."

"Perhaps." Sen-nedjem was silent for a moment then said, "Lord Ay wants his son-in-law to teach the boy driving and handling weapons."

"His son-in-law?" Hani's ears pricked up. That could only be Har-em-heb.

"Yes, the general. Which seems odd to me because Lord Ay has a son in the military himself." He looked at Hani with a trace of hauteur. "I'm their cousin, you know. I'm the king's cousin."

Hani raised his eyebrows in appreciation and said with his best diplomatic flattery, "A very handsome family, I must say. And talented."

Sen-nedjem shot Hani a skeptical look, but his manner softened marginally. "I suggest you start your lessons on the sixth day of the month, four days from now. Then every week at the same interval. I'll make sure the prince has a free morning."

"Will he be by himself?" Hani asked. "Or will there be other boys as well?"

"Probably some of the grandee children and maybe

some vassal princes. I hope that won't distract the Haru in the nest."

"It will certainly make it easier to converse when we reach that point." Hani smiled. "I'm eager to start." And he found that, in spite of himself, he really was.

Sen-nedjem bowed politely but without warmth, and Hani returned the courtesy. *He's insecure. I'll bet he's a harsh disciplinarian.* Then Hani made his way back to the cloister walk, the screams and laughter of the children fading behind him.

⊠

At Ptah-mes's villa, Hani encountered Maya and Mery-ra sitting in the garden, enjoying the bit of breeze that penetrated the walled enclosure.

"How did it go, son?" Mery-ra asked eagerly.

Hani seated himself on a low-backed chair at his side. "The young prince is a nice boy but lively, it appears. His tutor seems too humorless to engage the interest of a youngster. I'll bet his classes are boring."

Mery-ra chuckled. "Yours won't be, I'm sure."

"Oh, and guess who Lord Ay has chosen to teach the prince the arts of war? Our friend, Har-em-heb."

The two men uttered appreciative noises.

"Did he ever have that baby?" asked Maya.

Mery-ra shook his head. "He has no children, even after two wives. And I think he really loves them. It must be a terrible sorrow for him."

"Then this assignment may help him as well as the Haru in the nest. I hope he can gently steer the boy toward love of the Hidden One."

"You too, son. But be careful. I'm sure the king and her father will be keeping an eye on you."

"You know," Hani said, lowering his voice, "I don't think Ankhet-khepru-ra knows he isn't her son. Her love for him was touching and real. It makes me feel terrible to think someone is trying to deprive the boy of his mother." He remembered the pale mottling of the king's golden skin, so like that of the handmaids he had interviewed.

"Perhaps you should tell her about the poison. At least stop her from getting any more of it."

Hani nodded pensively. "That's what I think." *But I'm afraid of where the clues may lead us. May the gods forbid that Bener-ib was involved.* "Has anybody noticed any painting going on in this house? I need to know if there's any orpiment around."

"You think Lord Ptah-mes is the poisoner, my lord? But how?" Maya looked incredulous.

"No, no. I just want... I want to be sure the girls have nothing to do with this."

Mery-ra shot Hani a grim look. He clearly understood his son's fears.

Hani called Ptah-mes's steward. The man approached with a respectful bow, and Hani said in a quiet voice, "I'm involved in an investigation for the king, my man. Is there any chance we could look in your mistress's room? And Lady Bener-ib's?"

The steward looked surprised, but he would hardly dare refuse a friend as trusted by his master as Hani. "Yes, my lord. But they should be home soon, if you would prefer to have them accompany you."

"No, I rather need to do it immediately."

The steward led them through the magnificent house, where Hani saw no sign of any repainting anywhere. They passed down a broad, echoing corridor upstairs, lit by high clerestories, and stopped at a door of cedar wood.

"These are the mistress of the house's chambers, my lord."

"And her friend's?"

The steward dropped his eyes briefly but said without inflection, "They share the room, Lord Hani."

Hani pushed his way, gingerly, into the vestibule. The apartment was spacious and cool and extremely luxurious. Carved furniture inlaid with precious woods, bright imported tapestries, an open ventilator in the ceiling—despite the paucity of gold, the room wasn't much inferior to the chambers of the palace Hani had seen, although a bit on the austere side. He wondered how much of it was Neferet's taste in decor and how much had been there when she arrived. Feeling guilty, he combed the room with his eyes. A large chest caught his gaze, and he opened it, but there appeared to be nothing within but clothing and bed linen. In the sleeping chamber, he saw a single bed with two headrests, invitingly made up with fresh straw, the mosquito net drawn back. On the other side of the room was a vanity table, although he could hardly imagine either of the girls spending much time primping. But what really drew his eye was a larger table where various pots and faience jars were arranged, along with several mysterious-looking bronze instruments plus a sharp knife, a scale, and a mortar and pestle. *This must be where they brew their potions. I guess Bener-ib carved the toe with that knife.* Hani opened a jar and saw within some kind of granular substance that smelled like cedar sawdust. Another had dried insects inside. He closed it distastefully. A coffer of bark, baskets of desiccated flowers—the same array of ingredients he remembered from Khuit's but neater and better organized.

A little squat faience pot sat to one side—Hani could detect its unpleasant odor of sheep fat even with the top on. He lifted the lid and almost staggered back. Inside was a bright-yellow salve. "Mut the mother of us all!" he exclaimed under his breath, his heart sinking like lead within him. This had to contain orpiment—the color was unmistakable. Perhaps this very salve was what had been rubbed on the king's stolen toilet articles.

Feeling faint, he lurched from the room and shut the hall door carefully behind him. As he descended the stairs, he heard a feminine voice raised in laughter, and Neferet called out, "Grandfather! Maya! Where is Papa?"

His throat tight with fear, Hani clattered down the last few steps and emerged into the salon, where the young doctor, her capacious basket on the floor, had just greeted Mery-ra and Maya. "Here he is," he said, forcing his voice to sound calm. But what throbbed in his head was the refrain *One or both of the girls is involved.*

"Did you meet the crown prince today?"

"I did, my duckling. He seems like a nice boy." Hani watched his daughter closely. If she were up to no good, it would be written on her face.

"And the king is nice too. She promised she would protect Ibet and me from Mahu. I don't think she likes him very much." Neferet picked up her medical basket, preparing to go upstairs, but her father stopped her.

"Neferet, my duck, could I have a word with you before

Bener-ib gets back?" Hani drew Neferet away from the door. "My duckling, do you ever use a salve made of orpiment?" He wasn't able to conceal the anxiety in his voice.

"Not usually, Papa. We're doctors, after all, not cosmetics girls. But the queen wanted some undesirable facial hair taken off, and she trusts us more than anybody, so we made her some."

Hani was almost afraid to ask, "How long have you been making it?"

"About a week. Maybe less. Why, Papa? Are you tired of shaving?" Neferet looked up, a twinkle in her eye.

A great wave of relief broke over Hani, liberating his chest from the weight of unwilling suspicion. "No, my dear. Perhaps you shouldn't use any more of it. I'm told it's poison."

The young doctor's little eyes grew wide. "But a lot of medicine is poison, Papa, if you use too much of it. Do you think that's what's been poisoning the king? But we only gave her some a few days ago."

"Not exactly. But be careful nonetheless. And I recommend throwing that stuff away." *Before Mahu finds it,* he added silently.

Neferet shrugged, unoffended. "I'll ask Lady Djefat-nebty about it."

Hani asked, "How much longer will she be here?"

"Not long, I think. She only comes to the palace every few days now."

Hani nodded, not sure if he dared tell his daughter what he had discovered about the yellow pigment on the queen's toilet articles. "Just be careful. Wash your hands if you touch anything." Then, shaking off his fears, he said more cheerfully, "I'll be going to the palace day after tomorrow to give the crown prince his first lesson. Can I walk with you ladies?"

"Of course, Papa." She beamed, then little by little her smile faded into a wrinkled brow of concern. "Papa, would it be all right if I tell Ibet that you will be her father now?"

Hani was nonplussed. "She's been living in my household for five years. Surely she counts as a daughter."

Neferet shrugged. "I mean really, though. She's a complete orphan now, and believe it or not, she loved that awful father of hers. She's more broken up about his death than what shows. She almost feels she put a curse on him by repulsing him like that—she keeps saying, 'I shouldn't have.' And then, being accused of his murder—could anything be more awful? She's completely in shock, but one of these days, it will come down on her head, and she'll need someone there for her."

Hani felt his nose twinge. "That's very sensitive of you, my girl. Truthfully, I don't know what to make of your friend. I feel like I don't know her at all. She's hardly ever showed any emotion in my presence, although I hear her laugh with you. She's warmed up to your mama, but she seems shut against me. And I can't say I don't understand that..."

"She's always saying how lucky I am to have a father like you." Neferet took her seat on Hani's lap and stroked his cheek. "Please, Papa? It will mean so much to her."

Hani felt a little trapped. "What is it you want me to do? I'm afraid to touch her because it might scare her, especially after that scene at Lord Ptah-mes's house."

She dropped her eyes. "I thought of Lord Ptah-mes, but

I don't think he's the one she needs for a father. He's always so beautifully polite that it seems distant. He would never give her a hug—or me either, for that matter."

Don't try to hug him, he warned her silently. *You're in danger of making him fall in love with you. Thank all the gods he's so polite.* "You know I'm willing, my duckling. But it has to come from her, don't you think?"

She slid off his lap and said confidently, "It will."

After his daughter had flounced off up the stairs, Hani was left with his mortified thoughts. *How could I think that poor broken child might have murdered people?* But he couldn't shake the suspicion.

⊠

Two days later, the young doctors waited to accompany Hani to the palace. It was early, but the way was long, and Neferet wasn't one to use a litter or carrying chair. Mery-ra waved an affectionate goodbye to the little party as they left.

Hani had to admit to deep preoccupation as they walked. He so dreaded the thought that Bener-ib could be found guilty of her father's murder and the attempted poisoning of the king that it was almost a bitter taste in his mouth. Yet he couldn't forget that pot of yellow salve in the girls' room. *They must have orpiment in their possession.* Hani wished Ptah-mes was there with his clear intellect and court contacts, but—ever the gentleman—he had gone to Waset in order to leave his house in the capital to the young women.

They were close to the central part of the city, with its workshops and warehouses and modest artisans' dwellings hemming the street in tightly. It was one of those back lanes favored by the two *sunets*, and this early in the morning, there were few people abroad. Here and there, a craftsman was opening the gate of his studio for the day. Clanging and shuffling from within told of preparations for the morning's work. Shadowed as it was by the close-set higgledy-piggledy residences, the sun hadn't yet cast its rays over the narrow lane.

Little by little, Hani got the impression that there were more footsteps than there were feet. He strained his ears, thinking perhaps it was an echo off the crowding walls, but he couldn't be certain. His hearing grew more and more on edge until he was completely distracted from his thoughts. All at once, he stopped cold and held Neferet back. Bener-ib pattered to a halt in their wake. Hani was sure he heard a scuffle behind him. He whirled, but he saw no one. They'd just passed an intersection, though, and if anyone were trailing them, he might well have dodged around the corner.

His heart accelerating, Hani said under his breath, "I think someone may be following us." Neferet opened her mouth to say something, but Hani put a finger to his lips. "If anyone should attack us, I want you to drop your baskets and run like anything for the central palace. Nobody would dare to harm you there—there will be soldiers on guard even at this hour. I'll slow them down."

"But, Papa," Neferet said, "we can help you fight—"

"Don't argue, Neferet. Do what I tell you for once. You're the ones they're after." Hani's uneasiness made him sharp. Neferet's straight brows knit, but she said nothing.

So, those who wanted to silence witnesses to the prince's birth have finally decided to come after the girls.

Hani felt totally vulnerable. He was unarmed and hampered by his concern for his two young charges. Quietly, they began walking again, almost holding their breath.

The sound of footsteps grew suddenly nearer. Hani spun to see a big man, his arms corded with sinew, his face masked with a linen scarf, emerge from the shadows. He threw himself forward toward the three.

"Run!" Hani shouted at the girls. "Run! Now! Get the watchman!"

They disappeared from sight as Hani crouched low, braced against a blow. His heart was pounding, every nerve concentrated. With his squat, muscular build, he'd been a redoubtable wrestler in his student days, but that was a long time in the past. The man confronting him was younger and in better shape, with the catlike grace of a seasoned fighter.

The two men circled one another, hands crisped, waiting for the chance to grab hold of each other. Hani feinted, and the man lunged, but recovered before Hani could lock a leg behind his knee. They faced each other, panting. Hani had resolved to hurl himself at the man's legs and take him down, but the attacker reached to his waistband, and his fist came up with a glittering blade of bronze. Hani's throat constricted in fear. The fight had just become a lot less even.

"Look out, Papa!" Neferet screamed. "He's got a knife!"

Anger flashed through Hani's peripheral consciousness— the girls hadn't fled. His breath was rattling in his throat, and his eyes were fixed, unblinking, on his adversary. Now he dared not let the man overcome him, or the foolish youngsters would be imperiled. He continued to circle slowly, hoping for an opening to cut under the knife or to kick the man in the crotch—anything that might permit him to grab the weapon.

All at once, Neferet launched herself upon the attacker's back, locking her arms around his throat and her legs around his waist. The man staggered backward under her weight, his knife clattering to the ground. Hani scooped up a handful of dust from the road and threw it into the fellow's eyes. Blinded, the man doubled over, his hands to his face. Neferet slid from her perch and hit the ground with a thud. The attacker shook his head and scrubbed at his eyes, but he seemed to be recovering his eyesight only too rapidly. Hani darted in with a head butt. As he struck the man in the midriff, Hani could feel him arching backward, and the attacker dropped like stone into the street. Hani, who had fallen on top of him, picked himself up and scuttled back with the haste of fear, lest the man should rise and grasp him.

But the attacker didn't rise. He lay there, flat on his back, his sightless eyes fixed on the sky. One of them had a drooping lid. Neferet sprawled a few feet away, her own eyes round with shock as she tried to pull herself together. Hani, panting, looked up to see Bener-ib standing over the would-be assassin—timid, swaying, and stunned looking—and in her hand was the man's knife, crimson to the hilt.

Hani gaped. He was heaving, and his face was running with sweat, but that was nothing compared to the disbelief that chilled him. "Thank you, my girl. You, too, Neferet," he panted. They had just saved his life, he realized, in their providential disobedience.

Neferet, who seemed as unable to credit her eyes as Hani, scrambled to her feet and rushed to Bener-ib. The girl held out the knife at the length of her thin arm and stared at it in horror then let it drop to the ground. Suddenly, her eyes began to spout tears, and to Hani's utter amazement, she threw herself into his arms, sobbing, "Lord Hani! Thank the gods you're all right. I couldn't let you die too. I've already lost one father."

Hani, his nose twinging with tears, took the girl in a tight embrace. *Welcome back to the world of the feeling*, he thought tenderly. Behind her, Neferet clasped her hands and bit her trembling lip. Hani could say nothing, just let the little woman from Sau sob out her fear and sorrow. At last, he said in his gentlest voice, "Do you ladies think you can go on to the palace today or not? I need to find out who that was and why he was after… whoever he was after. He didn't seem to be one of Mahu's *medjay* thugs."

"Maybe we should go home, do you think, Ibet?" Neferet put a comforting arm around her friend.

"Do you want me to walk you back, my duck?"

"No, Papa. We'll be careful." She hesitated then wrapped her father in a crushing hug. Her voice was shaky when she whispered, "Thank all the gods for keeping you safe. I worry about you since you gave away your amulet."

Hani had left the amulet with a dying slave in Djahy the previous year and never gotten around to replacing it. He kissed his daughter on her shaven scalp, and she drew her friend back in the direction from which they'd come. The sun was already starting to rise over the roofs of the surrounding houses, and people would be walking the street before long. The girls picked up their big baskets and scuttled away. Hani needed to get gone too. He decided he wouldn't call the watch after all—that would surely lead to Mahu, and there were too many things he couldn't explain. He hurriedly peeled down the dead man's mask to reveal a squarish face with a long scar down the cheek, and he remembered, with a thrill of discovery, where he'd heard such a face described. Surging to his feet, he set off toward the palace.

He was still shaken—moved beyond words but also uneasy. It seemed Bener-ib did have the strength to stab a man. And she had pulled out the knife automatically, leaving no blood on her except for an easily washed hand.

The assailant, for his part, was clearly a professional, silent and masked like a robber. Had the attack been no more than an attempt at theft? Hani doubted it, although he wasn't sure if he were the object or the two young doctors, witnesses to a dangerous secret.

He couldn't get away from the scene of the attack fast enough. It wouldn't be a good thing for him or any of his household to be associated with a murdered corpse lying in the street. It seemed like a blessing that the girls had not alerted the watch. After walking fast for several blocks toward the palace, he began to encounter pedestrians. The workday had begun, and bureaucrats were making their way to the Hall of Royal Correspondence. Hani felt a sense of safety at last. But he kept walking, aiming for the north residence. He was late for his lesson with the Haru in the nest.

CHAPTER 10

Maya and Lord Mery-ra were hunched over a hot game of Hounds and Jackals when Neferet and Bener-ib came bursting into Ptah-mes's salon.

"Grandfather! Maya! You'll never believe what just happened!" Neferet cried excitedly. Maya saw that both girls' faces were tear streaked, and a chill of alarm rippled up his neck.

Mery-ra put it into words first. "Where's your father, my girl? Is he all right?"

"Yes, Grandfather. And guess what? Bener-ib saved him! She killed the man who attacked him!"

Maya and Lord Mery-ra exchanged a horrified look.

"Attacked him?" Maya gasped.

"Or us—but he was going to fight to protect us, of course. And the man turned out to have a knife, so I jumped on him, and Ibet stabbed him with his own knife! You should have seen it!"

"I think I'm glad I didn't," said the old man with

feeling. "You girls need to be much more careful. It seems someone is out to get you for sure."

"Where is Lord Hani?" Maya asked. Trickles of cold sweat made their way down his temples.

"He went on to the palace. He had a lesson with Prince Tut-ankh-aten."

"Perhaps I should go and wait for him, to walk home with him." Maya jumped to his feet anxiously.

Lord Mery-ra rose too. "I'll go with you, son."

But Neferet called after them in disappointment, "Don't you want to hear about what happened?"

"Of course," said her grandfather, clearly distracted by anxiety.

Neferet proceeded to tell about the attack with her usual verve, acting out the assailant's stealthy approach and Hani's quick defensive crouch. She showed how she had leaped on the man's back, and how Bener-ib had picked up his knife and as soon as there was an opportunity, had plunged it with all her strength into his back. As a doctor, Neferet reminded everyone, Ibet knew just where to strike.

After she had finished, Maya heaved a huge breath of relief. And of confusion. *What was that all about? Is the baby switcher after the girls? Or is someone after Hani, who may be getting too close to the guilty party in his investigation of the palace thefts?*

"And then," Neferet added, drawing Bener-ib to her proudly, "Ibet found out she loved Papa, and everything will be all right now." Her little brown eyes started to shrivel with tears.

"Well, of course she loves him," said Mery-ra kindly.

"Everybody does. And he loves you, too, my girl. You may be sure of that. And so do all of us."

To Maya's astonishment, Bener-ib stretched out her arms and hugged her friend's grandfather, murmuring in her little-girl voice, "Thank you, thank you, Lord Mery-ra."

Maya found himself choking and had to clear his throat, looking away in embarrassment. Something had ripped open in the girl. All those frozen years were melting away before their eyes. Eventually, he said, "We should probably get going, Lord Mery-ra. Lord Hani's lesson is brief. By the time we get to the north palace..."

"Yes, my boy. Let's go." Mery-ra patted Bener-ib on the back and gave his granddaughter a quick squeeze. "Don't leave the house, my daughters. Stay inside, and don't show yourself to anyone."

"Why don't you walk on the processional way from now on? No one would try anything against you in the public eye," Maya suggested. But in his heart of hearts, he wondered if that were true.

The two men called for Ptah-mes's litter and piled in, unspeaking. It was not until they had gone well past the central bureaucratic zone that Maya said, "I think Lord Hani shouldn't walk around by himself."

Mery-ra cut him a sharp glance. "You took the words out of my mouth, son. He needs us to act as bodyguards from now on."

Maya thought Hani probably needed someone more formidable than an old man and a small person like himself, no matter how brave the two of them were, but he just nodded.

They dismounted outside the pylon gate of the north

palace and took a seat in the road in the shadow of the wall. Maya was sunk in thought, but his reflections were muddled. *Bener-ib stabbed a footpad? That sheds a new light on her physical capacity to murder her father.*

Sometime later, Hani emerged from the gate, humming a badly off-key tune, and started down the processional way.

"Son! Hold up!" called Lord Mery-ra. He struggled to his feet with Maya's aid, and the two of them hustled to catch up to him.

"Father. Maya. Is anything wrong?" Hani's good mood turned serious. "Mahu hasn't showed up, has he?"

"No, but we thought you could use a little company on your way home," Mery-ra said with a significant lift of the eyebrows.

"Don't forget the litter, my lord." Maya pointed at the four bearers, who were stirring in confusion.

"Why don't you take the litter, son, and keep yourself out of sight?"

Hani snorted. "Nonsense. There's no danger on a major thoroughfare like this. You take it, Father."

After a bit of negotiating and stubborn refusals, the three men set out under their own power, with the litter bearers following. At least they'd be a stalwart defense if anyone tried anything.

"How did the lesson go, my lord?"

Hani laughed. "Well, Sen-nedjem was right about the prince being easily distracted. I have to see to it that something interesting is always happening. Then he gets eager and competitive. There's one boy a little older than the others who is extremely smart. I think he'll set a good example for the Haru in the nest."

"One of the vassals? Their language isn't so different from Akkadian."

"No. A young son of our own aristocracy. His name is Amen-mes son of Djehuty-mes. I don't know his parents, but they must be proud of him."

"We were always proud of *you*, my boy."

Hani clapped his father on the back with a grin. "When I wasn't up to my ears in mischief, eh?"

"I certainly never remember any of my teachers bothering to try to make class interesting," said Maya dryly.

"Unlike me, they weren't hoping their tenure would be over soon." Hani chuckled, then he turned serious. "Did the girls tell you what happened, Father, Maya? Someone who wants to see all witnesses dead is after them at last."

"Are you sure it's them he's after, Hani?" asked his father dubiously. "You've been asking a lot of questions lately. Perhaps you're getting too close to a solution."

Hani gave a sarcastic bark of laughter. "I wish someone would tell me what that solution is." He lowered his voice. "I wonder about Djefat-nebty. But my chief suspect is Bener-ib, and I'd rather do almost anything than see her put to death, the poor child. By the Hidden One, she saved my life."

Maya and Mery-ra heaved a big simultaneous *whoosh*.

"Is it ever the greater *ma'at* to let a criminal go? I could just warn the queen about the poison and name no names."

"They'd torture you to winkle it out," said Mery-ra grimly.

Maya, who had been silent, said, "What could the

girl's motive be, my lord? I mean, we know several possible reasons for murdering her father, but what about the king?"

"I'm sure I don't know." Hani gave a discouraged sigh. "That's something we need to find out. And I just pray that I'm wrong." He walked on in pensive silence. At last, he said, "Our attacker answered to the description of a fellow who bought orpiment recently. The merchant called him a servant of a rich man."

⊠

In the end, Hani concluded that—in conscience—he had to warn the king about the poison, but he decided to tell her just enough to make her cautious, without providing any details that might implicate the girls. He sent a message corroborating Nakht-ef-mut's finding and warned her about the orpiment, begging Ankhet-khepru-ra to wash her hands thoroughly before eating, especially after handling the stolen-and-returned objects. And then he sat, pondering the possibility that the king's eldest daughter might be behind the plot. No doubt she was in the king's apartment regularly. The idea lay heavily upon his heart. *How could a child do that to her own mother? The public image of the royal family has been so affectionate and close...* As often as he'd seen in his investigations that things weren't always what they seemed, it still pained him to discover this. *You're innocent, my boy. The world is full of liars.* And he dared not close his mind to other possibilities than Bener-ib.

He confided his disillusionment to his father, who said with a sigh, "Hani, you're a diplomat. What do diplomats do? They lie—they flatter, they conceal the truth, they try to make things look better than they are. Don't be too quick to put anything past the queen." He shot his son a meaningful look. "Or anyone else."

"You're right, revered Father. And while I conceal the truth from the Lady of the Two Lands, I need to find out for sure who is behind this attempt and why."

Mery-ra grinned beguilingly. "You know, son, the end-of-year holidays are upon us, and I thought I'd go back to Waset to celebrate with the family. Why don't you join me? I know that would make Nub-nefer happy."

Hani considered that. It sounded wonderful to get out of this city and Ptah-mes's stark, luxurious villa and settle into his own comfortable house for a while, with those he loved around him. Or at least, some of them—no doubt Aha would stay in the capital, and the girls might not be able to get away. Pa-kiki was in Waset already with his superior, General Har-em-heb. *But do I dare abandon my investigation for a week or more?*

"Sen-nedjem said the crown prince was sick, so I don't have a lesson this week," Hani said. "I believe I'll do that. Stepping back may help me think. I seem to be out of ideas."

He was tired. This case wasn't budging, and Ay's goodwill could only be counted on for so long before he demanded results. Perhaps Hani needed to sleep in a temple and wait for a dream from the gods. But none of the temples were open anymore.

⊠

Hani, his father, and Maya disembarked in Waset six days later, and when they entered Hani's door, they were greeted with delight by Nub-nefer. "Oh, Hani, I'm so happy you were able to get back for the Feast of Drunkenness. I just don't feel safe anymore after those riots a few years back." She tilted up her face to kiss her husband, who responded with fervor, drinking in the fragrance of her glossy natural hair, still dark.

"Nobody's happier than I, my dove. I just wish the stay were longer." He suspected the likelihood of violence might, in fact, be growing, since the death of Nefer-khepru-ra had given people hope of a change that still had not come under his successor.

Nub-nefer cast her eyes around as if someone might be listening and then whispered, "Amen-em-hut wants to talk to you."

Oh, no, Hani thought in alarm. *That's all I need, with Mahu out to get me and Ay seeming to know my every move.* "Is that wise?"

"What's wrong with you visiting your bereaved sister-in-law? Nobody needs to know he's back in the house with her."

Hani cocked a dubious eyebrow and said reluctantly, "All right. But not for long."

Nub-nefer's eyes lit up, and she pulled Hani's face down for a kiss. "I knew you'd say yes, my love." Still beaming, she headed for the kitchen to see if the men's meal was ready. At the doorway, she stopped and called back, "Didn't Maya return with you, Hani?"

"Indeed—and quite eagerly. He split off to go directly home."

"Sati has a little surprise for him." She disappeared through the door with a secretive smile.

Mery-ra chuckled knowingly. "Sounds like you're about to gain another grandchild, son."

◈

The next morning, Hani prepared to visit his sister-in-law and her concealed husband. It had been five years since Hani had laid eyes on Amen-em-hut. The former Third Prophet of Amen-Ra had done a remarkable job of staying hidden—Hani had never been sure who was actually sheltering him.

With mingled pleasure and uneasiness, Hani crunched up the neat white gravel path through Amen-em-hut's immaculate garden. Evidently, the priest had been back to his gardening—not a leaf was out of line. A drowsy late-summer morning laid its golden veil over the cicada-pulsing trees, and Hani could well imagine what a comfort it was to the man to be back with his family in this familiar place. Hani announced himself at the door, and his sister-in-law, Anuia, came hustling out into the vestibule, arms wide.

She hugged Hani, almost squealing with excitement. "Isn't it wonderful, Hani? Amen-em-hut is in the salon, waiting for you."

Sure enough, the small, good-looking figure of Nub-nefer's only sibling stood grinning in the doorway. "My brother! It's been too long."

The two men enveloped one another in a heartfelt embrace. Different as they were, Hani was fond of his brother-in-law. Amen-em-hut was a nervous, intense man, but Hani admired his fearlessness and refusal to give up. Despite the fact that Amen-em-hut was two years older than his sister, he and Nub-nefer looked so much alike that

Mery-ra referred to them as Shu and Tefnut, the divine twins.

"Are you sure it's safe for you here, my friend?" Hani asked.

"No one would think to look for me under my own roof." The priest's handsome face beamed. "It's good to see you again, Hani. I know how you've been working for the cause." He led his guest to a pair of stools, and they took their seats, Amen-em-hut still grinning.

Hani had to laugh. "You look mighty cheerful for a man with a price on his head."

"And why not? The abomination on our throne is gone. The gods have spoken. The present king won't stay with the Aten much longer, once she sees how little support she has. And why should she? Her husband, the heretic, is dead. What happens to all his fine theology now? And Lady Meryet-aten—or Meryet-amen, as she's starting to call herself in private—is ready to exalt the Hidden One as before. Things are happening, Hani. Everything is about to change at last. Why, there are rumors that the king's going to reopen the Ipet-isut."

The Ipet-isut, the Theban temple of Amen-Ra, was the greatest holy place in the world, built on the spot where the very first land had emerged from the waters of chaos. Hani remembered with longing the splendid liturgies on festival days, the river processions of the god in his ram-headed barque, the feasting.

"No one could be happier than I am, brother," he said with sincere joy. "Except maybe Nub-nefer. She's never stopped her singing practice, waiting for this moment."

Amen-em-hut laughed, his face flushed with exaltation.

"We're crossing the Lake of Flowers, my friend. The trials are past, and the Field of Reeds is almost in sight." He took Hani by the arm. "Come with me. I have something to show you."

Curious, Hani let himself be led across the side garden toward the impressive pavilion where Amen-em-hut's family was accustomed to gathering on a fine evening. The blinds were down. His host drew one aside, and Hani saw a group of people seated within. They rose at his approach.

Dear gods. What are these people doing here? Hani asked himself in astonishment. Because he recognized the men. Mai was there, and his Second Prophet, Lord Si-mut—which wasn't altogether surprising. But to Hani's amazement, he saw Lord Nakht-pa-aten, the vizier of the Upper Kingdom, the most powerful man in the Black Land after the royal family. And beside him, a group of army officers waited: Har-em-heb and Menna and another young man whom Hani didn't know. And then... there stood Mane, a big, mischievous grin on his face.

Hani's jaw dropped. His old friend, the former ambassador to Naharin, involved with these people? At last, Hani remembered to bow.

When he rose, Har-em-heb approached, and with a twinkle in his eye, he clapped Hani on the shoulder. "My friend. Welcome."

The other men chimed in, grave and elated at the same time.

What on earth is going on here? Something seditious, I'm almost sure.

"Hani," said the vizier in a warm voice. "We've never worked together, but my colleagues have only good things to say about you." Clad in the long kilt knotted across the chest that was the mark of his office, he was a tall, dark-skinned, well-built man who carried more than a whiff of the military about him.

What nerve, Hani thought admiringly. *Anyone who saw him would recognize him.* Hani felt his face growing hot. "My lord is too kind."

"I think you know everyone here," Mai said. "Except perhaps Har-em-heb's adjutant, young Pa-ra-mes-su."

"I'm a friend of your son-in-law, my lord," the young officer said respectfully. "Our wives are friends."

After the courtesies were exchanged, the men reseated themselves, beginning with the vizier, and Hani and Amen-em-hut pulled up their stools. Hani was still in shock. He'd had no idea that so many of his friends were part of the Crocodiles. "How can I be of service to you, my lords?"

In his deep voice, Mai said, "You're doing exactly what we want of you for the moment, Hani. As you know, the day will come—soon—when you are to make with Kheta a fateful alliance that will save our erring kingdom. As soon as Ay's attention is elsewhere—and we'll see to it that it is—you must go and leave to us the making good of your absence to the God's Father. We are already gathering rich gifts for your journey in the port of Per-nefer and identifying the appropriate staff for you so you'll be ready to leave on a moment's notice. Our friends Menna and Pa-ra-mes-su will lead your escort, thanks to the indulgence of General Har-em-heb."

"I've heard, Lord Mai, that our present king may reopen the Ipet-isut," Hani said, wanting to hear him say that if the Atenist tide began to reverse, they would back away from their violent plans and let the upside-down world settle naturally.

Lord Si-mut answered with a smile, "Yes. Our influence has already begun to dissolve her obduracy." He blinked—a soft, owllike man with dark-ringed eyes.

"It won't be long now," Amen-em-hut said, looking quite ecstatic. "It's a shame Lady Apeny isn't here to see it."

Hani wondered if Apeny's widower, Ptah-mes, were a part of this group or if he simply shared their general position. *Will he be glad to see a war between Meryet-aten and Ay when the king dies?* "I hope we can count on the army's support. Otherwise, nothing will come of this, Hittite or no."

Har-em-heb said, "The infantry is definitely ours. And while some of the cavalry will follow their commander, Lord Ay, there are many who have served the Aten only out of necessity and will rejoice to see the old ways restored. If it comes to a battle, they may turn."

"I... I wish us success." Hani fell silent while the others beamed at him. After a moment, he said, "The king is being slowly poisoned. Is that us?"

Mai and Si-mut exchanged a surprised glance—an answer Hani trusted more than words. "No, Hani. We have no hand in this. We draw the line at killing women and children."

"What's to become of the Haru in the nest when his sister is crowned?"

"He's young. Once out from under Ay's sway, he can be redirected in his loyalties."

He's old enough to know if someone pushes him off the throne he has always been promised, thought Hani, unconvinced. More and more, he was conflicted over the armed revolution these men espoused, even though it meant the return of the Hidden One.

"Gentlemen, perhaps Hani wants to get on with his day. It might seem suspicious if he spent too much time here. Mahu may be watching him." Amen-em-hut clapped Hani on the shoulder with a fraternal grin.

Hani could take a hint. He bowed low. "With your permission, my lords."

"I'll walk you home, my friend," said Mane in his loud, cheerful voice.

The two of them made their way across the garden side by side, in companionable silence. Once they had emerged into the street, Mane said jovially, "You didn't expect me to be here, did you?"

Hani laughed, but in his mind, he wasn't so unambiguously happy as his friend. "No. I've barely known you to express any opinion about the present situation."

"As long as I was representing the kingdom abroad, I felt I shouldn't show myself in opposition to it. But now that I'm retired"—Mane shrugged—"I'm my own man."

Hani walked on in pensive silence then said in a lower voice, "Are you ready to commit violence, my friend?"

"It need not come to that. If our timing is right, it may be a bloodless coup."

"I think you may be living in a dream world, Mane—you and all those intelligent men in that room. There's already violence going on. The Great Royal Wife once openly admitted to me that she wanted to hasten her father to the grave—it's very likely she did. And somebody is trying to assassinate the present king, life, prosperity, and health to her—and I think I mean that, in spite of everything."

Mane eyed his friend, suddenly concerned. "You're no longer with us—is that what you're saying, old man? You don't want to see the Hidden One returned to his heavenly throne?"

Hani shook his head as if to clear it of the confusion that had insinuated itself among his thoughts like a creeping mist, obscuring the right path. "I do. But it seems to me that that's already beginning to happen. It says something that the Ipet-isut is being reopened. I'm not sure I like the way our friends are going about things. Do you know that Lady Meryet-aten is planning to bring in a Hittite consort?"

Mane nodded, his face darkening.

"Har-em-heb and I are both teaching the crown prince," Hani insisted. "He's young and impressionable, and I think we can influence him toward the good, in spite of his grandfather. I'm afraid these people are too impatient. The Field of Reeds is approaching at its own pace. We can't just fly over the Lake of Flowers. Meryet-aten's naked ambition concerns me."

"Do you think Ay is any less ambitious, Hani?"

Hani raised his eyebrows in acknowledgment. "No, but he's less of an ideologue. I think he'll compromise if he sees that the infantry and the bureaucratic class are against him."

Maya gave a hum of consideration.

Hani dropped his voice even lower. "Lady Meryet-aten's excuse for crowding out the prince is that she thinks he's the son of a servant girl who was exchanged with the king's stillborn daughter."

"That's what Mai said, yes."

"What if it isn't true? What if Tut-ankh-aten really is Meryet-aten's brother?" Hani stopped and fixed his friend with a meaningful stare.

Mane looked at him, his tufty eyebrows raised, for the space of a heartbeat. "You know that to be the case?"

"I do, although Meryet-aten doesn't. I've hesitated to tell her... perhaps out of cowardice. I didn't want to be forced to see so clearly that preserving the dynasty wasn't her motive at all."

Mane, thoughtful, resumed walking, and Hani matched his stride.

"I think the prevailing sentiment," said the former ambassador, "is that seeing the Hidden One restored to his rightful place excuses almost any action."

That's the way it always is, Hani thought glumly. *As our old friend Keliya would say, "Kings are like that." And so, it seems, are revolutionaries.* With a creeping of the skin, he began to believe Lady Meryet-aten was a more likely suspect than Bener-ib in the gradual poisoning of her mother. Lord Mai might refuse to kill women and children, but Hani wasn't sure the same thing could be said about the queen. If that were so, where did his own loyalties lie? Where was *ma'at*?

Mane left him at the juncture that took Hani back to his own home. They parted fondly, but Hani could see that his words had tarnished his friend's bubbling good cheer, giving the former ambassador something to think about. Hani himself was pensive as he entered the house, which was strangely quiet. He had no sooner seated himself in the salon to greet Baket-iset than female voices chirruped from behind the door into the rear part of the house and Nub-nefer, Neferet, and Bener-ib irrupted into the room, full of laughter. They surrounded him in a flock, grinning mysteriously. Hani was aware of his father appearing in the doorway behind them, looking conspiratorial.

"Nub-nefer, my dove. Neferet. Bener-ib. What's this?" Hani asked. "I'm so irresistible that I draw women like flies?"

Neferet laughed. "No, silly Papa. We have a surprise for you." She drew from behind her back a packet wrapped in linen and, exchanging an excited glance with her mother and friend, handed it to Hani. "For you."

Hani unfolded the little packet and revealed a beautiful amulet of gold and carnelian. It was an image of a lion-headed woman on a throne—the goddess Sekhmet—not much longer than the joint of Hani's thumb but so beautifully carved from the pomegranate-red stone and set in such delicate bezels of gold at top and bottom, that it had to be the work of In-hapy. The chain was a kind of cord woven of fine gold filaments.

He looked up, shocked and delighted. "How magnificent! What's the occasion?"

"We were worried about you," said Nub-nefer, smiling. "Ever since you gave away your Serqet amulet."

Hani felt a blush heating his cheeks. "Oh, my love, I was afraid you'd be hurt by that—that I would part with the charm that was a gift from you." He had left it in Djahy at the bedside of an old servant whose testimony had helped him solve a gruesome murder.

But his wife caressed his face with a fond hand. "No,

Hani. I'm just proud that you're a man who would surrender his own protection to help a dying slave."

Hani folded her in his arms and kissed the top of her head. "Thank you, my dove," he murmured. "This must have cost quite a lot."

But Neferet interrupted, catching hold of his arm, "I was the one who had it made, Papa. Lord Ptah-mes said I could do it, even though it was expensive."

Hani recalled that In-hapy had told him long ago that Neferet's order was ready—he'd completely forgotten to pass that message along. Now he knew what the order had been for. Touched and grateful, he put an arm around his daughter and folded Bener-ib in with her. "Thank you, my girls. It's a priceless gift."

"After that stupid business on the street the other morning, I was afraid for you, Papa," Neferet said with feeling. "Somebody's after you."

Sobered, Hani said, "Or after you two. Don't let down your guard."

Nub-nefer helped him lay the gold cord over his head, and he tucked the amulet under his shirt. Almost immediately, its cool stone began to warm against his skin as the goddess claimed him for her own.

"Are you young ladies here for the festival?" he asked the two doctors.

Neferet beamed, a little sly. "Yes. We figured if the crowd got unruly, as it has lately, we could at least mend broken heads. Lady Djefat-nebty said we could come."

"I'm trying to convince them not to go out tomorrow," Baket-iset said. "Two women alone with everybody drunk..."

"But Pa-kiki and Mut-nodjmet are coming with us. Maybe Sati and Maya. We'll be re-e-edoubtable!"

Hani agreed with Baket-iset that it was a bad idea for them to be abroad in an uninhibited nighttime crowd. The setting would cloak any attack their unknown persecutor might spring on them. Still, he said nothing, just blew out a heavy breath.

"They're grownups, Hani. I've told them if things get out of control to get home as fast as can be." Nub-nefer tried to hide her anxiety, but Hani perceived it. She, too, was trying to be reasonable despite her misgivings.

"Very well, my duckling. I leave it to you to find the phallus clappers—or carve some."

Neferet laughed, baring the winsome gap between her teeth. "We're heading to the storage room right now."

The two girls scampered off to look for the holiday apparatuses, and Hani and Nub-nefer were left alone, each with an arm around the other's waist.

"Should we send one of the servants out after them just to be sure they're safe?" Nub-nefer asked under her breath.

"I think Hani and I should go along at a discreet distance," said Mery-ra from behind them.

Hani turned to his father—he'd forgotten the old man was present. He pondered the suggestion, but he didn't much like the idea of dragging a beloved elder out into a drunken crowd. "I don't know, Father. Maybe some strapping young servants would be better."

"I should think they'd rather be out enjoying themselves, son. This festival is mostly for young people."

Hani and Nub-nefer exchanged a look. He was a little anxious but close to being convinced. "Maybe Bin-addi could go with you," Nub-nefer suggested hesitantly. The stable man wasn't much past thirty, and he was certainly stalwart. "As a foreigner, he probably doesn't care about the revelry in honor of Hut-haru."

"All right, Father. We'll stay far enough back that they can't see us but close enough to intervene if there's a problem." It occurred to him that if there *was* a problem, poor Bener-ib might be traumatized back into her painful mistrust. He fingered his new amulet with a heartfelt prayer.

⊠

That evening, Maya and Sat-hut-haru came to the house, eager to get away from the children for a night of adult celebration. Along with Pa-kiki and Mut-nodjmet and Neferet and her friend, they armed themselves with clappers and a wineskin and trooped merrily into the garden. Maya shot a curious look at Hani, who was standing a little too quietly nearby with Mery-ra, but said nothing.

"Sati, my love, be careful," called Nub-nefer. "You don't want to lose the baby somehow."

"Don't worry, my lady," Maya assured his mother-in-law. "I'll take care of her."

A'a let the young people out the gate, and Hani could hear their laughter and the clacking of their clappers as they made their way down the street. It was still early, and not too many revelers had turned out yet, but hoots and salacious cries were breaking out in the distance as twilight descended.

Hani caught his father's eye. "Now, before they get too far ahead of us."

With Bin-addi at their heels, the two men slid out

into the growing festal crowd. They were without weapons because Hani was afraid that going armed into the celebration might attract trouble. In previous years since the coronation of Nefer-khepru-ra, a hostile atmosphere had replaced the usual uninhibited fun, and merrymakers had devolved into something not much better than a destructive mob. He kept his eyes darting between the laughing group of young people ahead of him and the swirling mass of celebrants that grew and grew as they neared the center of the city. A pair of hilariously drunken partygoers shook their clappers under Hani's nose and sang loud snatches of a bawdy song as they passed, reeling.

"I must be getting old," Mery-ra said under his breath, "but this seems a lot less entertaining than it used to. I'd rather just get drunk at home and fall asleep until the drums wake me at midnight." He elbowed Hani affectionately. "Although it may or may not be coincidence that you were born nine months after this date."

Hani smiled, distracted. Something had drawn his attention. Leaning over the parapet of a roof terrace was a figure he could barely see in the thickening evening. He was tall and heavyset. At the foot of the house wall, another man with a torch stood, gesticulating upward as if the two of them were in conversation. He, too, was a big barrel-shaped fellow, but the brand he held was too far away from his face to give Hani any ideas about his appearance. Hani couldn't hear their voices, but as the lower speaker's torchlight caught the face of the man on the roof, Hani realized there was something familiar about him. *Who is that? I've seen him before.* Yet he could think of none of his acquaintances who would live in this modest neighborhood. He stared at the terrace, his mind sorting rapidly through his memories for something relevant. The man stepped away from the parapet and fell back into the darkness.

"Come on, my boy. They're getting ahead of us." Mery-ra tugged at his elbow, and Hani followed him, still preoccupied.

Ahead, Neferet was clapping her clapper zealously in everyone's face. The men, on the other hand, surrounded their wives and sisters for protection as the festivities heated up. Girls threw off their clothes in abandon. Wild whoops of joy and arousal sounded here and there as the torch-bearing crowd swirled, shaking sistrums and beating on handheld drums. Hani realized that the youngsters were moving in a general way toward the embarcadero. His throat tightening, he remembered how rude and inebriated the boatmen could become and hoped the children knew what they were doing.

Mery-ra yelled over the noise, "They're heading toward the River. Every year, people fall in and are eaten by crocodiles and hippopotamuses, who are only too happy to have a nip of marinated meat."

"I think we need to steer them away."

The men began to push their way forward, but the partygoers around them seemed irritated by their urgency. "*Iyah!* Stop shoving, old man!" someone shouted and shoved back.

Mery-ra staggered awkwardly against Hani, a scowl on his face. "Whatever happened to 'Do not revile one older than you'?" he muttered.

Hani was becoming more and more concerned for his

father but even more for the children, who had disappeared into the press. He craned his neck and caught sight of Pa-kiki's head some twenty cubits away. "Bin-addi, catch up to the youngsters and tell them we're trying to get to them."

The servant pushed off, wielding his elbows against the crush of half-dressed people. In the flickering torchlight, it was hard to tell if the mood was uninhibited celebration or something closer to resentment. Hani was almost sure that there would be provocateurs among the crowd—for those opposed to the government, the chance to stir up some trouble in anonymity would be too good to miss.

Ahead, Hani glimpsed Pa-kiki's head swivel as Bin-addi drew abreast. Of the girls and Maya, he could see nothing at all. He and Mery-ra forced their way forward, and Pa-kiki, spying them, waved, his face anxious.

At last, Hani was able to put a hand on his son's arm. "Let's get out of here. I'm not sure there isn't going to be violence," he yelled over the din.

Maya, on the other side of the young women, looked frankly afraid. "This wasn't a good idea. We can't let anything happen to the girls."

Even Neferet was a little wild-eyed. "Papa, we're trying to get to Lord Ptah-mes's boat. We'll be safe once we're on the water."

Hani, the sweat beading his brow, just hoped the vessel was at the embarcadero and that Ptah-mes hadn't gone off to the capital or docked it at his private landing. He and his father linked arms and brought up the rear of the group while Bin-addi tried to clear a way.

They were near the River now, and Hani could see the forest of slender masts swaying with the current, lit by a lurid glare that had to be a fire—whether a bonfire or something more sinister, he couldn't be sure. Hands reached out to touch the well-endowed Mut-nodjmet and the beautiful Sati, who clung to her husband's grasp, tears in her eyes. There was an ugliness in the people around them—angry, perhaps, that the changes they'd hoped for at the death of Nefer-khepru-ra had yet to be implemented. The Thebans had lost more to the Atenist revolution than anyone.

The docks were full of people but not yet in the same number as farther inland. Sure enough, a small fishing boat that had been drawn up on the shore had been set on fire. By its flickering red light, Hani saw wild dancing and couples lurching off into the darkness. *Maya was right. This was a terrible idea.* Hand in hand, the little party scurried toward the River's edge, Hani scanning the horizon for a sight of Ptah-mes's yacht.

"There it is," yelled Neferet, pointing with the hand that still held her clapper.

They veered downriver, and Hani saw, in the darkness, the majestic silhouette of the great black-and-green boat with its tall papyrus-shaped stern. There were torches on board, he noticed with relief—a crew was present who could take them safely away from the bank. Hani was almost panting, and he could hear Mery-ra's sawing breath as they pounded down to the water's edge where the boat lay rocking.

"*Iyah!*" he shouted, waving his arms. "It's your mistress and her family. Let down the gangplank, for the love of all the gods!"

The silhouetted figures on the deck burst into action,

and the plank crashed out onto the land. Behind him, Hani heard yells and drunken imprecations. He turned around quickly, only to see a small gang of men armed with pales and the legs of broken furniture running toward them.

"Hurry, hurry!" he said, gasping. "Let the women up first!" He and Bin-addi hung back in case anyone tried to stop them.

At last, they clattered up the ribbed planks, stumbling over one another in their haste, and tumbled breathlessly upon the deck. Sat-hut-haru was whimpering with fear, her arms wrapped around herself as if to protect the baby. At Hani's heels, the sailors lifted the gangway just as the group of half-naked men, shouting and whistling, threw themselves into the shallow water—but the men's attempt was in vain. The yacht's crew had lifted its stone anchors, and it glided serenely into the stream as the sail filled.

Hani mopped his face, weak-kneed with relief, and looked up. Before him stood Ptah-mes. His demeanor was cool and elegant as always, but his eyes held a flicker of concern.

"My lord! Thanks be to the Great One you had your boat docked here," cried Hani.

Neferet threw herself upon her husband with such force he staggered. "Oh, thank you, Lord Ptah-mes! I don't know what would have happened to us if the boat hadn't been there!"

Stiffening, Ptah-mes looked nonplussed by her hug, and Hani would have sworn his face grew red. After a long uncomfortable moment, the grandee laid a tentative hand on the girl's back. "Thank the gods you're all safe," he murmured, seeking Hani's eyes nervously as if afraid he might see disapproval for touching his friend's daughter. "Neferet said she and her brother and sisters were going to join the celebrations, and I began to think it wouldn't hurt to be ready at hand. There's been some agitation here tonight—clearly the work of instigators."

"I was sure of it," Mery-ra said with feeling. "This wasn't just the usual holiday crowd. It was more like that mob the year we had riots."

"I suggest we return to my house and have a servant take Lady Nub-nefer a message telling her of your safety," Ptah-mes said. "It's too dangerous to try to get back inland to your place tonight."

"My thanks, my lord. Once again, you've helped my family," Hani said.

A thin smile twitched at the corner of Ptah-mes's mouth. "You mean *our* family?"

The young people drifted off to the other side of the boat to chatter and watch the dark water glittering under a half-moon.

Maya stayed back. "Well, Lord Hani, your fears were certainly founded. That was a terrible moment. It's a good thing you and Lord Mery-ra were behind us," he said, removing his wig and mopping his brow.

"You know, Lord Ptah-mes, I'm almost sure I saw Pentju tonight," Hani said under his breath. "Or maybe I'm completely wrong…"

"What would he be doing in Waset? I thought his family is from Sau."

"That's what I wonder. Whoever it was, he was talking to some fellow from the terrace of a modest house in the center city—not the sort of place a man of Pentju's status would be expected to visit."

Ptah-mes's arched eyebrows drew down. "Curious. I have no light to shed on that, Hani."

The four men stood gazing out at the torch-spangled shore of the city. The moon had not yet risen, and overhead stretched the milky River of stars, while raucous cries and drumbeats echoed across the water. Hani was still tense, thinking of Nub-nefer and Baket-iset at home alone, defended by no one but the servants, and Pa-kiki's and Sati's children in the care of their nurses. Hani's stomach clenched. Pressing a fist to his new amulet, he prayed fervently that the mob would stay localized in the city center and not spill over into the southern suburbs. He could see Maya's face fixed grimly on the shore and suspected he was having much the same thoughts.

"So, tell me, Hani. How are your lessons with the crown prince going?" Ptah-mes said after a while.

Hani forced himself to act cheerful. "Well, my lord. He and his little friends are lively, but they have fun using Akkadian as a secret code among themselves. There's one youngster who is especially good. He's a serious lad, about eleven, I should think—Amen-mes son of Djehuty-mes. I don't know his family."

Ptah-mes was silent, his face frozen. Then he said with a bitter twist of the lips, "But you do, Hani. He's my grandson."

Hani gaped at him, distracted from his concerns about the girls. "Your grandson?" he echoed stupidly.

"Yes. The youngest child of my firstborn—the one who turned on me because I accommodated the Atenist regime.

And here is his son, sent to grow up in the Kap together with the heretic's heir. I suppose the temptation to cultivate familiarity with a future ruler is too much for Djehuty-mes's idealism to resist."

How painful, Hani thought. "But that's not the boy's fault, my lord. He seems like a fine little fellow."

"I wouldn't know," said Ptah-mes acidly. "I've never seen him."

Hani became aware that the boat was angling toward the shore, and he was glad to leave this uncomfortable topic behind. The private jetty behind Ptah-mes's villa was lit by torches. Amid a dancing twinkle of light on the water that made it seem they were breasting the starry sky, the boat slid into its berth. The sailors heaved out the anchors and cast the painter to shore for their fellows to secure. As soon as the gangplank was out, Hani and his family followed their host to the land.

CHAPTER 11

THE NEXT MORNING, HANI AND Maya grabbed a bite of breakfast in Ptah-mes's garden pavilion. Hani was gazing in thoughtful distraction at his host's long pool, where the ducks—despite the manicured splendor around them—behaved like any ducks, messy and undisciplined.

"Ah, you're up already, my friends," said Ptah-mes as he emerged around the bushes and took a seat beside them. "You should have a quiet walk back—the revelers will all be sleeping off a hangover." He laid upon the table the chunk of bread he'd brought with him and began to break off pieces as if preparing to feed the birds.

"I've been thinking, my lord. Trying to make some sense of what's been happening. Perhaps I've forgotten to tell you this: the man who attacked the girls in the street also bought orpiment from a merchant in Akhet-aten. The old man said the fellow was the servant of a rich household."

"Well done, Hani," said Ptah-mes with a caustic twitch of the mouth. "As if the king weren't dangerous enough, you've incurred the anger of the rich."

Hani chuckled ruefully. "If only I knew *whose* servant, I would have a better idea of who was out to get Neferet and Bener-ib. It must be someone who had something to do with the exchange of babies. Maybe the same man is guilty of murdering the midwife. The lady-in-waiting seems to have died of natural causes. Although"—the thought struck him—"perhaps she died of the slow poisoning everyone else in the king's intimate household seems to be suffering from. As Ankhet-khepru-ra's dresser, she must have handled the jewel boxes and mirrors more than anyone."

Ptah-mes nodded, his mouth pursed thoughtfully, his eyes fixed unseeing on the distance. "Do we have one crime here or more than one?"

"I honestly don't know, my lord. You mean, are the poisonings intended to remove all the witnesses to the exchange of babies?"

Ptah-mes lifted an arched eyebrow.

Hani revolved this possibility in his mind. Neferet's description had suggested that there were few actual witnesses, although a bevy of handmaids hovering outside the door might easily have gotten wind of it. *I don't know what to think. I need to find out who that scar-cheeked servant belonged to.* "As soon as my father and Pa-kiki and the girls are up, we'll get out from under your feet, my lord. I want to go back to the capital to do a little snooping. For one thing, I'd like to know what Nakht-ef-mut was carrying when he was killed. Lord Pentju said something about having his—Pentju's—name on him. So there must have been a document, a letter of some kind. Who do you think would have his effects?"

"His widow, I suppose. Wasn't she on her way up here when he was murdered?"

Hani agreed that it was likely. He suddenly felt more hopeful. This could give him a new line of investigation, though Pentju's presence in Waset the night before still troubled him—if it had really been Pentju.

"Come on, Maya," he said, rising. "Let's go wake the family."

⊠

Nub-nefer greeted her husband as if she'd never expected to see him again. "Thank the gods you and the children are all right, Hani," she cried, throwing herself into his arms. "I'm so glad you sent us a message. We heard what sounded like rioting, and I was worried. The grandchildren were all here with their nurses—they just left this morning."

"You did well to gather them here, my dove. The servants would have protected you all." He held her to him, basking in her warmth and perfume. "The youngsters should never have risked going out into that drunken crowd."

"At least everyone is home now, safe."

Hani wondered just how safe Neferet and Bener-ib were, but he said only, "I can't stay long. I need to get back to Akhet-aten. I may finally have an idea for pursuing Nakht-ef-mut's murder."

Nub-nefer's face fell. Still, she was used to Hani's departures. "I understand. But I wish we could have you back for at least a few days, my love." She caressed his face hopefully with henna-tipped fingers.

"With any luck, I'll be back soon." He took her palm and kissed it.

A brief while later, Hani heard voices in the vestibule, and Maya appeared in the doorway. "Whenever you're ready, my lord."

They set off for the quay. "I want to talk to Nakht-ef-mut's widow and also the man who found him in the street," Hani said.

"Wasn't it that woman, the weaver?" Maya asked.

"She said a man rushed out right behind her, so maybe he, too, saw something from his terrace. There was a reason he came outside, surely. Just the sound of someone crying out would hardly be unusual in a busy city."

Maya nodded thoughtfully, and the two scribes made their way in silence toward the riverside.

⧗

In the late morning, five days later, the men disembarked and left their baggage in Ptah-mes's "modest place" in the capital. From there, they headed for the working-class neighborhoods south of the palace magazines, not far from the River. Up the narrow backstreet they marched with their mismatched strides. The area was crowded with people at that hour—boys making deliveries, workmen with their tools on their backs, women with baskets of bread balanced on their heads, and the inevitable donkeys. Maya vastly preferred this real part of the city to the broad, arid processional boulevard, which looked soulless without some pageant taking place.

They came to the house of the weaver. Maya could see the woman's head above the low parapet of her terrace, leaning over and leaning back rhythmically as she wove.

Lord Hani called up to her pleasantly, "Mistress, can we have a word with you?"

At his side, Maya planted himself, feet boldly apart, arms akimbo, looking as implacable as he could. Perhaps a little fear would spur the woman to talk if his father-in-law's affability didn't work. But the woman came to the edge, and her worn young face brightened. No doubt, she remembered that the scribes had made it worth her while to talk.

In her gritty voice, she yelled, "Be right down." She emerged from her gate with something approaching a smile. "My lords. How can I serve you?"

"Do you know the man who joined you in the street the night the priest was killed on your block?" Hani unobtrusively slipped her a bag of grain, and her hand closed around the mouth and moved it behind her.

"Of course. He lives right there." She pointed at a shabby house with a large courtyard from which a mixed aroma of barmy fermentation and the heavenly scent of baking bread wafted.

"A baker?"

"Has a brewery too. He employs quite a few people, although you'd never guess it from the state of his place."

"I think I'd like to talk to him."

She shrugged. "His name's Haya."

Hani and Maya thanked her and crossed the street, making their way through the stream of pedestrians as best they could. In the gate of the courtyard, several people stood, pot-shaped loaves of bread under their arms, chatting in a neighborly way with a man whose natural short-cropped hair revealed a bald pate. His cheeks were fiery red as if he'd stuck his head into his oven. The two scribes waited politely until the knot of customers drifted off.

Before the man could retreat into his house, Hani approached Haya, raising a hand. "Could we have a word with you, my friend?"

Haya looked up. He had a friendly, good-humored face, but there was a tinge of suspicion there too. "If you're looking for beer, come in. If it's bread you want, a fresh load will be ready shortly, my lord. Come back around lunchtime," he said, but his expression was suspicious. He clearly guessed that the two well-dressed men approaching him weren't after bread.

Hani introduced himself with a wide, gap-toothed smile that would have melted anyone's suspicions. "My name is Hani son of Mery-ra. I'm in the king's service—life, prosperity, and health to her."

The man looked unimpressed. In fact, Maya was sure his lip curled a bit at the end. "I suppose you're here about that man who was killed in the street a while back."

"That's right, my friend. Did you happen to catch a glimpse of the person who stabbed him?" Lord Hani asked, slipping a pair of inexpensive faience earrings into Haya's hand. Maya noticed he didn't use the word *man* or *woman*.

"Come inside, my lords," the brewer said, and the two men set off into his establishment.

The courtyard was filled with women. Some laboriously pounded grain to crack it in tall wooden mortars. Others were hunched over stone querns, grinding the cracked barley and wheat fine until a mist of flour hung in the air, whitening the workers. Men carried heavy jars back and forth or poured their contents through strainers into other jars. Toward the visitors floated a yeasty smell mixed with honey, and Maya snuffed with appreciation.

Seeing Hani's and Maya's interest, Haya said proudly, "This is top-rate beer. You don't even need a strainer to drink it—you can drink it right out of a cup. We add honey or dates to some of it, so it's like the stuff the king drinks. You won't find any better."

As they approached the door of the house, they passed long firepits, where men were stacking fresh wood in the bottom, preparing to relight for the afternoon's loaves. An array of pots stood against the wall, filled with rising dough. Maya, who had never given a thought to how beer was made or why it was often in the same establishment as a bakery, craned his head around to see everything.

The men passed inside the house, where the light and noise dropped off. It took a moment for Maya's eyes to adjust. The brewer bade the two scribes have a seat on a low masonry bench along one wall while he settled himself cross-legged on the floor, and suddenly, the little salon felt crowded. "I may've seen him, sure enough. I was on the roof terrace—it was around dinnertime—just leanin' over the edge, taking a breath of fresh air. Gets pretty murky down in the court all day, what with the fire and the flour and the heavy smell of yeast."

Lord Hani nodded sympathetically.

"It was late, and nobody was in the street, just a man walkin' past fast. But I didn't pay no notice to him except to see his head was shaven." He spread his hands as if in apology for observing such a thing. "I was looking straight down on him, you understand."

Maya thought approvingly, *The more observant you are, the better, my man.*

"And then I saw another person comin' up pretty fast behind him, with a big rock in his hands—big as my fist—and before I could even cry out to warn the bald fellow, the other man had thrown the rock at him. It hit with the sound of a melon being split, my lord, and the first man gave a big cry and dropped in his tracks. My eyes was buggin' out of my head by that time, believe me. Then the man who had pitched the rock threw hisself on the bald man lying in the street and stabbed him over and over." Haya drew a shaking hand across his forehead. "I was just struck dumb. I've never seen anything happen like that. Never seen anybody killed."

"I'm sure it was terrible," Hani agreed, his tufty eyebrows crumpled in sympathy. "Do you think the victim was already dead after the rock hit him?"

"No, my lord. He was still movin' a little, as if to get to his feet, before the big fellow punched holes in him. By that time, I'd come to my senses and yelled like anything. I started down the stairs two at a time and ran out into the street. The man was runnin' away by then and turned a corner as if to go down to the riverbank. One of the neighbors was just comin' out her door, and we both knelt there over the body, then I called the watchman."

Hani and Maya exchanged a look of suppressed excitement. "Did you get a glimpse of the murderer, master?"

"Not real good—only at the beginnin', when he was holdin' the rock, before I knew anything bad was going to happen. So I wasn't payin' all that much attention."

"But you did see him?" Hani pressed.

"Yes, my lord. A sturdy-lookin' fellow, maybe in his thirties, with this big scar down the side of his cheek and a kind of saggin' eyelid, like he'd been slashed in the face."

Maya's heart leapt to his throat. *The same man who attacked Lord Hani and the girls!*

Hani sat in silence for a moment, then he asked, "Did you tell the watchman this, Haya?"

"He never asked, my lord. The police come around later, and I said to them what I said to you, but they sort of pooh-poohed it. Didn't seem interested at all."

No, Maya thought contemptuously. *Mahu already knew who he wanted to blame, so he had no interest in any testimony that disproved it. The scum.* But that made him wonder why Mahu's men seemed to have lost interest in Bener-ib and Neferet after Hani had sprung them from the police tower. No doubt the king had put him under orders.

"Anything else you can remember?" Hani asked.

The man twisted his mouth and scratched his balding skull. "Can't think of nothing."

Hani got to his feet, and Maya and their host followed. "If anything comes to mind, leave a message with Lord Ptah-mes. I believe he calls himself Maya now. His villa is in the southern suburbs."

The brewer bobbed up and down, fingering the earrings Hani had given him. Then he looked up with a worried frown. "Nobody's gonna say *I* did it, are they?"

"No, no," Hani assured him. "We'll find that man you saw, and everything will be fine."

He and Maya made their way back through the

courtyard and out the gate. Once in the street, they stared at one another.

"We can't find the man, can we, Lord Hani? He's dead."

"True, but let our friend Haya be comforted by the thought that we will. It seems the scar-faced gentleman was busy in his last few days. He bought orpiment, he killed Nakht-ef-mut, and he attacked me and the girls. What ties all these things together, I wonder?"

"Well, the poisonings seem to link the pigment and the murder. But how do Neferet and Bener-ib get into the picture? Could it be they're not being stalked because of the baby switch after all, as Lord Ptah-mes suggested?" Maya pushed back his wig and scratched his head.

"I wish I knew." Hani brightened, with a determined hitching up of his kilt. "Let's go find Nakht-ef-mut's wife."

As they strode along, Maya pondered the fact that they had no idea where she might be. Hani seemed to have something definite in mind, however.

"Where are we heading, my lord?"

"Pentju's. They'll certainly know where their friend's widow is staying."

⊠

The sun was strong and warm by the time the two men stood at the red-painted door of the physicians' residence. The porter finally bade them enter, and they made their way into the elegant salon, now grown familiar. Little by little, the new decorations were proceeding. More of the murals had been whitewashed out. Hani saw Lady Djefat-nebty standing at the foot of the dais.

She came toward them, her face as severely expressionless as always. "What can I do for you, Hani?"

"My lady, as you know, I'm trying to get to the bottom of Lord Nakht-ef-mut's murder. I thought it might be helpful to talk to his widow. I wondered if you knew whether she's here in Akhet-aten yet and where she might be staying."

The *sunet* nodded. "She's here. In this house. I can have her summoned for you."

She called a servant, who disappeared into the back of the house and a moment later returned with a plump little woman in a short curly wig, who looked younger than her late husband. She had on a white mourning scarf and seemed unable to stand still without dashing at her eyes, blowing her nose, or clasping and unclasping her hands.

Looking from Djefat-nebty to Hani, she asked, "What's this about? The police have already talked to me."

Her hostess said evenly, "The king isn't satisfied with their identification of the murderer. Lord Hani has some questions for you." She excused herself and left.

"My name is Hani son of Mery-ra, my lady. First, I offer my condolences on the loss of your husband. It must have been a terrible shock."

"And then to find out that awful daughter of his did it..."

Hani bit back a response and said instead, "I'd like to ask you a few questions, if I may."

"I'm Sit-ah," she said, looking at him with suspicion. "I don't know anything about it. I wasn't even in the capital when it happened." Her little beak of a mouth trembled, and she dropped her eyes and wrung her hands.

"I was told the police found something on Lord Nakht-ef-mut that made them bring the news of his death here to Pentju—something with Pentju's name on it. It occurred to me that they probably gave you his effects, and I wondered if you still have them."

She broke out in a raw, fervent voice, "I burned every bit of his clothes, all covered with blood like that. Do you think I wanted to see those things and have to remember how he died?" She dabbed at her eyes with the back of a plump hand. "But there was a little piece of papyrus in his purse, yes. I can show it to you if you want."

"That would be most generous, my lady."

She turned and walked quickly from the room. Hani and Maya exchanged a look.

"She still thinks Bener-ib did it," Maya whispered.

Hani nodded noncommittally. He opened his mouth to speak, but Sit-ah had returned and approached him with her hand outstretched, a piece of papyrus in her fist.

"You can see it, but I want to keep it. It's the last thing he ever wrote."

Hani looked at the papyrus. It was a small square that might have been snipped from the margin of something larger. Three words were written on it: *Pentju and Djefat-nebty.*

That's all? Hani was confused and more than a little disappointed. He stared at the words, trying to fix in his memory the distinctive scribal hand of the dead man, assuming it was even his. "That's very helpful, my lady. Thank you. There was nothing else?"

"He had quite a bit of silver on him when he started off, I'm told, but you can be sure there was nothing left when they found him." Her voice grew higher, and she began to sniffle. "I don't know what to do. I don't have any friends here. I guess I'll go back to Sau and live with my children."

"Bener-ib is here in the capital. No doubt she—"

"No!" cried Sit-ah shrilly, almost spitting with vehemence. "Live with my husband's murderer? Never. She's humiliated and divided the family enough."

Hani forced himself not to respond. Maya's eyebrows had drawn down ominously. "I apologize for reopening your grief, my lady. Unless you have anything to say, that will be all."

She nodded curtly, her eyes starting to overflow, and hurried away.

Before Hani and Maya could make their own departure, Lady Djefat-nebty appeared once more. "Don't worry about her abruptness, Hani. She's barely in control of herself."

"I understand—no offense taken. With your permission, we'll be going now, my lady." Hani and Maya followed the *sunet* to the door. Suddenly, Hani remembered something that had all but slipped his mind. "Was Lord Pentju in Waset about the time of the Feast of Drunkenness?"

Djefat-nebty's eyebrows rose in surprise. "Waset? No. He went to Sau, to start preparing our home for our return."

Hani and Maya bowed their way out, and as soon as they stood once more in the street, Hani murmured to himself, "In Sau? Then I must have mistaken someone else for him."

"You notice how the stepmother assumes Bener-ib is guilty?" Maya said with a sneer. "She'd like her to be so she can get rid of her forever. I bet Nakht-ef-mut left the girl most of his property."

Hani shot his secretary a sharp, admiring look. "I never

thought of that. Do you think Sit-ah might have paid to have her husband murdered and might even be the one trying to kill the girls? The assailant was the same person both times." The thought appealed to him, although it completely undid every idea he'd had up to that point. *Still, what about the orpiment?* "We need to figure out whose household that servant belonged to and how a woman from the Lower Kingdom would have been able to connect with him."

"Maybe he only pretended to be someone's servant. Maybe he's just some killer for hire."

They fell silent as Lady Djefat-nebty emerged from the gate with her big physician's basket. She nodded at them and, in her long, brisk stride, marched off down the street. Hani stared after her. She looked competent and determined. *She's a strong woman. I hope the girls are up to being royal physicians without her supervision.* And then he thought, with a shiver up his neck, *Could she be the poisoner? But she's a follower of the Aten. What possible motive could she have?*

⊠

Hani and Maya walked the not-too-great distance back to Ptah-mes's house and headed for the garden pavilion. Hani plopped down in one of the chairs with a *whoosh* and stretched out his legs, while Maya hoicked himself onto a stool. The steward came hustling out of the house and bowed. "Would my lord care for any refreshment? Lord Maya said to tell you he has some date beer you might like."

"Yes, my friend. Thank you. That sounds like just the thing."

The man headed back into the house and Hani said to Maya with a twinkle, "What do you bet that beer was made by our friend, Haya?"

They watched in silent anticipation as a serving girl brought them a ewer and two tall cups—not a pot and straws. She poured each of them a big draft and then melted discreetly back into the house. Hani lifted his cup and sipped, eager. He almost swooned with delight as the rich, sweet liquid caressed his tongue. "This is splendid, Maya. So that's what the king drinks, eh?" He took another draft of the beer and let it sit inside his mouth. It was nearly syrupy, but there were no impurities—the beverage was clean and smooth as fresh bedsheets.

In wordless admiration, the two men drank. The majordomo reappeared and seemed anxious. "Does it please my lordship?"

"It does indeed. Your master has unimpeachable taste."

A thought came to Hani. "How well do the servants of one great house know those of other households?"

"That depends, my lord. Literate people like myself tend not to be familiar with the lower sort of servants. But I can ask around among the staff if you want me to. Who are you interested in knowing about? There might be someone here acquainted with him."

Hani's hope surged up like the Flood waters, but he managed to say evenly, "I don't know his name. He's a sturdy-looking fellow with a long scar up his cheek and a drooping eyelid. Probably about thirty or so."

The majordomo listened attentively, his hands folded at the waist. When he'd digested the description, he replied,

"I'll ask, Lord Hani. You don't know which household he serves, do you?"

"No," Hani said with a smile. "That's what I'm trying to figure out."

The servant bowed and departed for the house.

"Do you think we may find our murderer this way, my lord?" Cradling his cup in his hands, Maya leaned forward eagerly toward his father-in-law.

Hani shrugged, not altogether optimistic. "That may be too good to be true. But we need to turn over every stone."

⊠

It wasn't until the next morning that the steward approached Hani once more, a young woman in tow. "My lord, this girl may know your man."

Hani and Maya exchanged a hopeful glance.

The young servant looked at Hani nervously. She wasn't especially pretty, being a bit snub-nosed, but she had the freshness of youth and a nice figure. Her eyes were meticulously made up. She was probably a welcome ornament, handing out flowers at Ptah-mes's parties—although as far as Hani could tell, his friend hadn't had any parties since this girl was a toddler.

A soon as the steward had taken his leave, Hani said kindly, "Tell me, my dear, what you know about this man."

"If it's him, his name is Ba-ba-ef, my lord. We were going to be married." She lowered her eyes, and her mouth turned down unhappily. "But he left without a word. I guess I wasn't pretty enough for him."

Ah, poor girl. "He hasn't left you voluntarily," he said gently. "I'm afraid he has flown into the West."

The servant gave a cry, which she stifled with a hand over her mouth. Her eyes widened in horror and then grew sparkly with tears.

"Can you tell me anything about Ba-ba-ef? Where you met him? What he did? Where he was employed?" Hani regretted having to prod the unfortunate girl, but she seemed to be holding up pretty well. He hoped the knowledge that her lover had not jilted her after all was a consolation.

"He was a little rough-edged, my lord—that's what everyone said. Quick to get into a fight. That's where he got that scar—in a knife fight. My parents weren't so keen on him. But he was always sweet and gentle around me." She sniffed plaintively.

"What did he do?"

"He was a laundryman, my lord. I can't remember who for, but it wasn't for a business. He worked for some rich man and seemed to be very well paid—he always showed me a good time. We met at the riverbank once. I had gone down to cut some reeds for Lord Maya, and Ba-ba-ef was washing clothes. We flirted a little and met again and then started getting serious."

"Do you know if he hired himself out for other sorts of jobs than laundering? He was a well-built fellow." Hani hoped she would say that her beau did occasional assassinations, but it was unlikely that she would be aware of it.

"I don't know, my lord," she said. "Frankly, I didn't ask too many questions. Maybe not enough. We saw each other for five years at least, but I don't really know that much about him."

Despite Hani's prodding, the servant had no other information to share about the scarred man. At last, Hani let her go with a sincere "I'm sorry for your loss, my girl. If you should remember anything else, please let me know."

She bowed her way out, and Maya turned to Hani with a sneer. "A murder, an attempted murder, and purchasing poison? I'd say he *was* a little rough-edged."

"Well," Hani said mildly, "we're not altogether sure this was our man. There must be plenty of people with scars. What we need to know is who sent him on those missions. Regarding the orpiment, he might well have known nothing about how toxic it was and simply been following orders. People do use it for a pigment."

Maya gave a skeptical snort. "What do we do next, Lord Hani?"

"Let's lay out what we know and see if anything jumps out at us."

Maya seated himself on the ground and rifled through his writing case for a potsherd. When he'd prepared his ink and a pen, he looked up. "Ready my lord."

"First, we have the thefts of household articles from the queen's chambers. We know that the goal seems to have been to poison them and return them to their original places, where their use would slowly sicken the king and her ladies. Maybe her dresser already succumbed."

"And our friend Ba-ba-ef is involved in that? Do you think he works for the poisoner?"

"That's what it looks like, but we can't be altogether sure. It does seem likely that Nakht-ef-mut was murdered because he knew something about it. Or was it because his wife wanted to secure her inheritance? Or was Bener-ib trying to protect herself from her father's cruel good intentions? It may have had nothing to do with his reporting the poisonings as we've assumed."

"And what about the exchange of babies?" Maya asked. "Is that no longer an issue?"

Hani heaved a big, anxious gust of air. "I think it *is* still an issue. The midwife was clearly murdered, and the girls seem to be targeted. As for the queen and Lady Djefat-nebty, one can only hope they're protected. Although we know both Lady Meryet-aten and the God's Father Ay stand to lose if the information comes out—Ay if word is leaked that the crown prince isn't Ankhet-khepru-ra's son, and Meryet-aten if anyone should learn the lad really is her half brother. Meryet-aten may well be behind the murder and attempted murder."

"But didn't you say you never told the queen about the girl's real parentage?"

Hani stared pensively into his lap. "You're right. Although she could have known from some other source. But if Ba-ba-ef attacked the girls, then his master must be the one wanting to hide the baby switch. Do you think the poisonings are aimed at the same thing?"

Maya widened his eyes uneasily. "What if *you* were the target of that attack in the street, my lord, and not the girls?"

Hani was somber. "If so, we must be getting close to something important, something that worries the perpetrator of the switch or of the poisoning. Maybe they're the same person." He leaned forward, his forearms on his knees. "And what is it we know about either? What person has a connection with both events? How could someone smuggle the queen's objects in and out without being seen? Is it Meryet-aten? Is it... is it Bener-ib?"

"It could just as easily be Neferet or Djefat-nebty, my lord. The big baskets they carry would hide a lot— remember how Neferet brought you some of the things to look at? Or it could be some other tradesman the handmaids mentioned."

Hani pursed his mouth in pained thought. *Could it possibly be Neferet? She takes her healing so seriously I can't imagine her doing a patient harm. And if she had something to hide, it would show on her face. Djefat-nebty? She has nothing to gain by concealing the baby switch.*

No, the obvious candidate was Queen Meryet-aten. "But she wouldn't want to kill me," Hani murmured. "She wanted me to bring her Hittite to her."

"Who's that, my lord?"

"The queen. Both events seem to be pointing to her. In which case, it was definitely not me they were trying to kill but the girls." Hani stood up and stretched painfully. He felt as if he'd been sitting in a cramped cage for months, with the same few suppositions fluttering around him, squawking and shitting on him. "Actually, that wouldn't surprise me. But I'm not sure I want to call her out to Lord Ay, even though he'll expect some sort of resolution sooner or later."

Maya ranged his writing tools and scrambled to his feet. "So, what do we do now, my lord?"

"I can't help thinking that Nakht-ef-mut may be a clue.

What did he know, and how did a newcomer find it out? Who did he talk to the evening of the murder?"

"We know he talked to his daughter. He must have talked to Pentju." Maya scratched his head in confusion. "And maybe he knew something even before he came up here."

Hani remembered the mysterious paper in Nakht-ef-mut's purse. *Pentju and Djefat-nebty.* Did that mean something, or was it just notation of the house where he was quartered? "Pentju and the *wab* priest apparently had an argument before Nakht-ef-mut left the house to warn the king about the poisoning attempt."

"Political, maybe? He was a priest of Sekhmet, and Pentju is God's Father of the Aten."

Hani murmured that such a thing might well be. He was deeply confused. Something seemed to want to take shape within him, but he couldn't yet make it out.

The two men made their way up the gravel path toward the house, sunk in thought. As they stepped onto the porch, the serving girl Hani had spoken to almost collided with them.

She backed off and bowed in embarrassment. "Oh, forgive me, my lord. You said to tell you if I remembered anything else, and something just came back to mind. I thought you'd want to know."

Excitement lit a little fire in Hani's heart. "Yes, my girl?"

"I remembered who Ba-ba-ef worked for. Somebody named Pentju."

CHAPTER 12

Hani was not as shocked as he might have been, although a chilly seepage of disillusionment soured inside him. The crime seemed all the worse when committed by one who was sworn to heal. Doctors made an oath to Djehuty to do everything in their power to preserve life.

At his side, Maya gaped, round-eyed. "But why would he kill his friend?"

Hani recovered enough to thank the girl, and she scuttled back into the house. He was trying to lay to rest the squawking of his imagination so he could think. To Maya, he said, "We don't know that Pentju is behind Nakht-ef-mut's murder, only that the murderer was a member of his household. Perhaps the laundryman knew Nakht-ef-mut was carrying a lot of silver and decided to rob him."

Maya quirked a considering eyebrow.

"Perhaps he hired himself out for pay. He could have been acting on anyone's behalf."

"Maybe," Maya conceded begrudgingly. "I have to

admit Pentju has no motive for attempting anything on the girls or for poisoning the king."

"Quite the contrary. Remember, he's a priest of the Aten. Keeping Ankhet-khepru-ra on the throne and seeing her succeeded by her son are to his advantage. If he were prone to murder, he would have tried something on Queen Meryet-aten."

Maya blew out a discouraged breath. "So, this doesn't really give us any new lead after all."

"Not anything definitive," Hani had to admit. "Although it might be worth our while to talk to Pentju's other servants. One of them might know if Ba-ba-ef had a little mercenary business on the side."

He turned toward the gate and, with Maya in his train, headed out into the street. Hani's thoughts were in a turmoil. Before they had gone far, he stopped and said, thinking aloud, "What excuse can I give for interviewing the *sunu's* servants? It's for royal business, but do I want Pentju to know his man is under suspicion? He may be involved too."

"Or not... and he might be glad to know. He must realize by now that Ba-ba-ef is dead, even without knowing what he was up to."

"All right," said Hani with a sigh. "Here we go."

The porter let them in the door, where they had entered so frequently of late. Hani asked to see Pentju, but the man informed him apologetically that the master of the house was serving at the palace.

"Perhaps you would like to talk to Lady Djefat-nebty, my lord?"

"That would be splendid. Thank you."

While he and Maya awaited the mistress of the house, Hani looked around him at the progress on the wall painting. The new designs had been outlined in black, and the color men had begun to fill them in, using a lighter palette than the previous red-heavy images. There were birds and marshes, Hani noted with approval. Lots of pale blue and green and yellow. He drifted over to the pots of paint ranged against the wall behind the dais, and with a thrill of discovery, his eye fell on the sunny pigment he had come to know so well lately. He hoped the painters wouldn't suck their brushes. But his mind kept asking, *Is it Djefat-nebty, then?*

From the door, Djefat-nebty said, "Hani. What brings you here? Surely not to admire the murals?"

"No, my lady," Hani said, rising from his crouch. "Although they're very admirable."

"Ah, that's right. Neferet said you like birds." A faint smile twitched at the corners of her mouth.

"I'm here about the murder of Nakht-ef-mut. Do you have a laundryman named Ba-ba-ef?"

"We did," she said, bidding the men to stools. She took her place before them on another. "He seems to have gone missing. Perhaps something has happened to him." Her eyes raked Hani with cool curiosity. "Why do you ask?"

"A man answering to his description was seen murdering your friend from Sau, my lady."

Djefat-nebty's face grew pale. "Ba-ba-ef killed Nakht-ef-mut? Is your witness sure it was he?"

"No, but he described a man with a long scar on his cheek and a drooping eyelid. And the scar-faced man was killed recently, too, which would explain why Ba-ba-ef hasn't shown up for work."

She fell silent, staring into her lap, and finally said, "Why do the police insist it was Bener-ib, then, if there was a witness?"

"Apparently, Mahu wants it to be Bener-ib, and his mind is closed to any other possibility. I've seen this in him before." Hani tried to scrub his tone of the contempt he felt for the chief of police. "Of course, someone must have suggested the girl to Mahu."

"What on earth could Ba-ba-ef's motive have been?" With her brows knitted, the *sunet* rose to her feet, and Hani and Maya did the same.

"Presumably, he was acting for someone else. Do you know if he did jobs for people on the side?"

But Djefat-nebty shook her head. "I have no idea what he did in his free time. He certainly wasn't doing laundry for our household all day, every day."

"Did he do odd jobs for you, then? Maybe"—he shot a glance at the row of paints against the wall—"buy pigments for your muralists?"

"That's possible. You'd have to ask my husband. He's been keeping after the painters." She paced a few steps then turned back to Hani, her face grim. "But motive, Hani—what would his motive have been? Who would want Nakht-ef-mut dead? He had only just arrived in our city."

And who would want my daughter or me dead? Yet someone does, and Ba-ba-ef was his cat's paw. Is it necessarily the same person both times? Or... Hani lowered his voice. "Could it have been his widow, my lady? It's occurred to me that there may have been some conflict over his bequest.

Had he decided to leave everything to Bener-ib, and Sit-ah wanted to stop him before he could change his will?"

Djefat-nebty looked skeptical. "Hani, she was still in Sau when this happened. How could she have contacted a servant of ours, whom she'd never met, and ordered him to kill her husband?"

Hani had to admit that presented a problem. He heaved a sigh. "I have no other leads, my lady, so I thought it was worth talking to you. You and your husband seemed to know Nakht-ef-mut as well as anyone else in town. And Ba-ba-ef was in your employ."

Her mouth crooked. "Are you implying that we're somehow involved?"

"Not at all. I just thought you might have some insights into what was going on. My sole aim is to protect Neferet and Bener-ib by finding out who the real murderer is." Hani's face felt hot. He wondered what exactly he *was* trying to prove.

There followed an uncomfortable silence. Then Djefat-nebty said briskly, "Forgive me, Hani, but I have duties at the palace today. I'm afraid I'm going to have to say goodbye. You don't mind seeing your way out, do you?" She picked up the lidded wicker chest that contained her medical supplies and strode to the door. Hani and Maya bowed and trailed her out.

⊠

"Where do we go from here, Lord Hani?" Maya asked when they were once more standing in the street.

Hani scrubbed his face with his hands. "I wish I knew. How I long to be dealing with slippery vassals and murderous

303

hapiru once more—it's so much less challenging." He forced
a rueful laugh. "Well, come on, my boy. I think we deserve
to go home to Waset for a week or so."

Maya's heart rose in happiness. Sati was going into
seclusion soon, and he wanted to enjoy her company as
much as possible before she disappeared into her birthing
bower. "With pleasure, my lord!"

They collected their baggage at Lord Ptah-mes's villa
and, having left Neferet a note, headed down to the
embarcadero. There they found a ferry bound upriver, and
soon, the two men stood on the deck of the boat, watching
Akhet-aten recede behind them into a metallic shimmer.

Hani's thorny brows were contracted in thought, and
it was a long time before he finally spoke. "The effort to
silence witnesses to the exchange of babies almost has to
be spearheaded by Ay or Meryet-aten. But which one? The
poisoning of the king... not so clear. I would have suspected
the Crocodiles, but Mai seemed to deny that. Although it
could still be Meryet-aten, acting through someone else.
Is that someone Djefat-nebty? I think she would be very
unwilling to carry out a command of the queen."

"And the murder of Lord Nakht-ef-mut is undoubtedly
perpetrated by the same person, eh, my lord? Trying to
silence him." Maya gave a knowing nod.

"Unless it was Bener-ib, to assure her own safety, or
Lady Sit-ah, out of greed."

Maya rolled his eyes. "You're right, my lord. Foreign
service is much easier."

The rest of the five days' voyage passed uneventfully.
Maya and his father-in-law spoke little. Maya was thinking
almost constantly about Sat-hut-haru and the children,

wondering if the next baby would be a girl or a boy. *I need to have Khuit do a forecast. I all but promised her I would.*

When they finally disembarked in midmorning, he said, "I'm going directly to Khuit's, my lord. I want to tell her to cast me a prediction on the sex of the baby."

Hani, who was still pensive looking, brightened. "Why don't I go with you, son? Nub-nefer will be eager to know, and this will give me a little present to take her."

They picked up their baskets of toiletries and no-longer-fresh clothes and headed off into the working-class neighborhood where the old healer lived. Maya struggled to conceal a smile of pride as they passed his house. It was now the finest residence in the area, impeccably whitewashed, its gate painted red with *Amen-mes known as Maya son of Turo, royal scribe* neatly lettered over it and a fringe of foliage grazing the top of the garden wall. They turned left at the next corner and made their way down the half-uninhabited lane to the tumbledown residence of Khuit. Lord Hani rapped on the gate, and before long, the dark, shriveled old face of the healer appeared in the aperture.

"Why, if it isn't Lord Hani! And my little friend, In-hapy's son! Come in, come in." She opened the gate and stood back for them to enter—a shrunken, bowlegged nub of a woman not much taller than Maya.

"We have a request, mistress," said Maya, "and will certainly pay you for it. How much does it cost to have you make a prediction of the sex of my next baby?"

"Ah! What did I tell you! Your wife is expecting again." She gave a naughty cackle and poked Maya in the chest. "And she didn't do it by herself, did she, sonny?"

Maya was aware of Lord Hani suppressing a snort of

laughter, and his own face heated up. "So, what do you want in exchange?" he demanded with a lordly lifting of the nose.

"Oh, a little duck, or maybe a goose. There's nothing like goose fat for mixing salves." The old woman's toothless mouth spread in a sly grin.

Maya promised her the goose, and she rubbed her hands together as if she could already taste it. "I can't do it right now, you understand. The moon isn't right. But I'll tell you as soon as it's time. And if the little woman needs a midwife, I've been practicing again here lately. Sometimes, a skilled midwife can make all the difference."

"We'll keep you in mind," Maya assured her, thinking that with all the family women at her side, Sat-hut-haru wasn't likely to need anyone else once she squatted on the birthing bricks.

"Be careful, mistress," Lord Hani said with his amiable gap-toothed smile. "It seems midwives lead a dangerous life. One was murdered in the capital not too long ago."

"Oh?" Khuit's appetite for gossip was clearly awakened. Her little black eyes sparkled. "Murdered? Who was it? Most of them there came from Waset. Maybe I knew her."

"A woman named Tuy. I think she was originally from Seyawt."

"Tuy! Why, I knew Tuy! She sometimes worked at the palace with me when the court was in Waset. Some handmaid or other was always having a baby—and not always by their husband neither." Her bony shoulders bounced with a lewd chuckle. "She came to see me not long ago, in fact. Murdered, you say?"

"Yes." Lord Hani's face had grown suddenly keener.

He thinks she may have information we could use. A surge of excitement bubbled in Maya's middle.

"Her throat was slit, in fact. And then she was claimed by the Lord of the Waters. Have you any idea why someone would kill her so brutally and then throw her body into the River?" Hani was watching Khuit closely.

The old healer's mouth screwed up in thought. "Why, she knew about the little girl whose tongue's been cut out. She was there, same as me—that's what she came to warn me about. So they got her, did they?"

Iyi! Maya thought. *A witness of not just the crown prince's birth but his mother's as well!*

Hani was silent for a moment, then he laid a hand on the old woman's shoulder and said earnestly, "Please take her warning seriously, Khuit. If her murderer knows you were a witness, too, you may be in danger."

"Who else knows her identity, mistress?" Maya demanded.

"Oooh—it's been a few years, sonny. There must have been some other serving girls around. The doct—"

At that moment, a beloved voice called from the gate, "Khuit? Are you in there?"

"It's Sati!" Maya rushed to the door and through the courtyard, arms extended. "My love! Here I am! We just set foot on land, and I wanted to surprise you with a forecast."

He and his wife embraced, a hug a little awkward but full of love and joy.

"You're back, my lion!" she squealed. "I was just coming to have a prediction cast too! See how we think alike?"

Hand in hand, they walked through the courtyard to the door of Khuit's little house. Maya could hardly take his eyes off her. She was as delectable as cold water to a man dying of thirst.

"Sati, my swallow! Your papa's here too." Lord Hani stood grinning in the doorway, Khuit trying to peer around his broad bulk from the rear.

There were joyous greetings all around, and quite forgetful of the old healer and her curiosity, the three of them made their way back out into the street, where Hani bade them a beaming goodbye. Still holding hands, Maya and Sat-hut-haru headed home to the children.

⊠

A similarly warm welcome awaited Hani when he made it back to his own place. Nub-nefer, who was starting to build Sati's birth bower on the platform in the corner of the salon, flew to him, and he hugged her hungrily. Then he crouched beside Baket-iset and caressed her face. "How is my favorite eldest daughter?"

"We're so excited for Sati, Papa. She and Mut-nodjmet have been over here all morning, helping Mama with the construction." Her big kohl-edged eyes sparkled with excitement.

My noble little swan. I've never seen the least bit of envy in her. Her sisters' triumphs are her own. Hani swallowed hard.

With an arm around each other, he and Nub-nefer drifted over to admire the construction that was rising on the dais. Four sturdy bundles of lightweight reed marked the corners, kept upright by horizontal bars of the same material, top and bottom, all lashed together with cord. Hani knew that before Sat-hut-haru was ready to occupy it, the women would decorate the bower with fragrant flowers, and all the statues of Ta-weret and Bes, protectors of childbirth, and of Mesh-khenet, goddess of the birthing bricks, would be arranged around. From that point on, his male eyes would not be permitted to see inside until the mother's time of seclusion was over.

"Maya ran into Sati at Khuit's. They had both gone there independently to ask for a forecast," Hani told Nub-nefer, stooping to kiss the part in her natural long hair.

"Not that Sati really cares—she has a little girl, which is what she always dreamed of. Did you get done in the capital everything you wanted to, my love?"

"I think so, although the state of my investigations is unsatisfyingly far from a conclusion. Neferet and Bener-ib are doing well. No one has dragged them off to jail recently."

Nub-nefer laughed, but it wasn't an altogether happy sound. "It's sad when a good day is one on which you're not jailed."

"Khuit told me that the Osir Tuy had just visited her—to warn her. That would explain why Tuy's body was found upriver of the capital: she must have been killed here and washed down with the current."

"The poor woman," Nub-nefer said, her brow buckled with compassion.

⊠

Hani was relaxing in the garden when he heard Mery-ra enter the gate, warbling some unidentifiable tune at the top of his lungs. Then came a burst of jolly laughter in the voices of two men. "Father? Is that you? I'm back," Hani called curiously, rising.

A moment later, his father rounded the corner of the bushes with Pipi in tow. "Look who's here, son!"

Pipi cried simultaneously, "It's me!" He opened his arms to Hani, and the two brothers embraced, with much hooting and attempts at tickling one another.

"What brings you back to Waset, you reprobate?" Hani asked, his hand on Pipi's shoulder.

"I wanted to see Mut-nodjmet and the grandchildren. Things are quiet in the chancery until the old king is buried and the new king is officially installed."

Hani tried to keep his voice nonjudgmental. "So, you just left the office and took off? Is Nedjem-ib with you?"

"Yes, and the twins too. They wanted to see their sister."

"They went straight into the house," Mery-ra added.

An excited sparkle lit Pipi's square-jowled face and widened his little brown eyes. "Wait till you see what I've got, brother. It's the most beautiful thing ever!"

"More beautiful than your grandchildren?" Hani said dryly.

"Well, no. The most beautiful inanimate thing. You'll love it!"

I have a bad feeling about this, Hani thought in affectionate resignation. "Show it to me, man."

"After dinner, maybe, eh? We just walked from there, and I'm a bit thirsty."

Hani shot his father an inquiring look, but Mery-ra just waggled his eyebrows. "Let's go join the women."

Pipi crowded in after his brother and father, and inside, the men were greeted with the loud hide-and-seek of the twins and the eager chatter of Nedjem-ib. She was as plump and jovial as Pipi and crowned with a wild frizz of hair.

Nedjem-ib flew from Nub-nefer to Hani, crowing with good cheer, and threw her arms around him. "Hani! Wait till you see what Pipi's getting!"

Hani embraced her, but he felt uneasy about this "something" of his brother's. He caught Nub-nefer's eye across his sister-in-law's head. She shrugged, with an eloquent lift of her eyebrows.

"Isn't it nice, my swan, to have the family all here for a few days?" Hani said, kneeling at Baket-iset's couch and leaning in to kiss her cheek. As he drew back, he noticed a pair of cats watching solemnly from the foot of the bed. One he recognized, but the other, a handsome male with a big round head, was unfamiliar. "And who is this fine fellow?"

"That's Pa-miu, Ta-miu's son," Nub-nefer informed him.

Hani threw back his head and laughed. "Ta-miu and Pa-miu—she-cat and he-cat? Many wonderful things can be said about this family, but no one would say we're imaginative!"

Baket-iset said with mock seriousness, "Little Tepy named him."

Hani admitted that it was the perfect name. Before long, the servant girl came from the kitchen to inform them that dinner was ready, and several others hustled to set the tables around with two stools apiece until the whole family was accommodated. They settled to the abundant roasted sedge roots and green onions, and bread was circulated time and again as the supply disappeared. Pipi and his wife were hearty eaters, and their young sons seemed to be following in that tradition.

"So, what are you investigating, brother?" called Pipi from his table.

"Oh, some thefts. And Bener-ib's father died," Hani said vaguely. He saw Mery-ra watching him with a grin.

"I thought maybe I could help you, since I'll be here for a while with nothing to do," Pipi said, eagerness dyeing his chubby cheeks bright.

Oh dear. The last man I want to draw into a royal secret. "There's not much to do here in Waset, brother. Maybe later."

After they'd finished the meal off with some dried grapes, Pipi gathered the men, and while their wives cleared the salon and settled in for some fresh news from the capital, the three of them headed into the city. "We ought to blindfold him, oughtn't we, Father? So he gets the full impact," Pipi said, excitement trembling in his words.

"We don't want to give him a heart attack," Mery-ra replied dryly.

What in the name of all that's holy could this be? Hani had an idea, but it was too improbable. Yet once they turned toward the River and the quays, his suspicions grew. And sure enough, Pipi, beaming, led them down the row of boats bobbing at the water's edge to a lovely small yacht with an impish head of Bes leering from the prow, painted in bright colors that glowed in the gathering twilight.

Hardly able to control his pride, Pipi stretched out a hand. "What do you think of her, Hani? Nice, isn't she?" He waved up at the crewmen, who bowed.

Hani stared at the boat, sleek and graceful. While by no means as large as Lord Ptah-mes's, it was the same sort of vessel—luxurious, a status symbol. Expensive.

"You can't afford this, brother," Hani said flatly. He was so angry at the feckless Pipi that he didn't trust himself not to yell.

From Pipi's other side, Mery-ra heaved a sigh that spoke of his fruitless efforts to convince. "I told you so, son."

"I'm not bailing you out again. Remember what I told you after the horses."

"I can pay for it, Hani." Pipi looked up, pleading, from under his bangs like the pudgy little boy he had once been.

But Hani was adamant. "And can you feed your family too? No, man. Get rid of it."

"Still, you have to admit it's beautiful." Pipi looked from his father to his brother, hopeful. "We got here so fast, even without a night crew."

Hani sent a breath out his nose like a cloud of steam. "Well, at least you didn't pay a night crew. These men have to be supported, you know. The thing has to be maintained. You don't just buy a boat, and that's the end of it."

Pipi hung his head, all his pleasure drained out.

"How much did you pay for it?"

"I haven't paid all of it. They let me test it out on a trip from the capital. I have to have it back by the end of the month."

"Then take it back to the owner and say you've changed your mind. Make them give you your gold back." Even as he spoke firmly, Hani began to walk up and down the quay, observing the boat from every angle. It was a pretty thing—a little saucy, with its red-and-green designs and the long, folded sail on its yardarm resting at an angle. There were torches lit on deck where the crewmen lounged.

Ever since the king had made him Master of the Royal

Stables, Hani had considered treating himself to such a boat. But he was afraid of how it might hurt his brother if he, Hani, bought the vessel out from under Pipi's nose. It would dramatize painfully their respective levels of financial achievement.

He turned back toward the city, fighting his annoyance, and Pipi and Mery-ra followed in silence. Hani could all but feel his brother's dejected gaze on his back, and it sent a pang through his heart, but for Pipi's own sake, he couldn't relent.

It was evening, and the trudging of their feet on the earthen street was the only noise, except for distant laughter and the clatter of cooking pots from inside the houses around them. Painting long rectangles of orange on the house walls opposite, lamplight shone from the high windows and distracted from the emerging stars. Hani was beginning to regret his harsh words to his brother and thought that he'd come up with something kindly to say when they reached home—what good taste in boats Pipi had shown or how touched Hani was that his brother had let him see it first.

As they approached the intersection in the street that marked a turn into the more prosperous suburb where Hani's house stood, the sound of marching footsteps made him stop. He held up a hand for the others.

"What is it, son?" whispered Mery-ra.

"It sounds like a troop of people walking quickstep. Let's hang back and see where they're going." In the back of Hani's mind was the fear that Mahu had resumed his persecution and that he might have sent his *medjay* to crank information out of Hani about the girls.

Pipi squatted and peeked around the corner at low altitude. He turned back to the others, his mouth agape. "It's the police, Hani. And they're heading toward your gate."

My worst suspicion confirmed. Hani's heart began to pound. *I must get back before he harasses the women.*

But as if he had heard, Mery-ra cautioned, "Don't go back, son. It's you they're after. Let Pipi and me protect the women. You get yourself into hiding."

"Where? Khuit's again? Mane's? Ptah-mes's? Anybody who's watched me is aware I have relations with them."

"The boat!" cried Pipi excitedly. "Nobody knows it has any connection to you!"

Hani had to admit that was a good idea. He clapped his father and brother each on the shoulder and turned to leave.

Pipi called out after him in a loud whisper, "Aren't you glad I bought it?"

With considerable trepidation, Hani melted into the gathering darkness. He felt like a coward, abandoning his wife and daughter, but the fact was, as soon as the *medjay* discovered he wasn't there, they were likely to leave. If only Nub-nefer and Nedjem-ib would keep their mouths closed—they were women of forceful opinions, and Mahu didn't scruple to arrest wellborn ladies. Hani prayed his father and brother would successfully temper their heat.

Walking as quickly as he could without breaking into a run, Hani headed back to the quays, his breathing heavy and his thoughts wild. *What does this mean? Who's after me now? Is it the same person who tried to kill me in the road before—and how is it Mahu's in league with them? Or*

has someone told him I'm guilty of some crime? He would be
predisposed to believe anything terrible about me.

He crossed the open bank that sloped down to the River and made his way along the quay. It had grown dark, and he could hardly tell one boat from another. He watched the swaying masts anxiously, looking for torches lit on board. At last, he spied a small yacht with the Bes-head prow he thought he remembered, and called out in a stage whisper, "*Iyah*, men. Is this Lord Pa-ra-em-heb's boat?"

A dark figure rose from where it was seated on the deck and replied, "Yes. Who's there?"

"I'm his brother. I need to come aboard. Quick."

"He's not with you?" the man said, surprised.

"No." Hani offered no further explanation.

The sailor lifted a torch from its bracket, and he and his fellows slid out the gangplank. When Hani had galloped up and the plank had been withdrawn, the three men confronted him in confusion. "Where do you want to go at this hour, my lord?"

"Nowhere. I just need to stay here for a couple of hours." He clapped the first man on the shoulder with a comradely gesture. "Your master will be grateful—and so am I. We'll make it worth your while."

◻

Maya and Sat-hut-haru had brought the children by after dinner to see Gammother and Gamfather, only to find that all the men of the family had left.

Nub-nefer said, "I'd tell you to join them, Maya dear, but I don't know exactly where it is that they've gone. There seemed to be some sort of mystery. Pipi wanted to show them something, but he wouldn't say what."

"His boat," supplied Nedjem-ib, rocking with laughter. "It's always something with that Pipi, isn't it? I couldn't find it in the dark for you, though."

Maya was a little hurt that he hadn't been invited along, but he said lightly, "Then I'm sure I'll hear all about it when they get back."

He had just taken a seat on the floor, prepared to play with little Mai-her-pri until the lad's grandfather should return, when a furious knocking sounded at the gate.

Nub-nefer started up in alarm. "Who's that at this hour? Surely Hani and the others wouldn't have hammered like that. A'a would have let them in right away."

Maya scrambled to his feet, prepared to defend the women and children if need be. One never knew what sort of violence the night would bring in these times. *I hope Lord Hani and the others are safe.*

A'a appeared in the doorway of the salon, his face stiff with fear, but before he could even announce the visitors, a troop of four policemen and a baboon stormed in, the despicable Mahu at their head. Maya could feel his hackles rise. If he'd been a dog, his lip would have rippled in a growl.

"Well, well," Mahu sneered in his usual way. "If it isn't the half scribe. Where's your master, little man?"

"My father-in-law. He's not here," Maya said frostily, drawing himself up to his full height. *"Half scribe" indeed, the rotten son of a jackal.*

"What gives you the right to break into our home?" Nub-nefer demanded, positioning herself between the *medjay* and Baket-iset. Sati and Nedjem-ib stood shoulder to shoulder beside her.

"I'm the head of the king's police, that's what. And my job is to apprehend criminals."

Maya retorted, "The king's police in Akhet-aten. You're a little outside your jurisdiction, aren't you?"

Mahu stalked up to Maya, glaring down at him, and then jerked the neck of his shirt up so roughly with a fist that he almost pulled him off his feet. "How would like to join your master in the bottom of a well with your nose and ears cut off, little man? Just keep talking big." His face had grown apoplectically crimson, and his jowls quivered with barely suppressed contempt.

Sati gave a yelp of outrage, but one burning look from the police chief shut her up. The blood was mounting to Maya's face in a wave of heat. *Don't touch her.*

"Where is Hani?"

"Do you see him anywhere? He's not here." Nub-nefer crossed her arms and planted herself in defiance.

The children huddled around their mother, their little hands clinging to Sati's skirts, and Maya could see, with a breaking heart, the fear and incomprehension on their faces. Only Tepy looked fierce, with his small fists balled at his side. Things had reached a frightening pitch of tension, and Maya was fully expecting violence to break out, when Lords Mery-ra and Pipi burst into the room, red-faced and panting.

"What's going on here?" the old man demanded, staring from Mahu and his henchmen to the women.

Mahu sauntered toward Mery-ra in a way that was

intended to be intimidating. "We're here to see your naughty son."

But Lord Mery-ra wasn't easily frightened. "My son is neither naughty nor present," he said grimly. "You'd better have papers from the king to justify this invasion."

Mahu ignored the challenge to legitimate himself and snarled, "Where is he?"

"In the capital, I suppose—or on his way. That *is* where he works." Mery-ra managed not to radiate anger, as Maya was sure he himself was doing.

But Maya was afraid as well as furious. Confrontation didn't sit well with Mahu, and he already had a grudge against Lord Hani's family. The presence of the women and children upped the stakes considerably.

"It seems we do nothing lately but search your house, doesn't it?" Mahu made a quick gesture to his men, and they separated, overturning furniture and throwing around cushions. Two of them trooped upstairs, and Maya heard some of them in the kitchen, breaking pots—as if Lord Hani might be inside them.

"I think we have a right to know why you're looking for my husband," Nub-nefer said, her mouth trembling with suppressed rage. "The king has accepted the innocence of Bener-ib in the murder of her father." Behind her, Baket-iset watched, wide-eyed but unafraid.

"Sedition, my lady. Is that serious enough for you?"

Nub-nefer fell back, her eyes enormous. No doubt she feared he had been seen at her brother's house. As for Maya, he was gape mouthed in astonishment. *Is it the queen or Lord Ay and the king who are accusing Hani? Has he slipped from the knife edge of neutrality he's been walking between the two factions?*

Their search ended at last, the *medjay* made their exit, the baboon stopping to shoot a contemptuous stream of urine at the doorsill. Mery-ra called after them, "I didn't see those mission papers of yours, my friend."

Mahu never turned. When their thunderous footsteps had died away, and the gate had clanged shut and the bolt dropped safely into place, Nub-nefer turned to Mery-ra with panic in her gaze. "Where is he, Father?"

"Safe on my boat," said Pipi. His coppery face was pale and his little eyes wild.

Sat-hut-haru rushed to Maya and fell weeping onto his shoulder—*Please don't let this shock harm the baby*—and Pipi and Nedjem-ib clung to one another.

Mery-ra put an arm around Nub-nefer then turned to Baket-iset. "You were very brave, my girls. The police may be watching the house for a while, so we shouldn't try to get Hani back yet. I'll tell him what happened tomorrow."

Before Maya shepherded Sat-hut-haru and the children back to their own home, Lord Mery-ra took him aside and whispered, "Tomorrow morning, take a basket and pretend to go to the market. From there, make your way to the quay and ask for Pipi's yacht. Someone will be able to guide you. I'm afraid if anyone left this house, they'd be followed. All right, my boy?"

"I'll do it first thing. What instructions should I give Lord Hani, my lord?"

The old man wilted and said sorrowfully, "I have no idea."

CHAPTER 13

H ANI DISAPPEARED INTO THE CURTAINED kiosk on the deck and decided to stay there out of sight until someone in his household should send for him. He suspected he really should leave the city, but where to go? He didn't even know what he was being hunted for. Indeed, he wasn't sure it was he in Mahu's sights.

The thing that gnawed at him most painfully was not knowing what had happened to Nub-nefer and the rest of the family. He had abandoned them in danger, leaving their defense to his old father and his feckless brother. Hani took his head in his hands, weary of all the deceit and plotting and murder, fast or slow. He wanted to awaken and find that the last thirteen years had been nothing but a bad dream. That Neb-ma'at-ra was still on the throne. That the Hidden One was once again ruling the heavens, and that Hani's beloved family was safe and happy, untroubled by such as Mahu.

Hani thought he would never be able to sleep, but

when he finally popped up from his blanket on the deck, the sky was already light. A voice was calling, "Lord Hani?"

"Maya, my boy? Is that you?" Hani scrambled to his feet and parted the curtain of the kiosk.

Maya's grin was joyful, but there was concern in his wrinkled brow. "It's me, my lord." He slid into the tented enclosure with a glance around him, as if afraid he might be watched. "Lord Mery-ra told me to come this morning because they didn't think my house would be under observation."

"Did he tell you what happened last night?"

"I was there," Maya said with a lift of the chin. "Sati and I had brought the children over to see their grandparents. But then the police burst in and wanted to search for you. Your father and brother showed up next, and together, we held Mahu and his thugs off from anything too dire." He dropped his gaze in ill-concealed pride. "You should have seen how brave Tepy was."

"He takes after his father," Hani said, his voice weak with affection and relief. "Are they expecting me at home?"

Maya told Hani that no one knew what counsel to give him. It was hard to imagine Mahu wasn't watching the house, and it didn't seem safe to return home. "Mahu said you were wanted for sedition, my lord."

The hair rose on Hani's arms. Why had he suddenly been accused of disloyalty? *Does the king not remember I'm infiltrating the conspiracy of her daughter on her behalf?* "Then I'm taking Pipi's boat back to Akhet-aten. I'm going directly to the king to argue my case." *Of course, my case is what exactly—being a double agent? Guilty as accused.* Hani remembered what his father had said—that diplomats were liars—and hoped he could prevaricate his way out of this thicket.

"If I just go into hiding, things will get worse."

"Be careful, my lord. Mahu is no friend." Maya grasped Hani's hand earnestly. "Let me come with you."

"We won't have time to pack anything. I want to get back to the capital before Mahu, if possible."

"Should I tell the others where you've—"

"I think not. They'll figure it out when they see Pipi's boat has left."

Hani went out on the deck, only to see the sailors stirring about, stretching sleepily, and eating their breakfast. He called, "*Iyah*, my good men. We need to set off right away for Akhet-aten. Lord Pa-ra-em-heb will follow us."

The boatmen jumped up, cramming the rest of their bread into their mouths and, with much bowing, set off to ready the vessel for departure.

"May everything go so smoothly." Maya heaved an uneasy sigh.

The two men stood at the gunwales, staring out over the shore. The day was mild and a little hazy, as if something were blowing up out of the eastern desert. With deep pleasure, Hani inhaled the morning air, rich with the deep green musk of the River. Even knowing what might be hanging over his head, he found it hard to be too glum on such a morning, with the water swelling and foaming behind the stern as they pulled away from the quay. The sail, furled since they were going down current and against the wind, resembling a pair of outstretched arms like the sacred symbol for *ka*, the life force. A trio of spoonbills floated ahead of them as if to pilot them to the City of the Horizon—and perhaps across the Lake of Flowers to a happier life.

⌘

It took as long to reach the capital on Pipi's elegant little boat as it did on the meanest ferry, but Hani found the trip strangely relaxing. He was able to forget for those few days the fact that he was being sought for the crime of sedition, a capital offense.

Maya, on the other hand, seemed anxious as they thudded down the gangplank and onto the sloping bank that served as the embarcadero. "Are you sure it's safe, Lord Hani, just to go marching into the palace? What if the soldiers apprehend you before you can speak in your defense?"

"It's a risk I have to take. I haven't done anything new or suspicious." *Except that visit to Amen-em-hut's house. How could I have been so foolish?* "So I can't think of anything that would have changed Lord Ay and his daughter's minds about me."

"You don't think it's because you missed the crown prince's lesson…?"

"No. I was told he was ill and that there would be no class last week. That's why I felt free to head back to Waset." After a moment, Hani said pensively, "I hope no one is poisoning him too."

Maya's eyes widened.

The men strode on in silence. It was deep into the afternoon hours, and the streets were sparsely populated, everyone either still at siesta or avoiding the midday sun. The two men made their way beneath the Window of

Appearances and followed the long white wall of the central palace, reveling in the strip of shade it offered. Then they turned and headed toward the River until they had reached the majestic pylon gate, where, to Hani's relief, he could see against the glaring sky the red banners that proclaimed the presence of the king. Suddenly, he gave realistic thought to the danger into which he'd thrust himself—a foolish, greedy pigeon entering a snare in the hopes of one more grain. His calm dissolved, and his heart began drumming a frantic rhythm. *I should have run in the other direction.*

"Wait for me here, Maya. If they hold me, I don't want you implicated."

The secretary obediently seated himself along the north wall, and Hani heard him swallow painfully. It seemed Maya, too, was considering the possible consequences of Hani's present action.

How could it be safe to trust Lord Ay's daughter?

After a very anxious wait in the gilded reception hall, Hani followed the majordomo to the door of the residential suite where he had last met the queen's father. That was somehow more ominous than the throne room. He entered, saw the God's Father Lord Ay alone on a high chair, and folded himself to the floor in a complete court prostration.

"Oh, get up, Hani. I'm not the king," Lord Ay said in a humorous voice.

Hani hauled himself to his feet and bowed. "I come to protest my loyalty to the Black Land, my lord."

Ay laughed. "Of course you're loyal. I just had to get your attention. You seemed reluctant to come back and make a report."

Get my attention? Hani thought in surprise tinged with

resentment. *By terrorizing my family and destroying my household?* He managed to say in a neutral tone, "Then I'm not accused of sedition?"

"No, no. Unless you choose to be." Ay's reddish-brown eyes considered Hani with a sly twinkle. "No doubt Mahu was ham-handed as ever in delivering my message, but that's why we need other subtler agents, too, eh?"

Fighting back anger, Hani nodded. "How may I serve the Lady of the Two Lands?"

"Any progress on the matter of the thefts—or should I say, the poisonings?"

"No perpetrator yet. I trust Our Sun God received my warning to wash her hands thoroughly after touching any of the stolen objects."

"We did, we did. That was just the sort of revelation we've come to expect from your investigative skills. Now we need to know who's doing it." The God's Father's long mouth drew out into a charming smile that Hani couldn't help but consider sinister. "Do you have any suspects?"

"Too many, my lord. And remarkably few clues to give me a direction. But I assure you, the culprit will be found."

"I believe that." There was a long thoughtful silence, then Ay said, "How are my granddaughter and her pastimes these days?"

"I haven't so much as seen her, Lord Ay. I've been occupied with the crown prince's lessons and with... the other matter."

"No rumors, even?"

Dear gods! Does he somehow know about the meeting at Amen-em-hut's house?

"No, my lord."

Ay nodded, silent once more, his handsome head cocked. At last, he said, "You know, a great deal of Meryet-aten's dudgeon is without cause. The king has every intention of returning little by little to the old ways. But such sweeping actions can't be carried out overnight without terrible harm. We've seen that." He rose from his chair and stepped down from the dais. "We can begin the steps, but it will be the younger generation that shepherds it to its end. Hence the importance of the Haru in the nest's tutors." He flashed Hani a complicit grin.

He knows I want to influence the prince? He wants *me to?* Hani felt disoriented by this avowal. He tried not to let himself be seduced by Ay's charm and to remember how ambitious the man was. Ay had to know that Tut-ankh-aten wasn't his grandson, yet he continued to push him forward as a protégé. *Still, since the boy was Nefer-khepru-ra's chosen successor, it doesn't matter who his parents were. He's the legitimate heir.* Hani wondered if he should say he knew about the prince's birth, but it seemed to be moot.

Hani's loyalties had become a lot less clear-cut. He said, as if innocently, "Is the queen aware of this, my lord? Her goal seems to be to restore the Hidden One. Perhaps she would collaborate if she knew her mother's intentions."

But Ay gave a snort of cynical laughter. "I suspect you know the answer to your question, my friend. Meryet-aten has one real goal, and that is to sit on the throne. She was rather put out that her husband died before Ankhet-khepru-ra, since she might easily have moved into some rank higher than a dowager queen, much as her mother had done. Her only problem is that there's a male child ahead of her in line. So she has rallied her followers around the idea of overturning the late Nefer-khepru-ra's reforms. I think civil war is a radical solution to the problem, don't you?"

Hani dared say nothing, just raised his eyebrows in an ambiguous gesture.

Ay drew closer and laid a ringed hand on Hani's shoulder, as if they were comrades. "Especially since the end result will eventually be the same, eh." He stepped back and gave a cheerful laugh. "So, all you need to do is find the poisoner."

Hani fought with himself and finally had to say, "Was it by your orders that Mahu tried to apprehend the young *sunet* Bener-ib for her father's murder, my lord?"

"Not at all. Why would I have done that? The loss of Nakht-ef-mut was an annoyance but hardly grave. My daughter values her trusted physicians. In fact, she's protecting them from Mahu."

"Then who is Mahu working for besides you?"

Ay looked at him sharply. "Who indeed. Perhaps for the poisoner himself."

⊠

When Lord Hani finally emerged from the palace gateway, his square-jowled face was thoughtful, but it didn't look like that of a man who had been condemned for sedition.

Maya sprang to his feet and ran to his father-in-law. "How did it go, my lord? Did you convince her you were innocent?" he cried, tingling with anxiety.

Hani gave a bark of caustic amusement. "The charge was just a ruse to get me to come to Lord Ay. He's impatient for me to solve the case of the poisoner. He also said he didn't sic Mahu on Bener-ib, so the mystery thickens."

"A ruse? After all the damage that son of a hyena did to your house?" Maya was indignant. "Couldn't Ay have just summoned you?"

"Perhaps he did, and Mahu decided to even old scores while he was at it."

The two men set off at their mismatched strides, Maya fuming. *The injustice.* But at least Lord Hani was free. "Are we going to Lord Ptah-mes's house?"

"Yes. I need to do a little investigation while I'm here and also write Nub-nefer and the others—assure them I'm all right. You'll probably want to do the same."

Maya agreed and settled his writing case more securely over his shoulder. The police scare and flight were taking on more heroic lineaments in retrospect. He thought something gripping could be made of it in his Tales. He had, after all, stood up against the *medjay* and defended the women and children—not alone, of course, but still, Tepy would probably remember his father's courage the rest of his life.

"Who other than Lord Ay could be giving Mahu orders? Who told him to go after Bener-ib? He wouldn't obey just anyone." Hani's brow was creased with thought.

"Unless they paid him, perhaps. Or unless it was someone in the government. Mahu might have thought he was speaking for the king."

"Perhaps. But who would want to ruin a defenseless young woman?" Hani mused. "Was it to make it look like she murdered her father to try to hide her tracks in the poisonings? The obvious culprit is the real poisoner."

Maya looked up at his father-in-law from the corner of his eye. "Whoever that is."

They walked in thoughtful silence until they reached Ptah-mes's villa.

⌧

Hani gazed, as he had so often, at his friend's laconically inscribed gate. *Ptah-mes* had been scraped carefully out and *Ptah-mes known as Maya* chiseled somewhat smaller in its place, but apart from his name, there was no mention of any titles.

It's a kind of act of defiance, Hani thought admiringly. *His worth doesn't depend on the favor of the king.*

By contrast, Hani thought of other nobles' gates. Lord Pentju's, for example, was full of fanfaronade, listing titles such as *seal bearer of the king*, *sole companion*, *attendant*, *favorite*, *king's scribe*, *first servant of the Aten*, *royal physician*, and *chamberlain*. He wondered if such a man ceased to exist when his patron was no longer on the throne.

Hani had expected to encounter Neferet, but instead, Ptah-mes met the two scribes at the door of the salon. "Ah, Hani. Maya. What an unexpected pleasure. I thought you were spending the whole holidays in Waset. I had planned to myself, but some business arose." He gestured the two men in, obviously pleased to see them, and they all seated themselves in some of Ptah-mes's finely carved chairs.

Hani explained to Ptah-mes what had happened in the City of the Scepter, including Mahu's invasion of his home and his own precipitous flight. His friend's lean face grew hard with contempt. He had no love for Mahu, who had protected the murderers of Ptah-mes's wife.

The grandee said with a forced smile, "So your brother has bought a yacht, has he?"

"Yes, and I have to say, despite the foolishness of it, it was a good thing for me."

They sat a few cubits apart, Ptah-mes lost in pondering, while Hani recounted all his family's recent episodes of hiding. They put Amen-em-hut's to shame. But then Hani's thoughts drifted back to the night of the festival and the ugly crowds that had threatened the children. And from there, he remembered the barrel-shaped figure with a torch at the foot of the wall and the tall man on the terrace he had mistaken for Lord Pentju. It *had* been Pentju. And the man he was talking to had been Mahu. Hani was suddenly sure of it, as if the knowledge had been fermenting inside him for all those days until it had finally popped its sealed lid. He straightened abruptly in his chair as if someone had goosed him.

"What is it, my friend?"

"Pentju might have told his wife he was going to Sau, but he was in Waset, and he talked to Mahu. I saw them together," Hani blurted triumphantly. He explained what he had witnessed.

"A strange fellowship." Ptah-mes's black eyes sparkled as the implications of such a union dawned on him. "What were they doing there together? There certainly didn't seem to be any effective police presence during the festival."

"Could Pentju have been inciting trouble, to cast discredit on the opponents of the Aten? Maybe he ordered Mahu not to intervene. But I don't know if Mahu would have done what Pentju told him. Our friend's presumably at the orders of the king—and Lord Ay."

"Pentju's the royal chamberlain, you know."

All at once, a whole new array of possibilities started

unfolding in Hani's mind, like the wet feathers of a hatching bird, getting more and more voluminous until it was impossible to believe they had just been contained in a tiny egg. "Of course! Anything he told Mahu to do would have been seen as coming from the king. And so…"

"And so?" Ptah-mes prompted after Hani had hung there for several heartbeats.

"And so, Pentju might have been the one who told Mahu that Bener-ib was the murderer of her father."

"You think Pentju himself was the killer, then?" Ptah-mes's hands on his knees had grown white knuckled with tension.

But Hani shook his head, afraid he was getting swept up into a mirage. "It's true that he was the last person known to have spoken to Nakht-ef-mut the night the *wab* priest died. And the actual murderer was a servant of his. But what would his motive have been? They were friends."

"Different political camps, perhaps. Pentju is a high priest of the Aten. And in any case, the motive might have been something personal that we'll never know about. It's not unheard of for friends to kill one another over a bagatelle."

Hani surged to his feet, unable to sit still any longer. "Maybe his motive is what we've suspected all along of our phantom killer: to hide his own attempted poisoning of the king. Pentju's house is full of pigments, including orpiment, while it's being repainted."

"But how, my lord?" Maya spread his hands helplessly. "He's never in the king's apartments now that the king's a woman."

"Ah, but he must be. He's her chamberlain. Don't

they manage the household and see to it that supplies are maintained?"

"I think that position is mostly ceremonial, Hani. The vice chamberlain actually sees to the running of things. Plus, there's still the matter of smuggling bulky objects in and out of the royal residence." Ptah-mes seemed to be hovering between skepticism and conviction, his mouth turned down and his eyes fixed on his lap.

Yes, Hani thought in frustration. *There's that little problem. Unless Pentju had a cat's paw in the queen's household. That Sheshi, the vice chamberlain? Or...* And he felt he had always known this down deep. "Lady Djefat-nebty! She carries a big covered basket like our girls. If Neferet could fit a whole assortment of the stolen objects into hers, Djefat-nebty might have done the same. And she's trusted—no one would have searched her."

Ptah-mes stared at him, and Maya nearly bounced from his chair in shock. "Her, my lord? She's the king's physician. Why would she poison Ankhet-khepru-ra?"

"I don't know why, but I do remember one of the handmaids telling me Djefat-nebty had said all those strange pale marks on the girls' skin were nothing serious. Even I could tell it was something odd, but of course, if the chief *sunet* herself said not to worry, no one would have."

Ptah-mes rose slowly to his feet, still pensive. "How are you going to be able to prove this, Hani?"

Hani had to laugh, but it was a nervous burst. "Perhaps I'll ask her."

⊠

Hani stared up at Pentju's pompous gate, where all the man's honors were enumerated. Even if he had lost some of his luster with the death of Nefer-khepru-ra, the physician was a formidable opponent, against whom Hani carried all the weight of a sparrow. The porter admitted him and escorted him into the elegant salon, where the newly finished murals glowed with their fresh colors.

A moment later, the mistress of the house emerged from an interior corridor and said with a dry smile, "Hani. What can I do for you this time?"

She stood before Hani, a tall, mannish figure with severe features—a formidable woman—and much as he believed in her adamantine honesty, he wondered if he weren't about to make a fatal mistake. "I have a question to ask you, my lady."

She tilted her head attentively.

"Is it you who are poisoning the king?"

Hani expected an eruption of outrage or at least amusement, but Djefat-nebty's face grew grave, and she beckoned him to a pair of low chairs, where they sat knee to knee. After a moment, she said with profound earnestness, "Has there ever been something so important to you that you would do almost anything to see it come about?"

Hani was afraid to say a word lest he expose himself. Did she refer to preserving the reign of the Aten or to someone threatening the safety of her family? At length, he admitted, "Yes."

"How have you enjoyed these last thirteen or fourteen years, Hani? Did they overturn anything of value to you?"

Dear gods, is she trying to make me commit myself to being an opponent of the government? But he felt he could only be truthful where the honor of the Hidden One was concerned. "They've overturned everything and caused great suffering for those I love."

She smiled humorlessly. "From Neferet's comments over the years, I rather thought so. It may surprise you to learn that my husband and I, too, are... dissatisfied with the present order of things. We, too, would do almost anything to hasten the reign of the King of the Gods. Anything, Hani." Her dark eyes fixed his with a glitter like obsidian. "I didn't poison the king, no, but I know who did. And the person doesn't deserve to die for it."

Hani's jaw dropped in astonishment. "But Lord Pentju is a priest of the Aten!"

"A political appointment. One keeps one's opinions hidden, but in conscience, one cannot abandon them."

Hani wasn't sure what to say and suspected he was gawking at her stupidly. He both had and had not expected that she was guilty of the poisonings, but not at all that she and her husband were secret partisans of Amen-Ra—Crocodiles, like Hani.

"Then, can you condemn me for using my position to help undermine the Atenist regime?" she continued. "Because I did. I could see exactly what the poisoner was doing, yet I said nothing. I made light of the king's mottled skin, knowing it was a symptom of orpiment poisoning."

In fact, he realized he could not condemn her. He had done the same thing. "No, my lady. I suppose I can't. I should have seen this sooner, in fact. But I was so sure that you were what you seemed."

She gave a bark of unamused laughter. "And do I seem to you a person who would sell her conscience to maintain the favor of the king?"

"Never, my lady. I just confess, this revelation has left me disoriented. It's so contrary to anything I suspected."

"Good. Then we've been successful. I was getting a little worried that you were onto the person. You're rather more perspicacious than the king and her ladies."

Hani fell silent. *What should I do about this information? Does Lord Ay deserve to know?* "Is this... effort continuing? Was it on behalf of Lady Meryet-aten?"

"No and no. This was purely on behalf of my husband and myself, and even we operate with some degree of independence. It seems safer that way. I've never even spoken to the queen about her ideology. My husband and I, knowing our friend and colleague Nakht-ef-mut shared our views, told him what was happening. But to our surprise, he wasn't willing to turn a blind eye. He and Pentju had an argument about it, then our friend set off to tell the king what was going on. As it happens, the poisoner is now ill, too, and thus the poisoning will stop. So the king won't die. Little by little, the symptoms will go away, and they'll all be fine." Djefat-nebty spoke stiffly but without a trace of guilt.

Hani leaned forward in his chair. "Nakht-ef-mut sent a written warning to the king and then went to the palace to tell her the details. What would he have told her in person—that you and Pentju knew who was at the bottom of it?"

"No. After all, he was sympathetic to our cause, though not the kind of man to do anything dangerous or desperate himself. He swore to Pentju that no word of our awareness of the poisoning would pass his lips."

All at once, Hani remembered the papyrus scrap in

Nakht-ef-mut's purse. *No, he wasn't going to say anything, but he was going to show the king that written testimony. He probably thought they were really the poisoners.* "And you believed that?"

"We'd been friends for years. Why should I doubt it?"

Hani told her about the names found on the dead man.

Djefat-nebty made a sour, reflective expression as if considering some unpleasant smell. "He was always a weak man. I suppose he wanted to make a name with the king and crown prince as someone loyal to them, despite his better instincts. I'm disappointed. We would probably have been tortured to wring the name of the culprit out of us."

Hani wasn't sure just how to frame the next question. It seemed Lady Djefat-nebty had been ignorant of their friend's intentions, but Lord Pentju might well have been less trusting.

"One last question, my lady. Who killed Nakht-ef-mut?"

"I have no idea, Hani."

"Are you sure it wasn't your husband? The man who attacked him was your servant. Pentju certainly had a motive if the two of you were uncertain what your friend would reveal."

"I can't imagine that. They had been comrades since their student days. The desire to please was stronger than honor in the case of Nakht-ef-mut, but that certainly isn't true of my husband."

The two of them fell silent, and Hani was just scooting forward to rise and take his leave when the *sunet* said dryly, "What are you going to do with this information, Hani? Turn us in?"

"It seems you're not really guilty of anything except knowledge, my lady."

The two them rose, almost of a height, and Djefat-nebty skewered Hani with a penetrating stare. "At some point, you may discover who the actual poisoner was, so let me ask you this. If you were a soldier on the battlefield, and you killed an enemy, would it be murder... or heroism?"

He returned her stare with a lift of the eyebrows. He thought of all the things Lady Meryet-aten had perpetrated—the priests of Amen-Ra, even his own brother-in-law—and the answer was by no means clear. "I'll have to give some response to Lord Ay. He's starting to pressure me for a solution."

Her face cracked in a carnivorous smile. "My suspicion is it was Ba-ba-ef, acting alone. He would have known Nakht-ef-mut had silver on him."

Hani bowed, and with one last conspiratorial look between them, he left.

⌧

At Ptah-mes's villa once more, Hani was surprised to find Maya and Ptah-mes bent over a game of *senet*.

"Ah, Hani. Come join us. You can have my seat. I've lost my touch for strategy." Ptah-mes looked up, smiling.

"I've just learned something important, my lord, regarding the poisoning of the king," Hani said in a grave tone, and Ptah-mes's expression sobered quickly. Hani drew up a stool and spoke in an undertone. "Djefat-nebty and Pentju, the royal physicians, know who the poisoner was."

Maya's eyes flew open. "And they haven't turned him in? But why?"

"They're committed to restoring the reign of the Hidden One. She called it an act of war."

Ptah-mes lifted an arched black brow. "And so, I suppose they also silenced Bener-ib's father."

"Djefat-nebty says not. My immediate problem is what to tell Ay."

"I suggest you blame the fellow who actually did it. Ba-ba-ef's dead himself and can't suffer any harm."

Hani nodded uncertainly. "That's what Lady Djefat-nebty said about the death of Nakht-ef-mut. But the poisoning... I don't see how he could have done that." *It was bad enough to kill a grown man, but all those innocent women?* He couldn't help remembering the love between the little crown prince and his supposed mother. There would have been another victim.

As if he'd heard Hani's thoughts, Ptah-mes said, "No one has been killed, after all. Perhaps now your investigation will frighten the poisoner away, and Our Sun God and her ladies will be all right."

Hani nodded, still troubled. "Djefat-nebty said the poisoner was ill and that the poisonings would stop anyway." *But not because the man has lost his will to do harm.* Hani was once again confronted with the same problem he'd developed with the Crocodiles' movement as a whole. Things were getting violent fast. Was he ready for that, or was he really more of a mind with Lord Ay—assuming Ay was telling the truth? That was a big assumption.

Maya spoke up. "You're right, though—how could Ba-ba-ef have poisoned the king? You're going to need something more convincing than that, my lord."

"I have to think about this," Hani said dismally.

339

Ptah-mes shot him a sharp, compassionate look and said, almost as if to distract him, "Have you any real leads about the murder of Nakht-ef-mut?"

"None. We're back where we started. Unless Lord Pentju acted without telling his wife." Hani heaved a shrug. "And then there's the matter of who killed the midwife and why. Surely it can't be Djefat-nebty eliminating witnesses to the baby switch. She would have had so many opportunities to do in the girls if that was what she was after. And it's been nine years."

"Plus, you said she seemed to have participated reluctantly," Maya said, his brows wrinkled in puzzlement.

Hani blew out a heavy, discouraged breath.

Lord Ptah-mes rose, tall and elegant, his pleated garments barely crumpled, and Hani and Maya followed. "Perhaps her murder had to do with something else altogether. Is there someone among her family or friends who could tell you anything that might give you a direction?"

A light seemed to blossom within Hani's mind, and he said eagerly, "Why, Khuit, of course."

⊠

Hani and his son-in-law made their arrangements to depart the very next morning for Waset. Before he left, he planned to see if Pipi had returned to the capital, and if so, he would leave his brother the new yacht and take a ferry south. If not, he would return it to Pipi there in the City of the Scepter.

That evening, the two young *sunet*s entered, baskets in their arms. Neferet greeted Hani with a spate of chatter, but he detected something tight beneath her cheer.

"What is it, my duckling?"

"Nothing, Papa." But she disappeared into the house quickly with some sort of vague excuse. Bener-ib lingered before Hani with hands clasped, white knuckled.

What's going on? Have the girls argued? Hani wondered.

Ptah-mes rose and excused himself discreetly, and Maya followed with a quick, curious glance behind him as he trailed their host into the house. Hani gestured the girl kindly to a seat, and he and Bener-ib sat face-to-face in silence—one that ached for the relief of words.

At last, the young woman said in a small voice, "I have something to tell you, Lord Hani. Please don't hate me for it."

"Hate you? Never, my girl. You're part of our family now," Hani said with a fatherly smile. Bener-ib looked so vulnerable that his heart went out to her.

She twisted her hands nervously then whispered, "I... I wanted my father to die."

Dear gods, is this a confession? "But you didn't... you didn't actually kill him, did you?"

Tears filled her eyes and began to pour down her thin cheeks. "May the gods forgive me, I... I was just overcome with hatred when he showed up and tried to force me all over again. He had done that to me before. It was so horrible. I was so scared—and then he had abandoned me, sent me away, never said a word, never sent a note. I thought he'd disowned me, that he wouldn't forgive me for not being what he wanted me to be. And then he came back, and instead of showing me love, he started *that* again. I was afraid I could never be safe as long as he lived." She bit her lip and lowered her head into her hands, sobs shaking her shoulders.

Dreading her next words, Hani reached out and put an arm around her, and she clutched at him.

"And so, I prayed he would die."

"My poor girl," Hani said gently. "I don't think praying for something to happen makes you guilty of the act."

But the girl was so upset that she didn't seem to hear him. Bener-ib turned a ravaged face up to Hani. "Am I damned, Lord Hani? How can I honestly tell the Judge of Souls I've never wished anyone ill?"

Hani was silent for a moment, thinking what she needed was not a theological answer but a show of loving acceptance. "I think your father meant well, my dear. But it was a cruel thing to do to you. We can't judge you for your thoughts. My own father even said that *he* would have killed someone who had done such a thing to him."

"Did he?" She turned haggard tear-filled eyes toward Hani. "I know it's a terrible crime..."

"But what he did to you was a *real* crime, my child. If he'd only thought about doing it, you would never have suffered, would you?"

She buried her face against Hani's chest and sobbed. "He was the only parent I had left, and I wanted him dead."

"He had broken the compact before you did. Perhaps there was some peaceful way to settle your differences, but in a moment of fear and hatred, I can easily see why you felt the way you did. I'm sure *I've* wanted to kill quite a few people over the years."

"I even asked that servant of Lord Pentju if he would do it, just to know—he would do anything for gold—but I couldn't make myself give him the order. I could never really have done it. I kept seeing Father in my head. I kept remembering how he loved me when I was a child and…" She trailed off, smothering a sob with a squeaking noise that sent mucus out her nose. She dashed at it with a trembling hand. "I hate myself. I asked the gods to kill him, and they did. Who could be so wicked as to want to murder their own father?"

Probably Queen Meryet-aten. "So then…" Hani pondered a moment. "When the servant came after us in the street, was he after you or me?"

"Me, I suppose. I knew things about him, since he said he'd commit m-murder if I paid him." Her mouth trembled, and she seemed ready to start sobbing all over.

By the Hidden One, it had nothing to do with the girls being witnesses to the switch of babies, then. Hani gave the young doctor a squeeze and stood up.

"Are you going to report me, Lord Hani?"

"No," he said with a reassuring smile. "I don't think you're dangerous. You've done nothing wrong at all, my girl."

She kissed him and then fled as if she wasn't sure she could believe what he'd said and feared, if she stayed around, that he would unsay it. Hani was left pensive and sad for all the poor tortured souls in the world—for foolish parents and children tormented to rage.

A moment later, Maya appeared tentatively at the doorway. "My lord, weren't we going to see Lord Pipi this afternoon?"

"Oh. Yes, Maya." Hani got to his feet, preoccupied. "While we walk, I have a little something to tell you about the attack on me and the girls."

CHAPTER 14

Pipi was home, so Hani and Maya left him his boat and took off the next morning on a public ferry. Lord Ptah-mes had offered them his own yacht, but Hani had declined. "You may want to make the trip yourself, my lord. And I don't know how long I'll be there."

Five days later, Hani joyfully took Nub-nefer in his arms. There was something blank about her look that he couldn't quite place. "Everything is well, my dove?"

"Except for Ta-miu, Hani. She's gone to join her ancestors. Baket was desolate, you may imagine. At least, she has Pa-miu now to keep her company."

Hani was sadder to learn the news than he would have expected, and now he understood why his wife's eyebrows had been shaved off. Ta-miu had been a fearsome hunter and had subjected many a bird to a savage death. But around humans, she was soft and amiable, and Baket-iset had loved her.

Having departed in a whirlwind, he had no baggage to carry upstairs. "I hoped you'd figured out what had happened to me. I hated to leave you all in the dark, but I wanted to get out before Mahu started scouring the city for me."

"We did, my love, and I'm glad you could make such a hasty exit. That Mahu—I have no words for that abominable man." Her curved lips drew back in a snarl of contempt.

"How much damage did he do? He didn't hurt anyone, did he?"

"No. He just smashed a lot of crockery and threw all the furniture around. I was so afraid for Baket, but they ignored her. Maya and Pipi and your father defended us bravely."

Hani tightened his arms around her golden shoulders. *This must end*, he thought fiercely. *How can I live knowing someone is targeting my family?*

"I have to make a visit to Khuit, my dove. She may be able to tell me something about that midwife who was killed, now that I have a better idea of how to frame my questions."

Nub-nefer said with a laugh, "You may find her at Maya and Sati's. She's there drawing up her forecast for them. The moon is finally right."

"Excellent. I'll start there."

Later in the morning, Hani knocked on the stout gate of Maya's house. Tepy opened to them, a naked brown imp dancing up and down with delight at the appearance of his grandfather, setting his sidelock aswing.

"Gamfather! We missed you the other night at your house. It was scary, with that awful policeman. But Papa and Big Gamfather and Uncle Pipi and I defended the girls. You should have seen us!"

"I've heard you were all very brave," Hani said with tender pride. He gave the boy's lock a tug, and the lad drew him through the garden to the house.

"Papa! Mama! Look who's here, safe and sound!"

Maya and Sat-hut-haru were bent over a little brazier, watching it avidly, their younger children on their knees. Khuit crouched on the other side, feeding bits of something malodorous into the fire. Everyone looked up at the announcement, and their faces brightened.

Sati cried, "Papa! We were so afraid for you. That Mahu said you were wanted for sedition, but I knew it couldn't be true."

"Everything is taken care of now, my swallow. It was just an excuse to get me to the capital."

Hani observed Maya's flared nostrils of disgust behind Sati's head and settled himself at their side. "Don't let me stop you. It's Khuit I'm here to see when she's finished."

The ceremony, it seemed, was nearly over. After few more prayers and gestures, the old healer announced, "The signs all agree, my loves. It's a girl."

"But that's wonderful!" Sat-hut-haru leaned over and kissed Maya. "Henut-sen will have someone to play with. Won't you, my treasure?" She cuddled the dimpled seven-year-old to her.

Maya looked a bit less delighted, but he said gamely, "Yes, that's great news. Don't go away, Khuit. I have that goose for you that I promised." He scrambled to his feet, handing Mai-her-pri to the child's mother, and disappeared into the back of the house.

Hani rose. "Do you mind coming into the garden, Khuit? I have some questions that I think you can answer better than anyone."

The old woman toddled before him to the porch, where the two of them seated themselves on the masonry bench against the wall.

Hani said in a low voice, "How well did you know Tuy, the midwife who was killed?"

"Oh, we worked together for a long while, my lord. She was younger than me, of course. That's why they wanted me with her at the palace when there was a difficult pregnancy. Nobody knew more than me." She cackled conspiratorially.

"I don't suppose she was present with you at the birth of your servant—the girl with her tongue cut out?"

Khuit laid a gnarled finger to her mouth in a gesture that said she was consulting her memory. "Why, she was, Lord Hani. How did you know?"

Because that was the only event I could think of other than the girl's own childbirth. "Tell me, Khuit," he said, preempting her question with another. "Did Tuy know the real parentage of the girl?"

"Why, of course, my lord. The little one's mother wasn't shy about sharing that, though not in Queen Tiyi's presence. Not that we ever quite knew when something like that was true, did we?" She indulged in a toothless grin. "But maybe that's why they had two midwives standing by, eh. She wasn't just any old maidservant's child, eh."

Well, well. Another mystery very likely solved. "You've been most helpful, mistress. I'll see to it something nice is sent to you." Hani gave her a benevolent smile.

She plucked at his sleeve as he turned to go. "Why'd

you need to know, Lord Hani?" Her shriveled old face grew sly.

"Just look out for yourself, Khuit. If she was targeted, so might you be."

⊠

Maya made his excuses to Sati and the children and followed Lord Hani out. "What did you ask her, my lord?" he said eagerly.

"It turns out the Osir Tuy was present not only at the Haru in the nest's birth but at the birth of his mother as well. She knew the girl was a bastard of Neb-ma'at-ra."

"Then maybe it wasn't about the baby switch at all—" Maya blurted.

"That's what I think, too, my friend. And why did it become necessary all at once to obliterate the witnesses twenty-five years after it happened?" Hani shook his head. "What changed after so long a time that made it urgent?"

Maya wrinkled his brow in perplexity. "That's a long while to wait..."

But Hani looked up suddenly, his little eyes bright. "Think about this, Maya. Lord Ay and the king don't want it known that the crown prince is not Ankhet-khepru-ra's real son. That would downright please Lady Meryet-aten, of course. She'd love to delegitimize her so-called brother. So Ay would be open to eliminating anyone who was witness to the switch of babies, but the queen wouldn't.

"On the other hand, she would *not* want it known that Prince Tut-ankh-aten is in fact royal on both sides and is her real half brother—while Ay would probably like nothing better if he felt the switch was going to become known at all. So in that case, Meryet-aten is more likely to be behind a silencing of witnesses to the first birth."

Maya goggled at Hani then said uncertainly, "But Tuy was apparently a witness to both events. How can we know which one was the cause of her death at the hand of the queen or anyone else?"

"No one has tried to harm Neferet and Bener-ib or Lady Djefat-nebty. Remember, it was Ba-ba-ef, trying to erase a witness to his own criminality, who attacked the girls in the street."

"And the king's dresser either died of natural causes or was poisoned in the attempt on the king." Maya stroked his chin. "So maybe the mother's birth is the issue. But why *now*?"

"I think Lady Meryet-aten just found out about the identity of the girl and is trying to hush it up." Lord Hani glanced down at Maya with a triumphant grin.

"Whew." Maya pushed back his wig and scratched his head in confusion. He wasn't sure he was following everything. It was all a little overwhelming. "*You* didn't tell her, though, did you, my lord?"

"No, but I'd bet someone did."

Who could that be, though? Who else knew who wouldn't be afraid for their own safety if the queen found out? Maya strode along in silence for a few steps then said, "Do you have any suspects?"

"Alas, no." But then Hani gave a start of excitement. "Wait—remember when we all left Khuit's in a rush? She was just starting to say something about the doctor who was attendant on the girl's birth."

Comprehension dawning, Maya cried excitedly. "Djefat-nebty!"

Hani held up a cautionary finger. "I don't know yet, my friend. But she's certainly a fellow zealot of the queen. She might well have done so in the interests of the cause."

"Our cause," Maya added, but Lord Hani pursed his lips in a dubious expression, his straight, bushy eyebrows contracted.

"I think so. I'm getting to the point where I'm no longer sure. Lady Meryet-aten and her confederates are becoming quite ruthless. I ask myself if that's what's best for the kingdom."

Maya was a little shocked. He had heard his father-in-law express some reservations about the more radical partisans of the Great One, but this was an unsettling degree of disenchantment. "Maybe not," he said noncommittally. "But how else is the Hidden One going to return to his throne?"

Lord Hani heaved a sigh. "Perhaps I'm just innocent." Then he looked at Maya with a twinkle in his eye. "Back to Khuit's, I guess. Maybe I'll take her sack of grain to her in person. But let's wait until tomorrow."

⊠

When Hani had filled in his father on what they had learned, Mery-ra was eager to see the old healer once more. Hani invited him along. The two men set out for Khuit's house the next day, stopping by to pick up Maya en route.

"Sati's getting closer to going into seclusion, my lords," Maya said in a tone between pride and dread as they walked the few blocks to Khuit's. "So she'll be at your house, and I'll be left with the children."

"Send them home with us too," Mery-ra said jovially. "It seems bare without Pipi and his brood underfoot."

Maya shot Hani a questioning look.

"Of course, son. We'd love to have the presence of the world's most adorable grandchildren for a few weeks." Hani smiled, but in fact, he was preoccupied. He wasn't sure just what Khuit could tell him or how many of the unknowns that still haunted him she could provide. He weighed the grain sack in his hand, listening to the dry hiss of falling kernels. *Please, Lady Ma'at, let her tell me something useful that we may arrive at your truth.* She would at least know the name of the presiding doctor. If it was, in fact, Djefat-nebty, she might well have told the queen the servant's identity.

They knocked at the weathered gate as they had so often lately. Hani called out, "Is the mistress of the house in?"

No one answered. Hani hammered on the door again, thinking the old woman was probably a little deaf and might not hear them from the rear of the house. "Khuit?"

"She must be out caring for some patient," Maya said.

They had turned to go when the sound of bare footsteps coming at a run made them turn. Khuit's maidservant was pounding toward them down the street, her face distorted with fear.

"What is it, my dear?" Hani asked in alarm.

The girl threw herself at his feet, panting and making wild noises that might have been sobs. She stared up at him through her tears and made a cutting motion at her throat.

Hani's hackles rose with fear. "Someone's dead? Who?" He had to force himself to ask, "Mistress Khuit?"

The girl nodded fiercely. She was trembling all over. Behind her, Maya and Mery-ra exchanged a look of disbelieving horror.

Hani lifted the girl to her feet and said quietly, "And you're in danger, too, are you?"

She bobbed her head once more in frantic assent then tugged Hani toward Khuit's gate and pushed it open. They passed through the bit of courtyard and into the small house, the others at their heels. Hani was immediately conscious of a heavy, sweetish odor he knew only too well from the battlefield.

Maya saw the corpse first. "All you gods have mercy!" he cried in a high-pitched voice.

Khuit had fallen almost in the kitchen door, her skinny brown legs outstretched, her body half-hidden by a pile of baskets and bundles of herbs that had tumbled on top of her. The salon was in blood-spattered chaos, as if there had been a desperate struggle, and the cat had fled. Covering her cheeks with her hands, the servant girl looked, wild-eyed, between the slain healer and Hani.

"May the Lady of the West receive her gently," murmured Mery-ra, his nostrils flared in disgust. "Who could have done such a thing to a harmless old woman? Have people no respect for gray hairs these days?"

Hani and Mery-ra squatted at Khuit's side and freed her from the avalanche of herbs. Her throat had indeed been slit, and dried blood had dyed her down to the waist, leaving her little old face frozen in a toothless rictus of fear. *She must have been standing when this was done. Her captor*

*must have held her from behind and killed her with one hand.
It can't have been that easy.*

Hani rose, overcome by a wave of nausea and sorrow. To
the servant, he said, "Were you here when this happened,
my girl?"

She shook her head, made an arc like a basket handle
over her arm and pretended to walk.

"You'd gone to market?"

The servant nodded. She instinctively looked toward
Khuit's body but then turned away, tears flooding her eyes.

"If someone just broke in and murdered Khuit, and the
girl didn't see the killer, why does she feel she's in danger?"
Maya asked, scratching his head.

But the servant caught Hani by the arm and walked to
one corner of the room then turned and came back. She
mimed an expression of horror then ran away to the corner
again.

"You had just returned and found her while the killer
was still here, and you fled?" Hani guessed. "He saw you,
then?"

She shrugged in helpless ignorance.

"Go get the servants of Inpu and bring them here. She
should be embalmed right away. After that, go to my house.
We'll see to it you're taken care of."

The servant nodded and fled, leaving Maya and Hani
and his father alone with the corpse.

"Whoever killed Tuy finally found her colleague. We
know Khuit wasn't present at the crown-prince's birth, so
this had to be about the birth of his mother," Hani said
grimly. He wished the old healer weren't staring up at him.

"And that means it's Meryet-aten behind it, right?" asked Maya, a curl of revulsion at the corner of his mouth.

Hani said nothing at first, feeling disillusioned and depressed. "Does no one care about *ma'at*? It seems both sides want to reshape reality to suit them and will let nothing stop them."

Mery-ra laid a heavy hand on his son's shoulder and shook his head sadly.

After a moment of unhappy silence, Hani said, "You and Maya might as well go home, Father. I'll stay until the priests get here."

The other two departed reluctantly, leaving Hani alone with Khuit. He turned away so he didn't have to see her final indignity. *She never told me who the doctor was at that lying-in,* he thought, troubled.

⊠

When Hani returned home, Nub-nefer met him at the door, her eyes red. "Oh, my love, Father just told me about poor Khuit. Neferet will be so sad." She put her arms around her husband, and he enfolded her in turn. "Should we go into mourning for her? I don't know if she has any family."

Hani thought for a moment then said reluctantly, "We'll pay for her funeral, but I think it would be safer to act like we know nothing about this. I just hope our using her house for a hiding place didn't contribute to her death."

"We're a dangerous family," Mery-ra agreed, emerging from the salon.

"Is Maya inside?"

"No, he's gone back home to see Sat-hut-haru and the children." Mery-ra clapped Hani on the back in commiseration. The three of them made a small, mournful procession into the salon, where Baket-iset lay. Although she had never met Khuit, Hani heard her sniffling.

"I'm so sorry for the old woman," she said in a trembling voice. "She was Neferet's first teacher. Neferet will take it hard, I know."

"She will, my swan. But 'It is the god who judges the righteous.' Khuit was a good woman, and soon her soul will cross the Lake of Flowers and enter into its joyful home as a blessed *akh*."

Nub-nefer stooped to wipe a tear from her tenderhearted daughter's eye. "Let's just be glad evil didn't strike any closer to home, my dear."

They tried to eat lunch in the salon, but the still air was too heavy, and not a breath could be lured down the ceiling ventilator, so the family moved out to the garden pavilion. The cicadas made conversation almost impossible—not that anyone seemed much inclined to talk. Hani was lost in his own thoughts. *Who knows what else Khuit could have told me if I'd only known earlier what questions to ask? Now I've lost my chance.*

The servants had taken away the tables, and the family, already drowsy with heat and digestion, were preparing to go inside for their siesta. Baket was going to take her rest under the shade of the grapevine, with Pa-miu occupying his mother's place at the girl's side. Hani rose and stretched luxuriously with a satisfying roar. All at once, he heard excited voices at the gate with A'a's exclamations in reply.

"It's Sati and Maya," said Nub-nefer, her eyes brightening.

Sure enough, the young couple came barreling around the bushes, their rapid footsteps rattling on the gravel.

"My lord! My lord!" Maya cried. "Wait till you hear what Sati saw!"

Her mother pulled out a stool for Sat-hut-haru, who settled her bulk with a wince. She said eagerly, "This morning sometime, I was on the roof terrace, helping the cook shell cowpeas, when a pair of *medjay* came running past. I went around the side of the house and saw them going down Khuit's lane. They hammered and hammered on her gate, and as soon as she opened it a crack, they pushed their way in."

Hami felt a chill of uneasiness ripple down his spine. "*Medjay*? Why would the police have any reason to break into Khuit's house?" He glanced at Maya, who wore a look of triumph.

"Do you think we've found our murderers, Lord Hani?" Maya asked.

"Can you call the police murderers?" said Mery-ra acerbically. "Aren't their crimes 'carrying out justice'?"

"Against Khuit?" Nub-nefer cried, outraged. "No, it's just plain murder of a harmless little old woman by two strong men. How despicable."

"The servant wasn't there, and Khuit must have answered the gate herself." *Here's a complication,* Hani thought grimly. *Is it Mahu's gang eliminating the witnesses one by one? In which case he must be taking orders from Meryet-aten.*

⊠

That night after dinner, Hani and his father sat in the

breathless evening shade of the grape arbor, sucking thoughtfully on their pots of beer.

"What are you going to do now, son?" Mery-ra wiped his lips with the back of a hand.

"I'd like to talk to Ptah-mes if he's in town."

Mery-ra waggled his eyebrows. "He seems to spend more time in Waset than in the capital these days. There's the advantage of being retired."

Hani snorted darkly. "He's not retired. He resigned, although I suppose that it looks now as if he has simply been recalled, like all of us, until the king reassigns missions." He straightened up from his straw and folded his hands pensively across his belly. "Besides, he's trying to leave the house in the capital for the girls."

"He's certainly the perfect gentleman. I wonder if he ever regrets the conditions of his marriage."

Hani glanced up quickly. "Do you have some reason to say that, Father? Because I've noticed signs too. Perhaps his affection for her is paternal, but Neferet's definitely charming him."

"Well, of course she is. She's one of us," Mery-ra said with a complacent grin. "He seems almost happy these days."

Hani had to admit that that was true, and the gods knew he didn't begrudge his friend such happiness. He just hoped it didn't end in heartbreak. *Nothing is simple anymore—not even the most straightforward little family relationship.*

"I think I'm going to look for him—tell him about Khuit. Our best potential hope of information has been struck down. Who else could even tell us the name of the palace women's doctor twenty-five years ago?" He surged to his feet, blowing a great breath of discouragement out his nose.

"It wasn't Djefat-nebty? If she's about your age, she might well have been."

"Probably. I don't know. I don't know much of anything for sure." Hani dusted the breadcrumbs from his lap and started down the path toward the gate. "Tell Nub-nefer where I've gone, will you, Father?" He set out and made his way to the riverside.

When Hani reached Lord Ptah-mes's magnificent ancestral residence, the gatekeeper admitted him and said cheerfully, "The master of the house is in the garden, my lord."

Who isn't, in this heat? Hani asked himself in amusement, pushing back his wig and mopping his brow. The walk had restored some of his good cheer. He crunched through Ptah-mes's orchard and watched the ducks in the pond until he was feeling almost chipper.

Ptah-mes was seated in his pavilion, bent over a roll of papyrus, but as Hani's noisy footsteps approached, he looked up and brightened. "Ah, my friend. How are you doing after your brush with the law?"

"No side effects, my lord. But I wanted to tell you some sad news. The old neighborhood healer who has been such a source of information about the crown prince's real mother has been killed."

"Killed?" Ptah-mes's face sharpened as if he had whetted it.

"Yes. Her throat was slit, just like the other midwife's. And a witness saw two policemen doing it."

"Policemen?"

"That's what my daughter said. She observed them going into Khuit's house. And the servant witnessed the *medjay* in action, although she escaped, hopefully before they realized that she had seen."

Ptah-mes sat staring into space, his arched black brows drawn down in a frown and the scroll forgotten in his lap.

"I'm almost sure Queen Meryet-aten is behind these deaths, my lord. But suddenly to eliminate witnesses to the birth of the prince's mother after all these years? She's not even twenty-five herself. I don't know how she found out about the girl's identity. I never told her because I was afraid of what she might do with that information."

Hani saw Ptah-mes's face stiffening before his eyes, as if frost were creeping over feature after handsome feature, setting them rigid and brittle. The grandee said nothing.

Hani stared at him in concern. "What is it, my lord? Aren't you well?"

Ptah-mes gave a cynical laugh and said in a tight voice, "Well but not good, my friend. *I* told the queen about the mother of the crown prince." He looked Hani in the eye, and his mouth quirked in an expression of profound self-contempt.

Hani was stunned. To be sure, he'd never said, "Don't tell anyone," but Ptah-mes was usually closemouthed—and out of favor at court.

Ptah-mes said, "It didn't occur to me that you had never told Lady Meryet-aten what you discovered. She said something that made me think she knew, and so I spoke unguardedly." He drew a deep breath, his face set and bitter. "And I wanted to be approved for once, Hani.

The queen had shown me favor—the first royal favor in seventeen years—and I felt that deserved a certain loyalty. Now two innocent people are dead. There is nothing I can say in my defense." His eyes dropped for a moment, but he raised them and faced Hani, unflinching.

By the Hidden One, that took some courage to say, Hani thought, half in admiration in spite of his horror. "I never told you it was a secret, my lord. You did nothing terrible. How could you know?"

"I'm a diplomat, Hani. But alas, I am also a weak, self-interested excuse for a man."

Hani was almost pained more for his friend's contrition than for the sad deaths of the two midwives. He extended a hand and laid it on Ptah-mes's arm. "I might have done the same thing. Anyone might have."

Ptah-mes rose, scroll in his fist, as straight and graceful as if he hadn't suffered such a blow to his self-esteem, but his face looked strangely hollowed out. "You're too kind, my friend. You—and your daughter—deserve better. Thank the gods Apeny isn't alive to witness this. It would confirm all her worst suspicions about me."

Hani tried to plead with his friend not to be so hard on himself, but his words rolled off the grandee's back. Eventually, he took his leave, his heart filled with pain.

When he returned to his own home, Mery-ra met him at the gate. "Well, son, did he have any good advice?"

Hani heaved a sigh. "The poor man hates himself because he committed an indiscretion. Somewhere along the way, someone has convinced him he has to be perfect or he's a total failure."

Mery-ra rolled his eyes. "No mystery who that was. His

father was a flint-hard disciplinarian of the worst sort. No doubt he told your friend he should be ashamed of himself every time he stubbed his toe."

Hani stared at Mery-ra. "You knew Ptah-mes's father? I've never heard you say a thing about him."

"Old Bak-en-ren-ef? I didn't know him personally. He was a chariot officer, as so many of those grandees are. I saw him in action frequently—berating someone for a minor infringement. His men were terrified of him, but he certainly got their best performance out of them. I suppose he ruled his family with the same fist of bronze. And your friend was the only boy—he had a lot of weight on his shoulders."

Hani pondered this. "How is it that Ptah-mes didn't go into the cavalry himself?"

"Probably not good enough for Papa," Mery-ra said with a snort. "The only other honorable option was a post in the bureaucracy."

"Well, that explains a lot. Not least how he knows his way around arms and horses." *And why he started his rise in the royal service so young—mayor of Waset in his twenties, vizier, First Prophet of Amen-Ra. He must have felt driven to excel. These last fifteen or so years of public humiliation must have been devastating for him.* Sorrow simmered in Hani's middle, melting his heart around the edges. It struck him, not for the first time, that the hardest task under the sun was to be a good parent—to teach one's children values and still let them be who they were. He said with feeling, "Thank you for not being that kind of father."

Mery-ra tutted. "I rather think your mother and I erred on the side of not enough discipline. But as long as you boys weren't mean hearted, we didn't care if you were mischievous."

A warm wave of tenderness lapped over Hani. Swallowing hard, he gave his father a quick, somewhat embarrassed squeeze around the shoulders. The two of them drifted to the porch and took a seat on the step side by side. Between them stretched a long silence broken only by the razzing of the cicadas and the quiet twitter of sparrows in the bushes.

At last, Hani said, "Maya isn't here by any chance?"

"He is—he and Sat-hut-haru and the children. Sati's getting ready to go into seclusion."

As if summoned, Maya appeared in the doorway. "Ah! You're home, Lord Hani. I thought I heard your voice." He came over and sat on the edge of the porch with the others. "Too much girl talk going on inside."

"We need to wrap up our cases before Ay decides to arrest me for sedition for real. I think we can be sure it was Meryet-aten who was killing off the witnesses to our servant girl's birth. I've found out who told her about the girl's identity, and the queen wouldn't have wanted that to get out."

"Oh? Who is it, my lord?" Maya asked eagerly.

Hani made a noncommittal noise. "I'm going to keep that to myself, son, if you don't mind."

Maya's eyes widened in hurt surprise, but he said lightly, "Now we just need to give Ay some answer about the poisoner."

"Who's dead that you can blame?" asked Mery-ra, leaning forward, his elbows on his thighs.

Hani gave a bleak grin. "I'd really like to get Mahu accused of it. But I don't think he's in the king's quarters that often. Anyway, who told him that Bener-ib had killed her father, that he should come barreling over here to arrest her? Not Ankhet-khepru-ra, and Ay wouldn't even care." He stood up and brushed off his kilt. "I need to go in and say hello to Sat-hut-haru and the children. They'll think Gamfather is mad at them."

⊠

Maya set off back to his house alone that evening. Sat-hut-haru would be staying with Lady Nub-nefer for a few weeks, and the three children too. Maya felt a sense of freedom mingled with sorrow. To be sure, he could visit them every day if he chose. Still, returning to an empty house didn't sound appetizing. He decided to walk around first, enjoy the mild autumn evening, perhaps polish his latest Tale a bit in his head. He might even eat dinner at the neighborhood beer house, if that wasn't too working-class.

Adjusting his pen case over his shoulder and hitching up his kilt, Maya turned and made his way toward the inland side of the Hall of Royal Correspondence. There was, he knew, a respectable family tavern in the quarter, where he and Lord Hani had gone many times in search of information as well as beer.

A warm light shone from the doorway, where the mat was rolled up well over Maya's head, holding a cheerful promise of conviviality. Maya could hear laughter and the clink of crockery. He entered to see a merry crowd, mostly of men—probably laborers relaxing after a long day of manual work—plus a few women sitting with their husbands. At a discreet distance from the nearest patrons, he hoicked himself up on the masonry bench along the wall and ordered a pot of beer and some fried fish.

It wasn't a bad feeling to stretch and sink into the amiable atmosphere of a neighborhood beer house. A lot of royal artisans patronized this one. Two servants scurried about from table to table, carrying beer jars and stands or plates heaped high with steaming food. Maya attracted a glance or two at first—whether because of the writing case prominent over his shoulder or because he was a dwarf, he couldn't have said. But after that, people returned to their own conversations, and he was left to enjoy his meal in the invisibility of anonymity.

At the little table next to him, several cubits' distance away, two men sat, their heads together in talk. One was Egyptian, the other a dark man from the south. They were young and fit, but their movements were slowed by too many pots of beer.

"What did Lord Mahu tell you to do then?" one of them said in a voice that was perhaps not as low as it was trying to be.

Maya's attention pricked up immediately. *Are these off-duty policemen?* Out of the habit of gathering information for Lord Hani, Maya strained his ears toward them, even while he pretended to be engrossed in his meal.

"Stir up my trouble, and get out. I wasn't sure I was going to get away, frankly. That crowd was like dry tinder," said the other man with a drunken gurgle of laughter. "I'm tired of this town. We're practically in exile here. I want to see my family."

The other man responded with a laugh and some statement Maya couldn't make out clearly, but he caught the name "Lord Pentju," and it sent a chill up his spine. *Who are these people?* he thought, his heart beginning to pound. *Are they* not *policemen?* He longed to draw closer to the pair but feared that if they saw him show too much interest in their conversation, they would stop talking. He decided to give a big yawn and folded his arms on the tabletop then laid his head on them as if going to sleep, at an angle that pushed his wig away from his ear. They could no longer see his face, but he could hear them more clearly than before. He could even watch them through the lashes of one eye if he strained.

"Where'd that Ba-ba-ef go?" said the Egyptian. "I never liked that man. I didn't sign on to the *medjay* to work with the likes of him."

The darker man laughed, a little tipsy. "I hear he was found dead. Guess even Pentju couldn't protect him from all the people he'd made mad at him."

Excitement began to fizz in Maya's middle. He had to force his body to stay limp and not bounce up with elation.

The Egyptian said wryly, "I bet Pentju killed him himself. He wouldn't want anyone to know he knocked off that doctor fellow."

"If they didn't pay well, I wouldn't touch these people. I never know who we're working for."

"We're working for Lord Mahu. Let his conscience figure out the rest." The Egyptian sat back and took a slurp from his straw then, smacking his lips, leaned forward toward his fellow once more. Maya hoped fervently he hadn't looked suspiciously at the dwarf sleeping at the next table.

"You know what I don't like?" the darker man said in a

loud whisper. "It's being Mahu's assassin. It just isn't right to kill an old lady."

His heart in his mouth, Maya almost bounded up from his pretend sleep. *This must be the pair of policemen Sati saw going into Khuit's house!* He stretched his ears until he felt they might detach from his head.

The Egyptian's voice was becoming slurred, and Maya couldn't make out the next few words. But then he heard, "I bet old Pentju is just taking out all his competition! That *sunu* fellow, the midwife, and now a village healer. He wants to be the only doctor around, what do you bet."

"Yes, but what does this have to do with us? We're supposed to be chasing criminals, not helping them," the other said in a tone of disgust. "Who's Lord Mahu really working for?"

There was a space of silence that might have bracketed a shrug, but the men had sat back, withdrawing from Maya's line of view. "I've heard rumors he's not even officially head of the *medjay* anymore. Just hiring himself out to whoever pays the most—Lord Ay, the queen, Lord Pentju."

"And dragging us into it. We'll be the ones to lose our noses and ears if we get caught, not him."

"It's all a roll of the knucklebones, my friend. If the queen's party wins, we're heroes. If Lord Ay comes out on top, we're fried smelt," growled one of the men.

"How much do you reckon Ay knows?"

But the other policeman said nothing. Instead, the two pushed up from the table and made their none-too-steady way toward the door. Maya risked lifting his head a finger's span and watched them through one eye as they pushed back the mat and stepped out into the darkness. Once they had departed, he popped up and shoved his wig back into place. *I've got to tell Lord Hani this right away! Pentju killed Nakht-ef-mut. It only makes sense that Ba-ba-ef was doing his master's will.* But it occurred to Maya that the new information might mean Pentju was at the bottom of the poisonings after all.

Maya threw some faience beads on the table, headed quickly toward the exit, and plunged out the door in a state of such concentration that he looked neither right nor left. Suddenly, strong hands jerked him off his feet, pinning down his arms, and before he could cry out, someone whipped a rag around his mouth. He struggled mightily, trying to grunt out a scream, but his captors upended him and dragged him by his feet away from the beer house into the night. It was the two policemen.

Bes have mercy on me! Maya writhed wildly, but he was hampered by the pain in his shoulders and the back of his head as he was hauled rudely along the earthen street.

His captors stopped, and one of them said, "Look there."

Maya cast terrified eyes over his head and saw that they were in a work yard. A big storage jar sat outside the door of the house. He could barely make out the reed awning overhead, dividing the light of the rising moon into long shards, and a dark fellowship of jars in the shadow of the wall.

"Throw him in. He's drunk too much tonight and gotten pickled, poor little sod."

The two policemen slit the clay seal around the lid of the jar and peered inside. "Beer," said the darker one. The two of them laughed with the hilarity of intoxication, taking him by hands and feet, and dumped him headfirst into the jar.

Beer exploded out with a slosh, and Maya, who hadn't had time to gather a deep breath, found himself swallowing the sour liquid in a rush slowed only by his gag. Choking and spluttering, he managed to get his nose above the surface, only to see the moonlight eclipsed as the two policemen smacked the lid back on the jar.

Maya grunted furiously and tried to jump up and down to prevent them from enclosing him, but the jar was too big for him to get any leverage—he could barely touch bottom with one toe, since the vessel narrowed to a tapering bottom. "Help! Help!" he tried to yell, but his mouth was under the beer. Finally, in despair, he stopped fighting and concentrated on pushing against the walls to keep his face above the brew. *How, by all that's holy, do I get out of here? I'll drown for sure. Oh, inglorious end! Everyone will think I was drunk and fell in.*

Maya managed to fight off his gag, almost sinking in the process. His scraped back burned as if someone had lit it afire, and his eyes were stinging from the beer. "Help!" he tried to cry again, but he had swallowed so much liquid that his efforts ended in coughing. It began to feel as if he really were going to die here. He'd never see his baby daughter. Little Tepy and Mai-her-pri would grow up without a father to model manly behavior for them.

The beer was beginning to get to him—he felt strangely unmoored, his head floating lightly, his thoughts none too clear. He fancied that the too-often-breathed air was growing heavy, overloaded with yeast and fruity fumes, and the darkness spawned terror. If he weakened or fell unconscious, he would sink and drown. *Can I tip this thing over?* he asked himself in desperation. Trying once more to touch bottom, he hurled his body against one wall, and sure enough, the jar rocked. Encouraged, he heaved himself to and fro until he thought he was going to break his shoulder. Each time, the vessel staggered a little more, the beer slopping dangerously close to his nose.

Then, all at once, the whole jar toppled and hit the ground with a bone-jarring thud. Its thick walls hadn't broken, but the top fell off, and beer flooded out all over the earth in a foul-smelling inundation. Maya crawled out on shaking knees, breathing in deep, luxurious drafts of air at last. He felt as if the air circulating in his veins had become barmy so that he could smell nothing else—as if his very blood had turned to beer. He was covered in mud after his emergence, dripping with the horrible sticky brew. Gods forbid anyone should see him like this.

Maya hauled himself to his feet and found he could hardly stand upright. The courtyard seemed to spin around him, the moon sliding in and out of becoming two moons. He clutched gratefully at his amulet of Bes. *Where am I? This could be another beer house—who else would have such an enormous jar full of the stuff?* He balanced, teetering, until he felt he could trust himself to take a step. Around him stood other jars, lots of them, equally large. *Is this a brewery?* he asked himself groggily. In any case, he needed to get out before they made him pay for ruining their beer.

Ahead of him was a gate. Maya staggered toward it and tried to fumble up the bar with unsteady hands only to find it was already unlocked. Leaving the gate wide open behind him, he lurched out into the street. *Head for the River. You can find your way to Lord Hani's from there.*

CHAPTER 15

H ANI WAS STUNNED WHEN A sodden and reeking
Maya staggered into the salon, dripping beer and
mud, without wig or sandals, his shirt ripped and hanging
loose over his kilt. *Mut the mother of us all—has the boy
gone on a binge since he left the house? Is the responsibility of
a fourth child too much for him?*

Hani and Mery-ra, who had been talking in the evening
after the women and children had gone to bed, rushed to
him as he swayed on the threshold.

"Here, son, we have you. Sit down, and tell us what's
happened," Hani cried in concern, supporting his secretary
under the armpits and setting him down on a stool, despite
his trail of muddy brew.

"Maybe he needs a cold shower," observed Mery-ra.
"That should cure several things at once."

"Take a shower," Hani agreed. "There's water in the
bathing room. Do you think you're going to fall? Do you
need help?"

Maya rose and managed to shake his head, then he

convulsed and vomited a stream of foul liquid. Hani took him in his arms and carried him to the bathing room, where he sluiced him several times with cold water. It seemed to bring Maya to himself somewhat. Hani threw him a towel.

"Here are one of the smaller of the servants' clothes. Those had better go into the laundry, if they're even worth saving," Mery-ra said from the doorway.

Full of curiosity and disquietude, Hani managed to put on a smile. "Tell us what has happened, son—that is, if you remember."

Maya tied on the servant's kilt. He had to pull it up under the armpits, but it was clean and dry. He put his head in his hands as if to clear his thoughts then turned strangely excited eyes to Hani. "This isn't what it looks like, my lord. Some renegade policemen almost killed me. They tried to drown me in a beer jar."

Mery-ra chuckled, his belly bouncing. "That's what they all say."

"No, really, my lord. Wait till I tell you what I overheard, Lord Hani!"

They returned to the salon, where the servants had finished cleaning up the floor, but Hani led them to the porch. "Let's go into the garden. I don't want to wake the children."

The men trooped out to the pavilion. After the unseasonably hot day, it was a mild night, even though the Inundation was well past, and with the mats down, the pavilion was comfortable enough.

Maya was obviously bursting to tell what he had learned. The three scribes seated themselves on stools, and he began, almost babbling, still not altogether in control of his speech. "I went to the beer house for dinner—you know the one, where we saw the Mitannians before—and there were two off-duty *medjay* eating there, and I pretended to be asleep and heard them talking. Lord Mahu isn't officially the chief of police anymore. He seems to be working for whoever will pay him, including Lord Pentju, and—"

"Easy, my friend," Hani said, patting the air with his hand, but hope leaped up within him like a new-lit fire. *Mahu has gone rogue?* "Slow down."

And Maya began in a disjointed way to tell everything he had heard. "And you won't believe this: it was Lord Pentju who hired Ba-ba-ef to kill Nakht-ef-mut!"

"I wonder why, if he and Djefat-nebty are not the poisoners. Would it have been worth killing a friend just so the king didn't find out he so much as knew about the crime?"

"It was Pentju who had Khuit killed, too, my lord. These were the very men who did it! And Tuy as well."

Hani and his father exchanged a knowing glance. "We assumed it was the queen because it would be to her advantage to obliterate all the witnesses to the serving girl's identity. But anyone else in the anti-Atenist camp would have the same motivation as well. I don't know how independent Pentju's actions were, but Djefat-nebty seemed to suggest that they were working only for themselves and their ideas of right. I doubt if even she knew what all her husband was up to. Or maybe he was the poisoner after all, and she found out about it but took no part in the plot. I can well imagine she's too principled to violate her oath to Djehuty." Hani struck his thigh with a fist. "I need to let Lord Ay know at least about the possibility. And Pentju can no doubt point the finger at whoever is guilty, if he's only a witness."

"Then it must have been he who told Mahu to go after our Bener-ib. He wouldn't have wanted anyone to come snooping around him." Mery-ra waggled his eyebrows.

"Yet he urged you to investigate, my lord, remember? As if he really wanted to know who had done it."

"What else could he say without tipping me off? And maybe he didn't want Djefat-nebty to know he had killed their friend." Hani pursed his lips thoughtfully. "He was brazen, by all that's holy—and they're the dangerous ones."

Then Hani realized that this meant that whatever Lord Ptah-mes had revealed to Meryet-aten had not brought about the old healer's death. Pentju had probably told the queen, if anyone had—and perhaps no one had. She seemed not to have had a hand in what followed, at any rate. That made Hani feel a little less uneasy about her.

Maya continued breathlessly, "And Pentju and Mahu stirred up the trouble at the Feast of Drunkenness."

"Just as I suspected, although I couldn't think of a motive then," Hani said in satisfaction.

The three men sat staring at one another, and Maya looked pleased with himself.

Mery-ra said dryly, "What exactly can you do about these revelations, son? I'm not sure a conversation overheard in the beer house will be considered substantive evidence—particularly by a man who came home in the condition of our young friend here."

"I'll tell the king what I know, but I admit Pentju may be untouchable. And regarding the poisoning, I have to say it won't be a tragedy to let the guilty party escape—the king is still alive. Lady Djefat-nebty spoke of the poisoner's deeds as heroic acts of war, anyway. I suppose whatever either of them did to hasten the return of the Hidden One must be seen in perspective." Hani's tone darkened. "Still, I'm certainly not averse to planting a little doubt in Lord Ay's mind about the reliability of his henchman, Mahu. He's playing both sides." *As am I.*

Maya's eyelids began to droop, and he seemed to be maintaining his consciousness with effort.

Hani stood up and, with a paternal hand on Maya's shoulder, said, "You, my boy—away to bed with you to sleep off that hangover. You've done us an invaluable service."

Maya lurched unsteadily off to the bedroom he sometimes occupied, leaving Hani and his father eyeing one another with satisfaction.

"I'll bet it was Djefat-nebty who told her husband about the witnesses to the servant girl's birth and her real identity. She must have been the doctor in charge those twenty-five years ago. It's probably no coincidence that all this happened on the eve of their departure from the capital." Hani walked arm-in-arm with Mery-ra back to the house. "I think some of our questions have finally been answered."

⊠

Before he left for the City of the Horizon the next day, Hani dropped in on Ptah-mes, who was sitting cross-legged in his salon, writing on a scroll that appeared to be a ledger. He looked up at Hani's approach and got to his feet with remarkable dignity, a maneuver that Hani had never mastered. Not a pleat of Ptah-mes's immaculate linen was out of place.

"Ah, my friend," the master of the house said with a hollow smile.

Hani could hardly hold himself back from blurting out everything at once. "My lord, it turns out your conversation with the queen had nothing whatever to do with the subsequent murders—Lady Meryet-aten had no hand in them." And he recounted to his friend what Maya had overheard about the partisan activities of the chief physician. "Mahu has apparently taken the bit between his teeth. He's working for whoever will pay him. It's my understanding he no longer holds official rank."

Ptah-mes heard him out with interest, but he didn't seem any happier on his own account than before. His kohl-painted eyes were bleak. "What are you going to do now, Hani? What are you going to tell Ay about the poisonings?"

"I'm not sure. He won't be happy that I still don't have a name for him, but at least I can refer him to Pentju for the full story. Pentju'll most likely prove to be the culprit. And anyway, they're moving, and the poisonings have stopped." *And why is he giving up the highest position a* sunu *can hold? Djefat-nebty said he was ill.* It all made sense.

Ptah-mes nodded, expressionless. "I suppose that, with the news about Mahu, the God's Father may not probe any further into a crime that seems to be finished."

"We'll know soon," said Hani with a wry smile that was more self-assured than he felt. "I'm heading up to talk to him as soon as I leave here."

"May the gods be with you, my friend."

Hani took leave of his former superior with a comforting

clap on the arms, but his heart was heavy. Ptah-mes had clearly not forgiven himself.

⊠

The first thing Hani did upon his arrival in Akhet-aten was head for the palace. He needed to report to Lord Ay about all he had learned, but in fact, he had only a likelihood of the poisoner's identity. It might be a disastrous interview.

As he waited in the reception hall for Ay to see him, Hani was surprised to see Neferet walking quickly past, her basket over her arm and a mourning scarf around her shaven head. "My duckling!" he called out.

She stopped in her tracks and ran to him in delight. "Papa! Are you looking for me?" She threw her arms around her father in bone-crushing affection.

"I'm here to see Lord Ay, my little duck."

Neferet's face grew suddenly guarded. She dropped her eyes. "Lord Ay, eh?" But then a crafty look spread over her. "I have something to tell you too."

"What's that, my duck?"

"Ibet and I are officially the court ladies' *sunet*s now. Lady Djefat-nebty has moved back to Sau."

Hani took her in his arms and gave her a big squeeze, his heart burning with affection and pride. Here was his youngest—a grown woman and the king's personal physician. "Why, that's wonderful, Neferet! What an honor. Do you feel confident that you have enough experience?"

"Oh, yes, Papa," she said airily. "Of course, no one can control everything, but we're ve-r-r-ry well trained."

"Your mother and the other children will be extremely proud, I know. Have you told Aha?"

"No. He's off traveling somewhere, and I doubt if Khentet-ka would care." The relationship between Neferet and her sister-in-law was cool. "It'll be strange for everybody not to have Lady Djefat-nebty around. She's taken care of the palace women for nearly twenty years."

A sudden alarm flapped in Hani's gut like a duck taking off from the River just ahead of the snapping jaws of a crocodile. If Djefat-nebty hadn't been there at the birth of the servant twenty-five years before, she wouldn't have known the servant's identity and couldn't have told Pentju. "Only twenty? Who was the *sunet* before that?"

"Not a *sunet*—a *sunu*. You'll never guess... it was Bener-ib's father! She wasn't even born yet, of course."

Mut the mother of us all! He was the doctor who presided at the birth of the servant girl? Then he must have known who she was. If Bener-ib's father had mentioned it to Pentju, that could have been the reason for the *wab* priest's death—Pentju was trying to erase all evidence of the Haru in the nest's royal birth. And it would explain why all these murders started happening just recently—Nakht-ef-mut and Pentju must have been in communication about their transfer of duties even before the man of Sau had arrived in the city.

"And there's another thing that will interest you." Neferet tried to smile, but there was something ineffably sad about the pull of her mouth. "They've found out who was trying to poison the king. I'll tell you more about it later."

Hani's heart stopped. *They've identified Pentju?*

"It was one of the serving girls. They found jewelry on her, and then she confessed. I have to go now, Papa. I'll tell you more later." Neferet's eyes kept cutting away as if she couldn't wait to be gone. Hani felt a twinge of concern. Something strange was going on here.

His daughter had no sooner bounced away than a majordomo appeared to lead Hani to his audience. Hani swallowed hard and followed the servant, stunned. Trepidation weighed down his steps. *Surely Neferet had nothing to do with it.*

Through the tall doors into Lord Ay's small, luxurious audience room Hani marched. He made a deep court bow, hands on knees.

Bright-eyed and pleasant as ever, Ay greeted him from his chair. "Ah, Hani. I wondered when you were coming back."

Hani's heart began to hammer. He bowed silently, trying to think of how he could explain that he didn't really know who the poisoner was.

But Ay spoke first. "I know what you're going to say. And we've already apprehended her, so job well done."

Hani struggled to control his unease. "The woman confessed, I believe?" he said blandly.

"Yes. Caught in the act, in fact. She pretended that she intended to sell the pieces, but who would buy something with the king's name on it?" His reddish-brown eyes twinkled. "But then you know all this already."

Hani tipped his head again for lack of words. He needed to talk to his daughter. "There's something else I wanted to make Our Sun aware of, my lord. I've heard rumors that Mahu is no longer official head of the *medjay*, but I have proof that he has been acting on his own, using police resources, at the behest of whoever pays him. Several of his men were witnessed killing an old-woman healer and the late midwife as well."

Ay raised his eyebrows. "You're right about his status. Like everyone else, he has yet to be reappointed to his post... or not." He shook his head. "I'm distressed he's made himself a partner to crime, of course. Who all has he been working for—other than the king?"

"Let's say followers of the more extreme party of restoration, but their danger has been neutralized. And I'm convinced that many of his deeds have been on his own behalf." *Like harassing my family.*

The God's Father clucked his tongue. "Perhaps the time has come to let the man drift off into retirement or to service in some remote outpost— with the viceroy of Ta-nehesy, maybe. A change of regime often brings about such transitions. No dishonor in it." He bared his teeth in a foxy smile. "Well, there you are, Hani. My daughter will see to it you're rewarded for your troubles. Maybe even the gold of honor, eh? What's a king's life worth?"

Hani bowed low. "I am at my ruler's disposal, my lord. Her favor is the breath of life to my nostrils."

As Hani started to leave, Ay called out, "Oh, by the way. My granddaughter will be calling upon you soon to take a little journey for her."

Hani's blood ran cold. *He's aware of more than I am.*

"Let me know when you start off, my friend. We want to be sure you stay safe. Who knows what could happen up there?"

Once more, Hani had no answer but to bow.

⊠

That evening, when he returned to Lord Ptah-mes's villa, Hani was surprised to find the master of the house present, with Maya and the two young doctors at his side.

"My boat is faster than the public ferry, Hani. I seem to turn up unexpectedly," said Ptah-mes with his bleak smile. "I had some duties to see to—personal ones, of course— and young Maya came along."

"It seems the poisoner has stepped forward and confessed after stolen articles were found on her, my lord." Hani shot a glance at Neferet, whose eyes were suspiciously averted. Bener-ib's hands twisted nervously in her lap. *Something gives me a bad feeling.*

Maya cried enthusiastically, "That's the last of our unanswered questions! Who was it? Did the queen have nothing to do with it after all?"

Ptah-mes looked down, his face impassive.

"Why did Mahu let up on Bener-ib, though?" asked Maya.

"Ay or the king no doubt warned him to let her alone. Ankhet-khepru-ra seems never to have believed in her guilt." Hani added in a lower voice, "And the queen has apparently decided that this is the time to send for her Hittite. I have to admit, I'm much less ambivalent about serving her now that we know she wasn't behind some of the dark deeds of recent months."

Maya's eyes goggled.

"Ay told me, by the way. He seems to be fully aware of her activities."

Suddenly, Neferet blurted, "Papa, that poor handmaid who was arrested doesn't deserve to die."

"What do you know about this, my duckling?" Hani asked, dreading to learn her role in the affair.

With a glance at Bener-ib, who was chewing her lip anxiously, Hani's daughter said, "You remember I told you Ibet was staying late to take care of Weneb, that servant who'd had trouble with her childbirth?"

"Yes. Vaguely."

"The girl was... she was raped by a member of the king's family. More than once over a few years. He got her pregnant. She lost the first baby and barely recovered, and then it happened again. She's one of those people who just can't have children safely. She needed a lot of extra care. But she isn't well yet, anyway. I bet she dies in jail before they can execute her."

"How sad," Hani said, his heart heavy. How many attractive young women had had their lives ruined by the attentions of the royal men? "Why did she want to poison the king?"

Neferet turned to Bener-ib with a squeeze of her friend's hand. "Tell them, Ibet."

Bener-ib looked up at the men, her face pale and tense. "I wanted to take care of her because I understood only too well what she'd been through, my lords. She was just an adolescent when this started. Lord Ay took a fancy to her—"

"Lord Ay?" cried Hani and Ptah-mes simultaneously. Maya's eyes were round with shock.

"Yes, my lords. He must have seen her around his daughter's apartments and sort of kept her to... to enjoy whenever he wanted. She was terrified of him."

Maya said, "But I thought Ay had changed out the entire staff of the royal household at some point."

"All but her. He wanted her around. And she was a poor servant, my lords. She couldn't just resign from the king's service."

Hani caught a glimpse of Ptah-mes's expressionless face, which promptly took on a look of cold cynicism. "We knew Ay was a bastard. This shouldn't surprise us," the grandee said with a curl of the lip.

"She hated him," Bener-ib continued, her voice dropping and becoming hard as the blade of a knife. "She hated someone who would take advantage of her like that."

As you well know, my poor girl, Hani thought.

"She wanted revenge, but there was nothing she could do to Lord Ay. He didn't even live at the palace. And he came with soldiers and everything."

Neferet, too excited to stay silent any longer, jumped in. "So she decided to kill the king instead. But how? She finally decided to poison her little by little."

"But didn't that mean she would be poisoned too?" objected Hani.

"She didn't even care if she died," Neferet said defensively.

"She would've been happy to die," Bener-ib murmured, her eyes in her lap.

A moment of pained silence fell. Then Maya said, "But what made her think of orpiment? How did she know it could be used as a slow poison?"

Neferet crowed, "Lady Djefat-nebty told her."

The men stared at one another. Hani remembered Djefat-nebty saying she knew who the poisoner was.

"What?" Hani stammered. "She just went up to the *sunet* and said, 'What can I use to poison the king?'"

"No, no, Papa. I told you we made the king some depilatory salve, remember? Lady Djefat-nebty had made some for her a year or more ago too. She'd seen the servant with the stuff and told her to be careful because it could become poison if you got enough of it on the skin over time. And that gave the girl the idea."

Ptah-mes asked, "How did the servant manage to sneak the objects away to put the salve on them? Everyone must have been under observation."

"She was on the night shift—the one who put things up into their chests at night. Nobody was around to keep an eye on her, even though they checked her at the door. So she got this bag and tied it around her waist, hanging between her legs. She only took little things, one at a time. If it looked bulky or she walked funny, nobody thought it was anything odd because she was bleeding and had to wear a bandage of thick rags down there. She bought a pot of salve from some village healer, and while she had the pieces in her room, she rubbed it on the stolen articles wherever they would be touched the most, then she returned them as she had a chance."

"If she handled the objects with no one around, I'd have thought she'd be the first suspect. Did no one look in her room?" Ptah-mes asked.

"Of course. But she'd hide them under a pile of dirty bandages. It would be a rare man who would dare look under there, my lord." Despite the deadly seriousness of the conversation, Neferet couldn't resist a snicker.

No one said anything. Hani struggled to absorb this

strange new revelation. "Did Djefat-nebty know what the girl was doing?"

"I don't know, Papa. But I bet she figured it out."

And said nothing, of course. Watched the symptoms piling up and said nothing. Because this case of personal grievance suited her political ends well.

"Did the servant tell you all these things? Wasn't she afraid you'd report her?" Ptah-mes asked in his driest magistrate voice.

"She was afraid she was going to die after the last childbirth, my lord. She felt close to me because... because I understood her," said Bener-ib. She still seemed reluctant to look them in the eye. "And she wanted to unburden her conscience before she met the Judge of Souls. So she told me everything. I don't think she even cared if we let the authorities know."

Maya said bitterly, "I'm sure Lord Ay was delighted to be able to arrest and execute her, the son of a jackal. No more witness to his predatory behavior."

And he said she claimed to have stolen them to sell. He must have known exactly why she was doing it. "How long have you known about this, my girls? The thefts began at least a year ago."

"We just found out, Papa, when Weneb thought she would die."

Hani shook his head slowly, both relieved that he had at last learned who the poisoner was and discouraged about the arrogant amorality of men in power. And the desperation of the vulnerable, who had no recourse but their fatal vengeance.

More than two weeks had passed, and Hani was back in the capital. He'd heard nothing further about Queen Meryet-aten's commission, but Ay had made good on his promise to decorate him. Hani found it ironic that he had been rewarded for a "successful conclusion" to a case he hadn't even solved. He'd said nothing about Pentju and Djefat-nebty's complicity in any of the business after all. They'd gone off to the Lower Kingdom, and no one was likely to bother them. Mahu had been retired with kudos and given a nice plot of land near Seyawt to which he was expected to withdraw. Hani hoped he and his family had seen the last of the man.

After the bestowal of the gold-of-honor ceremony, the family had gone home to Waset, but Hani had stayed on a few days to conclude some chancery business. The vizier of the Lower Kingdom, Ra-nefer, was all aflutter. Missions were finally going to be reassigned, and the business of foreign affairs was to resume. He seemed hopeful that he might lose his burdensome post.

It was early evening, and Hani and Pipi were sitting in the garden of Lord Ptah-mes's villa. They were well into the season of Peret, but the weather was mild, and the air was as soft as the feathers of a dove's breast. Hani stretched out in his low-backed chair, head against the rear wall of the pavilion and fingers laced over his belly, gazing peacefully out into the garden. The setting sun caught the water of the pool with an occasional flash as of golden crystals.

"Did you ever get rid of that boat, brother?" Hani said at last, forcing himself to break the lazy silence.

Pipi heaved a sigh and shot Hani a worried look from the corner of his eye. "He won't give the down payment back, Hani. I'm going to lose all that silver and grain and have nothing to show for it."

"Is the boat still in your possession?"

"Yes, though I'm supposed to have given it back a long time ago."

Hani rolled his eyes hopelessly. He tried to make his voice sound nonjudgmental. "They're going to come after you for theft. You might as well pay the rest of it if you can't get your silver back."

"But I don't have the rest of it," Pipi cried. Once the surface was scratched, the cheerful mood of the recent celebration had cracked to reveal the desperation beneath. "I don't know what to do. They may empty my granaries or even take my house."

Hani sighed in annoyance. He'd sworn he wasn't going to bail his feckless brother out of difficulties ever again, but he'd just received a substantial supply of gold and barterable foodstuffs from the king's hand. *And I've always wanted a yacht...* "Listen, Pipi. I'll take the boat off your hands. This time only, you understand. No more of this irresponsible business, is that clear?"

Pipi hurled himself on Hani, enveloping him in his pudgy arms. "Oh, I knew you'd say that! My big brother is still looking out for me." His eyes were dewy with tears. "Thank you, thank you, Hani. Just tell me what I can do to make it up to you."

"You can make this your last extravagance, that's what." In spite of himself, Hani returned the hug with tenderness.

He could hardly stay mad at Pipi, who had no more sense of financial responsibility than a child.

They settled back into their silence, but Hani could almost hear the joyful hum of Pipi's thoughts. It was getting on toward dinnertime when Pipi rose and stretched. "I think I'll go wash up. You coming in?"

"Not yet. I plan to wait to eat till Ptah-mes gets back from the Hall of Royal Correspondence. He had an appointment."

Pipi lumbered off into the house, and Hani folded his arms over his head in contentment. He was picturing himself on the beautiful red-and-green yacht, with the wind in his face, heading down to Hut-nen-nesut to see the flamingos.

Voices at the gate pulled him back to the present. Footsteps crunched up the gravel path, and in a moment, Lord Ptah-mes appeared, graceful and erect as ever. His face was carefully devoid of any expression, which raised a prickle of unease along Hani's neck.

He got to his feet and smiled. "Lord Ptah-mes. How did your meeting go?"

Ptah-mes said nothing at first, just lowered himself deliberately into Pipi's abandoned chair and spread his long, ringed hands over his knees. Then he fixed Hani with a cynical stare. "I met with Lord Ay."

Hani's eyes widened in surprise, and he sank back into his seat. "All is well, I hope."

"I expected him to censure me for my allegiance to his granddaughter, but instead, he offered me a post in the government."

Hani stared at him. He managed to say, "Well, this is

the moment when assignments are being made. I suppose that makes sense."

Ptah-mes blew an explosive breath out through his nose. "He presented me with a great long rationale about how his and the king's gradual method of reintroducing the cult of the Hidden One was the only peaceful means to restore the old ways. He assured me that he was as eager as anyone to see the gods back in the heavens but that a step-by-step approach was prudent. He said he's thinking of moving the capital out of Akhet-aten, but that may have to wait until Prince Tut-ankh-aten is on the throne—the city has sentimental connotations for the present king. Our friend is eager to reach out to partisans of the 'more extreme' proponents of violent change, because we must cooperate for the good of the Two Lands."

"He said something similar to me, my lord. It seems he's fully aware of what the Crocodiles are up to." Hani nodded, reflecting. "I must admit, little as I trust Lord Ay, I have to agree that his is a better plan, even if it takes some patience."

"Of course," Ptah-mes said icily. "The question is, *can* we trust him? He's a slippery serpent of a man."

And worse, thought Hani, remembering the sad story of the servant girl who had tried to exact her revenge on the king.

"I might have agreed—with reservations—right there, but then the God's Father said to me, 'Think of all the advantages your grandson will obtain by being raised as a companion to the next king. It would be a shame to jeopardize that through some misplaced sense of righteousness.'"

Hani said in disgust, "He threatened you?"

Ptah-mes tipped his head in acknowledgment. "Not with a strike at me but at my grandson. How would Djehuty-mes like that? 'Here, son, I'm being true to my conscience and letting Ay take it out of your boy's flesh. Are you finally proud of me?'"

Hani fell silent. *He's in a terribly hard place. My problems with Aha were easier to solve—it just took a few gold collars around my neck for him to respect me.* He could think of no consolation to offer. After a moment during which Ptah-mes, too, said nothing, Hani finally asked, "Are you willing to become high commissioner again if nothing has changed in Djahy?"

"That's not the post he's offered me, my friend. He wants me to be the Master of the Double House of Silver and Gold."

The treasurer. Hani was stunned. The second highest position in the whole government, right after the viziers. "You'll make a good one, my lord," he said sincerely. "You're intelligent and honest."

"And I have all the spine of a worm. Perfect for an official."

"But there's really no reason you shouldn't accept anyway, is there, my lord? We're all collaborating so that good men are in key positions. I just publicly accepted Ay's accolades too. I hope, as you no doubt do as well, that things are changing. Within a reign, I daresay the world will be back to normal." Hani reached out and laid a hand of solidarity on his friend's arm.

"Didn't I say something about my loyalty to the queen the other day as an excuse for a terrible gaffe? Like a dog, I seem to be true to whoever pets me." Ptah-mes gave a bitter burst of laughter and surged to his feet. He began to walk back and forth, his hands clenched at his sides and his jaw set. Finally, he stopped and looked apologetically at Hani. "Forgive me. I have no need to burden you with all of this. I'm an adult. I should work out my own moral problems."

Hani, who had risen, too, out of respect, said kindly, "We all have moral problems these days. I find myself drifting further and further away from the violent faction of the queen and Lord Mai. I'm afraid of what they're going to provoke. And yet I find the God's Father an appalling man. But as a servant of the Great House, I have to be on some side. At least, Ay's not the king."

Ptah-mes made a clear effort to wipe his face of bitterness and said with a forced smile, "You're right, of course. I should have expected such wisdom from you." After an instant of stiff hesitation, Ptah-mes extended his arms, and for the first time in the twenty or so years that Hani had known him, the two men embraced. Hani found himself deeply moved.

"This is the Lake of Flowers, my lord. Our trials are ending, and ahead lies the Field of Reeds. We must have faith that that is true."

Ptah-mes said, with an almost sly twitch of the corner of his mouth, "We're not across it yet, my friend. I just hope you can swim."

THE END

Did you enjoy Lake of Flowers? Here is a sample from the next Lord Hani Mystery, _Pilot Who Knows the Water_

CHAPTER 1

SPRING HAD POURED ITSELF OUT generously over the Two Lands—harvest season for wheat and barley—and on the farm, the laborers were bent over, sickles in hand, a line of white and red and black, moving methodically across the vast golden fields. Despite his misgivings about the politics of the kingdom, Hani had to confess life was good. The harvest would be rich this year; his granaries would be full. He might even have to build another one.

At his side, his wife, Nub-nefer, slipped an arm around his waist and said in a dreamy voice, "It's been so nice to have you here in Waset, my love. It's been so good for the grandchildren. I hope the king never gets around to reassigning overseas missions."

They were standing in the road between the house and its vegetable gardens and the broader fields of grain. Overhead the sky stretched, a vast, piercingly blue canopy like lapis lazuli, shot with the bright flash of pigeon wings as a flock settled in the stubble to glean. Hani drew a deep breath of satisfaction, squeezing Nub-nefer to his side. Perhaps the queen had decided against her special assignment for him after all. Months had passed since she had last summoned him to say, "Be ready," and still no word had come that would send him on the long voyage north to Kheta Land.

In the same way, Hani's lessons with the crown prince had ended as other subjects arose with which the lad needed to be familiar. *Familiar, but certainly not expert. How much of a foreign language can you learn in a year? I'm afraid, as Sen-nedjem said, the boy's going to be half-learned.* Prince Tut-ankh-aten's tutor, Sen-nedjem, had never seemed enthusiastic about turning any part of the lad's education over to anyone else, and perhaps he had finally had his way. But the upshot was Hani had been able to enjoy these months of nearly uninterrupted leisure with his family.

And Waset had become an especially exciting place to be in the last year, because the liturgies at the Ipet-isut, the great shrine of Amen-Ra, had resumed. Hani glanced sideways at his wife, whose serene gaze told him how her years of anger and anxiety had melted away. Once more, she had taken up her duties as a chantress of the Hidden One; her brother had emerged from hiding and was again praising Amen-Ra in his office of Third Prophet. It was easy to believe all the chaos of the last reign was over, and that good times were on their way back, surging irresistibly up the River toward them like the golden barque of the Hidden One on festival days.

"Maybe we should turn back, what do you think?" Nub-nefer finally said. "The girls may be getting worried about us."

Hani doubted it, but he smiled tenderly at his wife and said, "Of course, my dear. It's hot out here in the full sun anyway. A suntan won't hurt me, but I'm sure you don't want one."

They turned and, his hand and Nub-nefer's linked like a pair of newlyweds', they began their leisurely way back toward the farmhouse. The couple had only gone a few cubits before a cloud of dust appeared ahead, bursting from the farmyard, which soon resolved itself into the running figure of their grandson, Tepy. The ten-year-old pounded down the road toward them, his elbows pumping, his Haru-lock flying. A chill of fear seized Hani by the throat. *Dear gods, has something happened to Sati or one of the children?*

But Tepy skidded to a halt in front of his grandparents, eyes bright with excitement not fear. Panting, he cried, "Gamfather, there's a messenger from the queen at the house! He told me to get you right away!"

Nub-nefer shot her husband an anxious glance. She knew as well as Hani what this meant. Hani could feel his happiness draining away like the receding waters of the Inundation, leaving cold trepidation in its wake. "Thanks, son," he said to Tepy with a forced smile. "Let's see what the queen wants."

The three picked up their pace and made their way through the rows of lettuce and onions and freshly planted cowpeas into the low-walled enclosure around the house. Geese scattered, squawking their indignation, as the humans entered, while Tepy danced around in anticipation of something momentous. In the salon, Sat-hut-haru sat with her children and her sister-in-law-and-cousin Mut-nofret. Baket-iset, Hani's eldest girl, lay immobile but bright-eyed and lovely, as she had for more than half her life after a terrible accident. The young mothers sprang to their feet, and it was only then that Hani saw in the shadows of the small room a rather splendidly dressed gentleman rising at the same time. Under a long court wig, his face had that look of sleek impassivity that said "high-level royal functionary." His hands were clasped loosely in front of him, but the man didn't look altogether at ease.

"Papa," cried Baket-iset, her voice pleasant but relief only too obvious beneath it. "This man has brought you a message from the Great King's Wife. He looked for you in Waset, but the servants told him you were up here."

Hani advanced toward the messenger and, being unclear about the man's rank, greeted him with a sketchy sort of bow. "You've had a long journey. I'm sorry you had to come this extra distance. How may I help you?"

The man's expression grew a little tart, as if he, too, were sorry about the additional *iterus*. "Our lady has a message for your ears only, Lord Hani. Where can we speak?"

Hani was on the verge of telling him, "These people can hear anything you have to say," but already Nub-nefer had discreetly begun to round up the children and their toys.

She said, "We'll go up on the roof where there's more breeze. You men say whatever you have to say right here." In a minute, the three women and the little ones had hustled up the stairs, and the servants carried Baket's couch up after them. Tepy gave a longing look of curiosity over his shoulder as he trailed in their wake.

With the disappearance of the family, a nervous silence fell. Finally, the messenger said in a low voice, "I'm sure you know what this is about, my lord. The queen our lady wants you to be advised that the time has come to make your… ahem… journey." He fixed Hani with his painted brown eyes as if to convey without words what they both realized this meant.

Hani did know only too well. A chill ran on spider feet up his backbone. He said in an equally guarded tone, "Is she satisfied that Lord Ay won't oppose us? He's aware of her intention, of course."

The servant tipped his head. "There's an uprising in Ta-nehesy. The God's Father Lord Ay and General Har-em-heb have gone south to put it down."

So that's why Queen Meryet-aten has chosen this precise moment to send me north. "Very well. I'll leave immediately. Does she want me to meet with her before I go?"

"No, my lord. She wants you to get outside the borders of the kingdom as soon as possible. Gifts of exchange, your military escort, and seagoing ships await you at Per-nefer. Speak to the garrison commander there."

"I have no reply, then. But I invite you to stay the night here before you start back to the capital."

The man bobbed a grateful bow, his cold expression thawing. "Appreciated, Lord Hani."

Hani called a servant to show the man to a guest room—that seemed more appropriate than a pallet in the servants' quarters—and he himself stumped heavily up the stairs and onto the roof terrace. "Nub-nefer, my dove. A word with you?"

She rose from where she sat on her heels on the smooth packed-clay floor, playing cat's-cradle with little Henut-sen. Her eyes were anxious behind the smile.

The two of them retreated to the stairwell, where Hani

took his wife by both shoulders and said gravely, "The queen has finally sent me on that mission I told you about."

Hope flared across Nub-nefer's golden face and her great kohl-edged eyes grew fierce. "At last! Now the Aten will go back where he came from, and the Hidden One will reign again."

Still, Hani wasn't so sure. His mission was to bring back to Kemet a bridegroom for the queen, so that as soon as her mother, the she-king, should die—and Queen Meryet-aten apparently had reason to think that would be sooner rather than later—the girl would share the throne with him and reinstate the old cults. But the bridegroom would be a Hittite prince. This was so unimaginable that Hani could still hardly believe the young queen was going through with it. Kheta was the rival of the Two Lands. While Hani himself was not opposed to more friendly relations between the kingdoms, there would be many, even devotees of the Hidden One, who would be scandalized by the plan. He only hoped it didn't end in disaster. Surely the Black Land had lived through more than its share of disaster over the past fourteen years.

"I need to leave immediately. I told the messenger he could stay the night, but as soon as I can pack, I'm taking off. I'll pick up Maya in Waset."

"All right, my dearest. Write to us often. I'll send the other children your love."

"Maybe I'll see Aha when I pass through Akhet-aten." *Or maybe not. This is hardly news I'd want him to think too closely about.* Aha, Hani's firstborn, was a devotee of the Aten. "And Neferet and Bener-ib. I guess Pa-kiki will be on his way to Ta-nehesy with our friend Har-em-heb." Hani looked around, suddenly missing a familiar face. "Where is Father?"

"He must be outside somewhere. Baket said a messenger brought him a letter, and he went to the garden to read it. You surely want to say goodbye to him. At his age, one never knows."

The thought sat chill as the walls of a deep well in Hani's gut. He had started thinking about this more and more. His beloved father, while healthy and strong for his age, was seventy-four, a ripe sum of years. Much as Hani hated the thought, Mery-ra wouldn't live forever. *And if I were to be gone when he passes over into the West?* He wasn't sure he could forgive himself. "I'll be sure to see him before I go."

Now, Hani told himself. *Before I get involved in packing.* He set off through the farmyard. Near the low wall that separated the little yard from the agricultural fields outside, Hani's father stood, his back turned, seemingly reading something. Mery-ra was an older version of Hani himself—broad to the point of squat, with powerful shoulders and a cheerful square-jowled face. Hani was overcome with a burning wave of tenderness. *No one could have had a better parent.*

Mery-ra turned as Hani approached, and he slipped whatever he had been reading behind his back. Hani thought from the glimpse he caught before the object disappeared behind his father's broad middle that it looked like a clay tablet. "Why, Hani, my boy. I thought you were out in the fields." The old man clapped his son jovially on the shoulder and smiled his welcome, but his eyes shifted sideways in a guilty glance.

"What are you up to, Father?" Hani couldn't resist a teasing grin.

"Oh, only a letter from an old friend. What leads you to prowl around the garden, son?"

Hani's smile grew tight as he said, "A messenger just came from the queen."

Mery-ra's thick black eyebrows rose. "I wondered whose big boat that was, tying up."

"She's ready for my mission to Kheta."

Mery-ra's small eyes widened, then narrowed in what might have been a considering look. After a moment, he said, "Ah, son, this could be dangerous. You need protection."

"Menna and Pa-ra-mes-su will be leading the escort," Hani assured him. "They're both loyal to the queen."

"Soldiers, yes, but who's going to be your eyes and ears?"

Hani had a sense he knew where this was leading, and he said firmly, "Maya. I need you to protect the women in our absence—which will certainly be a number of months."

"It seems to me, my boy, that what you need is an experienced spy and emissary at your side to feel people out. Someone with long experience dealing with foreigners. One who speaks Neshite." Mery-ra looked up at Hani with a sly grin that bared the gap between his front teeth.

But Hani was adamant. "No, Father. This is going to be a very hard journey—we'll be traveling as fast as we can with the fewest number of breaks. And the gods know how many people will be out to stop us from getting to Hattusha."

"All the more reason you need me. I've been to Hattusha." Mery-ra crossed his arms, triumphant.

Hani jerked back in surprise. "You have? I didn't know that."

"Trust me, son. There's plenty you don't know."

"No, absolutely no. This is dangerous. And by the Lord Djehuty, it's an official mission for the queen. I can't just bring my relatives along for a lark." Hani had an unpleasant feeling that his father had already considered such an objection.

Sure enough, Mery-ra said smugly, "You'll have staff, won't you? I'm a better scribe than most of those youngsters, whose script looks like they've written it with their left hand."

Knowing he was defeated, Hani shook his head, lips compressed and face starting to get hot with the pressure of all the ripostes that wanted to fly out. "Then we both need to pack. I'm leaving by mid afternoon, and anyone who isn't ready will be left behind."

"That's my boy. You'll be amazed at how useful your old papa is. People don't take a venerable gentleman all that seriously. They'll reveal things to me you'd never get out of them."

The two men set off toward the house stride for stride, while the geese and ducks scattered at their feet. Hani knew better than to hope to change his father's mind. He couldn't imagine what had put the idea into Mery-ra's head, but there would be no moving him. Mery-ra was as cheerfully stubborn as his granddaughter Neferet. And Hani could imagine that the old man would probably be helpful indeed. *Still, the danger...*

In Waset, they picked up Maya, who had gone home to supervise some workmen at the house while the rest of the family enjoyed their time at Lord Hani's farm. Although he'd expected the call to leave the Two Lands eventually, it had caught him by surprise. He trudged up the gangplank of Hani's boat feeling mildly disgruntled. The first thing he said to his father-in-law was, "I didn't get a chance to say goodbye to Sati and the children."

"She knows where we've gone, son. You can write to her when we put into shore tonight."

Maya sighed in resignation. Then, behind Hani's back, he saw Lord Mery-ra, hands on his hips, looking pleased with himself. Maya's eyes flew wide in surprise. "My lord. Are you accompanying us to Per-nefer?"

Mery-ra toddled forward and laid a conspiratorial hand on his son's shoulder. He said to Maya with a gap-toothed grin that split his cheeks, "I'm accompanying you to Hattusha."

Maya stared from one man to another. He didn't know what to say and eventually managed to stammer, "Oh?"

Unseen by his father behind him, Lord Hani rolled his eyes. "Yes. He's familiar with the city and has invited himself along as part of my staff."

Much as he loved the old man, Maya's heart chilled, suddenly grown heavy as a rock. He had looked forward to the uniquely close relationship to his father-in-law a long journey opened to him. They would have been on the deck of a ship for endless weeks together with only one another to talk to, play word games with, plan their course of action. They would have shared the experience of making land in exotic places together, forming memories that only the two of them would laugh over afterwards. Faced danger at one another's side...

Now, of course, Lord Hani would talk to and confide in his father. The two highborn men would share the jokes, enriched by their lifetime familiarity with one another. Lord Mery-ra would be sent on delicate fact-finding missions instead of Maya. Maya would be pushed to the side; he would be reduced to a mere secretary. And even there, who knew? Perhaps the old man would supplant him as Hani's amanuensis.

Disappointment crushed Maya to the ground, and he could scarcely make his face smile. "How wonderful. Welcome, my lord."

Hani caught Maya's eye with a penetrating look and quirked his mouth a little—in amusement or compassion or both—as if he could read his son-in-law's thoughts. "We'll join our party at Per-nefer. The commandant has staff and escort waiting for us and all the diplomatic gifts the queen has gathered for the negotiations. Meantime, we might as well enjoy our last sight of Kemet for a while."

The three men found a seat under the tented sunshade toward the stern. Hani's small yacht, which he had bought from his brother Pipi to save Pipi from bankruptcy, had no cabin like that of the much larger vessel of Lord Ptah-mes, his former superior. But it was still a vast improvement over a public ferry—cleaner, more private, decidedly more appropriate for the Master of the King's Stable. The sailors were well fed and respectful. And the voyagers could stop or even reverse course anytime they liked.

Besides, Maya reminded himself, fellow travelers would stare enviously at the jaunty, expensive-looking boat, painted bright red and green with a grinning Bes-head on the prow, and ask themselves what dignitary was passing.

They sat for a bit, cross-legged on the deck in the small square of shade, while Maya chewed over his disappointment. All at once, he remembered something he had meant to tell his father-in-law. "My mother said to tell you her chief workman was found murdered, my lord. That Ipy—remember? The one who made some of those daggers that Nefer-khepru-ra gave to his friends?"

"I'm sorry to hear that," Hani replied in genuine sorrow. "He was a real artist."

"And Mother had planned to leave the workshop to him when she retires." Maya had suffered pangs of guilt over this revelation. It should have been he, her only son, who carried on the family business of royal goldsmith. But of course, he had chosen the role of a scribe. Now, as In-hapy approached old age and the inevitable loss of keen eyesight that signaled the end of a jeweler's career, she didn't know what to do. She didn't want to close the shop and take jobs away from the men and boys who worked for her. Maya felt somehow obliquely to blame. Wouldn't a good son have abandoned his own ambitions to support his parent in her later years? It occurred to him that that was why he was in such a self-pitying mood.

"She, er, she was hoping we could find out who killed him—not that that would bring him back, but... you know. For his family's sake," Maya added. His conscience throbbing like a boil, he had almost stayed behind in order to perform this service for his mother. But the lure of adventure and prestige had been too strong.

And now, Lord Mery-ra.

Hani said reluctantly, "Much as I'd love to help her, I don't see how we can, Maya. It will be months before we get done with this mission. Unless you want to turn back..."

There they were: the words Maya had dreaded to hear.

"No, no. Official business comes first," he said hastily. "I just wanted you to know."

Eventually, his eyes squinted as he gazed across the bright water, Lord Mery-ra said, "It'll take us... what? A week or more to reach the coast of the Great Green?"

"I would think so," said Hani. "On the 'more' side, probably."

"And then, how many weeks to Kheta Land? Is the capital on the coast?" Maya asked.

"By no means. It's very far north, in the highlands. Days'—maybe weeks'—journey from the port at Ura." Lord Mery-ra's little brown eyes twinkled. "Unless they've moved Hattusha in the last fifty years."

Lord Hani laughed and shook his head.

"And if we put in at Adana and have to go through the land of Kidjuwadna, the mountains are even worse. You think you've seen mountains in Amurru—these are the grandfathers to those little hillocks." Mery-ra chuckled, shaking his head at the memory.

Maya said glumly to himself, *Are we going to be listening to reminiscences the whole way? Reminders that some of us haven't been to Hattusha?* He felt for the Bes amulet hanging around his neck, as if to send up a prayer for help.

Lord Hani breathed in an expansive inhalation of the

fine air. "You know," he said, "I don't think we're going to reach the capital before nightfall after all. We'll just stop in Seyawt or wherever we've gotten when dusk comes. There was no real reason I needed to go to Akhet-aten, except to say goodbye to the girls." His daughter and her friend were physicians to the ladies of the court.

"And we can write our wives tonight, right, my lord?" Maya said.

But Mery-ra looked sly. "Ah, who will read the letters to them, though? All of us literate fellows are here."

Hani gave a snort of laughter. "It was your choice to abandon them, Father. Aren't you ashamed? Maybe Amen-em-hut, now that he's back among the living. Or we'll have to have Pipi join them for a few months." His brother, also a scribe, normally lived in the capital, but wasn't above taking long periods of time off to return to his ancestral home in Waset. It happened less frequently now that Pipi's daughter lived in Akhet-aten too.

All we need is for the indiscreet Lord Pipi to start asking where the rest of us are. "Surely there's a neighborhood scribe somewhere around," Maya said.

"No doubt," said Hani cheerfully. His eyes were fixed over the water, on the flight of some kind of big bird with its long legs trailing out behind. Then he turned back to Maya with a more serious expression. "I think we need to write to Lord Ay, my friend. He made a point of telling me to let him know when we took off. I'm assuming that it will reach him in the field too late for him to do anything about it." He lifted an eyebrow.

Mery-ra slitted his eyes suspiciously. "What's he up to, the old fox? He can't really want this mission to succeed."

"I'm sure I don't know, Father. But whatever he has in mind, we're right in the middle of it. Don't say I didn't warn you."

☒

The journey downriver took every bit as long as Hani had foreseen—his new yacht might be more comfortable than a ferry, but it was no faster. By the time the men reached Per-nefer on the coast of the Great Green, they were already tired of being confined on a small deck. In relief, they disembarked at that last Egyptian port in the estuary of the River and struck off into the town to find the local commandant. It was here they would change to a seagoing vessel for the second leg of the journey and send Hani's little yacht back upstream.

The worst is yet to come. Hani sighed. *That endless voyage from one end to another of the Great Green across the heaving waves.*

He had to admit that, despite his reservations, his father was a delightful addition to the traveling party. As a former military scribe, Mery-ra was accustomed to bear difficult conditions without complaint, and his unshakably cheerful and humorous presence helped to lighten the hours. Hani observed, to his amusement, that Maya had been disgruntled at first—he was transparently jealous when it came to Hani's favor—but he was back to himself now, won over despite his insecurities.

The commandant of the port garrison was a burly man in his thirties with a big slab of a nose and ears to match. Firmly in the camp of the Hidden One, he seemed willing to put the queen's orders before any the king might have given him. The man drew Hani and his small entourage discreetly into his office, a rather nicer room than Hani remembered Har-em-heb occupying at a comparable stage of his career.

"My lords, we have gathered here everything you'll need. I'll introduce you to your staff and show you the gifts our lady has put aside for you whenever you're ready. Two young officers you already know will be leading the escort of a hundred troops."

"That's very generous," said Hani with a rise of the eyebrows.

"Your cargo will be valuable, Lord Hani. Going... but even more valuable coming back." The commandant fixed Hani with a knowing stare. "May the King of the Gods watch over you, my lord. There will be those who will want to stop you."

Hani thanked the man sincerely and let himself be led to the treasure room where the diplomatic gifts were being kept. Mery-ra and Maya trailed after him in silence. Hani whispered to his secretary, "We do have Lady Meryet-aten's letters, don't we? Signed with her seal?"

"Yes, my lord. In Egyptian and in Akkadian."

"Good man."

Their young guide led the three diplomats down a maze of hallways to a ponderous bronze-strapped door, sealed with a lump of clay and a string. From its bracket on the wall, he unmounted a torch, broke the clay seal and let the men into the room. Hani took the torch and held it up. In the small pool of orange light, he saw the rich glint of gold vessels, bolts of fine linen, elephant tusks, leopard pelts, bundles of ostrich plumes, inlaid chests. A fabulous treasure—like a glimpse into a storehouse of the gods—one that should soften the heart of the Great King of Kheta Land, no matter how obdurate he might prove to be.

"This piece," said the soldier, carefully opening a small enameled casket "is especially for the prince, I'm told. The servant who brought it said not to touch them—it will tarnish the silver." Hani saw by the flickering light of the torch a pair of magnificent cuff bracelets made of gold and silver inlaid with turquoise, carnelian, and lapis. They were the only things in the treasure trove that Hani wouldn't have minded having for his own—not that he wore much jewelry. But their value could have ransomed a king.

"This is perfect," Hani said to the soldier. "I'll want a detailed list of everything, of course."

"I'll have it ready for you, my lord."

"Could we see Menna and Pa-ra-mes-su this afternoon, or are they busy organizing their men?"

The young soldier assured him the officers of the escort would be more than happy to meet with him, and, with a brisk clap of a fist across his chest in salute, he turned and disappeared down the darkening corridor.

Once they were alone, Maya gave an appreciative whistle.

"Our queen was serious about those diplomatic gifts, wasn't she?" said Mery-ra with a waggle of his thick eyebrows. "If anybody knows what we're carrying, I'm not sure a hundred men is enough."

"Meryet-aten is trying to convince the king of Kheta to do something pretty extraordinary. This should help sweeten the request." In silence, Hani pondered the dangers inherent in traveling with such objects. Certainly, they were safer at sea than they would have been on the Way of Haru, but the increasingly large delegation would have to take two or even more ships, without a doubt. Hani wasn't sure what he thought about separating himself from the gifts for which he was responsible.

"Lord Hani!" cried a cheerful voice from behind him. Hani turned to see the welcome face of Menna, a man whose life he had saved as a young soldier and who was now devoted to him. Menna—who had to be forty by this time, Hani calculated—had been promoted to regiment commander some while back, but he was the same old lean, dark-skinned, bucktoothed fellow as always, his wide, frank eyes creased with joy. Behind him stood the good-looking Pa-ra-mes-su—General Har-em-heb's adjutant—with his predatory nose. It spoke eloquently of the importance of their mission that Har-em-heb had relinquished him in the middle of the Nubian campaign.

In genuine affection, Hani embraced both of the men in turn, and Menna nodded respectfully to Hani's father. "We have handpicked troops for you, Lord Hani. Each of them is sworn to fight for the glory of the Hidden One."

"Excellent, Menna. I can't tell you how much better I feel with you two on guard. I'm afraid we may encounter opposition, whether from the Hittites or our own government."

Menna lifted a knowing eyebrow. "Our men are all ready to go, my lord. We have three vessels secured and we'll split our forces so that each ship has an escort at sea, then when we stop for the night, we'll rejoin one another. Once we're on land, of course, we'll all be there to protect you."

"Do you know your way through Kheta, son?" asked Mery-ra.

"We don't, my lord," Menna admitted. "We'll have to depend on local guides. Surely the king will contact us as soon as he discovers an armed party of foreigners entering his territory."

Contact us or shoot us full of arrows, Hani thought grimly.

Beaming, Mery-ra said, "Lucky for you and Pa-ra-mes-su I've been to Kheta. I can guide you."

"Fifty years ago, Father. Things might conceivably have changed." Hani shot him a dry grin.

"Well, the mountains and valleys will be in the same spots, won't they?"

"Your help will be appreciated," Pa-ra-mes-su said diplomatically.

The two officers took their leave, and Hani and his party made their way back to the rooms that had been assigned to them.

"Who's ready for dinner?" Hani asked more cheerfully than he felt. "It's our last Egyptian meal for months. I hope the commandant has a good cook. What I wouldn't give for Nub-nefer's fried fish, or meat pies with cumin!"

Some benevolent god must have heard Hani, because when their meal was delivered to the chamber, it contained both steaming meat pies, fresh from the oven, and small fishes fried to a delicious crisp, along with stewed leeks and plenty of bread.

As he bit in, Hani could feel the saliva fountaining up appreciatively in his mouth. "Ah!" he cried, "Our commandant has an *excellent* cook. They're almost as good as Nub-nefer's."

"Why don't we just stay at Per-nefer for the rest of our lives?" asked Mery-ra with a chuckle. He brushed crumbs off his belly where they had sprinkled with his first bite of pastry. "My recollection of Hittite food is that it was pretty dull."

Maya said, his mouth full of leeks, "How are we going to divide the men up on the ships, my lord? Will the three of us be together?" A wrinkle of anxiety pleated the secretary's brow.

"I think the three of us and the treasure should be together, with about a third of the troops—we won't be attacked on the water, surely. The rest of the staff and the other soldiers will travel together and we'll all spend the night on deck when we dock in the evening."

"You know, there are such things as pirates, son," Mery-ra said, suddenly serious. "Maybe it would be safer to divide the treasure among the three ships. Surely you can trust our young officers to oversee its guard."

Hani considered this, gnawing his lip, then said, "I think you're right, Father. If we're attacked, we don't want to lose everything. That would end our mission right there." He reached out for the last fish and threw it into his mouth. "I'll talk to Menna and Pa-ra-mes-su in the morning and see what they think."

Once they had reduced the little tables to a litter of bones and crumbs and fruit peels, Hani rose and stretched with a satisfying roar. "I vote for going to bed. 'Man ignores how the morrow will be,' but I predict it will start early."

ACKNOWLEDGMENTS

THE AUTHOR GRATEFULLY ACKNOWLEDGES ALL those who have helped her in the production of this book. To the wonderful women of my writers' group, for their critique and encouragement, my thanks. To Lynn McNamee and her editorial team at Red Adept—Jessica, Sarah and Irene—profound gratitude (and Lynn, for so many other forms of help). To the flexible and talented gang at Streetlight Graphics for the cover and map. To my cousin and her husband, my technology guru: thanks, guys. To Enid, who urged me forward by her support, I can't thank you sufficiently. Also, to Joe and Maria and all the wonderful crew at Kommos all those years ago—you've taught me so much about the Bronze Age, and in particular a certain yellow pigment. And most of all, to my husband, Ippokratis, who put up with the months of fixation it takes to write a novel, many, many thanks.

ABOUT THE AUTHOR

 N.L. Holmes is the pen name of a professional archaeologist who received her doctorate from Bryn Mawr College. She has excavated in Greece and in Israel, and taught ancient history and humanities at the university level for many years. She has always had a passion for books, and in childhood, she and her cousin (also a writer today) used to write stories for fun.

Today, since their son is grown, she lives with her husband and three cats. They split their time between Florida and northern France, where she gardens, weaves, plays the violin, dances, and occasionally drives a jog-cart. And reads, of course.

Made in the USA
Coppell, TX
31 August 2021

61557736R00246